Praise for M

"Michelle Sutton's *It's Not About Me* tackles many issues: temptation, deception, forgiveness, and trust, to name a few. The story is most strong when its players are weak. Readers will identify with Annie, Dan, Tony, and maybe even Susie, because these characters struggle—as we all do—with very human failings. You can't read Annie's story without renewing your appreciation for our powerful and loving God."

—Trish Perry, author of *Beach Dreams*

"Michelle Sutton lives up to her tagline of Edgy Inspirational Author, tackling issues of desire, premarital sex, alcoholism and volatile sibling relationships in her debut novel, *It's Not About Me*. Michelle is not shy about detailing the main characters' feelings of desire and their battle against acting on their attraction, making this book more suited to those in their late teens and older. This may make some lovers of traditional Christian romance uncomfortable while generating a devoted audience in others who have been waiting for such 'real life' fiction. *It's Not About Me* sends a strong message about commitment, faithfulness, and the true source of beauty and love. Michelle is sure to make a splash."

—Rel of *Relz Reviewz*

"Michelle Sutton's *It's Not About Me* . . . is a book mercifully free of easy answers and tidy resolutions. Sutton paints with broad, bright strokes, introducing the reader to characters who are far from perfect, thereby allowing us to connect with them in very human ways. And because we can relate so strongly to their day-by-day battles between flesh and spirit, we can rejoice and ache with them, laugh and cry, and ultimately learn that perhaps it's when life is most messy that God's grace shines brightest. By allowing her characters to be fully human, Sutton delivers a story that glows with authentic holiness."

—James E. Robinson, author of *The Flower of Grass*

"Michelle Sutton's touching debut novel is truly a page-turner. *It's Not About Me* is filled with raw emotion and is a story that demonstrates pure love within its pages. It's a must-read for teens who are already saved, but more so for young adults who are 'on the fence' regarding their faith, or who don't know God at all."

—Sherri L. Lewis, *Essence* best-selling author of *Dance Into Destiny*

"Michelle Sutton's *It's Not About Me* is the bittersweet tale of Annie Myers, a young woman torn between the love of two brothers—and devastated by an assault that leaves her emotionally and physically scarred. Readers will weep with Annie as she struggles to come to a place where she can love herself again . . . and attempts to understand how God could let the attack happen. A heart-wrenching and inspiring read."

—Susan Lohrer, Write Words Editing

it's NOT about ME

Acknowledgements

There are so many people who have encouraged me in this writing journey over the past five years that I know I'll leave someone out. If I do, please forgive me.

To my Lord, who inspired me to craft life-changing fiction back in August 2003.

To my agent, Tamela Hancock Murray. You are an awesome person and have become a dear friend. Nobody has encouraged me more than you have by investing time in me and pressing on. I love how you'd say they rejected "us," like we're a team. And indeed we are. You're the best and I'm never giving you up!

To Sheaf House owner and editor Joan Shoup. You told me four years ago that you'd buy one of my books and publish it. At the time we both knew you were joking. Who'd a thought it would become reality? We're going places, lady, and I plan to enjoy the ride, so hang on!

To Cynthia Rutledge, Love Inspired and Silhouette Romance author. You've helped me with this vision and have been an encouragement to me to keep trying and never give up.

To my husband, who has read most of the stories I've written. You told me that you didn't understand why it was taking so long, and that people would be crazy not to want my books.

To my sons, particularly my oldest, who is a grammar whiz and proofed my original version. You were as excited about my story as I was. That encouraged me greatly!

To my mother, who has been with the Lord for ten years now. She had the gift of writing when she was younger, though I never saw anything she'd written. Must be in the genes.

To my dad, my sisters, my aunt, and my cousin, who have been instrumental in encouraging me. Thanks, Aunt Maureen, Cousin Mary Kay, and my sister Anna Marie, for reading this book and going nuts over it. And thanks, Suzette, for being an awesome support and believing in me.

To my ACFW original crit group members. In particular, Laura Hilton, Amy Wallace, and Dawn Kinzer. You guys rock! Thanks for beating me up and challenging me in love to excel.

To all of my published author friends and editor friends who have read either all or some of my manuscripts just because you wanted to and because you said you enjoyed reading my stories. And thanks also to those who have taken the time to edit scenes and offer great pointers. Thanks Robin Carroll (Miller), Nancy Toback, Deb Ullrick, Kathi Macias, Marylu Tyndall, J. M. Hochstetler, Sara Mills, Melanie Dobson, Susan Meissner, Sharlene MacLaren, Sherri Lewis, Deborah Piccurelli, Trish Perry, Siri Mitchell, Julie Lessman, Kacy Barnett-Gramckow, Cindy Woodsmall, Susan Lohrer, Bonnie Leon, Gail Sattler, Susan Page Davis, Cathy Elliot, Claudia Mair Burney, Victoria Christopher Murray, DeAnna Dodson, Deb Kinnard, Donald Parker, Kathleen Fuller, Kristin Billerbeck, Colleen Coble, Deb Raney, Randy Ingermanson, Marilynn Griffith, Mary Connealy, Nancy Jo Jenkins, Pamela Tracy, Tricia Goyer, Tosca Lee, Louise Gouge, Dorothy Clark, Betsy St. Amant, Cecelia Dowdy, Jill Eileen Smith, Melanie Carlson, Georgiana Daniels, and Nicole Baart.

To my not-yet-published author friends who are on their way and may even be published by the time this book comes out, and my avid reader/promoter friends. Thanks, Angela Breidenbach, Bonnie Engstrom, Carolyn Davis, Rhonda McKnight Nain, Crystal Laine Miller, Diane Moody, Deena Peterson, Ane Mulligan, Lisa Buffaloe, Gina Holmes, Greg Davis, Heather Tipton, Jennifer Keithley, Margo Carmichael, Scott Sutton, Tamara Cooper, Wendy Lynn Decker, Lynn Divoky, Shawneda Marks, Aida Bode, Bonnie Calhoun, Gina Conroy, LaShaunda Hoffman, and Tyora Moody.

To my awesome friends from church, work, and beyond. Thanks, Emily Plamondon, for reading everything I've ever written and getting more excited than I did. To Debra Mansker, Jessie Swierski, Priscilla McCarthy, Jenadee Webb, Michael Hutchinson, Ryan Gray, Amanda Smith, Sarah Gomez, Vikki Atkinson, Jane Hatfield, Diane D'Armond, Hannah Dodd, Pastor Dennis Nitchke, Diana Nitchke, Brittany Perkins, Mavis Perez, Barbara Welsh, Emma Kieninger, Adele Schloemer, Kathy Sokol, Kelly Lewis, Darby Mahon, Howard Gordon, Penny Heins, Jeannie Zick, Milagro Gessler, Navdeep Gupta, Rae Gibson Reynolds, Sandy Nelson, Sherri Higgs, Colleen Lomelino, Lorena Nevarez, Raquel Hoston, Sheila Schultz, Lori Andersen, Chris Cherry, Tony Lazok, Tim McBride, Lori Rubio, and Cathi Hassan.

A special thanks to Mick Silva for being the first person to lay eyes on this story and for encouraging me so much. Thanks for teaching me what *moxie* means. You're awesome!

Thanks also to David Gunckle for reading this book and getting excited about it. I'm taking you up on your offer to help me get it into Arizona's libraries. You are a fabulous encourager.

Of course, my acknowledgments couldn't be complete without including the experts who helped me with accuracy. Thank you, Dr. Myles Whitfield, neurosurgeon, for your knowledge regarding neurosurgery and your enthusiasm about my book. Thanks, Keith Plamondon, PA, for your knowledge regarding hospital procedures and transportation for a patient via helicopter. Many thanks also go to Benna Troupe, Cochise County Legal Defender, in regard to criminal court proceedings/procedure at sentencing hearings.

Lauren Heins, you are gorgeous and I'm thrilled that you've enjoyed my story and didn't mind all the attention directed your way as a result. Thanks for understanding that your pretty face couldn't be on the cover. I sure wanted it to be.

Last, thanks to Forrest and Devan for being my hunky models, and Katie, for your willingness to be my model for Annie. God bless you all.

It takes many friends to make a great novel. Thanks so much, everyone!

Michelle Sutton

it's NOT about ME

A Second Glances Novel
#1

Michelle Sutton

Charlotte, Tennessee 37036 USA

Library of Congress Control Number: 2008923548

ISBN 978-0-9797485-1-6 (softcover)

Scripture quotations are taken from the New English Translation.

Published in association with Hartline Literary Agency, Pittsburgh, Pennsylvania 15235.

Interior design by Keitha Vincent.

08 09 10 11 12 13 14 15 16 17— 10 9 8 7 6 5 4 3 2 1

MANUFACTURED IN THE UNITED STATES OF AMERICA

it's NOT about ME

Dedication

To the woman whose beautiful heart and tender spirit inspired this story. You took your tragedy and turned it into triumph. May God use the pain resulting from the traumatic event and the healing inspired by God's presence in your life to continually illuminate His amazing love.

Note: While some incidents in this story were based on true events, this novel is a work of fiction. All relevant information was changed to protect the people involved.

"God does not view things the way men do. People look on the outward appearance, but the Lord looks at the heart"
—1 Samuel 16:7*b* NET

Prologue

Ever have something happen to you that was so awful you wish you could go back and erase the memory? I did. But in a strange way I'm glad it happened. Not because I enjoyed the nightmares or the pain, but because it changed me and made me a stronger person.

On the inside.

I always thought life was about me. That behaving and being a good person were all I needed to do to be happy. But now I realize all I did was try to please other people, to make them happy.

I'm not sure why I felt compelled never to let anyone down. But what happened to me that horrible night forced everything into perspective. I learned something about myself that wasn't so pretty.

It's not about me.

Chapter 1

Annie Myers offered a shy grin to the congregation of First Christian Church as they applauded for her solo, "How Great Thou Art." She dipped her head until her shoulder-length hair covered her face and returned to her seat. She hated it when her cheeks burned.

She slipped into the pew and adjusted her black skirt as she settled beside her boyfriend, Tony. He slid closer until he eliminated the space between them. Draping his arm over her shoulder, he warmed her ear with his breath. Though she stared straight ahead, she could hear the smile in his voice.

"You sounded great." He lingered with his lips against her hair, the light scent of his musk aftershave invaded her senses, making her grin despite her effort to appear aloof.

"Not so close." She stifled a giggle with the tips of her fingers and tried to scoot away.

When he clutched her waist and inched closer, she stopped struggling, but sighed. While she didn't mind him displaying a little affection, she didn't appreciate him grabbing her in church. Not when her nosy neighbor Nancy, an elderly widow who rarely left her house except for church services, perched in the row across the aisle and scrutinized them with raised eyebrows.

Annie tried to pay attention to the service, but her mind couldn't focus. Between her neighbor staring and Tony's ever-increasing proximity, she struggled to keep her breathing normal.

Nosy Nancy had made it clear she didn't like their pastor's youngest son and shared her disparaging opinion of him with anyone who would listen. The old woman worked hard to collect evidence against him. For what purpose, Annie didn't know, nor did she want to.

On occasion she and Tony performed special music together. He was the one who had given her the courage to sing in public. And she loved it when he harmonized with her. His voice was smooth and enticing, just like his personality. And though every girl in church wanted to date him, Tony had chosen her to be his girlfriend.

Shuddering as he tickled her open palm, she tried to discreetly pull away from him, but he refused to let go. Nosy Nancy probably sensed Annie's not-so-pure thoughts and would scorn her like Annie scorned herself for allowing Tony such liberties. Rather than confronting him, however, she stared at the wooden cross behind the pulpit and ignored his sensual teasing.

During the closing hymn, he repeatedly traced *I love you* into her palm. Finally she leaned close and whispered, "Stop."

He shook his head. Wearing a mischievous grin, he dragged his fingers over her palm, and then trailed one up her arm. She shivered from the tickling sensation on her skin and glanced across the aisle. Nosy Nancy's eyebrows had climbed halfway up her prune-like forehead. Something in Annie's gut told her Nancy had seen Tony pawing her.

The moment the hymn concluded, Tony tugged her—feet dragging—across the carpet. He urged her toward the stairs that led to the Sunday school rooms below the sanctuary.

She dug her heels in and tried to pull away. "Tony, what are you doing?"

He pulled harder, refusing to let go. "Come on."

Not wanting to put up a fight in front of church members, she tried to not trip on the steps as she descended the stairs behind him, his hand still clutching hers. "We shouldn't be down here alone."

"I know. But I've got something awesome to tell you."

Not sure she believed him, she allowed him to drag her along the narrow hallway. "Why does it have to be so private?"

Tony laughed. "Come on. Loosen up. We're adults now."

Her spine stiffened at the way he emphasized the word adult, and she halted. "Wait a sec. Just because we're going to college in a few months doesn't mean we should start breaking all the rules. Your dad will have a fit."

"Naw. My dad's cool. Really." He winked.

She laughed at his obvious lie. His dad had a reputation for being overly strict with his sons. "You're nuts! He'll have your hide if he finds us down here alone."

Tony smiled and pulled her toward the door at the end of the isolated hallway. He yanked it open, propelled her inside, and slammed the door behind him.

The smoldering, sexy look on his face made her let out a high-pitched giggle. "Someone might hear and come looking for us. What will people think?"

He tipped his head, inspecting her with intense eyes, yet wearing a disarming smile. "You believe I care what anyone thinks?"

"You know *I* do."

He touched her chin, then tilted it up. "You're really gorgeous."

The way his eyelids lowered as his gaze lingered on her lips caused her heart to do little flips. "You're just saying that."

"Yeah, right. Like you were voted Prom Queen 'cause you're so ugly."

Annie forced herself to relax. They were in church. How much could he do? She fingered the collar of his tan dress shirt. "You're pretty hot yourself, Mr. Prom King."

Growling playfully, he backed her into the chalkboard. "Ooh, I like it when you say that."

One of the erasers hit the floor. Chalk dust exploded in a cloud, and as she bent to pick it up, she coughed. She wished their church would join the twenty-first century and invest in a dry erase board and markers.

"Grab it later."

He pressed her against the wall, not allowing her to reach down, his arms blocking her in. Gazing into her eyes, he tipped his head until their lips almost touched. Their breath mingled.

"Oh, Queen Anne, grant me one request?"

Her pulse hammered at his sensual tone, but she didn't hesitate. She needed to get back upstairs before anyone noticed them missing.

"Sure."

He kissed the tip of her nose. "Anything?"

She nodded and swallowed hard.

"You mean even this?" Closing his mouth over hers, Tony deepened his kiss until her knees turned to rubber. Yet the minty taste of his breath and the silky warmth from his lips made her crave more. Nobody looked or tasted as good. Not that she had anyone to compare him to. She'd never kissed anyone else.

Stopping suddenly, he gazed into her eyes and searched, as if peering into her soul.

The smell of chalk dust reminded her where they were. "I thought you wanted to talk." She found her hands had crept up to his shoulders, and she lowered them, pushing gently on his chest. "I don't like kissing down here. It's disrespectful."

"God invented sex. There's nothing wrong with it."

"Not if you're married. But . . ." *Why does kissing always make him think of sex?*

"Mmm . . . But nothing."

His soft lips moved rhythmically over hers in an intimate dance until she thought she'd faint. She had to escape.

Lately he wanted to make out every chance they got and let his hands roam further and further. Though she knew it was wrong, she didn't hate it. In fact she enjoyed it. Too much.

"Let me show you how much I love you," he whispered against her lips and melded his body to hers.

Panic forced the air from her lungs. She shoved him away. "Are you crazy?"

He laughed. "Not here."

Relief whooshed through her. Then he lightly brushed his index finger down her nose.

"Later. Tonight."

She frowned. He had to know how she felt, so why did he keep pushing the issue?

"We've talked about this before."

"I want you, Annie. I love you. I'll be careful."

She crossed her arms and stepped back. "And I love you. You know I'm fine with kissing, but I'm waiting until I'm married for the rest."

He huffed and raked his fingers through his hair. "That won't happen for four more years! Not if we graduate from college first. I can't wait that long."

What happened to the old Tony I knew? The sweet, patient one?

"If you love me you'll wait." Her voice wavered despite her resolve to remain firm.

"But your parents won't be home until tomorrow night. Don't you see? It's so perfect." He tried to cup her face, but she swatted his hands away.

So that was why her nosy neighbor had been giving her such rapt attention. She must be spying for her parents. They've never been out of town overnight before.

The thought gave her the shivers. What would Nancy tell them? What would they think? Her first time home alone, and she had her boyfriend over—yeah, that would go over well.

"No way. My parents would find out. They trust me."

"They don't have to know. You're the perfect daughter. No one would suspect a thing." He touched her hair and tucked a lock behind her ear. "Come on, babe. I'll leave early so no one will know I was there. I promise."

His manipulation caused a tumult of confusion to swell in her breast, weakening her resolve. Then logic assured her that Nosy Nancy would certainly be aware of his presence, which would earn them serious consequences.

"I said no. If that's all you wanted to tell me, then I'm out of here before someone sees us and starts talking." She tried to push past him, but he stepped in front of her.

"Is that all you care about? What people think?"

She stared into his eyes, where hurt danced with annoyance, and a lump clogged her throat. "No."

He moved closer and whispered, his voice desperate, "Don't you care what I think?"

When he looked at her like that, she wanted to throw caution to the wind and give in, but she had to be strong. "Of course I do. But why is this so important to you all of a sudden? You haven't been yourself lately."

She hesitated at the soft, yet passionate gaze in his eyes, wanting him to love her, but not push her so hard. How could she keep him in her life and keep her reputation at the same time? It seemed impossible, and it frustrated her.

Tony closed his eyes and puckered his lips, teasing her like he always did when she got mad at him. "Plant one right here, baby." He pointed at his mouth.

Annie sighed, then leaned toward him and offered a quick peck. "There. No more."

"That's more like it." He opened his eyes and grinned. "Now add a little warmth."

She scowled. "Tony . . ."

"I was joking." The corner of his mouth rose. "You can't blame a guy for trying."

She stared into mischievous brown eyes. "Think I'll change my mind if you keep this up?"

"I hope you will."

His eyebrows zipped up and down in a suggestive manner. The gleam in his eyes and his lopsided grin dissipated her anger.

"You kiss nice, but not enough to persuade me."

With his eyes thinned into slits, he observed her for a second. "Um, yeah. Hey. Listen. That's not why I brought you here. My news is . . . guess."

"You know I hate guessing games. Just tell me."

He captured her hands and smiled. "If you give me another kiss, I'll tell you."

"Just spit it out."

"Come on, hot stuff. One little kiss?"

She rolled her eyes and imparted another innocent peck.

Mimicking her, he rolled his eyes too. "That the best you can do?"

"You said one little kiss." She giggled. "You didn't say make it sloppy."

The look on his face was priceless. She could tell he wasn't sure if she was serious or not.

"Are you saying I'm a sloppy kisser?"

She laughed. "Maybe."

His now-wide grin assured her he understood her teasing. "All right, you kept your end of the bargain, though it *was* pretty lame. . ."

"My bad." She covered her mouth with her hand.

"All right, I'll just tell you. I got my acceptance letter from Northern Christian. I'm in!" He rubbed his hands. "Now we can go to the same college. Isn't that great?"

Her heart pounded and she stiffened. Fear and joy merged as she considered their recent struggles over sex—or the lack of it. She groaned inwardly at the thought of having to put him off for four more years.

"Sure," she answered, her smile weak.

He stepped back. "You don't sound excited. Aren't you happy? If we're at the same college, we can be together every day."

If they attended separate schools, it would be easier for her to deal with his burgeoning desire. Especially since it now mixed with the newly heightened awareness of her own.

"Yeah, I'm glad."

Tony squinted. "You're not happy. You're scared."

She shook off her doubts and brightened her smile. "Of course I'm glad. You know I'd love to spend every day with you." She touched his smooth chin, following the line of his jaw. "Why wouldn't I be happy? I was just a bit stunned at first."

"Good." Touching her hair, he whispered, "You're so beautiful."

Her body warmed as he inched closer.

Pressing her against the wall, he kissed her hungrily. His fingers combed through her hair and his lips found the hollow of her neck. Though she intended to behave, if he up kept up the passionate kissing, she didn't know how much longer she could keep her resolve.

Just as he slid his other hand under her shirt, something creaked behind her. *Someone walked in on us!*

She shoved Tony away and hastily wiped her mouth with the back of her hand. Smoothing her hair, she noticed Dan lurking in the doorway. Tony's nearly six-foot-tall, brown-haired, blue-eyed older brother stared at them, his mouth gaping in shock.

Dan blinked, then stepped inside. "Dad's looking for you."

Tony stuffed his hands in his pockets. "So?"

"You better find out what he wants. He's not happy you disappeared after service."

When Dan glanced at Annie, her neck flushed red-hot. Despite her embarrassment, relief washed over her at the interruption.

Tony touched her cheek. "Talk to you later, sweet stuff."

He sprinted up the stairs, leaving Annie out of breath and staring at his older brother. Dan shifted his feet as he fixed his gaze on her.

"Hi."

His frank stare evoked a shiver. What had he seen? What did he think of her?

She glanced away, running her fingers through her long hair. Dan appeared more handsome than usual today, and more like a man than a teenager. She hated that she noticed that about him.

Why wouldn't he go away? He'd delivered his message.

Dan's intensity puzzled her. He'd always been nice, yet extremely attentive, which made her anxious. Several times this past month, she'd caught him staring at her in church.

Tony had mentioned that Dan had graduated from college last month and returned to Boise to find a job. For now he lived with their parents. But that didn't explain his obvious interest.

"You sounded great today." Dan's voice dipped lower.

She peered at him while nibbling her lower lip. The compliment sounded sincere and unfamiliar warmth filled her chest.

"Um, thanks."

He scanned the length of her, then pointed at her skirt. Annie glanced down.

"What?"

"You're covered in chalk dust."

Her mouth curved in a wry smile, though her pulse hammered. "I, um, was looking for my . . . Bible and I . . . I guess I bumped into the chalkboard."

She slapped at the dust and fumbled through a stack of books on a table. He remained in the same spot, his hands stuffed in his back pockets. Straightening, she surveyed him from the corner of her eye.

"Need help dusting off?"

Was he serious? "No thanks."

His neck reddened and the color spread to the tips of his ears. He cleared his throat.

"I'm sorry. I didn't mean it like . . . Ah . . . never mind. I better go." He turned and disappeared down the hall.

Seconds later, her friend Susie Ziglar popped her head into the room. "There you are. I've been looking all over for you, girlfriend."

Annie tried not to appear flustered. She cleared her throat and tugged her skirt down as far as it would go.

"Just looking for my . . . Bible. Can't find it."

And you're lying. Nice, Annie.

"That's 'cause you left it upstairs, you nut."

Annie laughed and lightly slapped her forehead. "Oh, yeah. Duh!"

She sure would miss Susie when she left on the upcoming missions trip that would take her away for several weeks. At least Annie had Tony to hang out with. As long as she could keep him at bay.

Susie leaned close, her dark hair hanging in her face. "Why were you alone with Dan?"

"I wasn't alone. Not like—"

"Yeah, right. I just saw him looking all red-faced and running up the stairs like the building was on fire."

Glancing at her skirt, Annie smacked at the chalk dust. "He came to get Tony."

Susie took Annie by the shoulders and turned her around to get a better look. "Boy, what a mess. You want some help?"

"No, thanks."

Susie smirked. "I won't ask how you managed to get all that chalk on you."

Annie raised her brows. "I didn't plan it, you know. It just happened."

"Yeah, yeah, I know. But what I want to know is why the good stuff always happens to you. Why not to the rest of us average people?"

"Come on, Susie. There's nothing average about you."

Susie rolled her eyes. "Whatever. But you know I'm right. It's so unfair." She tapped her chin. "Do you think if I prayed and asked God to have Dan notice me, He'd answer my prayer?"

"It can't hurt to try, right?"

"I suppose. Come on. Let's get out of here before people start talking."

Annie followed her friend up the stairs, thankful for the continual interruptions despite how uncomfortable they made her feel. She didn't know how much longer she could deny Tony's insistent demands, and that scared her even more than her parents' finding out about their rendezvous in the church basement.

She didn't want to disappoint them. But more than that, she didn't want to betray her own plans for her future.

Something in her gut told her things were slowly unraveling in her relationship with Tony. And she had no clue how to make things right again.

Chapter 2

Annie wiped her hands on the kitchen towel after finishing the dishes. She surveyed the results of her work. Not a speck of grease on the stove. The floors had that fresh lemony-pine smell from the floor cleaner. Even the coffee pot sparkled.

Perfect.

While her parents always said Christians should never work on Sundays, she knew they'd be pleased to find the house spotless when they arrived home tomorrow night. No need to mention what day she actually did the cleaning, right? It was the result that mattered. Besides, she had to keep busy or she'd dwell on Tony and their earlier encounter.

Closing her eyes, she imagined her parents' surprised expressions. She really didn't mind doing her part. Her parents denied her nothing, so it was the least she could do. Unlike most of her friends, she truly was thankful for what she had.

Her mom's excuse for not keeping up on the housekeeping was she didn't have time now that she worked full-time. Maybe so, but they both knew she simply couldn't stand housework. She'd never liked tidying up, even when all she did was help out at the church office.

Annie had agreed this summer to volunteer in her mother's place. She didn't need to earn money for college. Her parents had saved for her education so she wouldn't have to. But it couldn't be that hard helping out if it was just office work. Her mom had said it might even be fun. She'd find out tomorrow when Tony's dad picked her up to take her there and get her started.

While changing into her favorite blue sweatpants and white T-shirt adorned with several tiny holes in the front, Annie thought about Tony's implied proposal. They'd dated nearly four years, and up until last month he'd been great about not pressuring her for sex.

He had surprised her on prom night when he told her he wanted to marry her after college graduation. Once he saw her in her white gown, he raved that he couldn't stop picturing her in a wedding dress. He actually got down on one knee and pretended to propose.

At least she thought he pretended, but after this morning in the church basement she was starting to think he might be serious. Although being a beautiful bride was a lame reason to marry, she had to smile at his compliment.

Despite his flattery, she still hadn't seen a ring, so nothing was official. Yet she longed to be his wife . . . someday. Sometimes with Tony it was hard to know when he was serious and when he was just trying to get to her. Even after four years of dating, he still caught her off guard.

She recalled him playing with a loose strand of her hair on prom night, staring into her eyes as if he could drink her up. Once they left the banquet hall, he'd taken her to a dark area in the parking lot and pressed his lips against her bare shoulder. He'd trailed sensuous kisses up her neck and told her he wanted her more than any woman he'd ever known.

She sighed at the memory. He sure knew how to make her feel beautiful and special.

Turning Tony down when he showed her a key to a room he'd reserved for them had been difficult. He could be very persuasive, but Tony finally relented after she insisted he take her home or she would tell his father about his proposition.

It took him a few days to work through what he referred to as her rejection, before he warmed up to her again. If anything, Tony persisted when he wanted something. But at least he didn't break up with her over it like the boys she'd heard other girls talk about in the locker room at school. She worried about that happening but wasn't about to let him know or he'd try harder to win her over.

To her amazement, he hadn't called begging to come over tonight. That had been his MO for the past month. She chuckled and spoke to her reflection in the mirror. "That's because he knows I won't give in."

But he knows he's wearing me down.

She shrugged off the thought before she dwelled on it too much and walked into the living room. Frowning, she considered watching one of her many Cinderella stories on DVD. Too bad real life didn't always have happy endings. But if she had anything to say about it, Tony would be happy with her despite her refusal to have sex with him. After all, he was her Prince Charming.

She scanned the shelf, admiring her growing collection. She probably owned every variation of the Cinderella theme ever filmed.

Plucking a new selection from the shelf, she crossed the room in her pink bunny slippers. She planned to make herself comfortable in her father's favorite chair before her cat, Persnickety, nabbed it.

When she glanced over at her father's chair, she chuckled. Sure enough, Snicky had beat her there. The cat licked her paw, glancing up every few seconds with a sly grin, as if daring Annie to kick her out of her comfy seat.

She turned on the TV and slipped the DVD into the player. She grabbed a green afghan from the couch and eased into her mother's chair. The creak of the springs comforted her, almost like Mom was there.

A sigh escaped as she cranked up the volume so she wouldn't miss a word. Nothing beat a yummy love story.

About ten minutes into the show, she heard someone banging on the door. Grumbling, she paused the DVD, tossed off her comfy blanket, and went to the door. She peeked through the lace curtains that covered the window.

Tony! I can't have Nancy see him. But how can make him leave without hurting his feelings?

She yanked the door open, forcing a smile. "I'm surprised to see you here. I thought we talked about this."

"We did. But that was before I planned to give you a special gift."

She frowned. "Don't think you're getting inside by conning me with a present."

"Of course not." He grinned. "But I hope you'll let me in because you love me, and 'cause it's kind of cold out here."

As if to prove his point, a gust of cool air whipped through the door and invaded the holes in her shirt. The unseasonably cool breeze prickled her chest. She was glad she'd kept her bra on.

She rubbed her skin to ward off the goose bumps now traveling up her arms and glanced over Tony's shoulder. No lights illuminated Nancy's windows. Either her neighbor wasn't home, or she had gone to bed.

"All right. You can come in, but just for a minute."

He followed her gaze. "No worries. I parked around the block to be on the safe side, but Nancy's in the hospital. My dad was talking to someone on the phone about it."

She raised her eyebrows. "Really?"

How could he be so casual about something like that? Then again, he had no reason to like Nancy, nor did she.

She opened her mouth to point out that he needed to show a little compassion, but then decided against it. No way would she nag him again. She'd done too much of that lately.

"Maybe I'll send her a card."

Tony strolled past her and entered the living room wearing his usual combination of blue jeans, a concert T-shirt, and an overly confident grin. He reminded her of a clean-cut biker as he turned and plopped onto her parent's new southwestern style couch.

"Come here, babe." He held out his hands and wiggled his fingers.

"I'm not a two-year-old," she sniffed, annoyed.

He glanced down at her fuzzy bunny slippers. "Are you sure about that?"

She peered at her feet. She felt herself smiling despite her intention to keep a safe emotional distance between them.

Tossing aside her concern for a moment about being caught with him alone, she placed her hands on her hips and leaned teasingly forward, pushing her lips into a pout. Before she could move away, he grabbed her hands and pulled her toward him.

"I love it when you're all feisty with me."

She giggled and fought him, but not very hard. "Tony!"

He propelled her down, flipping her over like a rag doll on his lap. "Now that was easy."

Seeing the lusty gleam in his eyes, she said coldly, "You know I'm not."

His smile faltered. "Never said you were."

Raising an eyebrow, she grunted. "Didn't have to. Coming over here after I asked you not to tells me exactly what you think."

"That is *so* not true. I came over 'cause I brought you something." He stuffed his hand into his back pocket and whisked out a shiny object. "Here."

She gasped. Unable to speak, she stared at a silver-colored ring with a solitaire diamond. When he slipped it on her finger, it was so snug he had trouble getting it past her knuckle. But it fit.

"Sweetness, I've gotta marry you. We've been together almost four years. Put me out of my misery. Tell me you'll say yes."

Her gaze darted between the sparkling diamond and his twinkling eyes. Now she had every reason to believe he meant what he said.

His face lit with expectation. She didn't want to hurt his feelings by saying no, but she wasn't exactly ready to say yes, either. What to do?

We'll have four years to fine-tune the details. I love his family, and it would be nice to marry a pastor's son. I can't bear the thought of losing him.

She nibbled on her lower lip. Finally, in spite of her reservations, she chose what would make him happiest.

"I suppose we can be officially engaged four years."

"You will?"

"I think . . ."

Tony's warm lips covered hers as he wove his fingers into her loose hair. While his enthusiasm excited her, it also struck a chord of terror deep inside her. Did he think his proposal and her acceptance gave him permission to indulge sexually? Had she made a mistake?

His silky kisses grew more intense, and he eased her back on the couch. Usually when they kissed they stood upright. She suddenly felt vulnerable as he pinned her with his weight. He shifted and propped his head with one hand, adjusting so he wasn't directly on top of her.

His free hand slipped from her hair and wandered to the front of her shirt. Her breath caught as he began to gently massage her breast.

He'd tried the same thing before, and she'd always managed to stop him. This time she hesitated too long. She shouldn't have let him in.

While her mind flitted between choices, his touch grew bolder. At first she enjoyed the sensations, but when she thought about having sex with him, and in her parents' home, she couldn't breathe. Things were happening too fast.

She'd told him many times she wasn't ready for sex, that she wanted to be married in the eyes of God when she entrusted her heart and body to a man for the first time. She wanted something precious to offer her husband. Something pure and beautiful that couldn't be taken from her. That included no regrets.

His finger dipped inside the waistband of her sweats.

Obviously he didn't plan to stop, so she would have to stop him. She tried to push him off, but he wouldn't budge. His muscular arms clasped her tight. Finally, she shoved him hard enough to demand his attention.

"Stop!"

With a heavy sigh, he shuddered and finally relented. "You are too hands-off."

"Well, you're too touchy-feely. I think you'd better go."

She glanced away, unable to watch his reaction for fear she'd weaken. Those warm brown eyes always caused her to melt inside when he smiled. She needed to be careful. What if her parents arrived home early? What if she lost control and didn't stop him?

"I'm not ready to leave. Come on, you know I won't bite. We've been going out forever, and I've never forced you to do anything you didn't want to do, right? I'll hold off if you give me something else to do with my hands."

She wasn't sure she believed him, but the innocent look in his eyes persuaded her to give him the benefit of the doubt. "All right, but one more slip and you're out of here, mister."

"Deal. So you got anything tasty to eat?" He rubbed his hands together. "I'm starved."

She snickered. "I was going to nuke some extra-butter popcorn. Would that satisfy your manly appetite?"

His mouth curved into a wry grin. "I thought we weren't going there."

"Um, yeah. I didn't mean it that way."

He snorted, "Yeah, right. I think you enjoy teasing me."

Placing her hands on her hips, she snapped, "I do not. That was a mean thing to say."

"Whatever." He smiled again, his eyes holding a wicked gleam.

For an instant she wanted to smack the smirk off his face. He had some nerve bossing her around. But then again, she'd let him come inside. She snorted and left the room to make popcorn before she said something she'd regret. Returning to the room a few minutes later with a hot bowl of popcorn and two drinks on a tray, she gestured for him to scoot over.

"Man, you want to take the fun out of everything, don't you?"

She giggled at the funny look on his face. "I'm just trying to keep you from messing with me." She set the tray on the coffee table.

"I told you I won't as long you keep me busy." He cupped his hands. "Fill 'em with that delicious popcorn and I'll be respectfully occupied, I swear."

"You shouldn't swear."

She sighed at how lame she sounded. And so goody-two-shoes. Handing him the bowl, she slid over beside him, making sure to leave a few inches between their legs. Reaching for the remote control, she pushed play.

The movie resumed. He watched for a few seconds, then groaned.

"A chick-flick!"

"What else is there?" she asked with a laugh.

"You're teasing me again. Watching all of that hugging and kissing will drive me crazy."

He stuffed a handful of popcorn into his mouth. Before he swallowed, he gave a broad smile, exposing the chewed contents of his mouth.

"You're so uncouth." She poked him in the chest. "You know that?"

He took a gulp of his drink and set it down. "Is there anything you like about me?"

"Sure. Just not watching you grin with your mouth full. Now be quiet and watch the movie, will you?"

"If that's all you don't like, there's no way I'm watching this flick when I could be kissing your hot lips instead."

"Tony—"

He shoved the popcorn bowl out of the way. "Please, just one more kiss? Then I promise I'll back off."

She rolled her eyes. "You don't know how to stop. You think I'm stupid enough to let you get started again? My parents would die if they found out I had you in their house alone, not to mention if I actually did . . . stuff with you."

"But we're engaged now. And you love me, right?"

Her eyes narrowed. He was trying to trap her again.

"You know I do."

"Then kiss me. Please."

She sighed. "It's not about that."

"So who cares what your parents think?"

"I do. They trust me."

"But what about me? Don't I matter?" He cupped her cheeks in his hands and whispered, "I need you. Can't you see that? I only want what's best for you. For us."

Staring at him, she contemplated his words. Technically if they got married he would be the only man she'd ever have sex with. But how would going against her beliefs be best for her? And so many things could go wrong. She wanted to insist they wait, but that wasn't what slipped out.

"I suppose we—"

He pressed his lips against hers. Slowly opening his mouth, he explored hers with such abandon she sensed he wouldn't stop despite what he promised.

Their heated exchange sent her mind into a tailspin and further eroded her resolve to remain pure. Before she lost all sense of self-control, she shoved him away and stood.

"I told you no more! I . . . I can't let you stay."

His face reddened. "See, you *are* a tease. Don't deny it anymore. I'm on to you."

His accusation stung. "W-what?"

The hurt look in his eyes made her pause. He clenched his fists and shook with anger, or frustration. She wasn't sure which, but it scared her. She started to move toward him—to calm him—but stopped herself.

His eyes flared. "You're no different than I am. You know it, so stop pretending."

He made no sense. Now he was attacking her? What was wrong with him?

"I don't know what you're talking about."

"You're such a faker. You're pretending you don't want me, just like you pretend to love God when you're in church. But it's not real. You just want to look good."

Shocked, she stepped back, trembling. "Where is all this . . . this anger coming from?"

He leaned toward her and pointed, but didn't say anything. She stepped back.

Is it that obvious I have doubts about us, about God?

Tony must've known he was losing his edge because he switched to a softer tone and poured on his usual charm. "Come on, babe. Let's get married this summer and live together at college. Then it'll all be okay. You won't feel like you're sinning with me."

That I'm *sinning? What about you?*

She blinked. "You want to marry . . . this summer?"

"Yeah. Why wait, right? Besides, I heard they give you more financial aid when you're a married student." He wiggled his brows. "Not to mention the other benefits."

"I don't know, Tony. Marriage is forever. What if it's a mistake?"

"Being with you could never be a mistake. Think about it, babe. And think about this—did you know the Bible says it's better to marry than to burn with lust?"

She searched his eyes in hopes of finding the old Tony she loved. This sex-obsessed man was not the same guy she'd fallen in love with.

"I think I've heard that before."

"Well, I'm burning for you, Annie, and I can't stand it anymore. I think about making love with you all the time."

His eyes softened and passion exuded from him. He touched her hair, sending delicious shivers down her back.

Her heart warmed and she closed her eyes. She really did love him. God help her, but she wanted him too. But was that a good enough reason to marry him? What did God want?

As he drew her close and caressed her mouth with another kiss, her mind returned to his earlier accusation. A faker? Not a real Christian? What did he mean? She broke the kiss and glanced up at him.

His eyes had welled with unshed tears, making her heart go out to him. A tear slid down his cheek.

"I want you, Annie," he whispered huskily, "I want you so much."

She warmed from head to toe at the sound of his breathless voice, intense with emotion. She'd never seen Tony so distraught before, needing her so much. How could she continue to turn him down and reject him? It seemed unfair to hold out on him. They'd be married soon anyway, right?

But still . . . it was wrong. Against everything she believed in. Her eyes stung and her throat tightened.

"Did you know in Bible times being engaged was the same as being married? That's why it says Joseph planned to divorce Mary quietly, and that he didn't lie with her until after she gave birth to Jesus."

She blinked the tears back before they could spill over. She needed to be strong.

"I'm not sure." Her voice sounded thick, raspy.

"But it's true." He gazed into her eyes. "You're just supposed to be with only one man or one woman. The marriage itself is just a legal ceremony, a piece of paper. God knows you're the only one for me. I don't need a certificate to prove that to anyone. Neither do you."

Her chest tightened as her doubts increased. Maybe she was wrong to deny him what he wanted. She wanted it too, but more than that, she didn't want to lose him. He already had a long line of female admirers. Any one of them would jump in to take her place if she broke up with him over sex. And now he was making too much sense. She'd heard the same argument from friends at school. Of course, they weren't Christians, but maybe he was right . . . and he looked so good with his lover-boy grin and bedroom eyes begging her to love him that way.

Her heart pounded. She wanted to make him happy. She wanted to share something special with him that would make him love her even more. Wouldn't having sex with him seal their relationship in a special way since they were both virgins? She bit her lip and offered a shy smile despite her reservations.

Again he leaned toward her. She sensed from the gleam in his eyes that he perceived her change of heart. Electricity crackled around them.

"I know you'll enjoy this. It won't hurt. I promise."

Warmth coursed through her again until the seriousness of what he'd said registered. She stiffened.

"You sound like you have experience. I . . . I thought you said were just like me. That you planned to wait."

"I have waited. I'm still waiting. Too long. I've read up some on what to do, but I haven't actually done it yet."

He touched her lower lip, tracing it to the corner as he smiled. Planting another feather-light kiss on her lips, he said, "I want you to be my first, my only."

His words were so persuasive. Especially when he said he'd saved himself for her. Didn't every woman want to hear that? And what if she didn't do what he wanted? What if he couldn't take the rejection this time and dumped her over it?

He seemed so vulnerable as he offered his heart. How could she stomp on it?

Truth be told, she wouldn't. A smile crept across her face. With no one to stop them, it seemed inevitable. That was why her parents warned her about spending time alone with Tony. They probably sensed she didn't have the strength to deny him for long.

She no longer worried about betraying her parents' trust. She wanted to make Tony happy.

"Okay," she whispered, trembling. "I'm scared, but I—"

Tony kissed her as he tugged at her clothes until he'd freed her T-shirt. He slipped his hands underneath and worked on unclipping her bra. He seemed to know right where to go to find the hook.

"You won't regret this, I swear."

Every muscle in her body tensed. What if he'd lied to her about his experience? Would she come to regret it?

Not if I can keep him.

Once he succeeded at releasing the clasp, she felt her bra loosening. He paused, peering intensely into her eyes as if gauging her response. He closed his eyes and kissed her again.

She couldn't believe she was about to give him her most precious gift. What was she thinking? She had to find a way to stop him.

"Relax." He whispered against her lips.

"Wait! What if I get pregnant! I'm sorry, I can't—" She whimpered, now trembling to the point her teeth chattered.

He patted his back pocket. "I've got something. Trust me."

He came prepared? What if it fails? It isn't a guarantee.

A sense of foreboding snaked up her spine, and her shaking grew more pronounced. He must've thought she wanted more because it seemed to increase his fervor. He unsnapped his jeans and gently nudged her with his hips.

"I can't!" she squeaked out.

She wanted to please him but couldn't see past the fear. Squeezing her eyes tight, she felt tears slipping from her lashes as she shot up a quick prayer.

Help!

No matter how much she tried to rationalize it, she simply wasn't ready. But she also didn't have the courage to disappoint him when he was so eager.

God, what should I do?

Tony paused his frenzied kissing and with a serious look in his eyes said huskily, "If you're really worried . . . there are other things we can do . . . you can do. It's not exactly sex, but you won't have to worry about getting pregnant."

She understood exactly what he meant and it grossed her out to think about it. Maybe some girls were willing to experiment, but she could never do that.

"No. That's . . . gross. I'm sorry I'm being such a baby."

"All right then, we'll do it the regular way."

He kissed her neck and slipped his hand into her sweat-pants, past the elastic band of her panties. Just then the phone jangled, and she jumped at the sudden noise.

He ignored the sound and with a grunt slid his hand farther down. "Let the machine get it."

She grabbed his hand to keep him from reaching his goal. "Wait."

His mouth traveled down her neck, making her shudder. She relented and released his arm. His gentle probing created warm sensations as she relaxed more and allowed him to explore.

When he began touching her in places he'd never reached before, she dissolved into the passion of the moment. She knew it was wrong, but it felt so good.

In the background, the phone stopped ringing, and the answering machine clicked on. Her father's recorded voice telling the caller to please leave a message snapped her back to the reality of what she was about to do.

The machine clicked off. Then the phone started ringing again.

"Wait! I have to get the phone. It might be my parents, and I'm supposed to be home."

With a frustrated groan, he moved away from her and threw his hands in the air. "Fine, get the stupid phone, but hurry back."

"Okay." She hopped up and grabbed the cordless. She pressed one arm against her chest to stop her body's trembling.

"Hello?"

"I need to speak with Tony this instant. And don't cover for him. I know he's there."

A lump formed in her throat, and she swallowed hard. "Oh, okay." She held out the receiver. "It's your father. He sounds mad."

Tony's eyes widened. He snapped his jeans and jumped from the couch to receive the phone.

"Hey, Dad." He winced. "I'll be right back . . . I'm sorry . . . Yeah, I borrowed the car. I didn't think—"

Handing the phone back, he frowned. "Dad hung up on me."

"He did? Why?"

"I borrowed his car. Now he's ticked off because he needed it. I thought he was in for the night. I didn't think he'd notice."

"You took his car without asking?"

He hung his head. "Yeah. And now I'm dead."

Chapter 3

Once Tony left her house Annie didn't feel like finishing her chick flick. She scooped Snicky from the chair and trudged to her bedroom. She couldn't help wondering what Tony was thinking about her now that she'd let him do things they'd never done before. She could never go back, and her heart ached with a deep sense of loss. Their hot kissing and touching—frightening and yummy as it was—left her feeling a bit dirty. And cheap.

She doubted their time together affected Tony the way it did her. He seemed encouraged every time she allowed him a bit more leeway.

Maybe he'd never be satisfied with less than the whole thing. And once he finally got her to give him what he wanted, how often would he want more? Maybe the only solution was to marry him, because a future without Tony seemed bleak and depressing.

A future she couldn't imagine.

While worried about his being in deep trouble, she was relieved at the same time. She knew their family rules. If his dad grounded him, then they couldn't get together unless one of his parents was present. The bonus would be no more pressure.

Snicky purred nonstop once Annie tucked them both in. The Siamese snuggled Annie under the chin—the one place her cat loved to burrow her face even more than her dad's chair.

The more Annie scratched her cat's ears, the more Snicky sounded like a high-powered engine revving for a drag race. She propped herself on one elbow and stared into her cat's perpetually crossed eyes.

"You know what I don't get?"

Snicky blinked as if she were listening and clung to Annie's every word.

"Of course you wouldn't know. How could you? There isn't a male cat howling at your door, you lucky girl."

Her sweet crossed-eyed, narrow-faced cat was so ugly she was kind of cute as she stared intently at Annie and crooned.

She nuzzled Snicky's neck. "I'll bet Tony's in big trouble. So why does he think he's grown up enough to marry me when he can't even borrow his daddy's car without getting punished?"

Annie chuckled at the irony. "I wish my car wasn't in the shop again. Then I wouldn't need a ride to the church tomorrow, and I wouldn't have to talk to Pastor. Tony would die if he heard half the stuff his dad says about him when he isn't around."

Snicky stretched her neck as Annie's fingers worked their magic under her chin. "What am I going to do, Snick? I love him and I want to be with him in every way, but my parents would be furious if they found out I had sex with him. I always promised myself I'd wait, but I don't want to lose him . . ."

With that question still burning in her mind, she drifted into a fitful sleep.

Right after supper Monday night, Pastor Lane picked up Annie for her first day of volunteer work as the church's secretary. "Have you eaten?"

"Yes, I had a sandwich. Thanks for asking."

Silence ensued for several minutes. Pastor finally spoke. "I want to apologize for Tony's behavior last night."

Her breath caught. What did Tony tell him? "You do?"

"It's just that I don't believe a lot of what he says anymore. Ever since he started hanging out with the college kid who moved in next door, he's been staying out late and sneaking around. I think the guy is a bad influence on him. I can only imagine what they're up to."

"I don't know who you're talking about."

"Hasn't he told you about Sam, the guy he met over spring break? As far as I can tell, Sam isn't a Christian. Tony started hanging out with him when Sam and his family moved here from Salt Lake City, and he's been sneaking around and lying ever since."

The month after spring break was right around the time Tony started pushing her to do more than kiss. She couldn't help wondering if Sam had a sister, which might explain Tony's sudden interest in sex.

"I've never heard of Sam. Does he have a younger sister or brother?"

Pastor Lane raised his brows. "As far as I know he's the only child. Well, he's more of an adult than a kid. I'm surprised Tony never mentioned him."

She shrugged. "He doesn't tell me everything."

"Has he gotten serious with you?"

Why all the questions? "He didn't tell you?"

Pastor Lane stole a glance at her. "Tell me what?"

A nervous chuckle escaped as she held up her hand and wiggled her ring finger to draw his attention to the diamond. "He asked me to marry him."

His brows knit together as if he didn't approve, but he kept his eyes on the road. "After college graduation, I hope?"

"He talked about getting married this summer, but the more I think about it, the more I think he's in over his head there."

"Have you told your parents?"

"Not yet."

She had no idea how they'd respond. Most likely in shock and ready to dish out a lecture about how she had her whole life ahead of her and how Tony was the only guy she'd ever dated so how could she know he was the right one. She'd heard all that the last time she hinted she might marry him.

When Tony's dad braked at a four-way stop, he glanced at her hand. His eyes widened.

"He gave you his grandmother's ring?"

The shocked look on his face caused her stomach to cramp. She peered at her finger and admired the ring.

"He didn't say whose it was when he offered it to me."

"I'm surprised. That ring is worth a lot of money. I knew my son thought highly of you, but I'm truly impressed."

Annie's chest tightened. "Why?"

He patted her hand as he drove. "I didn't mean it like an insult, honey. It's just that Tony has always been a bit self-centered. If he parted with his grandmother's ring, you must mean the world to him. He adored her and was devastated when she died."

"That happened just before I moved here, right?"

He nodded. "He was smitten with you right away. You really helped pull him out of the dark place he was in."

She twisted the ring. "How did you know he was at my house last night?"

"I called Sam's and he hadn't seen Tony. Your house was the next logical place."

"Did he get in trouble?"

"I told him we're not giving him the car he wanted for college, and he's grounded from using my vehicle. His mother and I work too hard to be tossing money at him, not when he pulls stunts like this. From now on he has to tell me where he's going. If he needs to borrow one of our cars, it better be for an emergency, and even then he needs permission first. If he breaks that rule, he'll lose the privilege altogether."

"Did you ground him from anything else?"

As they approached the railroad tracks by the church, a train siren blasted. The signal lights flashed on, and the crossing arms jerked downward.

Pastor Lane pulled up to the crossing and stopped. Annie could feel the pulsing throb of the engine shake the vehicle as it sped toward them.

"No. His mother and I decided to limit his grounding to the use of our cars since that's the privilege he took advantage of. But I think that's enough to make him sweat this summer so he knows we mean business."

The train roared by, the wheels of the cars clicking against the tracks, drowning out all other sound. Silently Annie watched it pass, thinking that Tony's punishment wasn't as bad as it could have been.

"By the way, thanks for offering to help at the church. I have a lot of catching up to do since I was out sick all last week."

"No problem," she said with a smile. "It doesn't seem like work when you're serving God."

The train had passed, and he drummed his fingers on the steering wheel, waiting for the crossing arms to swing up. "Just be careful."

"Be careful? About what? Tony?"

"That's not what I meant." He glanced at her from the corner of his eye. "Has he done anything you need to be careful about?"

Annie shifted in her seat. "Um, not really."

When the crossing was clear, he stepped on the gas. They bumped across the tracks and headed toward the church.

"I meant be careful about how you view your walk with the Lord. It's not about what you do as much as it's about your relationship with Him."

She glanced at Pastor Lane, surprised he stated the obvious. "I know that."

"You know that in your head, but do you really understand? Doing good things won't get you into heaven."

"Yeah, but it can't hurt to be good. Right, Pastor?"

"You've got a point there." He chuckled. "Here we are."

He parked in the church parking lot. As they walked to the entrance, he pulled the keys from his pocket. Unlocking the door, he ushered her inside.

"I'll be in my office if you need me for anything. Go ahead and file those papers, type the bulletin, and take messages while I prepare the eulogy for the funeral I'm conducting tomorrow. Can you do all that?"

"Sure. Sounds easy enough."

"Great. Oh, if you run out of things to do, you can always shred the paper in that box over there." He gestured to a box heaped with papers in the corner of the office.

"I'll take care of it."

"Don't forget I have to go to the hospital tonight before visiting hours end. If you plan to stay later, that's okay with me. Just be sure to lock up before you leave. You have a ride, right?"

"My parents are picking me up on their way home from the airport. But I don't have a key to lock the door when I leave."

He went to the outer door. "You don't need one. Just twist the handle like this, and it'll lock when you pull it shut." He demonstrated. "Easy enough?"

Annie nodded.

"Thanks again for your help." He gave her a nod as he went into his office.

The moment Dan walked in the door, his brother advanced on him. "You're a real jerk, you know that?"

Weary from fighting traffic and interviewing all day, Dan frowned and loosened the tie around his neck. "What's your problem, Tonc?"

"You are, you stinking narc. Why'd you tell Dad about Annie and me in the basement? Were you jealous? Wishing it was you kissing her instead of me?"

Dan stiffened at the accusation. He tried to remain calm, refusing to let Tony provoke him again. He'd been home less than a month, and the constant antagonism was getting old. He pressed past Tony and headed for his bedroom.

"Now you're getting ridiculous."

Tony pushed his way into Dan's room. "Hey, I'm talking to you. I see how you look at her. You think I'm stupid?"

Shrugging out of his suit jacket, Dan tossed it on his bed. "No. But I think she's too good for you. You're just using her."

His brother's face turned crimson and the veins in his forehead pulsed. "That's outta line. I love her."

Dan smirked as he kicked off his dress shoes. "Yeah, right. I found your collection of hottie magazines. You're trying to wear her down so you can get some action."

Tony shoved Dan's bicep, making him turn and face him. He growled, "What were you doing in my room?"

"Just looking for a clean pair of socks."

When Tony headed out the door to his bedroom, Dan followed. "I thought I'd borrow a pair of yours. I couldn't believe what I found instead."

Leaning against the door jamb, he watched Tony paw through the bottom drawer of his dresser. When his brother found the magazines still there, he straightened, eyes narrowed.

"You have no business getting in my stuff."

"Don't worry. I didn't say anything to Mom and Dad about them. Who's this Sam guy they're addressed to anyway? Did he give them to you?"

Tony scuffed his foot on the carpet and avoided eye contact. "Yeah. He's letting me borrow them for a while."

"Those pictures are sick and perverted, maybe even illegal. You better give them back. Mom will have a heart attack if she finds them. You're playing with fire, you know that?"

Tony huffed. "I know what I'm doing." He lay on his bed, grabbed a ball, and bounced it off the bottom of the top bunk.

"No, I don't think you do. Because if you did, you wouldn't treat your girlfriend like you're a hungry dog and she's a side of beef."

"You're so full of crap. Get out of here! This is my room and I don't need you preaching at me." He pointed at the door while bouncing the ball with his free hand.

"Whatever, Tone. You know the deal. You are so busted if mom finds your stash."

"Yeah, well, I'll get rid of them . . . soon. But if she finds them before then, I'll know who told her. So don't even think about it."

"Whatever. It's your neck. I'm not the one who's gonna swing."

The phone rang. Dan left Tony's room and hurried to the kitchen. He grabbed the phone.

"Hello?"

"Tony?" The girl's voice sounded a bit scared.

"No, it's Dan. Is this Annie?"

"Yeah. Where is he? He was supposed to be here at eight. My parents had to take a later flight, and Tony said he could pick me up here at the church and take me home."

"I don't have a clue, but I'll ask him." He strolled into Tony's room. "It's Annie."

Tony's eyes widened.

Dan pressed the phone against his chest and whispered, "She said you were supposed to pick her up at eight."

His brother jumped off his bed and dropped the rubber ball. "Crap! I was so ticked at you I forgot all about it." Plunging his fingers into the hair over his forehead, he paced. "Dad's not home. Where's Mom?"

"She takes an aerobic class every Monday night. How could you not know that?"

"Just shut up." Tony thrust his hands out, clearly frantic. "How am I supposed to pick up Annie with no car?"

Dan shrugged and stuffed the phone into Tony's open palm. "Not my problem."

Tony covered the mouthpiece with one hand. "Can you give me a ride?"

Dan grinned, glad to have the upper hand for once. "I suppose. But you owe me big-time."

Tony's shoulders slumped as he pressed the phone to his ear. "We'll leave right now. You don't mind if Dan drives, do you? Good. It shouldn't take more than twenty minutes if the traffic isn't too bad. Hang in there, okay?"

Tony hung up and quickly whipped off his shorts. He jammed his legs into a pair of tight jeans and tugged on clean socks.

Stomping his feet into shoes, he groaned. "I can't believe I forgot. She sounded upset. Oh, she's gonna kill me."

"If Mom doesn't kill you first."

Dan walked out. He needed a quick change too and grabbed a pair of jeans and his sneakers. Once he finished dressing he popped his head into Tony's room.

"Let's go."

"Give me one more sec." Tony grabbed a clean T-shirt from his closet and tugged it over his head. "Come on, let's hurry."

੨੨੨੨

Annie stared at the clock. Ten minutes after eight. She sighed and peered out the window. The sun was almost down and it was getting harder to see.

Of all the times for Tony to forget, why her first day? She'd called him as soon as she found out her parents wouldn't be able to pick her up, and that was over two hours ago. Was she that insignificant to him?

A chill irritated her spine, and the hair on the back of her neck bristled. Pastor had left twenty minutes ago, believing Tony would pick her up shortly.

The air was so still, and it was becoming dark outside. With every passing minute, she became increasingly uneasy.

It had always bugged her that First Christian lay nestled in an obscure cul-de-sac down by the railroad tracks. The building faced an open field, and the house closest to the church was about two city blocks away. The location had infrequent traffic, especially at night.

Pastor had told her that sometimes homeless people who lived in tents on the other side of the tracks would come by and ask for food. She just prayed they'd stay away tonight.

Watching the clock only made time drag, so she entered the kitchen and put clean dishes away. She sang a love song to distract her from the empty building's eerie quiet.

After finishing, she returned to the front office and shredded paper. The hum of the machine broke the frightening silence and provided a measure of comfort. In ten minutes Tony should arrive and pick her up. She wasn't a baby. She could make it till then.

Shivering despite the warmth in the room, she sucked in a cleansing breath and tried to block her fears. If she could just hang in there until they arrived without calling 911. She grinned at the thought.

She crossed the room and admired the Pastor's now immaculate desk. Convinced he'd be impressed with her work, she straightened the bulletins and selected one to show Tony.

Behind her she heard the door click. "Miss?"

The sound of a harsh, gravelly voice made her jump. She swung around to find an old man with mussed hair and a scraggly gray beard standing in the open doorway. He wore torn jeans and an oil-stained jacket.

Startled, she dropped the bulletin clasped in her hand. How did he get in? She thought she'd locked the door after Pastor left.

He dropped a dirty gray backpack on the floor and approached her. Without thinking, she backed up. The man's glassy hazel eyes fixed on hers and she stared back. It was like looking into an empty soul.

The stench from his unwashed body violated her senses. Her stomach roiled.

The door. Why didn't I lock the door?

She opened her mouth but couldn't speak. The man's eyes turned to slits and his sour, alcohol-saturated breath expelled when he huffed, making the foul odor pour over her face. She could barely breathe without the urge to vomit.

One of his large hands tugged on his greasy beard. "You deaf, woman?"

She shivered at his harsh tone and shook her head slowly.

He inched closer, until he nearly stood nose to nose with her. An inner voice screamed, *Run! Get out!* But her legs were riveted to the floor like steel pillars.

"Then speak, girlie."

"Uhhhh . . ."

"What's your problem? Never seen an old man before?"

He snorted and wiped his nose with the back of his hand. His eyes darted around the room, and he went to tug on the top drawer of one of the filing cabinets next to the desk. It was locked.

"I'm grubbing for food. Got anything to eat or drink?"

When he returned to her, she pressed her trembling hand against her neck. "Ah, no, sir. I . . . I don't . . . maybe tea, I think."

"Then just give me money." He breathed in her face.

She stepped away from him until her back pressed against the wall. He followed. Jerking her face away from his rancid breath, she stifled a fearful sob.

This can't happen, not to me! "I . . . I don't have any."

"Liar. Every church has a money box."

A hand like steel grabbed her elbow and wrenched her against him. He was far stronger than he looked.

"Get me the cash box!"

She recoiled from his touch, breathing in short, sharp gasps. "I don't know . . . about any money box. I . . . I don't have a key. I don't know . . . please, sir."

He tightened his grip, his fingers burning her skin. Spittle flew from his mouth with each word.

"Then look in your purse. A rich girl like you has to have cash. Now get it!"

He shoved her toward the desk, and she lost her footing. "Okay. Okay."

With fumbling hands, she grabbed at her bag from the desk, but it slipped out of her fingers and crashed to the floor. A whimper escaped her. He loomed so close she could feel the malevolence radiating from him.

She scooped up her purse and reached inside, fishing around for her wallet. *Please let there be money in here!*

The man snatched her purse from her hands, dumping everything inside onto the floor. He fell to his knees and rifled through the contents.

Get out while he's distracted!

Her body trembled uncontrollably. A gust of cool air drew her gaze to the black rectangle of the open door. Heart pounding, she baby-stepped toward it, but he easily blocked her way.

He glared at her, then grabbed her wallet and flipped it open. There was nothing inside except her high school ID and a few bank cards.

Emitting a guttural snarl, he lurched to his feet and hurled the wallet at her. It smacked hard into her chest.

She gasped and froze, terrified she might anger him further.

Cursing, he stomped on her makeup bag. She could hear her compact crunch under his heel. With a swift kick, he flipped her purse over with his foot. A leather coin pouch sprang free. Snatching it from the floor, he dumped the change into his palm.

"This it? Fifty cents?"

His mouth twisted, and he tossed the coins in her face. Shrinking away, she covered her eyes and watched through shaking fingers.

He paused and fixed his stare on her engagement ring. Panic constricted her chest.

"I'm sorry. I . . . I never carry money." She eased her hand behind her back.

He reached for her arm. "Show me your hand."

Shaking her head, she took several steps back. "No. Please."

The man charged at her.

Startled, she tripped over the wastebasket and fell against the desk. She spun and clutched the sides with both hands as she slid to the floor, sobbing.

"No—"

He grabbed her hair. Yanked her to her feet. Hissed, "Is it worth your life, rich girl?"

She screamed and fought, twisting against him. Her scalp burned. Sobbing from the pain, she clawed at his fingers.

"Don't—please—"

He swore and released her hair, shoving her to the floor. With both hands, she clutched her head and rubbed her scalp, then scrambled to her feet and stumbled away from him.

Since she couldn't get past him to run out the door, she glanced wildly around the room seeking anything she could use for protection. Her eyes fell on a letter opener on the desk. She lunged for it.

He blocked her path, roaring, "Give me the ring!"

Whipping out a knife, he shoved her to the floor and hunched over her. She drew her knees to her chest. Her heels dug into the carpet.

"Oh, God, help me!"

"Give it to me."

Stifling a scream, she whimpered, "It's not mine."

"I don't care whose it is. Hand it over." He leaned menacingly into her face. "Or I'll cut your pretty little—"

"No! Please." She scooted into the wall and squeezed her eyes shut. "Somebody, please help me!"

She felt the knife press against her neck, stinging the first layer of skin. "Shut up, rich girl, and give me that ring!"

White spots danced in front of her eyes. Her heart beat wildly. *Please don't faint. Please don't faint.*

Her ears were ringing. Deciding a ring wasn't worth dying for, she clawed at it, but it wouldn't budge. Gritting her teeth, she prayed for it to slide off.

Through the open door, she heard the distant rumble of an approaching car. The man darted a glance over his shoulder and momentarily froze, eyes widening.

Swinging back, he spit on the carpet beside her. "Come on—come on! I don't have all day."

"I'm sorry . . . it won't come loose," she sobbed, now hysterical. "I can't get it off!"

He gave her leg a vicious kick. "Give it to me!"

Shaking violently, she fought to yank the ring over her knuckle. "Please don't hurt me!"

God, where are You? Help me!

"Hurry up."

The roar of the car's engine was louder now. It had to be at the entrance to the parking lot.

"I—I'm trying. Please, I can't get it off." *God, let it be Tony and Dan.*

He bent over her, so close she could see the spidery red veins in his eyes. Baring his rotted teeth, he hissed, "Then I'll just take it off myself."

"No!" Her finger was turning purple from her efforts to remove the ring. Choking on a sob, she wailed, "It's stuck. I can't—"

Please, God, help me! Where are they?

The car swished past along the street. The sound of its engine faded until she heard nothing but her pulse hammering in her ears.

No . . . come back!

He grabbed her with his filthy hand and jerked on the ring. Still it wouldn't budge. Howling like a madman, he lifted the knife.

"*I want that ring!*"

Bitter bile rose in her throat as the knife plunged toward her. Dumb with terror, she tried to wrench away from the shining blade's downward path.

I'm going to die . . .

From the corner of her eye, flashes of metal penetrated her line of vision. He struck again and again, the blade tearing into her cheek and the side of her neck.

For an instant she felt nothing except the blunt force of the blows. Then white-hot pain exploded as the knife ripped repeatedly through skin and muscle. Warm liquid trickled down her neck.

Faint and nauseated, she collapsed against the floor. *Mom . . . Dad . . . somebody help me* . . .

Dimly she felt her attacker grab her hand, spread her fingers, and yank. A burning sensation seared through her hand and up her arm.

He let go of her and shoved her hard. She rolled onto her side, her hip crushing her throbbing hand. Uttering a curse, he tossed something onto the floor beside her bleeding cheek.

She was vaguely aware of heavy breathing. Footsteps fading away . . .

Silence descended. All she could hear was the faint throb of her pulse. Unable to move, she lay suspended in a haze of agony, clinging to consciousness with all the strength she had left.

After what seemed like hours, the sound of a truck engine drew closer, then abruptly halted. If she could just move . . . or call out for help. But she struggled for every breath.

Her last conscious thought was, *Why, God, why?*

Then she slipped into utter darkness.

Chapter 4

Dan wondered how Tony could pout the entire drive to the church without speaking a word. He usually had plenty to say even if only to brag.

It took longer than Dan expected to get there, and the tension thickened between them. Being busted with porn in the house and having to beg for a ride probably didn't help. His little brother had a lot of growing up to do.

Pulling his extended-cab pickup into the dark church parking lot, Dan wondered how Annie had kept busy while waiting for them. Being all alone in a dark, empty building had to be scary, especially down by the railroad tracks.

He parked in the first nonhandicapped spot closest to the entrance. Tony grabbed the handle and shoved the door open.

"Be right back," he muttered

As Tony sauntered toward the building, Dan noticed the church office door was already open. He was getting bad vibes, and when Tony went inside, Dan stepped out of his pickup, a warning going off in his mind.

A piercing scream erupted from inside the building. Dan slammed the truck door shut and darted toward the church.

Tony shot out the door and dropped onto his knees on the grass. The sound of violent retching evoked a shiver, and Dan's mouth filled with saliva. He forced the sensation down and darted toward Tony.

"What happened?" He knelt beside his brother. "Where's Annie?"

Tony clutched his stomach, shook his head, and heaved again.

Dan glanced at the door, his heart hammering. "Is she—"

His brother sobbed, "She's . . . she's . . .oh, God!"

On wobbly legs, Dan stood and raced for the door. Peering inside, he found Annie lying on her stomach with her head cocked to one side, surrounded by a pool of blood.

"Annie!" He rushed to her side.

He knelt to check her pulse, his stomach roiling as the metallic odor of blood assaulted him. He could feel the cool wetness seeping through the knees of his jeans. His stomach clenched as he gently moved her long, auburn hair, now sticky with gore.

The sickening sight of the wounds laid open along her cheek and neck made him lightheaded. For a moment he was certain he was going to pass out.

Please don't let her be dead, God. Please.

Afraid of hurting her, he carefully slid his fingers down her bloody neck, searching for signs of life. He felt a faint pulsebeat, and she moaned, a faint, agonized sound.

His heart leaped. *Thank You, Lord. Thank You!*

Peering around, he took in the horrific scene. Blood was everywhere.

"Annie, can you hear me?" He gently shook her shoulder, but she didn't acknowledge him.

His stomach contracted. This time he tasted a peculiar bitterness rising in his throat, burning like acid. Who could do something so violent to such a sweet, innocent girl?

Suddenly it occurred to him the person who did this might still be in the building.

The police. I need to call the police.

He grabbed the phone, but it slipped from his blood-slick hand. "Stay with me, Annie. Stay with me."

Stretching to reach the receiver, he scooped it from the floor, his hand shaking, and punched 911. At the first ring, he muttered, "Come on. Answer!"

He felt Annie's side to make sure she was still breathing. Her ribs made a slight rise and fall under his hand.

"You're going to be okay, Annie. Hang in there. I'm calling an ambulance."

Another slight moan escaped her. Thank God she was still alive.

"What's your emergency?"

"She's been hurt. Annie Myers. Bleeding really bad. We just found her. It looks as if she's been stabbed, and there's blood everywhere. She's so . . . pale. Oh, God! She's barely breathing. Please hurry!"

He wiped moisture from his eyes with his free hand. He'd never been so scared in his life. What if she died before they got there?

"Who am I speaking with?"

"Daniel Lane."

"What's your location, Daniel?"

"First Christian Church on 7th Avenue and Railroad. Please hurry!"

"Is anyone with you?"

"Just me and my brother. He's outside."

"Is it safe? Was the attacker still there when you found her?"

"I don't know. I didn't see anyone."

"Hold on, Daniel, while I send for EMS and a patrol car. Don't hang up."

"I won't." He touched Annie's shoulder. "Help is on the way, Annie. Stay with me now. Stay with me."

Stroking her silky hair, the color of fox fur, he whispered, "Jesus, be with her."

He switched the phone to his right ear and placed his finger just over her top lip. He held his breath and waited. A faint puff of air brushed his fingertip.

Thank You, Lord.

Exhaling in relief, he glanced around, taking in as much of the office as he could. When he turned back to Annie, his attention settled on a white object about three inches long that lay beside her cheek. He hadn't noticed it earlier, and he leaned closer to inspect it.

To his horror he saw it was a severed finger. The contents in his stomach clamored in his throat, but he forced the bile down. He turned his face away so he wouldn't lose control.

Awareness made the hair on his arms rise. *What if the person who hurt her is still here?*

He noticed a bloody footprint embedded in the carpet on the other side of her body. Several more fading prints led away from it, headed toward the rear exit. His shoulders slumped at the realization that her attacker must have gone.

Clutching the phone, he prayed as he glanced around the room. *Jesus, help her.*

After a moment, he touched her shoulder. "I'm still here. Hang in there."

In the distance, the shrill pitch of sirens pierced the still air., steadily drawing closer.

"They should be arriving any moment," the dispatcher said in his ear.

The sirens ceased, and within seconds police officers and medics crowded the room.

"They're here," Dan told the operator. Without waiting for a response, he hung up.

One of the officers said, "Sir, please step outside."

Dan whispered to Annie, "I'll meet you at the hospital. You're going to be okay now."

He stood and left with some reluctance. Outside he found his brother engaged in a conversation with the police, crying hysterically.

"I'm serious. I don't know what happened. I just came to pick her up and . . . and I . . . we found her like that."

Tony peered at Dan with frightened, desperate eyes. Dan hurried over to him. Surely they didn't think his brother would have attacked Annie.

Around the side of the church, a different officer yelled, "Look at this." With a plastic-gloved hand, he lifted a bloody knife out of the bushes.

Another officer snapped photos of the area and of the knife before heading into the building with his camera. The first officer dropped the knife into a bag and sealed it.

Dan placed his hand on Tony's shoulder. Tony grabbed him and sobbed, clutching at the neck of his T-shirt and pulling it down as he shook.

The odor of vomit on Tony's shirt caused Dan's stomach to lurch. As he clung to his little brother, Dan wanted to cry too, but the shock of finding Annie in a pool of blood had numbed him. He'd never witnessed anything so gruesome in his life.

Dan's chest tightened as his brother clung to him with all his strength. "She'll be okay, Tony. We gotta believe that."

But will she be okay? Oh, Annie. Why would someone hurt you like this?

Tony suddenly wrenched away, his chest heaving as he sucked in big gulps of air. His face contorted with grief as he shoved his finger into his own breastbone.

"It's *my* fault. I should have been here on time to pick her up. Oh, God . . ."

He moaned and crumpled once more into Dan's arms.

Tears erupted in Dan's eyes at the realization that his brother blamed himself. Though Tony often drove him crazy, Dan still loved him deeply.

"Mind if I pray?"

Tony stiffened and shoved him away. The veins in his neck bulged as he clenched his fists.

"Don't you dare. God could have protected her. I'll *never* forgive Him if she dies!"

As if suddenly realizing the truth in his words, Tony groaned, eyes wide. "What if she dies? Oh, Dan. I couldn't take it. I couldn't!"

He backed away, panic marring his face. Then he turned and dashed into the inky blackness.

Tempted to run after him, Dan resisted the urge and stayed with the police instead. He had to make sure Annie would be okay. His brother just needed time to grieve.

A police officer approached. "Sir? Did you see what happened?"

"Huh? Um, no." Distracted, Dan glanced at the officer, then back at Tony as he slipped farther into the night. "Is it okay for my brother to just leave?"

"Yes. We got a signed statement and have no evidence against him, so he's free to go."

Dan's shoulders sagged in relief. *Thank You, Lord. Please keep Tony safe.*

"Now tell me what you know."

Sucking in a breath, he blew it out slowly. "We found her like that. My brother was late picking her up. And because he needed a ride, I brought him here. That's all I know."

"Did you see anyone outside when you drove up?"

"No one. It was already dark when we got here."

"Thank you. Can you please write your statement here and sign below?" The officer held out a form on a clipboard and offered Dan a pen. "Make sure to write a number where you can be reached for further questioning if needed."

Dan wrote quickly and signed his name, then handed the clipboard and pen back to the officer.

"Thank you."

Medics emerged from the office with Annie on a stretcher. Police had taped off the building and snapped more pictures. An undercover squad car appeared with a single light flashing on top. A man in a suit got out and joined the group of officers huddled near the entrance. Speaking into a police radio, he walked around the building.

Dan glanced at Annie. She appeared so vulnerable on the stretcher, and so pale. He went to touch her hand and reassure her, and found her left hand heavily bandaged. It looked like a bloody boxing glove.

The other appeared fine, so he grasped it instead. "Annie. I'm going to follow you to the hospital. I'll see you there."

She nodded. The movement was so slight because of the neck brace she wore, he wondered if he had imagined it. Glancing again at her bandaged hand, the image of a finger lying in a pool of blood flashed through his mind. He recoiled as he realized with a shiver that it was her detached finger he'd seen. A wave of nausea bowled over him, and he clutched his stomach.

While the medics loaded her into the ambulance, he forced himself to breathe slowly. He glanced around once more in search of Tony. Not seeing his brother, Dan climbed into his truck and prayed for Tony's safety. Who knew what he would do in such a distraught condition?

Fighting to keep the panic from overwhelming him, Dan turned the key in the ignition. For the first time he became aware of the blood congealed on his hands and smeared across his shirt. His focus shifted to the dark stain on the knees of his jeans.

Unable to control the next wave of emotion slamming into his chest, he covered his face and wept bitterly. *Oh, Annie. How could anyone do this to you?*

Dan pulled into the parking lot of the emergency room, wishing he'd invested in a cell phone so he could have called his father on his way to the hospital. He headed for the courtesy phone on the wall.

While dialing, he wondered again where Tony had gone. At first he thought maybe his brother had headed to the hospital on foot. But he wasn't there.

"Hello?"

Dan closed his eyes, dreading telling his father what happened. "Dad?"

"Dan? What's going on? Where are you?"

"I'm at the hospital . . ."

"At the hospital? What happened? Dan? You still there?"

He swallowed the lump of excruciating pain clogging his throat. "It's Annie. Tony and I went to pick her up. She was—"

"What? Was there an accident? Is she okay?"

"I don't know if she's going to make it." His voice broke. "She . . . she was hurt bad."

"I'm on my way."

After he hung up, Dan realized his father would probably make a wrong assumption. He might assume Annie had been in a car accident with them and that she was hurt the worst.

But he would know the gruesome truth soon enough. There was no point calling back to explain.

Dan paced around the far end of the emergency room, determined to pray until his father arrived. Every few seconds he glanced toward the sliding glass doors, hoping the next set of headlights coming toward him belonged to his father's Suburban. Or rather, his mother's, since her accountant's salary paid for all the luxuries they owned. If they had to exist solely on his father's income, they'd be lucky to have one car.

He spotted his dad coming toward him and ran into his arms. "I'm so glad you're here. They won't tell me a thing because of that stupid HIPPA rule."

"How is she?"

"I just told you. I don't know. They won't tell me."

His father's eyes widened as he took in the blood on Dan's clothes. "Are you okay?"

"I wasn't hurt. It's Annie's blood." He choked on the words.

"I'm her pastor. Maybe they'll talk to me." He grabbed Dan's shoulders. "Where's your brother?"

"I haven't seen him."

Dr. Scott Roy, an ER doctor and family friend, approached them. "Pastor Lane. You here to check on Annie? I'm one of the doctors assigned to her care." He glanced around. "Are her parents here?"

Dan glanced toward the entrance. "I haven't seen them. They were out of town and due back tonight. I doubt they even know yet that she's here."

Their doctor friend nodded. "Sorry I can't tell you anything. But her parents can. Please have me paged when they arrive."

"Please, I need to know. Is she going to make it?"

The doctor turned away without answering.

Dan's father grabbed Dr. Roy's sleeve. "Please. We're worried about her."

Scott lowered his voice. "I shouldn't say this, but . . . she's in the OR. I'm praying the surgeon can save her finger."

Dan's father paled. "Her finger? What happened?"

"Her ring finger was completely severed." Dr. Roy raised his left hand and pointed at his wedding band. "The medics said they found it near her body. They brought it in a cooler."

Dan's stomach squeezed as he fought off the image of her slender white finger streaked with blood. His thoughts shifted to the blood-soaked bandages around her hand.

Dr. Roy's pager beeped. He unclipped it and peered at the number.

"I have to run. Keep praying." He patted Dan's father on the arm and offered an empathetic smile.

His father turned and stared into Dan's eyes. "What kind of accident was she in? It wasn't a traffic accident, was it?"

Dan cleared his throat. "Someone went into the church office while she was waiting for us to pick her up. That psycho stabbed her a whole bunch of times. The police found the knife in the bushes. But why would he cut off her finger?"

His father turned sheet white and covered his mouth with his hand. "It's my fault. I should never have left her alone. Oh, I'm just sick over this."

Grabbing his father's shoulders with both hands, Dan asked, "Why?"

His dad ran his shaking hand across his forehead. "I think I know what happened. He must've wanted the ring." His pinched face made him look close to tears.

Dan stared at his father until his eyes lost their focus. "Wanted the ring? What ring?"

"Last night Tony asked Annie to marry him. She was wearing your grandmother's ring when I brought her to the church office."

"That huge rock?" Dan gasped. "Tony gave it to her?"

His father nodded. "I saw it on her hand. She said Tony had proposed, and she was wearing it."

"Oh, man! Tony was already upset. Now he's really gonna freak."

"Where is he?"

"I don't know, Dad. He ran off and I haven't seen him since."

A faraway look came into his father's eyes. "Son, before her parents arrive let's pray for everyone involved."

Exhausted, Dan sighed. "That's the best thing we can do right now."

An hour later, Dan and his father were standing against the wall under a portrait of horses running across the desert when John and Jayne Myers entered the emergency room. Their business suits were wrinkled, their expressions strained. Jayne's contorted face was streaked with tears. Her husband scowled.

While Annie's mother looked like an older version of her daughter, her father just seemed . . . old. His frown aged him further.

"Pastor Lane." Mr. Myers approached, his wife's hand clasped in his. "We heard there's been an accident. Is Annie going to make it?"

His face matched his pale dress shirt. Annie's mother cried and clung to him. She didn't speak, but the haunted look in her eyes told Dan she feared the worst.

"Please, Pastor, tell us what happened," Mr. Myers asked in a shaky baritone. "At least tell us if she's still alive."

Giving the couple a brief nod, Dan's father ushered them to a group of matching orange chairs in the empty back corner of the ER waiting room. "Last I heard, she's still hanging in there, thank the Lord."

Annie's mother moaned and sagged against her husband.

Dan's father cleared his throat. "Dan and Tony found her. Someone attacked her . . . with a knife . . . while . . . while she was in the church office."

Annie's mother gaped at Dan and scanned him from head to toe. Her eyes glazed as she focused on the blood that splattered his clothing. Annie's blood.

"With a knife? At the church office? The message said she was in a car accident."

"My father didn't know what happened until he got here. I'm sorry."

She sputtered, "What was she doing there alone?"

"She was helping Dad, but he had to leave early. We were late picking her up." His voice hitched. "I found her . . . on the floor. She was stabbed in the face and neck . . ."

His throat tightened. Unable to finish, he glanced helplessly at his father. The doctors would have to explain the rest.

"Our church has been located in that part of town for over ten years. I never suspected . . ." Pastor Lane rubbed his face and glanced up. "Who would have thought something so horrible would happen in a church?"

Mrs. Myers wailed and grabbed his father's arm. "Please tell me she's not going to have permanent damage. Tell me she's going to live."

Dan's father closed his eyes. "We're all praying. I'm so sorry, John, Jayne. I truly am. I'll have the doctor paged so he can answer all your questions."

"We'll take care of it." John Myers stood.

For several moments, no one spoke. Annie's mother sobbed.

Patting her on the back, her husband led her to the information desk. Dan didn't mean to eavesdrop but couldn't help overhearing their interaction.

"Why did I encourage her to volunteer?"

"Shhh, Jayne. It's not your fault. No one could have predicted something so awful."

He kissed his wife's hair. "The doctor will be back any minute. Then we can talk to him about how Annie . . . how she's doing."

Dan exhaled with a silent prayer on his lips. *Please, Lord. Don't take Annie from her parents. She's all they have.*

When Dr. Roy and Dr. Perry entered the waiting room, Dan's breath caught. He couldn't tell anything from their stoic expressions, but he hoped they weren't bringing bad news.

Dr. Perry shook hands with Annie's father. "I'm sorry to have to meet with you under these circumstances."

Annie's father asked Dan and his father to join them. They followed the doctors to an exam room located off the main lobby. Two empty plastic chairs stood against the wall, but no one sat down.

Dr. Perry offered a warm smile to Annie's parents. "There's good news. I conducted a thorough exam of Annie's face and neck. Several of the knife wounds went fairly deep into her muscle tissue, but none struck her spinal column or vocal cords, and none of her bones were chipped."

Annie's father sucked in his breath and blinked several times as if struggling to take it all in. But Dan was overjoyed to hear Annie had no permanent damage. He would've broken into a happy dance, but he suspected her parents wouldn't understand his joy. Of course, they hadn't seen her in the bloody state Dan had found her in.

"She'll have scarring on her face and neck no matter how good the plastic surgeon is. But she has no permanent or life-threatening injuries that we are aware of at this point. We've sutured the face and neck wounds, but we're most concerned with saving her finger. There will definitely be nerve damage, but we're pretty sure it can be saved. Right now, we have it on ice. Fortunately, when she collapsed on her hand the pressure was enough to cut off the flow of blood. The weight from her body stopped the bleeding."

Annie's parents stared, mouths gaping, and obviously horrified. When their faces crumpled, Dan's heart contracted painfully.

Mrs. Myers covered her mouth. "On ice?" she squeaked. "Our baby's finger is—"

Dan was afraid she was going to faint as she swayed toward the doctor. Mr. Myers drew his wife to him, whispering reassuringly to her while tears rolled down his cheeks.

Dr. Perry cleared his throat. "There's nothing more we can do here. We'll transport her to Boise General by helicopter to avoid delays. A hand surgeon will examine her within the hour."

Dr. Roy added, "She'll need to see a plastic surgeon as soon as she's strong enough to handle more surgery. Boise has one of the best. In fact, the doctor who did the emergency surgery on your daughter tonight trained under him."

Mr. Myers nodded and tightened his arm around his wife's shoulder. "We can't thank you enough for all you've done for our—" he cleared his throat. "Our precious daughter. God bless you both."

The doctors shook everyone's hands. As they walked away, Mr. Myers hugged his wife and they both wept.

Chapter 5

Dan and his father arrived home exhausted. Tony still hadn't returned. Concerned about his fragile state of mind, his parents decided to search for Tony while Dan waited at the house.

Once his parents left, Dan entered the bathroom to clean up. Tears formed in his eyes as he peeled off clothes encrusted with Annie's blood. Shock from what he'd witnessed returned like a potent drink, numbing him. On trembling legs, he stepped into the hot shower. As the stinging spray heated his skin, he inhaled the moisture and scrubbed.

Glancing at his feet, Dan stared in horror as the water turned pink, then red. He still couldn't believe that Annie had been so savagely attacked.

The dam restraining his grief burst open. He sobbed, pressing his forehead against the still-cool ceramic tile on the shower wall, and released the overwhelming pain inside. He didn't move until the water turned lukewarm.

About ten minutes after Dan dried himself off and dressed, Tony stumbled through the door reeking like he'd drunk a case of whiskey. Pinpricks of anger stabbed at Dan's heart. How dare his brother drink himself into near oblivion, especially when Annie almost died because of his desertion. If he hadn't been with Tony at the church . . . He shuddered.

Dan stepped in front of Tony and attempted to look him in the eyes, but his brother avoided his stare. He shoved Dan as he tried to push past him.

"Move it, Danno."

Refusing to let him go, Dan grabbed the sleeve of his brother's T-shirt. "Where were you? Mom and Dad are going nuts."

Tony ripped his arm free and lumbered along as if he hadn't heard a word.

"I'm talking to you!" Again Dan stepped in front of his brother and blocked his exit. "What happened?"

Tony ignored him, stumbling again as he tried to pass by.

Disgust over Tony's immaturity fueled Dan's anger. He grabbed his brother by the shirtsleeves and slammed him against the wall.

"I said where were you?"

"None of your businesssss."

The pathetic slur in his brother's voice made Dan want to smack some sense into him. Dan shoved him again.

"Of course it's my business, you reject. You left me to clean up your mess. How could you take off on Annie like that? Huh?"

Tony's face contorted. "Don't talk about her. I can't deal."

"What?" Dan screamed in his Tony's face. "You're a real wuss, you know that? You're going to have to deal, like it or not. Your girlfriend almost died. You hear me? She was stabbed, Tony. Stabbed! She's lucky to be alive, no thanks to you."

"Bite me." Glaring, Tony tried to push him away.

"I'm not moving. Not until you hear everything I've got to say."

Tony tried to wriggle out of Dan's clutches, but Dan slammed his brother harder into the wall. He fought the urge to put his hands around Tony's throat and choke the life from him.

"You listening? Like it or not, you're gonna hear it all."

Tony closed his eyes.

"She was stabbed at least four or five times. She needed hours and hours of surgery. The hospital flew her to Boise General so she could have her finger reattached by a hand surgeon."

Tony's eyes snapped open and a confused expression marred his face. "Her finger?"

"Yes, you jerk. Her finger was cut clean off. Her attacker wanted the diamond. Remember the ring you used to manipulate her into having sex, you freaking dog?"

Tony choked. "Someone cut her finger off and stole Gram's ring?"

Dan squeezed Tony's arms and yelled in his face. "Is that all you care about? The stupid ring? What's your problem, you self-centered piece of garbage?"

To avoid throttling his brother further, Dan punched the wall next to Tony's head.

With a yelp, he stepped back and shook his hand. A flaming sensation caused his hand to throb like crazy. He rubbed his knuckles, immediately regretting his action.

Tony scowled and tried to bull past him again. "You're outta line, you jerk. I love her."

Ignoring the pain in his hand, Dan shoved Tony, then grabbed his chin and forced him to meet his stare. He wanted to pummel Tony's face in, but prayed for the strength to hold back. If he hit his brother once, he didn't know if he'd be able to stop.

"Then why did you leave her to die?"

"I didn't . . ." Tony flinched.

Dan's voice hitched and the fight left him. He just wanted to cry.

"How could you do that to Annie? Huh?"

"I'm not . . ."

Disgusted, Dan let go of Tony's shirt and stepped back. He plunged his fingers through his hair, trying to swallow the lump in his throat and sucking in tears. He refused to humiliate himself by crying in front of his little brother.

His shoulders slumped, Tony leaned against the wall, moaning. "Stop—"

"How could you walk away from her when she needed you, Tony? How?"

"I said stop!" Tony sobbed, flinging his arms in front of him as if to shoo Dan away. "I don't know! Just leave me alone!"

He whipped around and jostled past Dan, stumbling twice as he sped down the hallway. The soles of his sneakers squeaked against the hardwood floors. Slamming his bedroom door shut, he put an end to the conversation, and a quiet *click* told Dan his brother had locked him out.

He approached the door to Tony's room and stopped cold. The sound of his brother's pitiful wailing hurt like a swift kick in the ribs. Remorse caused Dan's chest to squeeze. His brother needed prayer more than he needed condemnation right now.

He leaned against the door. "I'm sorry."

He waited several seconds. Tony didn't reply.

"I said I'm sorry, bro."

Tony snapped, "And I said leave me alone."

Dan hesitated as a strangling sound emitted from inside Tony's room, followed by a loud bang. Terrified that Tony had tried to harm himself, he sighed with relief when he heard the sound of his brother retching into his wastebasket. His brother was too drunk and preoccupied with getting sick to do anything stupid like killing himself.

The next morning Dan avoided speaking with Tony at breakfast. He didn't want to rehash their argument from last night, if Tony even remembered it.

His father didn't even glance up when Dan entered the kitchen. The strained smile on his mother's face told him his little brother was in for a serious lecture.

The tension was so thick he briefly considered moving out and renting his own place, but he dismissed the thought. He'd only been back from college a month. Until he found a job to support himself, paying rent wasn't an option.

Dan peered at his mother. She hadn't spoken to Tony yet but stared at him with her mouth open, as if she planned to confront him but couldn't decide where to start.

Part of him wanted to butt into the conversation to make sure they got their facts straight. On the other hand, if he left the kitchen before an argument ensued, he wouldn't need to worry about further upsetting his parents. They already had enough to deal with in trying to comfort Annie's parents.

Finally his father glanced up with eyes so bloodshot he looked like he hadn't slept. Rubbing his forehead, he heaved a loud sigh.

"Son, we need to talk."

Tony nodded, eyes cast down. *Click. Click. Click.* He tapped his fork against his plate. Each tap grew louder until Dan thought he was going to break it.

"Tony!"

His mother imparted "the look." Tony set his fork down and clenched his hands together, still avoiding eye contact.

"I think we should talk in private." His father glanced from Tony to Dan.

"Just do what you've gotta do, Dad," Dan agreed. "I can leave."

Their mother straightened in her chair. "No, Daniel, I want you to stay. This problem involves the whole family. You need to be part of the conversation." Her brow furrowed, and she stared at their father as if daring him to challenge her.

Tony's head popped up. "No! I don't want that jerk here while we talk!"

Dan wrinkled his nose. His little brother's breath smelled of stale liquor. The alcohol Tony had consumed the night before must still be seeping from his pores. His parents would have to be clueless to not notice.

His mom shook her head. "We're going to get to the bottom of this. I want him to stay."

"You heard your mother," their father said, his eyes narrowing. "He stays."

"Whatever," Tony huffed. He slunk down in his seat.

"Sit up!"

Tony obeyed his mother, his head still bowed.

"Go ahead. You start." She nodded at their father.

He cleared his throat. "All right. First, Son, I want you to look at me when I'm talking to you."

Tony raised his head. His mouth tugged into a tight frown.

"I smell alcohol on your breath this morning. Want to tell us what happened?"

Tony tipped his head in Dan's direction. "Why don't you ask him?"

Dan startled. "Ask me?"

"Yeah, Danno. Go ahead. Tell them whatever you want. They'll believe you."

His parents fixed their eyes on Dan. "You know what's going on with your brother?" his father prompted.

"No!" He glared at Tony. "He can tell you about his problems himself. That's a real cop-out, Tone, asking me to tell Mom and Dad so you don't have to own up to anything."

"Own up to what?"

Dan shrugged. "Don't look at me, Dad. He needs to tell you himself."

"Okay. Let's start with the obvious one, Tony. Where did you get the booze?"

"A friend. We went back to his house. I only planned to have one to help me calm down. But then I kept seeing . . . kept thinking about . . . ." He choked on a sob and shook his head. "Just forget it."

Their mom placed her hand over Tony's. "We not going to 'just forget' anything, Tony. We want to help you through this. Talk to us."

Tony pulled away his hand and clutched his head. His voice shook.

"I—I can't."

"What do you mean you can't?" Dad frowned.

His parents fixed their eyes on his brother, but he didn't respond.

Since they'd reached an impasse, Dan decided to help. "I can tell you one thing. When Tony found Annie at the church, well, that spooked him pretty bad. He thought she was dead. We both did."

Tony glanced up, his eyes full of tears. "It's my fault we were late. There! Are you happy now? So Annie is in the hospital, and it's all because of me." He covered his face with his hands. "Why did God allow this to happen? She didn't deserve it!"

"No, she didn't, but it happened," Dan retorted. "Now you need to pull yourself out of your funk so you can help her. Getting drunk doesn't solve anything."

Tony clenched his fists. "I know that," he snarled.

"Why are you so angry?"

"Isn't it obvious, Dad? Everything has changed. Everything!"

"But Annie still loves you, Son. I doubt that's changed."

Dan's chest tightened at the thought of Annie still loving Tony, especially after he had abandoned her when she needed him most. If Tony had gone to pick her up alone, Dan didn't doubt for a second that she would be dead.

He had sensed his brother's insatiable desire to conquer her for weeks and watched over them the best he could to protect her, if needed. Finding the porn had only heightened his concerns. He wondered if keeping Tony's unsavory habit a secret had been the right thing to do—for Tony's sake and for Annie's.

"There's another thing your mother and I are very concerned about." Their dad got up and left the room. He returned with Tony's illicit magazines. "Can you explain these?"

Tony squinted, shooting daggers at Dan with his angry gaze. "I knew you couldn't keep your mouth shut for even one day. You're such a narc."

Their father raised his hand. "Hold on a sec, Tony. Your mother found these last night when she was putting your laundry away. Dan had nothing to do with it."

"Yeah, right!" Tony scoffed.

Mom stared at Dan, a hurt look in her eyes. "You knew he had these?"

"I only found them the other day."

"And I'll bet you really enjoyed them, didn't you, bro?" Tony sneered.

Dan's neck heated. "Hey, I resent that."

Their father sighed. "Tony, no Christian man should keep that kind of temptation around. It doesn't glorify God and makes you dwell on things that are reserved for marriage. And honestly, most of the stuff in those magazines incites lusts that are unnatural."

Before Dan could put a rein on his tongue, he snorted, "Why do you think Tony wants to marry Annie so bad?"

Tony jumped from his seat, his chair scraping the floor as it crashed behind him. "You better cut it with the wisecracks or I'm gonna nail you."

Dan stood. "You're just mad because you got caught."

"No!" Tony pounded the table with his fist. "I'm mad because you don't understand me. I do love her—"

Tony turned his face away. His shoulders shook with racking sobs.

Dan stared at his brother, overcome by remorse. *I'm sorry, Lord. I shouldn't have pushed him so hard.*

Their mom whispered, "If you love her, Tony, then come visit her with us. I'll bet she wants to see you."

Tony swung around, his eyes widening with panic. "No!"

"You can't avoid her, Son. She needs to see you."

Tony's mouth thinned. "Dad, I'm not going."

"What are we supposed to tell her if she asks about you? Sorry, Annie, but Tony couldn't stand the idea of seeing you? Come on, Tony! Grow up."

"Tell her whatever you want, Dan. But I'm not going. Nobody can make me."

Tony stormed out of the kitchen, slamming the door behind him.

Dan sucked in a breath, let it out. "If we're done, can I go? I need to visit Annie. She deserves some moral support, and I'm going to see that she gets it. I have a bad feeling that when she figures out Tony's avoiding her it's going to hit her hard. I want to be available . . . as a friend, you know?"

Their father nodded, his expression sad. "Thank you, Son."

Annie's eyelids fluttered. It took several seconds for her vision to clear. The dank taste in her mouth made her want to lick her lips, but they seemed glued together.

She needed a drink of water. When she eyed the water pitcher on the table, she noticed the fuzzy outline of her mom sitting in a chair next to the window. Her father sat on the other side of the bed, his chair reclined. He had his arms crossed and his eyes closed.

Why would her parents be sleeping in chairs? Her gaze darted around, taking everything in. She focused the IV pole next to her bed. A bag of red fluid hung next to a bag with clear fluid. Tiny tubes connected them to her right hand. Then it struck her despite the haze fogging up her mind. She was in the hospital.

"Dad?" she whispered.

Her father's eyes snapped open, and he sat up. "Look, Jayne, she's awake."

"Thank you, Jesus!" Her mom stood and approached the bed.

"Can . . . can I have a drink?"

"Sure. Anything."

Her father reached for the pitcher, poured a small amount of water into a cup, and lifted it to her mouth. She emptied the cup and wiped her lips with her right hand. The tubes made the movement awkward, and her hand ached from the IV needle.

"Thanks, Dad." She attempted a smile, but it hurt the left side of her face.

"Sure, honey." He set the cup back on the table.

She adjusted her hips on the bed. A stabbing pain shot through her face and radiated down her neck. A whimper escaped. She glanced up to see that tears soaked her mother's eyes.

Annie's gaze was drawn to the thick bandage that swathed her left hand. She gasped.

"Why is my hand wrapped up?" She tried to move her fingers, but the makeshift cast immobilized them.

Her father cleared his throat. "Don't you remember, sweetheart? You were attacked at the church."

Annie closed her eyes. Recalling the horrible smell of the old man's breath, she shuddered. Her stomach cramped at the memory of him screaming in her face, the repeated flash of the knife, the searing pain.

She touched the side of her head and explored the bandages covering her cheek and neck. Her fingers trailed up her left cheek until she reached the smooth skin near her eye. The gauzy feel of the cloth and the tape over it made her think of a mummy in a cheesy horror flick. But why would she have those types of bandages on her neck and face? Unless . . .

"No. No! That horrible man, he didn't. Did he . . . he . . . cut my face?"

The fuzzy shape of her mother's head nodded ever so slightly. Annie's vision blurred further as tears streamed down her face.

"But why would he do that to me?"

She surveyed her hand and her chest tightened. *The ring.*

No one answered. Maybe because it was too inconceivable to say out loud.

"He didn't . . . did he—" Nausea crawled up her throat. "Rape . . . ?" she whispered.

"No!"

Both her parents shook their heads with vehemence, and more tears flooded Annie's eyes.

"Where's my ring?"

Her parents peered at each other, then her father stroked her arm. "The police think the man who attacked you stole it. Do you remember what happened?"

"But . . . he couldn't have taken the ring. It wouldn't come off."

Her father grimaced. "He cut your finger, Annie. The surgeon had to reattach it."

Vivid images of the attack overwhelmed her. The world tilted on its axis.

Through the memory's horror, a pleasant-sounding man's voice penetrated her consciousness, comforting her. *Stay with me, Annie. You're going to be okay.*

The voice sounded deeper than Tony's. Was Dan the one who had spoken to her? But what had happened to Tony?

She opened her eyes. "Does Tony know what happened?"

Her mother nodded. "He found you after . . . what happened. His brother called the ambulance and followed you to the emergency room."

"Tony and I are supposed to get married. I was going to tell you . . ."

Her parents glanced at each other as if shocked, then peered at Annie. "What?"

Her chest tightened. "Why are you looking at me like that?"

Her parents' mouths hung open. They looked unsure of how to answer. Something was wrong, but what?

Then she remembered the horrific sound of Tony's screams . . . and the way everything had faded into blackness.

"Where is Tony? Is he okay?"

"I don't know, sweetheart," her father crooned. He stroked her hair. "No one's seen him."

Her mother blinked back tears and pressed her fingers over her lips. Swallowing hard, Annie gazed into her sad eyes. *Tony, where are you? Why didn't you stay with me?*

Chapter 6

Dan drove to Boise General alone. He'd told his parents he wanted time to think, so he left before they did. The truth was, he also wanted the option of choosing when to leave. He thought about his schedule and decided he could visit Annie daily until the three interviews he had lined up for next week.

Of all of his interviews so far, the job in the lab at the hospital sounded the most lucrative and interesting. His internships before graduation qualified him for the position. He hoped they'd offer him a job soon so he could support himself and move out on his own.

The added bonus of the job at the hospital would be working near Annie. A smile spread across his face at the thought of seeing her every day. He'd make her feel better somehow.

He almost missed his exit because his thoughts were so wrapped up in Annie and how he could cheer her up. And though the savings in his bank account had dwindled, he still wanted to buy Annie a special gift.

His heart lifted at the thought of seeing her for the first time since her surgery. Stab wounds wouldn't change her beauty in his eyes.

But would the trauma somehow change her sweet personality and make her bitter? And how would she react to Tony's continued absence? Dan envisioned her despair, which evoked his suppressed rage and made him want to throttle his brother all over again.

Dan had always kept his distance from Annie due to her age and his brother's relationship with her. But when Annie turned nineteen last month, her age no longer factored into the equation. He couldn't see any reason why developing a friendship with her wouldn't work. Except the fact she was now engaged to his brother.

He sighed, wishing there was a way he and Annie could become more than friends. But he didn't see how that was possible without someone getting hurt in the process.

For now he'd keep a safe emotional distance for both their sakes. Their relationship would have to center on friendship. As long as her heart belonged to his brother, it would never belong to him.

The trouble was that his love for her ran deep. He couldn't stop how he felt. A lump formed in his throat while he parked his car and prayed for her like he'd done every day for the past four years. Sucking in a deep breath, he stepped out of his truck and headed for the gift shop. There had to be something he could purchase to brighten her day.

After browsing several minutes, he spotted a stuffed cat. He remembered Annie mentioning how much she loved cats because they had that in common. Actually, he had a soft spot for most animals, and he suspected she felt the same way. He decided to buy her the stuffed cat to snuggle up with since the hospital wouldn't allow real pets.

As he paid for his purchase, he smiled. Oh, how he envied the stuffed animal. No doubt Annie would cuddle the cat, her fingers gently roaming over the silky fur. And the animal's body would fit perfectly under her arm while she slept.

While he waited for the elevator, he closed his eyes and imagined her cuddling him instead. Warmth coursed through him and ignited his senses. He quickly redirected his thoughts so he wouldn't get too stirred up right before he saw her.

Lord, help me be a blessing to Annie today. Please help her to see me as a friend and not just as Tony's brother. Thank you, Lord, for being faithful and for answering my prayer. Amen.

The elevator dinged, and the doors slid open. He stepped inside, riding to the third floor alone. His hands started trembling and sweating, as if he were about to get in front of his graduating class and give a speech. He wiped one palm on his leg, and then transferred the gift to his free hand as he wiped the other.

Relax, he chastised himelf. *You're not proposing anything but friendship here.*

He exhaled when the doors slid open, then sucked in a nervous breath as he caught sight of Annie's parents heading toward him. His heart thumped at the sight of their worried faces.

"Is Annie okay?"

Mrs. Myers' eyes shone with tears and she smiled. "I think so. She's dozing right now, so we thought we'd go to the cafeteria and get something to drink. Would you like to join us?"

"No thanks. I'll just wait in her room until she wakes up."

"Thank you for coming to see her," Annie's mother added softly.

"No problem."

She glanced at the stuffed cat. "How sweet of you to bring a gift. I'm sure she'll love it."

Her father fixed his attention on Dan. "This is going to be very hard for Annie. We don't want our daughter hurt any more than she already is."

Dan's throat tightened with unexpected emotion, and he coughed. He hated being so transparent.

"I know. I'm so sorry this happened to her. I'll do my best to help her heal."

"We appreciate that. She needs someone like you in her life. Someone who truly cares."

He wondered if they were trying to imply something about Tony. Mrs. Myers hooked her arm through her husband's elbow.

"Let's give the young man some time alone with Annie."

Wearing a forlorn-looking smile, Mr. Myers squeezed her hand. "Sure. Let's go."

If Dan hadn't known better, he'd think they were trying to set him up with their daughter. Frowning, he went to tap on Annie's door.

No one answered, so he slipped into the room and eased himself into the vinyl chair next to her bed. The bandaged half of her neck and head faced the wall. The untouched side remained closest to him.

As he watched her sleep, he remembered getting into his mother's closet when he was about four or five and rubbing her fox fur against his face. Annie's hair was the exact same color, and he wanted so much to rub his face against it. If only he could touch her smooth skin, or caress her cheek with his hand . . .

He imagined gazing into her eyes and telling her she was still beautiful to him. The ache in his chest grew so strong he squeezed his eyes shut to keep from crying.

After a moment he opened them and focused on the stuffed cat on his lap. He was eager to give it to her. He played with the nylon whiskers and tried to imagine the look of pleasure his gift would bring to her eyes.

While lost in thought, he heard her stir.

"Ummmm . . ."

A whimper of pain escaped her lips as she tried to adjust her body. He held his breath as she opened her eyes.

Her head turned in his direction and she stared for a moment, a questioning look in her eyes. When she spoke, her lips barely moved.

"Dan? What are you doing here?"

Not at all the reception he had imagined. "I wanted to see how you were doing."

Pain from her comment must have registered in his eyes because she quickly apologized. "Sorry, I didn't mean to be rude. My parents told me you found me and called the ambulance. You saved my life. I want to thank you for that."

"You're very welcome. Here." He offered the stuffed cat. "I brought you something."

She started to smile, then yelped with pain.

His muscles tensed. "Want me to call a nurse to bring you pain medicine?"

Her head bobbed slightly and she winced, tears escaping.

"Hold this. I'll be right back." He handed her the cat.

Tears rolled down her cheeks. "Sure."

He scoured the halls until he found a middle-aged RN counting meds and placing them in cups. "Annie Myers is in a lot of pain. Can you bring her something?"

The heavy-set nurse squinted. "I'll check her chart. Give me a minute to finish up."

He waited for what seemed like an eternity until she finally checked Annie's chart, then prepared something to ease her pain.

When he reentered the room with the nurse, he found Annie petting the stuffed cat. She glanced up and her lips twitched slightly.

"Thanks for the gift. It was sweet of you."

Dan's face heated at the compliment. His heart thrilled at the smile he'd brought to her eyes.

"I thought you might like it."

He eased into a chair while the nurse injected a clear medication in the tube of Annie's IV.

"In a few seconds you should be feeling better. If not, just push the call button."

"Thanks, I will."

Annie's attention lingered on Dan. He grew antsy under her scrutiny.

"Is something wrong?"

"Why'd you come?"

Words escaped him. How much should he divulge?

"I hoped we could be friends."

Her eyes clouded. "That's nice, but I don't know if—"

"Just friends, Annie. Don't worry about my brother. He can deal with it."

"Where is he anyway? My parents said they haven't seen him. Is he all right?"

Another question with a difficult answer. "Um . . . Tony's fine. He's just having trouble dealing with what happened to you. He's not ready to visit yet."

She squinted. "What? Tony loves me. Of course he wants to see me. We're engaged."

Annie didn't believe him. He tried to not focus on the pain her words caused.

"He should be coming to see you soon." He offered a feeble smile. "I just don't know when."

She leaned back on her pillow. "He'll visit soon. I know he will."

His heart squeezed at the way she said it, as if reassuring herself. If Tony would grow up and be the man she needed, Dan would let it go.

Something in his gut told him his brother wouldn't change and in the end would devastate Annie. Dan was overwhelmed with the longing to protect her.

The rich scent of meat wafted through the room as an orderly entered with Annie's meal. The moment the woman set the tray down, Dan could hear Annie's stomach growl.

He grinned. "Hungry?"

Annie quirked a tiny half smile in return. "Starving."

"Need some help?"

"That'd be nice." Her warm response caused his heart to do a little flip.

He lifted the lid from the dish. Annie sniffed and peered at the items inside.

"Smells a lot better than it looks."

Taking in the solitary bowl of broth and a tiny cup of Jell-O, he couldn't help snickering. "Still hungry?"

"Now I'm not so sure." She giggled. "Let's give it a try. If it stinks, you can have it."

"Gee, thanks. How kind of you." He dipped the spoon into the bowl and raised it carefully, blew on the broth, and held his free hand underneath to prevent a spill. "Ready?"

When she offered a tentative nod, he eased the spoon to her open mouth so she could sip the warm liquid. Never before had something as normal as eating appeared so sensual to him.

A grimace wrenched her mouth. "Ah . . ."

"That bad, huh?"

Her eyes opened and she whimpered, "It hurts to swallow. The muscles in my neck are so sore." She touched her neck. "But I guess I should be thankful my throat wasn't cut or I wouldn't be able to swallow at all."

His eyes burned at the memory of her lying in a pool of her own blood. He glanced away so she wouldn't see the tears forming in his eyes.

"Tell me about what happened," she whispered.

He set the spoon down. "What part?"

"When you found me."

He exhaled. "You sure you want details?"

She nodded, wincing at the slight movement.

"Do you need more medicine?"

"I'm okay. Tell me what you remember."

His eyes stung and he blinked back tears. "Well, you—" his voice cracked. "I'm sorry. It's hard for me to talk about it because I—I thought you were dead."

Her eyes widened.

"Tony freaked out and started screaming when he saw you, so I ran into the building to see what upset him. I found you, and blood was everywhere."

She whispered, "I think I remember that."

He cocked his head. "Remember what?"

"Tony screaming. The horrible screeching sound. I thought maybe someone had hurt him, but I couldn't see."

"I called 911 right away. A couple of times you stirred, but your skin was ghost white—" His voice caught. "I'm sorry. I don't know why I can't talk today. What I'm trying to say is I was afraid you'd stop breathing."

Her mouth formed an O shape, and her eyes clouded over. He waited until she was ready to hear more. The sound of her stomach rumbling made them chuckle, relieving the somber moment.

"Want to try some Jell-O? Maybe it'll slide down easier than the soup." He balanced a chunk of the red gelatin on the spoon.

"Sure." She moistened her lips.

As he watched, a jolt of warmth shot through him. Lifting the spoon to her mouth, he tried not to obsess on how full and pink her lips were.

Annie closed her eyes for several seconds before swallowing. She sighed.

"Much easier than hot broth."

"Good."

He enjoyed the task of feeding her. It pleased him that she seemed comfortable accepting his help.

She met his gaze. His pulse jumped at the gratitude reflected in her gorgeous blue-green eyes.

"Ready for more?"

A tentative smile curved the undamaged side of her face. "Yeah."

"Knock, knock." Dan heard his father's voice behind him.

Annie glanced at the door. "Tony?"

As Dan's parents entered, he watched for their reaction. His mother avoided eye contact with Annie. Not a good sign.

"He's not with us, but I'm sure he'll come if he can get away," she said.

"Get away?" Annie's voice sounded hoarse.

Dan's father cleared his throat. "Tony's having trouble accepting what happened to you, Annie. He blames himself."

A puzzled expression came over her face. "Why?"

His parents studied each other, then his mother answered, "He thinks it's his fault."

"That's crazy."

"To him it's not. He was late picking you up, and you were attacked because of the ring he gave you."

"But it's not his fault. Tell him, please. And tell him I love him. Will you do that for me?" Annie spoke softly, tears streaming down her face.

Dan's mother offered a weak smile. His father nodded and patted Annie's good hand.

"Sure."

Annie closed her eyes. "Thanks."

As Dan watched her expression transform, he wondered why she needed so much to believe in his brother. The glazed look in her eyes struck him like a kick to the chest. She reminded him of a person in shock, and it made him break out in a cold sweat.

"I better go. It's getting crowded in here." Dan stood.

Annie's lips formed a pout as if she hated to see him leave. "Come back and visit again."

Placing his hand over her good one, he allowed himself to linger for a few seconds. The feel of her soft skin sent shock waves up his arm until they reached his heart.

He loved her so much. Why did he think he could handle being friends when he wanted so much more?

Be patient, Son.

He gently squeezed her hand. "I will. See you soon."

Her eyes twinkled as he let go, and she reached for the stuffed cat. "Thank you. I'm naming her Purty."

"It's the least I could do." He waved one last time and walked out before anyone could notice how emotional he'd gotten over her grateful smile.

When he exited the building he spotted Tony. His bother stood at the far end of the parking lot, gazing up at the hospital's windows. Had he changed his mind?

Dan approached without speaking and lightly touched his brother's arm. Tony jumped. Swaying slightly, he shoved his hands in his pockets and stared at Dan for several seconds.

"So how's she doin'?" he slurred.

Anger squeezed Dan's chest. Tony was drunk again.

"Why don't you freakin' go see for yourself?" he spat.

He stormed off without looking back, praying that Tony would either do right by Annie or get out of her life before he broke her heart.

Chapter 7

Visiting hours were finally over. Annie's eyes burned. She'd wanted to cry for the past hour. The lump in her throat strained against the sutures in her neck, but the physical pain didn't come close to the ache in her heart.

"Tony, why didn't you visit me?" she whispered in the empty hospital room. "Why?"

Seconds later, her phone rang. *Tony!*

A sense of urgency grabbed her when she realized she couldn't reach the phone. Ignoring the stabbing sensation in her neck, she lunged for the call button and pressed it.

Hurry . . . please . . . !

Five rings.

Six.

Where is everyone?

Seven.

Please, somebody come!

Footsteps.

Eight.

A young brunette sporting white pants and a green scrub shirt with a jungle pattern entered the room. "Can I help you?"

"Yes! Hurry! Answer the phone."

Grinning, the nurse picked up the receiver. "Hello?"

Annie held her breath and prayed it was Tony.

"Yes, she's right here." She covered the phone with her hand and whispered, "Whoever this is, he sure has a sexy voice."

Dan's hands were sweating before he'd even picked up the receiver. He needed to talk to Annie tonight. Not just out of genuine concern for her well being, but he wanted to find out if she'd seen Tony.

The moment he heard Annie's greeting his bravado plummeted.

"Tony?"

I should hang up. Spare myself.

"Hello? Is anyone there?"

Dan pinched the bridge of his nose between his thumb and index finger. "Hi, Annie." To cover the hoarse sound of his voice, he coughed. "How are you feeling?"

"About the same. Have you heard from Tony?"

His chest tightened. He understood why she'd want to know, but it still hurt.

"Yeah. I did."

She sighed. "And?"

"And I'm not sure what you want me to say."

"Start with telling me why he won't visit. What's keeping him away?"

"It's like my dad told you. He's having a hard time with guilt. He feels responsible."

"I said it didn't matter. Did you tell him I love him and that it's not his fault?"

"Didn't get the chance."

He thought he heard a whimper and a sputtering sound. "You upset?"

"Wouldn't you be?" she replied with a sad squeak.

"I suppose. Dumb question, huh? I'd better let you go."

"No! Don't hang up. I'd love to talk." She sounded almost desperate.

His heart danced a little jig. He was making progress.

"What do you want to talk about?" *Crud, I sound breathless.*

"Whatever you want." In spite of her giggle, she still sounded on the verge of tears.

"Can you be more specific?" He teased, trying to keep their conversation light.

"I don't know. Why don't you come up with something to discuss and I'll follow."

She must be so lonely. "All right. I enjoyed hearing you sing Sunday."

More whimpering sounds. *I upset her. I'm such an idiot.*

"I'm sorry. I didn't think about how you'd feel."

"It's okay," she sighed, "I'll have to get used to it. I won't be singing in church again."

"Why not? You have a beautiful voice."

"That was before," she whispered so low he had to strain to hear.

"But your voice sounds fine."

"It's not about my voice. It's my face. Even with plastic surgery I'm always going to have scars. I won't sing in front of people with my face all messed up." Her voice cracked.

Oh, Annie. "You'll always look beautiful to me."

She gasped. "Dan?"

I can't believe I just said that out loud.

A door slammed behind him. Tony stomped up the steps and pushed past Dan.

"Move it, bro."

Dan stepped aside, praying Tony would be quiet, that Annie hadn't heard his voice.

"Is that Tony? Can I talk to him?"

Too late.

"Sure. Hold on a sec."

He might as well make his brother face her now, so he shoved the phone in Tony's face. "Annie wants to talk to you."

Tony scowled, but grabbed the phone.

"Hel-loo?"

Dan leaned against the wall and folded his arms. He watched his brother try to keep it together. But Tony couldn't stand without swaying.

"Me? Drinking? Um . . . why do you think that?"

Dan snorted.

Tony glared at Dan, and then winced. "I'm sorry, babe. No, I don't think you're stupid. I just . . . I'm having a hard time."

He could barely hear Annie through the phone, but her tone sounded angry.

His brother's eyes widened. "No. I mean . . . sure, everything's great. It's just . . . you know . . . we were getting married. Then this happened."

Tony winced again. "I mean we *are* getting married. Gosh, Annie, you know what I meant. Don't get all upset."

Dan rolled his eyes.

Tony's mouth pressed into thin line. "Maybe tomorrow. Yeah, I think I can. Bye."

He shoved the phone at Dan and the sudden movement made him lose his balance. He fell against the wall.

"You jerk!" he growled. "Now I *have* to go see her."

Dan gaped as Tony stumbled down the hall. He raised the phone to his ear, praying Annie hadn't heard.

"Annie? You still there?"

The sound of her sobs told him she'd heard every hostile word. He wanted to pound his brother's face in for hurting her again.

"Annie, he's drunk. He doesn't know what he's saying." *Why am I making excuses for him?*

"I don't want to talk about it."

"Okay. We don't have to." *I don't want to talk about Tony either.*

"And I don't want to talk to you anymore either."

"Me? What did I do?"

"You're trying to break us up, but it won't work. He's marrying me. He will."

Dan's heart twisted at the desperation in her tone. "I know. Tony loves you. I'm sure this will all work out."

Her voice softened. "I'm sorry. I didn't mean to snap. You've been a good friend. Forgive me?" She drew in a shaky-sounding breath.

"Don't worry. Nothing will jeopardize our friendship. I promise you that." He swiped moisture from his brow, relieved still to be on speaking terms with her.

"Good. I need a friend. Night." *Click.*

"Night," he muttered as he stared at the receiver.

Right before she'd hung up he'd heard someone in the background offer her more pain medication. She probably needed it too.

If Annie needed to believe Tony, Dan would indulge her. But once she got stronger and realized the truth, he'd be there to hold her when his foolish brother broke her heart.

Eventually Tony's true intentions would come out. She might be devastated at first, but in the long run, she'd be better off.

He hated to think that way about Tony, but his brother's relationship with the Lord had always been questionable in Dan's mind. Tony's latest transgression just firmed up his theory.

Dan mentally added Tony to his prayer list. If God chose to move in a way that would change his brother for the good, he would not get in God's way. Tears formed at the thought of losing Annie, but he had to trust God, his Cornerstone.

I can't lose what was never mine, now can I, Lord?

The next afternoon two police officers woke Annie from her midday nap.

"Sorry to disturb you, Miss Myers, but we need to ask you a few questions about the other night. Are you able to talk right now?"

Annie blinked. "Sure."

The female officer drew a small notebook and pen from her pocket. "I'm Officer Grady, and this is Officer Briggs. I'll be conducting the interview and writing down your statement while Officer Briggs records it. Is that all right with you?"

Officer Briggs held up a mini voice recorder, his look questioning.

Annie swallowed hard and tried to calm her breathing. Thinking about the attack made her hyperventilate.

"I . . . think so."

"Good." Grady clicked her pen and wrote something in her notebook.

Briggs spoke into the voice recorder. "Testing, one two. Testing one two." After playing it back, he smiled at Annie. "All set."

He sat in the chair next to the bed. Annie clutched the sheet with her good hand, shaking in spite of her attempts to remain calm.

"I want you to describe everything you remember about the man who hurt you," Grady told her. "Take as much time as you need."

Her eyes quickly saturated with tears. "He, um, he looked about fifty years old and had a . . . a . . . white beard. He was dirty and smelled nasty. His voice was deep and scary."

"I have photos of three men to show you. Do you think you could tell if he was one of them?"

Fear seized her chest. Could she look at him? "I . . . I'll try."

"That's all we ask." Grady slid three mug shots from the back of her notebook and passed them to Annie. "Is one of these the man who attacked you?"

Her attacker stared back at Annie from the center photo. He appeared even meaner than he had in person. Bitterness surged in her throat.

With her good hand shaking, she pointed. "Him. He's the man who—"

She shuddered and turned her face away. Tears cascaded until they dripped from her chin.

"I'm sorry. I can't stand to look at him."

"I understand." Grady patted Annie's good hand and passed the photos back to her partner.

How could she? Her face isn't destroyed. Annie closed her eyes and tried to relax.

"I'm sorry if we upset you."

Annie's eyes sprang open. "How would seeing that horrible man *not* upset me?"

The officer nodded. "Right. Well, thank you for your time."

Briggs stood. "I hope you'll be well enough to go home soon."

"Thank you." Annie hesitated. "How did you know he was my attacker before I described him?"

"He pawned the ring for five hundred bucks," Grady answered. "The pawn shop owner reported it. He claimed the ring was worth an easy ten grand and if the man hadn't stolen it, he would've known that."

Briggs added, "Plus, we found specks of blood on it."

"So he's in jail?"

Grady nodded. "Yes, and he isn't going anywhere."

"Will I have to see him again?"

"If you want him prosecuted? Probably, though the county prosecutor may be able to get by with just your statement and the evidence we collected."

"I don't want to testify if it means I have to see him."

Someone rapped on the partially open door. "Annie?"

Dan. The sound of his voice stirred her heart.

He stuck his head inside. Seeing the officers, he said hastily, "Oh, I'm sorry. I can come back later."

"No, come in," Annie urged. "They were just leaving."

Dan waited until the officers left before he entered. He took the chair next to the bed.

"What did they want?"

"They took my statement. Guess what?"

"What?" He grinned in anticipation.

She held his gaze, and her pulse sped up as she wondered what it would be like to kiss him. *Wait! I can't think that way about Dan. I love Tony. And he loves me.*

She redirected her thoughts. "They found the man who attacked me."

Dan's smile broadened. "That's great, Annie."

He grasped her good hand in his and squeezed, causing warm sensations to shoot up her arm. The delicious heat went beyond anything she experienced when Tony touched her, and that made her shift uncomfortably. She didn't want to feel attraction toward his brother.

Annie stared at his lingering hand until he tore it away. "Sorry."

"It's okay." She cleared her throat. "Can we be friends?"

The tender look in his eyes melted her heart.

"Definitely."

Chapter 8

Dan took the stairs two at a time. He was flying high, and taking the elevator would have slowed him too much.

Annie had responded to his touch. He couldn't miss the emotion in her eyes. It was as if she saw him as a man and not just as Tony's brother.

For a moment he allowed himself to hope. But when he was tempted to confide his feelings to someone, his conscience reminded him she might never be his.

The bounce in his step diminished to a lifeless thud. His head hanging, he plodded across the parking lot.

He couldn't hope for her love. Not as long as she loved his brother.

His shoulders sagged and his pace morphed into slow motion. Pushing his leaden feet the rest of the way to his truck required enormous effort.

With a defeated sigh he pulled his keys from his pocket and opened the door. His gaze locked on a bloodstain that had soaked into the gray velour seat cushion on the driver's side.

He cringed. That bloody scene would be forever etched in his mind.

He turned the key in the ignition and the truck's engine hummed to life. If only love were so easy to engage. If only he could find the key to unlock Annie's heart, to make her want to love him.

He clicked on the radio. A song from his favorite Everyday Sunday CD was playing For a moment he listened to the lyrics to "Herself (I Want a Girl)."

"What does Annie believe, Lord? I don't see how she can cope with what happened to her if she doesn't know You. But maybe I don't know her as well as I should. I'm not sure about her faith. She goes to church, but a lot of people do that and they don't know You."

Ask her.

Dan hesitated, unsure whether the quite whisper in his heart was God's voice. "Ask? Hasn't she known You for years?"

She doesn't know Me. Not like you do.

A tremendous ache for Annie—deeper than the one he already carried—settled like a heavy burden on his heart. "All right, Lord. I'll ask," he decided. "Nudge me when the timing is right."

On his way inside the house, Dan tripped over a pair of Tony's sneakers. His brother often kicked his shoes off, leaving them wherever they landed until someone forced him to pick them up. Dan had several pet peeves, and this one topped the list.

Growling, he kicked the sneakers out of his way. At least now he knew where to find his brother.

"Tone, you better quit leaving your shoes in front of the door, or else."

He stopped to listen for a snappy comeback. Instead, he heard a pitiful, strangled sound. Curious, he followed it toward the back of the house.

When he came to the kitchen door, the nauseating smell of vomit slammed into him. He detoured into the kitchen, willing his stomach not to heave. Grabbing a dishtowel, he threw it over the reeking puddle on the floor.

He had never known Tony to drink before. Not even one beer. Tony's getting so bombed that he'd been sick three days in one week was insane.

Bristling, Dan headed for the bathroom. He found Tony hunched on his knees, arms draped around the toilet bowl as he paid homage to his latest idol. Dan gagged and tried to focus on something else until Tony finished heaving.

Mom and Dad will kill him if they find him like this. Not that Tony would care.

He stood behind his brother, hesitating, finally squatted next to him and placed his hand on Tony's shoulder. "You gonna be okay?"

Tony shook his head and heaved again. By now, all that came up was a dribble of clear fluid. His face was white and slick with sweat. Dan had never seen his brother look so awful or so miserable.

"How much did you drink?" he demanded in alarm.

Tony tipped up his head, his eyes glassy. "A pint."

"A pint of what?"

Tony wiped his mouth. "Southern Comfort."

Panic raced through Dan and he swore. "What are you trying to do? Kill yourself?"

Tony shrugged, then gasped and hung his head in the toilet again.

"Well, if puking your brains out is the kind of comfort alcohol brings, I don't see why you keep going back for more."

Tony straightened and glared. "Shut up!"

Dan winced. While justified, his condescending attitude was anything but helpful.

"Sorry, Tone."

"Whatever," his brother muttered, before retching again.

Lord, he's scaring me.

Watch over him.

Running his fingers through his hair, Dan heaved a sigh. The Spirit spoke to his heart again, but this time so clearly, Dan couldn't believe he imagined it.

Take him to the hospital.

The nearest hospital is Boise General, Lord. Where Annie is. I mean he looks bad, but he isn't that bad, is he?

Immediately he was overcome by the certainty that he had to take Tony to the hospital. There wasn't a minute to waste.

Shaking with the urgency of the impulse, he placed his hands under Tony's arms and yanked him to his feet. *I trust You know what You're doing 'cause I sure don't.*

"You probably feel like you want to die, bro, but we're going to the hospital. You need to see a doctor."

Tony didn't argue, and Dan half carried, half dragged him to his truck. It took all Dan's strength to shove his brother up onto the seat. As they raced to the ER, Dan saw that he had passed out.

Dan braked to an abrupt stop in front of the hospital doors. He shook Tony's repeatedly, calling his name and slapping his face, but nothing roused him. Panicking, he slammed out of the truck and ran to find someone to help get Tony inside.

The emergency crew tried smelling salts without success. His brother was dead weight when they lifted him out of the truck. They lowered him into a wheelchair and rolled him inside. Tony only stirred long enough to retch a thin stream of stomach acid down the front of his shirt.

A Hispanic triage nurse squinted at Dan as she took Tony's vitals. "You were smart to bring him here."

"Do you think my brother has alcohol poisoning?"

The nurse nodded. "He needs to have his stomach pumped. This kind of drinking kills because people pass out and suffocate in their own vomit."

She clucked her tongue. "This is going to take a while. You may want to call your parents." Turning, she pushed the wheelchair toward an available room.

"I plan to."

Stunned, Dan watched her wheel Tony down the hall. Could Tony die from drinking too much alcohol? He couldn't imagine his brother actually dying, though he knew it was possible. The thought scared him.

The nurse returned shortly with a physician. "I need you to sign your brother in, please. Then you can come back in a few hours, and we'll give you an update on how he's doing."

I hate giving my parents bad news about Tony all the time, but someone has to let them know. I just can't watch out for him anymore.

He called his parents. The answering machine kicked on. He alternated rubbing his sweaty hands on his jeans as he juggled the phone from one to the other.

"Mom, Dad, Tony's in the ER at Boise General. They think he has alcohol poisoning. He told me he drank a pint of whiskey, and he was really sick so I brought him here. I'll stay with him until you come. Bye."

While he waited for news about Tony and for his parents to arrive, he could pace the ER or visit Annie again. Talking to her would be a nice distraction, though he hoped she wouldn't think him a nuisance for coming back so soon. The idea of seeing her again made his heart lift until he thought about his brother's condition.

Lord, what should I say? Gee, Annie, Tony won't be coming to see you again. This time he's in the ER having his stomach pumped.

Despite his concern about her probable reaction, he chose to visit Annie and see how she was doing anyway.

Tapping on the door to capture her attention, he teased. "Knock, knock."

The sultry alto voice he'd grown to love responded with a giggle. "Who's there?"

He hoped she was teasing. "It's me, Dan."

Annie glanced over at him and smiled warmly. "You don't have to introduce yourself. I know who you are by the sound of your voice."

She recognizes me. That's a start.

Annie peered at him for a moment, quirking a grin. "Why are you back so soon?"

Though her tone sounded annoyed, the pleased look in her eyes when she gazed at him warmed him to his toes. Then it occurred to him if he answered her question, the truth would hurt her a lot.

Explaining his presence would mean telling her about Tony. The light in her eyes would dim, and he hated to steal the little bit of joy she possessed.

She scrunched her nose and sniffed. "What's that gross smell? It's kind of sour." Her gaze drifted to his sleeve. "You have something wet on your shirt."

He glanced at his arm. The contents of Tony's stomach had gotten on his clothing.

"Um, Tony got sick at the house. I guess some got on my shirt when I tried to help him." He held his breath for a moment, then decided it would be best to tell her the truth. "He's in the ER right now having his stomach pumped."

Her eyes widened, and then they glazed over as if her mind were engaged elsewhere. Dan didn't dare speak for fear he'd say the wrong thing. So he prayed for Annie and for his brother.

Touch their lives, Lord. If they don't know You, use these tragic circumstances to reach their hearts.

After long seconds of staring at the wall, she finally blinked. Tears fell from her eyes.

"He's destroying himself over what happened to me, isn't he?"

"Sure looks that way."

"I've seen Tony get tipsy a few times, like on prom night. But he only had two or three drinks. He was never like this."

"Yeah. He's starting to scare me. His behavior is getting more and more reckless."

"Looks like he won't be coming to visit anytime soon, will he?" Her chin trembled.

Dan shrugged. "Probably not."

"Do you think it's intentional?"

His voice lowered. "I don't know."

She twisted the sheet between her fingers, blinking back tears. "It's my fault he's acting like this."

"No, it isn't. He makes his own choices."

"Maybe." She peered up at him. "I wish there was something I could do to help him, but how can I when I'm stuck in bed?"

Talk about Me.

"Have you tried praying?"

Annie averted her gaze. "God never listens to me."

Her honesty amazed him. "Ever talk to God when you're alone?"

Her head moved slowly from side to side. "Just when I'm with a group."

"It's worth a try, isn't it?"

She met his gaze with a blank one. "I guess I don't know what to say."

"You ever read your Bible?"

She sighed. "I'm usually busy with other stuff. What's with all the questions?"

For several minutes they sat in silence, glancing at each other every few seconds. *Talk about Me.*

"When did you become a Christian?"

She stared, her eyes confused. "I don't know. I've always been a Christian."

"But when did you first realize you needed Christ as your Savior?"

"I'm a good person. I don't do anything bad, so I never think about it."

"Have you ever prayed to receive Christ as your personal Lord and Savior?"

She smiled. "Yes. I prayed the sinner's prayer once with a group of friends. I was in the seventh grade, I think."

"Did it make a difference in your life? Did anything inside you change?"

Her smile faded. "I don't remember. I don't think so. I prayed because I was told that's all I had to do to be saved."

"Do you want to know Him personally? Like a true friend?"

Her cheeks flushed. "I already do. I mean, I've served God for years. He should know me by now, right?"

"That's not what I meant. You can go to church and do things for God. Anybody can. But it doesn't mean you know Jesus on a personal level."

She chuckled, but her face grew taut and she appeared unsure. "You're being weird."

"Think about it, Annie. Let's say you've been a Republican all your life. You majored in political science in college. You know all about what the party stands for and have faithfully attended every rally. You even sang a solo at the Republican national convention. The whole nine yards.

"Then one day you hear that the president is having a party and every devoted Republican is invited. So you decide to go to the White House to meet him in person. But if you've never once spoken to the president face-to-face, would he let you in?"

Her eyes clouded.

When she didn't answer, he asked again, "Would He let you in? Would He know you?"

Her brow furrowed. "What are you getting at? Are you saying I'm not a Christian?"

Dan didn't answer, but held her gaze, unwavering. She shivered and closed her eyes.

"Listen to me, Annie. You can know all about Jesus in your head, just like you might know everything about the president. But if He doesn't know you personally, you won't be let in."

Her mouth tugged downward. "I'm tired. I want to rest."

He hadn't anticipated her sad response, but he refused to push the issue, so he rose to leave. "Okay, Annie. Get some sleep. I'll come visit again tomorrow."

She stared out the window, not acknowledging him.

"So I'll see you later?"

Still nothing.

He heaved a sigh and walked out, his hands plunged deep in his pockets.

Lord, how can I get her to see her need for You?

❧❧❧

Dan met his parents in the lobby of the emergency room. "Is Tony going to be all right?"

His father looked like he'd been crying. He nodded.

"His blood alcohol was .29. Three times the legal limit. He could've died. He's not a drinker, and they said his body couldn't handle it. I thank God you had enough sense to bring him here."

"Actually, I prayed and asked God what to do. He told me to bring Tony here." Dan's chest tightened. "Man, what if I hadn't listened? What if I'd let Tony rot in the bathroom with his head in the toilet?" His eyes misted.

Dan's mother patted his arm. "You couldn't walk away from him. You've never been able to pass by someone in need."

He stared at his mother. "Really?"

"Never." She smiled. "You know, when you were only two you used to hug the new kids when they arrived at the nursery and started to cry. You did a better job at calming them than the adults did."

"You never told me that before."

"There are lots of things you don't know." Her eyes flooded with tears.

Dan put his arm around his mother's shoulders. "Like what?"

She covered her face with her hands and tipped her head down. "I'm ashamed to tell you this . . . but my father . . . he was an alcoholic when I was growing up."

Rubbing his face, Dan exhaled. "Grandpa? No way."

She nodded. "Why do you think I had to work so hard to earn my education? I didn't have any help, not like you boys have. I had to make every nickel to pay for my accounting degree."

"How come nobody ever mentioned it before?"

"He quit drinking around the time you were born, and we all wanted to forget about the past. You know, Dan, he almost died from drinking too much. Just like Tony."

"You think he got the tendency from Grandpa?"

"I don't doubt it for a second. It's a difficult thing to break once you start."

His dad interjected, "Which is why your mother and I are going to give Tony a choice once he's feeling better. He can either be admitted to the Teen Challenge program when he sobers up or he can move out. We won't enable him to throw his life away. And though what happened to Annie was horrible, your brother would have found a reason to start drinking eventually. If not over Annie, then because of something else."

"Wow," Dan muttered, "I can't believe we had an alcoholic relative and I never knew."

His mother whispered, "I never wanted to talk about it because it was so painful. This problem with Tony just brought it all back. I can't avoid it anymore. At least, not if I'm going to help Tony. But I need to help myself so I can help your brother recover."

Dan nodded. "I understand."

His father placed his hand on Dan's back. "Pray for your brother."

Chapter 9

Annie stared at the television above her bed without really seeing it. When another stupid sitcom began, she turned the tube off. Her dark mood wouldn't allow her to laugh.

Just when she thought she and Dan could be friends, he pulled the I-don't-think-you're-really-saved garbage on her. Who made him her judge?

In the midst of her troubled thoughts, a smiling nurse entered the room. "How are you doing this evening? Are you comfortable?"

Annie turned her face away and muttered, "I suppose."

Minutes later her food tray arrived. Her stomach growled.

She lifted the lid with her good hand and stared at the contents. Ugh. More spuds. The nurse hadn't elevated the head of her bed. How would she slide the runny potatoes into her mouth without spilling gravy on her gown?

Annie pressed the call button. No one responded, and her food grew cold.

With a sigh, she lifted the spoon off the tray and tried to scoop up some of the now-cold mashed potatoes. Her plate slid across the tray as she chased her food.

Frustrated, she dropped the spoon. It bounced off her tray and hit the floor.

She picked up a fork, hoping she'd at least be able to eat some of the Jell-O. Each time she stabbed one of the squares, it broke in pieces. After demolishing about half of them she began to cry.

"I wish someone would help me!"

She tossed her fork. It clinked as it ricocheted off the tray to join the spoon on the floor.

Dan stepped into her room. "Did I hear you say you need help?"

Now desperately hungry, the irritation she'd felt toward him earlier evaporated. "Yes, I'm starved and I can't eat without spilling or mutilating my dinner. It's so frustrating!"

When his eyes warmed with affection, her mouth went dry. Tony never looked at her with such adoration, and her attraction to Dan bothered her. It felt . . . wrong.

Why is Dan always hanging around? No wonder Tony's been angry with him.

Scowling, she bit her lower lip.

He sobered. "Is something else bothering you?"

His expression was so tender she couldn't imagine him hurting his brother intentionally. But wouldn't Tony be hurt just knowing Dan spent so much time with her?

Should she encourage or discourage their friendship? Her heart squeezed as she struggled with what to do.

"Annie?" He touched her hand.

Tingles raced up her arm. Her physical response to his touch frightened her.

"Please, Dan." His face blurred as her eyes flooded with tears. "Please . . . d-don't touch me."

He wrenched his hand away, then stared at his feet. "Sorry. Um, should I go see if someone else can help you with your dinner?"

He's even kind when I'm rejecting him. She swallowed hard and offered a tentative smile.

"No. I'm sorry. Sit down. I don't know what's going on with me. I'm way too sensitive."

"No, you're not. I'd be upset too, if I were you."

Her chin quivered and a lump clogged her throat. "Why are you always so nice to me?"

He moved to reach for her hand, but stopped himself. "Because I'm glad you're alive. I've always cared about you. You're special, Annie, and not just because you're pretty."

She grunted. "Well, that's not even an accurate statement anymore. The plastic surgeon showed up to examine my face this morning. He told me he'd do the best he could to hide the scars, but some of them will always be visible because of the way my skin was . . ." Her throat tightened.

"I hear what you're saying. But I still think you're beautiful."

Warmth shot through her chest and her cheeks heated. *Why does he like me? I look ugly. Maybe that's why Tony won't come see me.*

A tear rolled down her cheek and she closed her eyes.

"Don't cry. I'm sorry if what I said upset you."

She sniffled and opened her eyes. "It's all right. I know you're just trying to be nice. You're a sweet guy."

He stared at her, his mouth agape. Then he clamped his lips together and turned his face away for several seconds. She heard him take a breath, then clear his throat.

When he turned back to face her, his eyes glistened. The emotion she glimpsed in their depths both frightened and thrilled her.

"I'm not just being nice." His voice sounded hoarse.

She hadn't meant to hurt his feelings. The soft look in his eyes made her insides mushy.

"You can't. . . . You can't like me."

He offered a weak grin. "Too late."

His blue eyes and tender expression stole her breath. She closed her eyes and willed herself to speak, then captured his gaze.

"I don't know if we can be friends. I—"

His eyes widened. "Don't say that, Annie. I'll keep my distance from you. I won't do anything. You can trust me."

She sighed. "Okay. We can try . . . this."

But can I trust myself?

⋇⋇⋇

Dan tossed in bed half the night. It seemed like his obsession with Annie was starting to affect his walk with the Lord. Every time he tried to read his Bible, her face would come to mind. When he tried to pray, he'd hear her sweet voice in his head.

He finally got up and went into the kitchen for a glass of milk, hoping it would help him relax enough to go back to sleep. When he entered the kitchen, his mother was standing by the stove.

"Goodness, Daniel, you scared me."

"Sorry, Mom. I need a glass of milk. I can't sleep." He yanked open the fridge and hauled out a full gallon.

She frowned as the teakettle whistled. "Me either. I'm worried sick about your brother."

"Yeah. He's a real mess." He grabbed a glass from the cupboard and filled it with milk. "At least they're keeping him overnight. By morning he'll be more coherent. Then you can talk to him about Teen Challenge."

"I suppose. But what if he refuses? What if he decides he would rather stay with his horrible friend instead?"

She poured hot water into a mug and stirred. The rich scent of hot chocolate filled the air.

"You mean Sam?" He shoved the milk carton back in the fridge and shut the door.

His mom nodded and lifted the mug to her lips.

"At least he'd live next door. Then you can still keep an eye on him. He wouldn't be all the way across town."

"Pray for him, Daniel. Pray for Tony." She sat at the table, her eyes unfocused.

He eased into a chair across from her with his glass of milk in hand. *Maybe that's why I can't sleep. I haven't prayed for Tony. But part of me doesn't want him to get better. Then I won't have a chance with Annie.*

He became aware that his mother was staring at him. "What?"

"You care about Annie, don't you?"

He tipped his head down, wishing his feelings didn't show.

"You're treading on dangerous ground, Daniel. Of all the women in the world, why her? Why your brother's girlfriend?"

"I've been asking myself the same thing. I don't know, Mom. I wish I did."

"You need to pray about this whole situation. I'd hate to see a rift develop between you and Tony over a girl, even if she is a Christian and a real sweetheart."

"Yeah, I know. But I don't think she knows the Lord."

His mother's brows rose. "Whatever gave you that idea?"

Dan downed the entire glass of milk, and then set his glass on the table. "I was praying about it so I asked her."

"And what did she say?"

He wiped the milk off his upper lip with the back of his hand. "She said she wasn't sure. She was tired, so I dropped it."

"That doesn't necessarily mean she's not saved. Everyone doubts from time to time. You know how it is."

"It not about her doubting, Mom. I don't think she had a personal relationship with Jesus in the first place."

She took another sip of her drink. "Be careful not to judge her. Only God knows her heart."

"True. But I'd rather assume she doesn't know Jesus and help lead her to Him than assume she does and have her end up condemned for eternity because I didn't care enough to lead her to the truth."

His mother frowned. "That's a pretty radical stance you're taking."

"Not radical, Mom. Why do you always say that? It's what I call real love."

He rose from his seat to leave before they got in another argument about the way he viewed things. His mother was the one person who made him feel stupid when it came to his faith.

"Let's talk about this another time when I'm not so brain-dead, okay?"

"Sure."

He loved talking about the Lord. Just not with his mother. He needed to be more patient with her.

"Good night, Mom."

"Night, Daniel."

He plodded down the hall with a prayer on his lips. "Lord, make me more like You, no matter what the cost."

Give Me everything.

You know I will.

Even Annie?

Dan's chest tightened. *You're asking too much.*

Something he'd read in a devotional reverberated in his mind. *The Lord wants all of you, or He'll say, "You'll have no part of Me."*

He winced, then whispered, "Yes, Lord. I'll give You Annie too."

Trust me.

His chest tightened. "I'll trust You, Jesus, but I'm scared. Help me not to be so afraid."

❧❧❧

Dan followed his parents' Suburban to the Teen Challenge facility, where Tony had been admitted last week. He planned to visit Annie once he found out how his brother was doing. She still asked about him, but less often now.

When they arrived, Dan glanced at the graffiti on the brick wall by the entrance and thanked God that he'd purchased a truck with an alarm. Without the device he'd undoubtedly be hoofing it home later.

How Tony had gone from being voted most popular in his graduating class and elected prom king to graduating from the Teen Challenge inpatient program mystified Dan. But if in the end his brother had a strong relationship with the Lord, it would be worth it. And Dan would do most anything to see that happen. He just hoped he wouldn't be required to give up the special place he kept in his heart for Annie.

He followed one step behind his father, who obviously knew where he was going. Before they could knock, a short man with numerous tattoos on his forearms opened the door. Dan guessed him to be one of the residents.

"Welcome to Teen Challenge, Pastor Lane. It's good to see you again."

"Good to see you too, Bob." The two men shook hands.

"And you are?" Bob offered his hand to Dan.

"I'm Dan Lane, Tony's brother."

"Ah, so *you're* the big brother."

The way Bob glared at him made Dan wonder what Tony had said about their relationship. Did his brother still harbor ill feelings toward him? They hadn't spoken since the night he'd hauled Tony to the emergency room to save his life, and Dan missed the camaraderie they had shared in the past.

He and his father followed Bob to a shabby visiting room, which contained several old couches and a scarred coffee table. The mismatched furniture looked like it had been donated to the program back in the 1980s. Dan considered giving to the ministry so people would at least have a decent room to visit in. Once he got settled in a job anyway.

Several minutes into their wait, Tony strutted into the room wearing jeans and a white T-shirt. He looked like his old self again, until he noticed Dan.

Then he stopped in his tracks and scowled. "What are you doing here?"

Dan swallowed hard. "I thought I'd come see how you're doing."

"You're lying," he sneered. "I know what you're really doing. You're spying on me so you can go back and tell Annie how screwed up I am."

His father cleared his throat. "Boys, I don't want to be placed in the middle of an argument. If you start verbally tearing each other apart, I'm going to leave."

Dan thrust out his hand. "No, Dad. If anyone leaves it'll be me."

"Go ahead and leave, Danno. I don't want you here anyway."

"Why all the hostility, Son?" Their father reached over and placed his hand on Tony's back. Tony hunched his shoulders and covered his face with his hands.

Dan froze. Something was seriously wrong with his brother, and he suspected it revolved around his relationship with Annie.

Tony raised his head and stared at Dan, a miserable look in his eyes. "Stay away from her, Dan. I don't want you visiting her."

"Now wait a minute. Your brother has been good to Annie. He's visited in your absence and helped cheer her when she was having bad days. That's something you should have done. I'd thank him, not harbor anger against him."

Tony squinted at him with suspicion. "Just *how* good have you been to her, bro?"

Dan's muscles tensed. "What are you implying?"

"You think now that I'm out of the picture you can zoom in for the kill. You think you can win Annie for yourself, don't you?"

Dan opened his mouth, but Tony cut him off. "Don't even try. In the end, she'll dump you for me anyway. I'm the one she loves. You'll always be second in line."

Dan's face flamed. "What kind of crap is this coming out of your mouth?"

Their father stood. "I told you boys I'm not getting involved in this mess. Annie is going to be with whomever she chooses. Fighting over her won't solve a thing. And you, Tony, aren't helping your case by ignoring her and then fighting with your brother about it."

"Whose side are you on, Dad? Dan's again?"

Their father sighed. "You know I love you both."

Tony snorted, "Yeah, right."

"What are you getting at, Tony? I've visited you eight times, and this is the first time you've been hostile toward me. What have I done to offend you?"

Tony's face crumpled and he glanced away.

"What is it?"

"It's not you. It's just—" Tony's voice broke and his eyes locked onto Dan's. "Danno's right. I'm a lousy, stinking dog. If I hadn't gotten caught up in wanting Annie so bad, none of this would've happened. I know she says she loves me, but now every time she looks in the mirror she'll be reminded of what a jerk I am. I can't marry her. I just can't!"

Dan's heart soared to the heavens until he considered his brother's despair. "What? Why not?"

Why am I saying this? I don't want him to marry Annie.

Tears spilled from Tony's eyes. "I'm not good enough for her. I'll never be good enough."

"Aw, come on now. Get over yourself. Once you pull out of this funk you're in and get back on the narrow road, you'll be fine. Annie's very patient, Tony, but she can't wait forever. If you want her, you need to stop avoiding her."

His brother's face brightened. "Maybe you're right. Do you really think she'll see past what happened and forgive me? You think there's hope for us?"

Watching the interaction between them, their father smiled. But inwardly, Dan cringed. He'd just encouraged Tony to win Annie back.

Lord, I'm getting deeper into this mess the more I try to help. I'm giving this entire situation over to you because I can't handle my confused emotions anymore.

"Aw, Tony, there's always hope. As long as you trust Jesus you can't go wrong."

"That's right, Son. Put your faith in God. Give your heart to Him. He'll change you and give you a brand new life. He'll give you hope and peace beyond description."

Tony's eyes clouded. "I don't want to trust God. He can take a hike for all I care. I'm done visiting." He hopped up, yanked the door open, and disappeared through it.

As the door banged shut, Dan peered at his father, who appeared as baffled by Tony's behavior as he was.

One minute Tony was hot, the next he turned cold. Dan had never been more confused about their relationship in his life.

"Do you think he's going to stay in the program?"

His father rubbed his forehead. "I don't know. But I don't feel very hopeful about it right now."

"Me either. What do you think about my staying away from Annie?"

"It couldn't hurt to consider it. Why don't you wait and see if she contacts you. If she does, you'll know she wants to see you too."

His father made a good point. So far Dan had initiated every contact with her. But he worried it would take a miracle for her to start contacting him.

"All right, Dad," he sighed.

Please, Lord. I need a miracle!

Chapter 10

Annie became conscious of a feeling of nausea. Every breath brought the heavy floral scent of her mother's perfume to her nostrils. Feeling groggy, she grimaced and licked her lips.

"If all goes well, Annie may be able to go home in a few days. She'll only need to return for follow-up appointments."

The disembodied voice sounded like her plastic surgeon. Suddenly she remembered her face and neck had been operated on for the third and final time that morning.

Her mother's squeal brought Annie fully awake. Her eyes popped open and, blinking, she took in her surroundings.

"Isn't that great, honey? You'll finally be coming home!"

Frowning, Annie felt around for her stuffed cat. Somehow Purty had wedged between her mattress and the side rail while she slept. She pulled the soft ball of fluff free.

Her father squeezed her good hand. "Don't let this bring you down, sweetheart. Your face is healing better than expected. Right, Doctor?"

Dr. Bang nodded. "I've done this type of surgery many times. Your skin is healing exceptionally well."

"See?" Her mother patted her father's back. "She'll to be back to normal in no time. We should start taking her flowers home now, shouldn't we? It'll take several trips."

Annie peered at the wide assortment of flowers and gifts she'd received. The scent she'd inhaled hadn't been her mother's perfume, she realized, but the fragrant blooms surrounding her.

She glanced at her injured hand. The surgical dressing had recently been removed, and although swollen, her ring finger was starting to look more like a normal finger every day. Two slender K wires, as the surgeon referred to them, protruded from her skin, stabilizing the severed bone ends so they would eventually heal together.

She'd been told the hand surgeon and physician's assistant had spent nearly five hours in surgery reimplanting her amputated "digit." Her finger did seem to relax more as the days progressed, a fact she found very reassuring. She looked forward to the day six weeks from now when the pins would be removed and she could begin therapy in earnest. A large ring should hide the scar.

Three times a day the nurses cleaned the pins and surrounding skin with hydrogen peroxide to reduce the risk of a pin tract infection. The occupational therapist visited her daily to work on the finger's range of motion. So far it refused to bend like it used to, and it curved less than the rest of her fingers when she attempted to make a fist.

According to the hand surgeon, the digital nerves, so painstakingly repaired under a microscope, were starting to heal as evidenced by the sensation of pins and needles. Annie swallowed hard. Her finger retained nerve damage, but at least she could still use it, though she had been told it would never function normally, even with therapy to stretch the tendons.

Annie pulled from her thoughts and glanced at the plastic surgeon in time to catch the end of his comment to her parents. She wondered what other pieces of their discussion she'd missed, but decided it must not have been important or the doctor and her parents would have included her in their conversation.

Her father nodded at Dr. Bang. "Thank you for your time, Doctor. We're very grateful for all you've done."

Dr. Bang smiled. "Just doing my job. She's a beautiful girl."

"Thank you." Annie's mom wiped a tear from her cheek. "We think so."

Annie rolled her eyes as the doctor left her room. She'd seen her face before the latest surgery this morning. The gash on her cheek would never completely disappear, and the scars on the left side of her neck looked like she had some horrible cancer surgically removed. She didn't dare hope ever to look normal again.

"Guess who we saw today, Annie?" Her father said.

Her heart leapt for joy. *Finally!*

"We saw a handsome young man who misses you very much," her mother added.

Annie's brows shot up. "You saw Tony?"

Her father's face fell. "No. I was referring to his brother, Dan—who is much more together, thank the Lord."

"Dan? He told you he misses me?"

"Umm hmm." Her father quirked a mischievous grin.

"Funny he'd say that to you. The last time I heard from him he said he was sorry he couldn't come by to see me. Said he'd call me later. That was four days ago. I haven't heard from him since."

Annie's throat tightened and she willed herself not to cry. She missed their talks and thought about Dan a lot. Too much.

Someone rapped on the door. "Can I come in?"

Tony! Her lungs sucked air and she nearly choked. He'd finally come to see her. Against her will, Annie's eyes flooded with tears.

Her mother covered her mouth with her hand and glanced at her father, who scowled. They didn't look like they appreciated Tony's sudden appearance.

Annie cried, "Please do!"

She could barely breathe from the anticipation. The last time she'd seen Tony, he'd nearly gotten her to give in to his wishes. How she missed him despite his pushy ways.

Tony stepped into the room looking even more handsome than she remembered. He wore a tight T-shirt and blue jeans that emphasized his muscular build. He smiled briefly at Annie, then stuffed his hands in his back pockets and stared out the window.

The ache in her heart threatened to overpower her. He couldn't even look at her for more then two seconds.

Her parents rose to leave.

"Tony." Her father nodded toward him, then turned to offer Annie a weak smile. "Your mother and I are going to grab something to eat. We'll be back in about an hour."

Without another word to Tony, her parents walked out.

"It's good to see you." She willed him to face her.

He turned, peering up for a second before dropping his gaze to the bedrail. "Hey, Annie," he whispered, his voice hoarse. "Sorry it took so long."

"No-o, it's o-kay," she assured him, so excited her words came out choppy. "I'm so hap-py you're here! I for-give you. I do."

He glanced up at her. "Have you seen Dan?"

"Um, not in the last four or five days. Why? Is something wrong?"

A strange smile appeared on Tony's face and he exhaled. "Good."

He stepped closer, reached for her right hand, and grasped it. "How are you feeling?"

She attempted to capture his gaze, but he looked everywhere but at her. Was she so hideous he couldn't stand the sight of her? The notion made her want to bawl like a baby.

"Tony." Her voice wavered. "Why won't you look at me?"

He stared for a moment before again glancing away. "I feel bad about what happened. It's just . . . When I look at your face, it reminds me."

"Oh." She cast her gaze down.

Silence reigned as she listened to the sound of her heart beating in her ears.

Finally she glanced up. "You know they caught the man, right?"

His eyes widened. "No one told me. Did they find the ring?"

"Yeah, that's how they found him. He tried to pawn it."

"Oh," he exhaled.

A lump grew in her throat, making it difficult to swallow. "Why don't you sit—"

"No!"

His forceful reply startled her. He ducked his head and rubbed his forehead.

"I mean, no thanks. I'll be leaving soon."

A strangled sound came from her throat as she fought back tears. He didn't want to be with her. Maybe he didn't even love her anymore.

He shifted on his feet and coughed. "I'm sorry. I can't do this. I just . . . I can't stay."

His eyes welled with tears as he bent over her bed and kissed her good cheek. "I'll try to come see you again."

His words escaped in a hoarse squeak. Before she had a chance to say good-bye, he darted out of the room.

The dam holding back her tears burst, and her shoulders shook. "No-o-o!"

He can't stand to look at me. I've lost him. He says he's coming back, but he won't. I know he won't.

After completing his second interview at the lab, Dan returned to his parents' home. He'd had a difficult time walking away from the hospital and not stopping to visit Annie, but he'd kept his word about not seeing her unless she contacted him first. But with everything in him he wanted to see her.

The past four days had been more difficult than he'd imagined. Not knowing where his brother had gone when he left the rehab center didn't help.

Tony had signed out of the program after their visit, just like Dan and his father suspected he would. No one had seen Tony since. His parents were worried sick. Dan felt partly responsible since his visit at Teen Challenge had seemed to set his brother off.

Just as Dan opened the fridge to get a drink, the phone rang.

"Hello?"

"Dan? This is Annie's father. Would you mind stopping by to visit her? She's very lonely and she misses you. She mentioned that several times."

Dan wasn't sure what to say. He had promised to wait for Annie to contact him, but her parents had called instead. Did that count?

Without consulting God for fear his request would be denied, Dan answered, "Sure. I'll be there in about ten minutes."

"Thank you."

Dan heard what sounded like a relieved sigh. He hung up the phone, a broad grin covering his face.

When Dan arrived in the hospital parking lot, he saw his brother exiting the building. Tony hopped into an old pickup truck resembling their neighbor Sam's and drove away.

What was his brother up to now? Maybe Tony had finally visited Annie. Dan's chest tightened at the thought.

He debated the pros and cons of going to see her. If Tony had just visited, then Dan was setting himself up for more pain. He ran his fingers through his hair in frustration.

"Please, Lord, give me peace. I really need it if I'm going to see her."

The elevators took forever to arrive. He stepped inside and exited on Annie's floor. On his way to her room, her parents intercepted him.

"Annie's very upset. Give her a minute."

"What upset her?"

Mrs. Myers' eyes were saturated with tears. "Tony came to see her, and she hasn't stopped crying since."

"Do you think you could cheer her up?" her father asked.

"I can try. Pray for me."

"Will do. Just give us a second."

Mr. and Mrs. Myers entered Annie's room again. Her sobs caused Dan's chest to clench. She had already suffered so much, and now Tony had made things worse.

"We'll come back later tonight, okay, honey?" he overheard them say.

Her parents stepped back into the hall. "Thanks for coming, Dan," Mr. Myers said in a low voice. "You're so good for her."

Unlike Tony.

The gleam in her father's eye caught Dan off guard. If he didn't know better, he would think Annie's father was trying to get them together.

"Sure, anytime." Dan sucked in a deep breath before popping his head in the door.

Okay, Lord. Here goes nothing.

"Hi, Annie. Can I cheer you up?"

A choked sound between a laugh and a sob came from her throat. "You could try."

He crossed to her bed. "What happened?"

She cried harder and turned her face away.

You sure know how to say the wrong thing, bozo.

He handed her a tissue, cringing inwardly. "I'm sorry. I didn't mean to upset you more."

"N-no, it's o-okay. It's not you, really."

"Then what is it?"

He eased onto the chair next to her bed and waited until she finally glanced up at him. Seeing her pain made his chest ache.

Wiping her eyes, she took a shaky breath. After letting it out, she reached for his hand.

Her fingers found his through the bedrail. Warm tingles shot up his arm, making him flush. Such a small yet intimate gesture touched him deeply, and a profound sense of gratitude filled his heart.

Her reaching out meant so much to him. But he reminded himself that from her viewpoint it probably meant nothing more than "thanks for being here for me."

Her hand squeezed his. After a moment she sighed.

"Tony stopped by to see me today."

Dan closed his eyes as she confirmed his worst fear. His brother had caused her this pain.

"He couldn't stand to look at me."

His eyes snapped open. The ache in his heart expanded as he watched her shed silent tears.

She bit her lip. "He thinks I'm ugly now. He doesn't want me anymore. I just know it."

While true that her face was swollen and bandaged, as far as Dan was concerned she was still the same lovely Annie. Why did Tony have to act like he couldn't look at her? What was he thinking?

Dan wiped away the stray tear making its way down her cheek. She sucked in a breath and fear appeared in her eyes. He was afraid to move.

"Why are you looking at me like that?"

Her mouth opened, but for a moment she didn't answer. Then she said, "Thank you for coming to see me, Dan. It means a lot that you can look at me."

His brow furrowed. "You didn't answer my question."

"Let's talk about something else, okay?" A feeble grin spread across her face as more tears slid down her cheeks.

Keeping his hands to himself this time, Dan willed himself to relax. "Okay. So what do you want to talk about?"

"I read something in the New Testament my mom brought me. I have a question." She wiped her face with her hand, then reached into the side of her bed and pulled out a small book. "See. I can actually hold it. It's not too heavy like my regular Bible."

His heart thumped harder. "What did you read?"

"There's something I've heard but never really understood. It's about how man looks at the outward appearance and God looks at the heart."

He smiled. "That's in First Samuel. It's a great verse, but it's the Old Testament."

Her chin quivered. "That isn't the one I read recently. This one was about the bones, when Jesus is calling the leaders hypocrites."

"You mean where Jesus says they are like whitewashed tombs. They look beautiful on the outside but inside are full of dead men's bones and everything impure."

She nodded. "Especially the part after, you know, where Jesus said on the outside they looked upright and pure but inside they were fake and rebellious or something like that, I think."

"That's a great passage."

"It forced me to think about what happened." She heaved a sigh and glanced away.

He watched her closely. "Why?"

"It sounded kind of like my situation. I thought about how I never had any real problems before. I had a good life. Everything seemed great on the outside, you know? But when I really think about it, my life was still empty on the inside. That makes me sad."

Despite his intention of keeping his hands to himself, he stroked her knuckles with his thumb. "That's good, Annie. Realizing you're empty is supposed to make you feel sad."

Her brows knit together. "It is?"

"Yes. It means you recognize that God knows the true condition of your heart. If hearing that makes you sad . . . if it makes you realize you need the Lord . . . then it's a wonderful thing."

His eyes misted at the thought. Every day he'd prayed that God would minister to Annie as she lay in her hospital bed. He understood prayers were never wasted, but this rush felt a lot like winning the lottery. He rubbed his eyes with his hands.

"You gonna cry?"

He cleared his throat and chuckled through tears. "I'm trying not to."

A nervous-sounding giggle bubbled from her. "You're so sweet."

His chest squeezed. At least she hadn't mocked him for being so sensitive like his mother often did.

"Thanks. What you said touched me."

"It did? What did I say?"

"That you're thinking about your relationship with the Lord. That you recognize something is missing in your life."

"Hmmm. . . . I did, didn't I."

"Yeah, and it's wonderful, Annie."

"Glad you think so." She rolled her eyes.

He grew serious. "Have you considered talking to God about how you feel?"

Her chin quivered again and she looked away. "I . . . I'm scared."

"Don't be. Jesus has been waiting for this moment. He wants your heart."

"I don't know why He would. It's pretty broken."

"That's what's so great about God. He wants a broken spirit and a contrite heart. When you're soft toward God, that's when He can help you."

A tender smile formed on her lips. He loved her so much he had to look away. He wanted to kiss her lips, to indulge for a moment and drink in their sweetness.

In my dreams.

Annie either didn't notice his distress or pretended to be oblivious. "Tony, can you bring me a cup of water?" She nodded at the pitcher on the table by her bed.

His face fell.

"What's wrong? A minute ago you were smiling."

He shook his head, not wanting to admit how easily her mistake had wounded him.

"Come on," she urged, her lips forming a pout. "Tell me why you're sad."

Pinching the bridge of his nose, he said, "You called me Tony."

She gasped. "I'm so sorry. I didn't mean to."

He slumped, clasping his hands between his knees. "It's okay. I know you miss him and you're sad because he's not here."

She glanced away, fixing her gaze on the wall for a moment. "I do miss him," she admitted.

They sat in silence for several moments. She bit her lip and searched his eyes.

"But when you didn't come see me . . . I . . . I missed you more."

Chapter 11

The affection in Dan's eyes struck her heart like flint lighting tinder. It felt like sparks flew and set her soul on fire. So much hope gleamed in his eyes. He looked as if he yearned for something he couldn't have, and that made her breathless with longing to know what he desired.

Dan's eyes probed hers with tenderness. She longed to touch him, to hold him close. But then she reminded herself that he wasn't just any man. He was Tony's brother.

"You really miss me when I'm not here?"

A shy grin tugged at her mouth, and her cheeks heated. "Yeah."

I can't lead him on. It'll never work between us. He'll always be Tony's brother.

"I've missed our talks, Dan. You're such a good . . . friend."

The light in his eyes dimmed, but he kept his smile. "So are you. You're the best . . . um . . . friend a guy could hope to have."

The sad lilt in his voice made her eyes burn. Disappointment weighed heavy on her heart. At least he enjoyed spending time with her, though she only offered friendship. She hated to let him down, but it was obvious they could never be more than friends.

Then why do I feel bad?

She needed to deflect the vibes between them. "You're too nice, you know that?"

"So I've been told." His weak grin told her he didn't see it as a compliment.

"I mean that in a good way." She perked up her tone. "Look at you. You're sitting in this depressing place talking to me when there are plenty of other things you could be doing."

He frowned. "Why do you always say things like that?"

She blinked. "Like what?"

"Implying visiting you is the last thing anyone would want to do."

"But it's true. Look at me. People feel sorry for me because of what happened. Nobody wants to sit here and just visit with me. It's too depressing."

Dan leaned forward. "I think people worry about upsetting you, so they avoid discussing it."

"Maybe I want to talk about it."

"So shoot, then." He grinned.

"Okay. I've been thinking about something Tony said to me the night before this happened. He said I was just like him, that I was a faker and just pretended to be good. Do you think that's true about me?"

She could see his neck muscles tense. "It doesn't matter what I think—or anyone else, for that matter. What do you think, Annie?"

She stared down at her clenched hands and whispered, "I think maybe he was right."

Afraid of his reaction, she shot him a quick glance. The warmth in his eyes encouraged her to continue.

"Before this happened," she lightly touched the bandages on her neck, "I worried about what people thought about me. I never realized I lived like that until I got hurt."

His eyes brightened. "What about now?"

Annie nibbled on her lip. "I'm wondering if anything I did before was real. I mean, the reason I went out with Tony in the first place was because he was so popular and good-looking. The girls at school were jealous he chose me. It made me feel good, you know?"

He looked stunned, as if what she said bothered him.

Taking a shaky breath, she rushed on, "When he asked me to marry him the same thing happened. I said yes to please him because that's what he wanted." Her cheeks heated. "Well that's not all he wanted, but . . ."

Dan glanced away for a moment but quickly returned his steady gaze to her, his expression troubled. She avoided his intense scrutiny.

"I'm not sure I would have agreed if I were a stronger person. I just wanted to make him happy."

"I'm glad you're starting to think about what *you* want instead of how to make others happy all the time. But there's still a problem with that."

"There is?"

He rested his chin on his hand. "God made us all with the same needs. We aren't truly happy unless we're pleasing Him. So what you did wasn't wrong, just misdirected."

Understanding dawned. "You think the love I had for Tony was really supposed to be for God?" she questioned, hope stirring in her heart. "Like Tony was so important that God couldn't have a place in my life?"

"It sounds like it."

"So if that's true, if I want to please Tony more, I won't want to please God?"

He nodded. "I'm afraid so."

She gave a soft moan. What was wrong with her?

"I want to please God, I do. But when I try, something stops me."

"Only God knows what's holding you back. I can't explain it to you. You need to take it to Him to learn what it is."

"I know I'm not supposed to love anyone more than God. But how do I love God more than people when He feels so far away?"

Several tears rolled down her cheeks. She hated to admit how she really perceived God, but Dan was so strong, so supportive that everything seemed like a safe subject.

Now I'm shifting from Tony to Dan. I still don't love God more. Something is wrong with me. Why can't I feel love for God? Why am I so dead inside?

Dan touched her hair, pushing several loose strands off her face. He stroked her cheek, setting her skin on fire. He was being way too intimate. It was more than she could handle.

"Please don't touch me like that."

I feel something for him. So why not You, God?

He snatched his hands back and clenched them on his lap. "I can't believe I did that again. I really don't want to make you uncomfortable with me. I'm sorry."

"I forgive you, but you can't touch me. It's not right. I want to figure this out and I can't keep replacing my need for Jesus with my need for the love of a man. Any man."

Understanding swept over his gaze. "You're right. You should never love anyone more than Jesus."

Her heart lifted. He understood. He didn't make her feel guilty for her honesty.

"And another thing I'm starting to understand is I can't accept the Lord to please you, either. I have to want Jesus on my own, or it won't be real."

His mouth curved into a contented smile. "You're so right on."

She grinned. "Glad you think so."

"I'm glad you're starting to understand. I have a feeling it won't be long until you'll be His. I'll keep praying."

"Thanks. You really are the best friend a girl could have."

His gaze softened. "You don't know how happy it makes me to hear you say that."

She chuckled. "I think I have some idea."

He leaned over and kissed her on the cheek, making her blush. Such a tender, friendly gesture, yet it melted her insides.

"Love you, Annie. See you later."

He got up and walked out, leaving her stunned. Before had time to think about what had just happened, her friend Susie Ziglar from church burst into her room.

"What was Dan doing here? He's floating on a cloud."

Annie stared at her, unsure of what to say.

Susie clapped her hand over her mouth. "Oh, Annie. You look so . . . I couldn't believe what I heard when I got back last night from the missions trip. I had to come see you right away. To see how you're doing."

Annie's cheeks heated. "I'm doing okay."

She still felt mushy inside from Danny's kiss. It must have shown in her eyes because Susie studied her with a curious look on her face.

"Don't tell me."

Annie chuckled. "Don't tell you what?"

"I can't believe it. I go to Mexico for three weeks and I come back to find out you've not only broken up with Tony, but now you're in love with Dan."

Annie's chest tightened. She whispered in a strangled voice, "I'm not in love with Dan. We're just friends. And who said I broke up with Tony?"

"Yeah, whatever," Susie huffed. "Deny it all you want. But I can see the truth in your eyes. What I want to know is how you do it."

Annie blinked, now confused. "Do what?"

"How you make the guys fall in love with you. Even with your face all messed up you—"

Her friend's words cut deep, and Annie burst into tears. Susie's eyes widened with remorse.

"I'm sorry, Annie. I didn't mean that like it sounded."

Annie couldn't stop crying. *I have to figure this out. I can't do it with Dan in my life. She's right. I'm distracted. I'll just call him and explain. He'll understand. He always understands.*

༝༝༝

Dan hung up the phone. He shouldn't have kissed her cheek. On impulse he'd taken things too far and now he would pay for it.

He'd agreed he wouldn't visit Annie unless she was ready to see him. What possessed him to agree to such difficult terms had little to do with pleasing himself. He chose to agree out of love for Annie. She needed to find a place in her life for Jesus, and he committed to praying for her every time she came to mind until it happened.

So far that evening he'd already prayed for her at least twenty times. The increasing ache in his chest reminded him of how unselfish true love was supposed to be. Sadly, in his heart of hearts he realized he'd never have her, at least not unless God performed a miracle. And how he longed for that miracle.

Yes, he loved God with all he had in him. But he loved Annie too. Loved her enough to let go, to let her choose.

His throat tightened as he hauled his basket full of dirty clothes into the laundry room. As he sorted them into separate piles, his thoughts shifted to Tony and the night he'd found the magazines in his brother's drawer. He had snatched one out, the temptation too great to resist.

After flipping through several pages, he had cringed and stuffed the magazine back under the clothes. He felt dirty looking at pictures of women reduced to nothing more than objects of lust.

In his way of thinking, women were supposed to be treasured, not used. How could Tony enjoy looking at those women when the photos degraded them so much?

A new swell of anger rose in his chest when he thought about how Tony's lust for Annie had triggered the entire tragedy. First Tony lost his driving privilege because of his irresponsibility, and then he was late picking her up. As a result, she'd been attacked, the engagement ring he gave her savagely severed from her hand.

Dan grabbed soap and filled the measuring cup, pondering the way God could take a dirty heart and clean it from the inside out. He slammed the lid of the washer.

Just then he heard loud bangs coming from the direction of the back door. It was almost midnight. He couldn't imagine anyone pounding on their door at this late hour unless it was an emergency. Without hesitating, he raced down the stairs. When he peeked out the window, he saw Tony standing outside.

"Hey Danno, let me in."

Dan hesitated before opening the door. "Shhh. Be quiet. Mom and Dad are trying to sleep."

Tony lowered his voice, but not much. "I really need help," he slurred.

So what else is new.

Dan frowned at his brother. "What do you need this time?"

To his surprise, Tony ducked his head, shame and remorse coming over his features. "I need to get sober. This is eating me up. I can't live like this anymore."

Dan blinked. Had he heard his brother right? "Well, it's great you see that now," he said, uncertain whether he believed him.

"Yeah, I can't hang out with Sam anymore." For a long moment, Tony stared at his feet. "He's not good for me."

Dan cleared his throat. "How'd you figure that out?"

Tony shrugged. The movement caused him to lose his balance, and he propped his body against the wall on the landing for support.

"I can't let this guilt eat me up anymore. I want Annie in my life, but I can't stand to think about what happened to her. I keep blaming myself and it's making me crazy."

"Makes sense. So what can I do about it?"

"Take me back to Teen Challenge. I need to get sober so I can figure this out and be the kind of man Annie needs. I'm no good for her like this. I'm no good for anybody."

Dan's chest tightened. He wanted to rejoice because his prayers were answered and Tony finally admitted he needed help. But if he changed, then he'd win Annie's heart back.

They had almost four years of history between them. So where would that leave Dan?

But he loved his brother. He wanted to see him succeed and get his life together. The rest was in God's hands.

"All right, Tone. I'll drive you there. Let me grab some things for you to take with you."

"Thanks, bro. I owe you big-time." Tony's eyes shone with tears.

Dan touched Tony's shoulder. "You don't owe me anything. Just take care of yourself, okay?"

Tony nodded. A flash of unspoken understanding passed between them, as if Tony had confessed with his eyes, "I forgive you Dan, and I'm sorry."

Dan lunged up the steps, and then crept the rest of the way on light feet to avoid waking his parents. He entered his room and dragged out a duffel bag, then searched Tony's room for clean clothes and underwear. He noticed the magazines were no longer in the drawer.

A half hour later Dan knocked on the front door of Teen Challenge. The tattooed man who had greeted them before offered his hand to Tony.

"Mr. Lane. Good to see you back."

"Is there anything I need to do?" Dan asked.

"No. Tony can to sign himself in, but rules are he can't contact anyone in person or by phone for the first thirty days. Family members can visit after the first ten days, but Tony can't leave. It's one of the rules we have for people who leave and come back."

Tony's head rose and he glanced at Dan with sad eyes. "I can't see or talk to Annie for thirty days, and college starts in forty. I still plan to go to college, and I hope Annie does too. Tell her I love her, will you? Tell her I'm doing this for her, and for us, okay?"

The vulnerable look in his brother's eyes helped firm up Dan's resolve to place his future in God's hands. He wanted Annie in his life, but ultimately God knew the future and what would be best for all three of them. Dan just needed to trust Him.

"Sure, Tony."

Tony's face crumpled. He grabbed Dan and pulled him into a bear hug.

"Pray for me, Danno. I need it. I feel so lost."

"Then you're right where you need to be, bro. You can't be found if you never knew you were lost in the first place."

Tony offered a feeble grin. "I guess you're right. Tell Mom and Dad to pray for me too."

Dan's eyes welled with tears. "Take care of yourself. I'll pray for you every day."

Tony chuckled. "You better. I need your support. I really do."

He scooped up his duffel bag and followed the man inside.

Dan walked slowly to his car, his heart pounding. He couldn't help thinking that every step Tony took toward recovery would also take Annie that much further from him.

Chapter 12

Annie sighed. "Good night, Mrs. Lane. Thanks for filling me in." She hung up the phone and lay back in her twin bed, pulling her rose print covers up under her chin until she could feel the soft pink flannel blanket against her good cheek. The sore side of her face and neck had not healed enough yet to remove the bandages.

She stared at the eight-by-ten photo on the light oak dresser in the corner of her room. Tony stood next to her on prom night. They wore their king and queen crowns and broad smiles. Such a perfect couple, at least on the outside.

Poor Snicky didn't understand why she couldn't snuggle under Annie's chin. The ornery cat meowed until her mother finally removed her from the room so Annie could asleep.

As she lay in the dark, still wide awake, she reflected on her conversation with Tony's mother. Apparently Tony had admitted himself to Teen Challenge, hoping to finish the program before heading off to college.

Annie hadn't allowed herself to even consider going to college this year. Even if her face totally healed, the idea of being around so many people so soon after her injury frightened her. Tony didn't need to know that though. Not if it might cause him to drop out of the program before finishing. He needed to graduate and she didn't want to hold him back.

A lump knotted her throat as she stared at the wall. So far her first night back in her own bed had brought more heartache than pleasure. The familiar surroundings should have comforted her, like sleeping with her favorite pillow. Instead, they magnified her loneliness.

She glanced back at her dresser. On the opposite side from the photo she'd laid some of the things she'd brought home from the hospital.

A smile covered her face as she studied the stuffed cat Dan had given her. He truly was the nicest man she'd ever met. True to his word, he had stayed away from her while she figured things out. She wondered if he thought as much about her as she did about him.

A gentle rapping sounded on her door. "Annie?" Her mother popped her head in the room. "Still not sleepy yet?"

"I don't think I can sleep alone. Can you hand me Purty?"

Her mother walked across the room to retrieve the stuffed animal. A flash of delight shone in her eyes as she handed the cat to Annie.

"Didn't Dan buy you this?"

Annie chuckled. "Yeah. I slept with it every night so I wouldn't feel alone in my hospital room. I think I'm going to need it for a few more days to help me fall asleep."

"Purty is kind of cute." Her mom giggled. "Your dad got me a gift, too, when I had to go to the hospital to have my tonsils out. I was a junior in high school and so embarrassed. Most kids had their tonsils out long before they turned seventeen."

"What did Dad give you?"

"A fuzzy monkey, kind of like a chimpanzee."

Annie laughed. "Dad gave you a stuffed chimp?"

Her mother blushed. "It was a joke. Whenever we went out on a date my dad would always say," she tucked her chin and deepened her voice, " 'Remember kids, no monkey business.' "

A snort erupted from Annie before she could stop it. "Gramps used to say that?"

"Yeah." Her mother wiggled her brows. "He didn't have anything to worry about though. Your dad was a perfect gentleman."

"He was?"

"Yes. Your father would never push me. He wouldn't even kiss me unless I wanted him to." Her mom grinned. "Unlike some of my friends' boyfriends, he never pressured me for sex."

Annie's eyebrows rose. "Guys did that when you were in high school?"

Her mom feigned upset and put her hands on her hips. "I'm not that old."

Annie giggled. "I know you're not. I just, well, I have a hard time imagining things being the same when you were in school."

"Honey, men haven't changed since the beginning of time. They know what they want and they'll do anything to get it. I'm just glad your father wanted me more than he wanted momentary pleasures."

"Why not have both?"

Her mom studied her for a moment. "Sleep with your father before we married? Never."

"Why not?"

"Have you done that, Annie?" Her mother frowned. "I thought we discussed this."

"We did." Annie touched her mom's hand. "And no, I didn't."

"Whew! Thank goodness. You had me going for a minute."

Annie's chest squeezed. She tried to blink back the tears pooling in her eyes.

Her mother sobered. "Oh, sweetheart, what's bothering you?"

"It's hard to explain." *How do I tell her I've been a faker all this time?*

Her mother drew her into a warm, gentle embrace and stroked her hair. The sensation soothed Annie until she calmed. She moved out of the embrace and peered into her mother's eyes, also wet with tears.

"Talk to me, honey. Say whatever is on your mind. I'll pray for whatever is worrying you."

"Okay." Annie's throat tightened. "All my life I thought I was a Christian because I went to church. I believed the right things about God, and I said the sinner's prayer."

Her mother looked worried, but she didn't speak.

"I . . . I think maybe I was wrong. Until this happened to me, everything in my life was perfect. I didn't need God, or at least I didn't think I needed Him."

She pressed her lips together to try and keep her chin from quivering. "I think Dan is right. I never knew the Lord. I wanted to believe, but I know I don't. I want to love Jesus more than anything but I don't know where to start. I told Dan I couldn't see him until I figured this out."

Her mother encouraged her to continue with a smile. "Don't be afraid, honey."

Deciding to trust her mom, Annie blurted out, "I think I'm lost. I want Jesus to change me. I want to know Him like Dan does. I want Him to be my best friend."

"Have you talked to the Lord about this?"

"That's just it, Mom. I can't bring myself to do it. I don't know how to start."

Her mom's eyes welled with tears. "I'll help you if you want me to. Will you let me?"

Annie trembled. "Yeah. I do. I'm just so scared."

"What are you afraid of, honey?" Her mother tucked Annie's hair behind her ear.

"I'm afraid if I pray with my whole heart . . . I'm afraid nothing will happen. That God won't want me." Annie leaned into her mother's embrace and sobbed.

"Shh." Her mom patted her back.

When Annie calmed, she wiped her wet cheek with the sleeve of her pajamas. Her mom cupped Annie's chin in her hand.

"You know your father and I love you, right?"

Annie nodded, her throat still tight.

"You need to know that Jesus loves you more than your father and I will ever love you. He won't reject you. He said if you feel weak and heavy burdened, He will give you rest."

Annie chuckled through a sob. "That describes me, all right."

Her mom reached for her good hand. "Then let's pray."

"Okay." Annie bowed her head.

Her mom urged, "Say whatever is on your heart. If you really mean it, then God will hear you. Jesus won't turn you away."

Annie inhaled deeply and slowly released her breath. "I want to know You, Lord," she whispered. "Change my heart and make me a new person. Please direct my life from now on."

Her heart felt like it was on fire. She couldn't say another word.

"Yes, Lord." Her mother gently squeezed her hand. "I agree with Annie. She needs You, Lord. And You said whoever hungers and thirsts for righteousness will see God. Show Yourself to her, Lord. Touch her life and let her know You love her.

And most of all, Lord, give her a peace that can only come from You. Let her know in her heart of hearts she is Your child. In Jesus' name, Amen."

Warmth flowed from Annie's chest and a love beyond description flooded her soul. When she opened her eyes, joy bubbled up from within.

"I feel it, Mom. I feel Him in my heart. He heard my prayer. Oh, Mom—"

Annie sobbed and clung to her mother. Only this time she wept tears of joy.

Dan had never been more excited and scared in his life. His hands literally trembled as he tied his sneakers. Annie had called him. She wanted him to come over.

The last five days had nearly driven him mad with wondering what she had decided. He hoped and prayed that the news she wanted to tell him today was what he wanted to hear.

If not, he would be devastated, but he'd live. The Lord had assured him this morning that He had everything under control if Dan would put his trust in Him. Dan vowed to do just that.

As he drove across town in his pickup truck, his mind charged forward with thoughts of Annie's smile, her laugh . . . her sweet nature. A lump swelled in his throat.

Please let this be good news, Lord!

Dan drove up the narrow driveway and parked. Annie's family had a beautiful, ranch-style split-level home. He'd never been invited inside before. The garage door was open, but he didn't see a car parked inside, which gave him the impression she was home alone. The notion excited and scared him at the same time. Did her parents know she'd called and asked him to come over?

He stepped onto the porch and curled his hand into a fist to knock. Through the window he could see Annie walking toward him with a smile on her face. She tugged open the door.

"I'm so glad you came."

His heart felt about to burst as he followed her inside. "Like I'd stay away . . ." he muttered under his breath.

She turned and glanced up at him. "Hmmm?"

"Nothing." He chuckled nervously as her gaze captured his.

The gorgeous sea foam color of her eyes pulled him like a strong tide. Her navy blue cotton dress shirt made her irises seem brighter. A tan silk scarf tastefully covered the scars on her neck. She'd parted her hair on the side so her fox-red locks covered the gash on her cheek. He could tell she'd worked hard on her appearance, and that gave him hope.

She stood in front of him, her mouth slightly open as she gazed into his eyes. Her inner beauty paralyzed him for a moment.

"You're so gorgeous," he whispered, unable to hide the longing in his voice.

Her cheeks flushed and she turned her face away.

Calm down. Your eagerness is going to frighten her off.

When she faced him again, he noticed the tears in her eyes and cringed. "I'm sorry, Annie. I didn't mean to—"

"No, it's okay. I believe you meant it sincerely. I . . . I think maybe it was just hard for me to hear . . . at first."

"You know you've always been beautiful. But there's something about you today . . . I can't put my finger on it. Something about your eyes . . . I'm not sure what it is, but you look even more beautiful than I remember."

Her lips curled into a shy grin. "Thanks. I think I can explain it."

"So I'm right? Something's changed?"

She stepped closer. "Umm-hmm."

He swallowed hard. She stood so close he could smell the fragrance in her hair.

Gazing into his eyes, she moved closer still. He had to fight the urge to stare at her lips.

Her chin trembled as she broke into a wistful grin. "Inside my heart . . . has changed."

It took him a moment to catch her meaning. The look in her eyes and the tender, loving expression on her face shook something deep inside him. Yes, it was the Lord's love he saw shining in her eyes. It couldn't be described or explained, only appreciated by fellow believers.

"Are you saying what I think you're saying?"

She nodded and a few tears slipped down her cheeks.

He wanted to shout, but held back. "That's so awesome."

She walked the rest of the way into his arms.

He wrapped her in his embrace and thought he'd die from the sheer pleasure of holding her in his arms for the first time. He'd dreamed of this day but never thought it would actually happen.

As he rested his head on her silky hair, he inhaled her intoxicating, sweet scent. His heart thumped so hard that even if she didn't hear it, he feared she'd soon feel it pounding through his shirt as she clung to him.

He needed to push her away before he devoured her like a fruit smoothie. He stepped back and felt a slight tremor, but wasn't sure if it came from him or from her.

"I'm so happy for you. When did this happen?"

"Let's sit down and I'll tell you everything."

He followed her across a formal living room that looked like no one ever used it. The modern furniture faced the back wall. Next to large bookcase, a television set was tucked inside the entertainment center.

Annie led the way down several steps, and they entered a large game room. A pool table and a foosball table stood next to each other on one side of the room. A comfortable-looking black velour couch with white chenille throw pillows stood on the other side, directly across from a large plasma screen television. A pitcher of iced tea and two glasses waited for them on the coffee table in front of the couch.

She smiled. "Like the TV? My dad got it for me as a coming-home present. Now I'll feel like I'm at the movies whenever I pop in a DVD."

"Nice gift. Very cool."

Easing onto the sofa, Annie patted the cushion beside her. "Sit by me."

His mouth went dry. The smile on her face and gleam in her eye made her look ravishing, and though he had no experience with women, he didn't trust himself. What to do?

Her lips curved into a pout when she noted his hesitation. "Don't you want to sit by me?"

He answered a little too breathlessly, "I do."

"Then please sit." She grinned. "I won't bite you, I promise."

Dan's gaze strayed to her lips as he settled next to her. Her teasing caused him to sweat even more. He'd love for her to bite him. Maybe a nibble on his ear. . . . His neck warmed and he cast his gaze down before his eyes betrayed him.

She touched his hand, making his skin tingle. He cringed inwardly. His attraction to her was going to make him nuts, especially now that her newfound love for the Lord made her seem even more beautiful.

"What's going on? I thought you wanted to talk."

He cleared his throat and pulled away from her hand. "I . . . I do."

"All right. You asked me when this happened. Still want to know?"

His heart pounded. Being alone with her in her home, sitting so close, was like a dream come true.

"Yeah. Sure."

Her soft lips curved into an enticing grin, beckoning for more than just a sweet kiss on the cheek like he'd offered while she was in the hospital. This time he wanted to indulge in a real one, just like he'd fantasized about doing for the past three years.

Silently he berated himself. *Get a grip! You may have saved yourself for the woman you marry, but you don't have to act like such a novice. She doesn't need to know you've never kissed a woman before. I doubt she's even thinking about doing anything but talking to you.*

"Are you okay? You look kind of pale. Do you need a drink of water?"

He swallowed, the sound echoing in his ears. He'd inherited his mother's Italian skin tone, which was slightly darker than Tony's, and he'd never been told he looked pale before. Did he really look sick?

Fear seized his chest. He jumped off the couch and wiped his sweaty palms on his thighs.

"I need to use the bathroom."

His voice squeaked and he winced. She must think he was a total idiot.

"Sure. It's over there." She nodded toward the other side of the room.

"Be right back," he called over his shoulder.

Annie waited for what seemed like forever. She hoped Dan wasn't physically ill, but he seemed queasy before he hopped off the couch. There was a stomach bug going around. Maybe he'd been exposed.

Dan opened the bathroom door and combed his hair with his fingers. "Sorry. I was a little dizzy, but I'm okay now."

"Do you think you have the stomach flu?"

He shook his head. "Nah. I jumped up too fast."

She blinked, not sure how to read him. "Okay."

He perched at the far end of the couch and crossed his leg over his knee. He still faced her but his leg separated them by several feet.

"Tell me. When did you receive Christ?"

"The day I came home from the hospital. It was so exciting. Mom and I were talking about guys and one thing led to another."

"You were talking about guys with your mom?"

"Yeah. Like about waiting until you're married and all that."

An adorable flush traveled from his neck to his ears. She'd probably embarrassed him.

"I'm sorry. Did I—"

"No. So what did you conclude?"

"About waiting?"

"Yeah." The red hue of his face darkened.

She winked at him. "I want to, of course."

He looked a bit breathless. "Me too."

A chuckle escaped her. *He's waiting? Goodness, he's so good-looking.*

A hurt, confused expression passed over his face. "You find that funny?"

She shook her head. "No. It's just . . . you're so good-looking I never would have guessed."

He raised a brow. "And your point is?"

Annie covered her mouth and giggled at how stupid she sounded. "Point taken. Sorry."

Silence lingered until Dan finally admitted, "I've never even kissed a girl before, not really." He blushed an even deeper shade of red. Then he tapped his cheek. "The one I gave you didn't count."

She wasn't sure she heard him right. He had virgin lips? Was that even possible in this day and age?

"Are you serious?"

"Yep. I'm waiting for that special person."

"Wow. That's great."

Delight made her heart swell. And suddenly she envied the lucky girl who would receive his first kiss.

They talked for about an hour. Finally Annie invited him upstairs. The warmth in his smile made her feel like they were best friends.

"Want to stay for lunch? I make a killer milk shake."

"What flavor?"

"Banana."

"Yummm. My favorite. Sure, I'll stay."

With her good hand Annie prepared two turkey sandwiches. She slathered extra mayo on the bread, just how she liked it.

"Go ahead and start eating while I make the shakes."

"I'd rather help you. What can I do?"

She thought a moment. "You can peel the frozen bananas. It's hard to do one-handed."

Dan peeled the three dark brown bananas into the sink with a knife while she scooped ice cream and poured milk into the blender. He pretended to bite one.

"Hmmm . . . I love monkey food."

His comment reminded her of the conversation with her mother, and she burst out laughing.

He squinted as he held the banana over the opening in the blender's lid. "Why do you keep laughing at me?"

Annie opened her mouth and tried to speak. She couldn't force the words out, which only made her laugh harder.

Smirking, he dropped the banana into the blender and touched the on button. As the bananas slowly mixed with the ice cream and milk, he fed the other two in.

The blender slowed. He set the lid on the counter and stuffed the bananas down with the long wooden spoon. Before she could punch the stop button, the spoon hit the blade. Milk shake and bananas sprayed in all directions.

As the cold, wet shake splattered across Annie's face, she blinked in surprise. Dan's shocked expression was priceless. His mouth gaped and she burst out laughing again.

Reaching over, he plucked a piece of frozen banana from her hair. He studied it for a moment—like a monkey at the zoo—then flicked it into the sink.

He exploded in a fit of laughter, which got her started again. She giggled and lifted a chunk of frozen banana from the front of his shirt.

Grinning down at her, Dan removed another piece from her hair, this time pushing the wet, loose strands away from her face and tucking them behind her ear. Shivering with delight, she stared at him with new eyes. He made her so happy, and she felt so comfortable with him.

Dan chuckled. "Sorry, Annie. I was just trying to help."

"I know. I'm sorry I didn't catch you in time. What a mess, huh?"

"What was so funny anyway?"

She smiled back at him. "Before I prayed with my mom to ask Jesus to come into my life, we were talking about the stuffed cat you brought me. You know, Purty."

"Yeah?" His grin broadened.

"She told me Dad got her a stuffed chimp for a gift when she was in high school. She said—" Annie clutched her stomach. "I can't—say it—"

"Yes, you can. Come on, tell me."

"Okay. Her dad used to tell her before they left the house—" She covered her mouth with her hand and snorted, then stood up straight, trying to be serious.

"Go on," he teased.

"He said, 'Remember, kids, no monkey business,' when she went out on a date with my dad. Isn't that just hysterical?"

Dan gave her a blank stare.

"Don't you get it?" She giggled.

"Um, yeah. I think so."

She slapped his arm. "Come on, it's so obvious."

His eyes clouded. Annie stepped a little closer and plucked banana from his shirt. With a grin she popped it into her mouth.

"Mmmm . . . still tastes good."

An unmistakable look of longing came into his eyes. It made her skin tingle. She had the distinct impression he wanted to kiss her.

She moved closer and lifted another chunk of frozen banana from his shirt. Holding it in front of his lips, she whispered, "Want a taste?"

As though hypnotized, he opened his mouth, and she popped the morsel in. When he closed his lips and slowly licked them, she followed her impulse and stood on tiptoe, cupping his face in her hands.

She wanted to be his first kiss. God help her, but she couldn't stand it anymore. She needed to know if the chemistry she felt between them was real.

He held her gaze, looking startled at first. Then his eyes darkened, but he didn't move.

Overwhelmed by his scent, his closeness, the need to know what it would be like to kiss him, she leaned into his broad chest. Time froze. She brushed her lips against his mouth, terrified he'd pull away, somehow sensing he wouldn't.

He didn't kiss her back at first. Hesitating, she pulled back slightly to gaze deep into his eyes. In their depths she found the same hunger that burned in her heart.

She closed her eyes, her lips again seeking his, savored the taste of him as she found his upper lip. Sliding her mouth across his, she tugged on his lower lip, silently teasing his senses, aching for his love.

She sensed clearly that something profound had awakened inside him. With a low moan, she kissed him deeply until he responded with like passion. His sudden fervor surprised her, yet pleased her beyond anything she'd imagined.

As she reveled in his kisses, the strength of his arms around her gave her a rush like no other. Passion exuded from him as his mouth met hers kiss for kiss. The unspoken longing that released in their embrace was so intense she was certain they'd burst into flame.

When she finally ended the kiss, Dan gave a low groan. Delight rippled through her as she acknowledged his desire. There was definitely chemistry between them and she wanted more. But would he give it?

"Oh, Annie . . ."

Now devouring her like a starved man, he pulled her back into his embrace, exciting her even more. She could feel him tremble as his lips moved gently over hers.

Her legs threatened to collapse beneath her. Never before had a kiss shaken her so deeply that it made her dizzy.

Tony was the only guy she'd ever kissed before, and he seemed more like a boy than a man. Considering Dan had never kissed a woman before, he demonstrated impressive skill.

He finally released her. She could tell he was as breathless as she was. His gaze revealed the same wonder she felt at what they had discovered in each other's arms.

Something wet trickled down her cheek. She lifted her hand to wipe her face.

"Wait."

He captured her hand and held it until she relaxed. Then he slowly untied the scarf from her neck and let it drop to the floor.

Tipping his head down, he kissed her cheek. His kisses slowly traveled the length of the scar. He nuzzled her neck, gently licking rivulets of milk and ice cream from her skin before returning to her cheek.

He sighed and whispered against her face, "You're so beautiful."

She shivered with delight. Nothing in her life had felt more wonderful than this moment.

He stepped back and cupped her scarred cheek with his hand. "I love you so much."

His words touched her so profoundly she couldn't find her voice. He had seen the ugly slashes on her skin, and he'd kissed her scars. He found her beautiful and told her he loved her. But how could he?

"I . . ." Her throat closed, and tears flooded her eyes.

He brushed the moisture away with the pads of his thumbs and traced her jaw, finally settled one thumb gently on her lower lip. She stood still, transfixed by his eyes. The expectation and hope she read in them stole her breath.

"Say you love me, Annie."

His husky voice, full of emotion, washed over her soul. His words warmed her to the very core. And she believed him.

"I love you, Dan," she breathed.

His mouth captured hers again. He slid his fingers into her hair as he drew her against him, tasting her lips until they set on fire.

Warning bells clanged in her brain. The point of no return was within reach.

Although she trusted Dan more than she'd ever trusted Tony, she worried about becoming physically involved with him. She had no intention of doing more but knew all too well how kissing could get out of hand when emotions ran high.

Instant regret for allowing Tony to explore her body made her throat ache. She wished she could erase the mistake because her experience with Tony had taught her how powerful such intimacy could be.

She forced thoughts of Tony from her mind as she gazed at Dan. If she had known he'd be this wonderful, she might have broken up with Tony and pursued him long before.

With Dan she found herself longing for something she couldn't have. But it was too late for them to go back to friendship. Not after such an amazing connection had occurred between them.

The stark realization hit her: She loved him.

He's so wonderful, Lord. Bless our relationship. Help us be strong and honor You.

His kiss interrupted her prayer. Caught up in the moment, she startled when she heard someone cough behind them. She felt Dan stiffen.

"Annie?"

Pushing Dan hastily away with a soft gasp, she turned toward the familiar voice.

Chapter 13

Dan nearly choked when he saw Susie standing in Annie's kitchen with her mouth agape, her gaze darting from one to the other.

"I—I knocked, but no one answered. The door wasn't locked . . ."

Annie waved her hand in the air and gave a nervous-sounding giggle. "Uh, we were just busy making milk shakes, and ice cream went flying everywhere."

His chest tightened. "H—hi, Susie."

"You guys looked busy all right." Sobbing, her hand pressed to her mouth, Susie ran out the front door.

The interruption hit Dan like a bucket of ice water and was even less pleasant. He'd known for some time Susie had a crush on him. She was a nice girl, but he'd made it clear to her several times that he wasn't interested in a relationship.

Obviously Susie had been hurt by what she had witnessed, however. Annie's face looked just about as stricken.

"Annie?"

She blinked several times as if snapping out of a trance. "Yeah?"

"What do you think she'll do?"

"Hopefully, nothing. We're friends, but she's been in love with you for a long time."

"I know," Dan sighed.

Annie's brows rose. "You do?"

"Yeah. I could tell by the way she stared at me whenever she thought I wasn't looking."

"She's gonna take this hard, I'm afraid."

He nodded. His mind whirred with terrible scenarios.

"Do you think she'll tell people at church?"

He cringed. "I sure hope not. Would she do something that low?"

Annie shrugged. "I don't know."

They stared at each other for a minute. Finally Annie asked, "Why didn't you ever ask her out? She's very pretty."

"Yeah, she's pretty, but I only have eyes for one girl." He winked.

"But why didn't you date other people since I was already taken?"

"I've never wanted anyone else."

Her brows rose. "Never? Not even in college?"

"Nope. I was a bit of a late bloomer. By the time I really cared about relationships with girls, I'd already met you."

"But I was only fifteen," she said, her eyes widening.

Reaching over, he prodded a now mushy bit of banana out of her hair. "And you're tastier than a banana milk shake."

Her sly grin made him want to kiss her again. She attempted to pull several more chunks of banana off his shirt, but only succeeded in smashing them into the fabric.

His jeans had very little on them, but by now his skin was starting to itch from the milk and fruit soaking through his clothes. "Hold on a sec." He pulled his shirt off over his head.

Her face reddened. "What are you doing?"

Ah, and she's modest too.

"Can I get a washcloth? Maybe wash my hair? And do you think I can borrow a T-shirt of your dad's if I give it back by Sunday?"

Her eyes shifted to his chest, then quickly away. "Um, sure. I'll be right back."

After she left, he glanced around the kitchen and grimaced. Not one square foot of the room remained unscathed.

What a mess!

Annie returned with two T-shirts. "I think either of these will work."

He selected the navy blue shirt. "I'll borrow this one if you don't mind."

"Not at all. Just hurry up and put it on."

Dan flexed his pecs and chuckled. "Why? Does this bother you?'

Annie giggled. "Very much."

"Cool." He grabbed the wet washcloth and wiped his chest.

She blushed and left the room, returning after a moment with a towel and some shampoo. "Here, wash your hair first so you don't get Dad's clean shirt wet."

She turned on the tap water and gestured for him to stick his head under the faucet. He adjusted the knobs to find the right temperature and leaned over the sink.

He always had trouble crouching over the sink to wash his hair and grunted his frustration. Annie readily volunteered to assist. When the cool shampoo touched his head, he sucked in his breath. Annie giggled.

"Relax. This should only take a minute."

She rubbed the shampoo around in his hair with her good hand. He savored the sensation of her massaging it into his scalp.

After she rinsed his hair, she turned off the water and tossed him the towel. "Here."

When he straightened, he found her staring at him. With ice cream and banana stuck all over her, she looked good enough to—

Quickly he quashed the thought.

"Thanks." He slipped the T-shirt over his head. "I better go now."

"Okay. I'll clean this up later. Right now I need a shower."

"Hey—" Dan opened his mouth to make a wisecrack about helping her but decided to shut up while things were still in his favor.

"Hmmmm?"

"One more thing."

Her eyes widened. "Yeah?"

He swallowed hard. "One more kiss?"

Raking her lower lip with her teeth, she looked up at the ceiling as if pretending to think about it.

"Please?"

She sidled closer and tipped her chin up. He carefully covered her mouth. Once more, her kisses transported him to a magical place he had never realized existed. He broke their kiss before he allowed his thoughts to stray.

"I need to leave before your parents get home."

"Why?" She placed her hand on his chest. "They know you're here."

"They knew I was coming over and we'd be alone?"

She giggled. "Of course. They trust me. But I don't think they'll allow me in the kitchen anymore when guests come over."

The tension in his shoulders eased. "How about I stay and clean up this mess?"

"Sure, but I'm starting to itch, so I'm going to wash up first. I'll be back to help as soon as I can, okay?"

When she left, he filled the sink with soapy water. By the time Annie emerged from the bathroom, he'd cleaned the kitchen so well that even he couldn't tell they'd made a mess.

She came up behind him and hugged him around the ribs.

He glanced back over his shoulder. "Like it?"

She grinned. "Like it? I love it."

He laughed and tossed the washcloth into the sink. Turning, he took her chin between his fingers.

"And I love you." He bent and kissed her until his brain turned all muzzy inside.

The front door shut. Someone stepped into the kitchen. "We're home."

Dan's head jerked around. Annie's parents were staring at them, mouths gaping. Dan dropped his hands, and Annie stepped hastily away from him.

Her mother gasped, "What in the world? Annie, I thought we talked about this."

Annie's father shot them a stern glance. "I thought you were better than your brother. How dare you take advantage of our daughter?" He pointed at the door. "Get out of my house."

Dan was too disturbed by his implications to speak. He threw a sidelong glance at Annie, who was now sobbing.

"It isn't what you think."

"You think I took advantage of Annie? I can't believe you'd think so poorly of me."

"Explain the wet hair," her father demanded.

Annie choked out, "We were making milk shakes and I had him peel the frozen bananas. He kidded about liking monkey food and I started laughing."

She finished in a rush of words. "So he put the bananas in the blender and shoved them down with a spoon, and milk shake sprayed everywhere. I just offered him a clean shirt, and I took a shower."

Her mother gradually relaxed and finally giggled. "No monkey business, then?"

Her father shot her mother a sharp glance. "You told her our story?"

Annie's mother nodded, her hand covering her mouth.

Dan looked down at his pants and found a stray chunk of banana he had somehow missed. He plucked it from his jeans and held it out on the tip of his finger.

"Here's the evidence."

Annie's father guffawed and came to grab Dan in a head-lock. "Sorry I didn't trust you, son. And, please, call me John."

Dan crouched out of the hold and offered his hand. "All right, John."

But her father bypassed his hand and grabbed him in a manly hug. "Glad to see you and Annie finally got together. Sorry I doubted you."

"No problem. You can trust me with Annie. I would never take advantage of her." Dan glanced in her direction.

Annie smiled. "Yeah, Dad. He wouldn't even touch me. I had to kiss him first."

Her mother's eyes widened. "Annie!"

"Oh, it's all right, Mom." She giggled. "He wanted to."

When her father shot him a questioning glance, Dan raised both hands. "I didn't plan to start anything. Honest."

"Besides, he never kissed anyone before me."

Dan's neck heated and he cleared his throat. "I hope you don't share that with anyone else, Annie. That's personal."

"That's right, sweetie. Never tell a man's secrets." Annie's father winked at Dan and slapped him on the back. "You're all right, son. You're all right."

The following Sunday Annie worked hard on her makeup and parting her hair just right. She wore one of the neck scarves her mother bought to match her long, black sleeveless dress and tied it in an attractive knot. Nodding at herself in the mirror, she smiled.

"Not bad."

"You almost ready?" her mother called from the other room.

"Just another minute," she answered.

A little less than two months ago that man had attacked her, and she'd thought her life was ruined. Now, she was ready to return to church. In less than a week Tony would be out of Teen Challenge, and ten days later he'd be on his way to college. So much had changed in such a short amount of time.

So far neither she nor Dan had been able to figure out a way to tell Tony about their relationship. But they both agreed on the most important thing. They would say nothing until Tony finished the program and was in a better position to handle the news.

Last night they debated on the phone about whether they should sit by each other in church. Dan said to do whatever made her most comfortable. She decided they'd sit together.

He met her on the church steps and reached for her hand. Her parents waved them on.

"You two go on ahead."

Dan leaned over and kissed her cheek. He led her inside and they slipped into a back pew.

She sighed with relief at his wise choice. She'd wanted to slink in and out and go as unnoticed as possible. Despite their plan, several people stared at them. A few turned away without smiling.

Annie blinked back tears and leaned into Dan. "Why are people staring at me? Do I look awful? I thought I hid the scars pretty well."

"I don't think that's what's going on at all." His voice sounded tense.

Then Annie saw what captured his attention. Across the aisle, Susie and several of her friends kept glancing over at them and snickering.

Annie's throat tightened. "They're talking about us, aren't they?"

"Sure looks that way."

Near the front of the sanctuary, Dan's mother turned until she saw them. Her eyes widened, and she snapped her head in the other direction.

Annie sighed. They hadn't informed Tony's parents about their relationship. After seeing the look on Mrs. Lane's face, she got the impression they wouldn't approve.

She exhaled slowly. She refused to obsess over what other people might be thinking.

Right after the offering, Annie got up to use the restroom. When she returned, one of Susie's friends leaned toward her.

"One guy not enough for you?"

Annie blinked back tears. While she and Tony hadn't formally broken up, she thought Tony had made it pretty clear he didn't want to see her anymore. The moment the service ended she begged Dan to take her home.

"Okay," he agreed, "but I don't see what the big deal is."

He reached for her hand as they headed for the door. She jerked away from him.

When they reached Dan's truck, he muttered, "Thought you were done caring what other people think."

"I am . . ." How could she explain?

"Then why pull away from me?"

"I'm scared."

"Of what?"

She inhaled deeply. "On the way back from the bathroom one of Susie's friends said, 'One guy not enough for you?'"

Dan raised his eyebrows. "She said that?"

"I don't want Tony hurt, but I'm afraid it's too late—that he's going to hate us both."

"People shouldn't talk about you like that. You haven't done anything wrong."

She scowled. "Guess it's a matter of opinion. Everyone here thinks I'm still going out with Tony. If he loved me and still wanted to be with me, he would have told me so, right?"

Dan stepped back, his face blanching. "There's something I haven't told you, Annie. But I didn't mean to keep it from you. I just forgot all about it."

He combed his bangs with his fingers and heaved a sigh, glancing everywhere but at her. Her chest squeezed.

"If it's important, how could you just forget?"

He hung his head. "I guess I didn't want to remember. I've been so happy . . . I didn't want the feeling to end."

The forlorn look on his face frightened her. She stepped into his arms and leaned on his chest.

"Nothing you say will make me angry."

Glancing up, breathless, she remembered their first kiss. Her lips had tingled for days wanting another. He seemed to read her mind because he hesitated, then nudged her away. The concern in his eyes worried her.

"Wait! Don't say anything yet. Kiss me first. I've been missing you."

"I don't know." He flushed and glanced around.

She followed his gaze. Only a few elderly people stood within hearing distance. Susie and her friends were nowhere in sight.

"Who cares if anyone's looking. I love you, Dan. Kiss me, please." *If this is it, I want one last kiss.*

He stepped back. "I don't know—"

Now panicked, she grabbed his suit jacket by the lapels and tugged him closer.

"Don't look at me weird. You're scaring me." Her voice squeaked. "I need you."

The love in his eyes darkened until all that remained was sadness. He rubbed his forehead and sighed.

"I love you, Annie. I'm so sorry. I don't want to lose you, but . . ."

"Kiss me. Please, just kiss me." She raised her chin and parted her lips.

His eyes darkened with the desire she longed to see, and when he lowered his mouth to hers, she reveled in the feeling. Her heart pounded until he released her, breathless and wanting more.

"You're such a good kisser."

Dan offered a sly grin. "Thanks, I try. You're hard to resist."

"Glad we've gotten that taken care of." She straightened his collar. "Now what did you plan to tell me that you think will make me so mad?"

The stricken look returned. He cleared his throat.

"I promised Tony something and I didn't keep it. I got so caught up in my feelings for you . . . I put it out of my mind. That was wrong." He stuffed his hands in his pockets and turned his back to her.

She tugged on his arm, trying to turn him around. "What are you talking about?"

He finally faced her, the haunted look on his face making her stomach quake. "What is it?" she whispered. "What could be so bad?"

"I—I'm sorry. I—" His face looked pinched.

"Just say it."

He swallowed. "I forgot to . . . I mean I didn't tell you . . . I promised Tony—"

"What? You promised Tony what?" She tensed, sensing his agony. "Spit it out."

"He asked me to tell you he loves you. I promised him I would when he went into Teen Challenge. He admitted himself so he could be with you again when he got out."

"What?" It would have stung less if Dan had slapped her. "Are you saying Tony admitted himself thinking he's going to be with me in four days when he graduates? That's what you forgot to tell me?"

Her entire body shook. How could he have failed to mention something so huge?

He stared at her, his eyes unfocused.

"I can't believe Tony is sitting in a rehab right now thinking I'm going to welcome him with open arms when he gets out."

"I'm a horrible brother. I can't believe it myself." His voice broke. "I'm sorry, I—" He turned away from her again and rubbed his face.

She stared at his back. As long as she believed Tony didn't want her it had been easy to love Dan. But now . . .

He turned. His face blurred as her eyes filled with tears.

"How could you do that to me? How?"

"I'm sorry. I just love you so much. There's no excuse." He reached to touch her cheek.

She thrust his hand away. "Don't touch me. I need a minute to process this." She pursed her lips. "Are you saying you manipulated me? You allowed me to think Tony didn't care, when all along he's been in rehab thinking I'll take him back. How cruel and insensitive! How heartless!"

Dan winced. "I know. But I thought you loved me too."

Her lungs squeezed at the forlorn look in his eyes. But he'd just admitted he'd kept this from her.

Yet she could tell he felt remorse for his actions. And she still loved him . . . a lot.

"Oh, Dan. What a mess we've gotten ourselves into." She searched his eyes. "What am I gonna do? I feel so bad for Tony."

Several tears rolled down her cheeks as she watched fear and relief pour from his eyes. He was obviously as confused and conflicted as she was.

"I know. I do too," he said in a hushed tone.

She believed him. He hadn't meant to hurt his brother. And she still loved him, more than she believed was possible.

Her insides quivered as she reached for his hand to reassure him. His eyes softened as their fingers clasped.

"I never meant to hurt you."

She pressed his hand against her cheek. "I love you so very, very much. I don't know how, but we'll figure this out together, okay?"

He drew her against him and sighed into her hair, making her shiver. "Thank you for saying that. I don't want to lose you."

As she leaned into him and snuggled close, he kissed her head several times. His masculine scent comforted her.

"You won't lose me, I promise. What you did is very upsetting, but I still love you."

His muscles stiffened when she said *I promise*. She had the sense he didn't believe her.

She didn't understand the depth of emotion Dan stirred in her. How could she show him she loved him more than she loved Tony?

Or do I?

Doubt penetrated her heart. *When Tony finds out I'm in love with his brother he'll feel so betrayed. But it's too late to go back. God help us all.*

Chapter 14

Dan woke in the middle of the night, his eyes swimming in tears. As he sat up, the familiar pine dresser with his high school diploma hanging on the wall above came into focus.

Sighing with relief, he whispered. "Thank God it was only a dream."

He flopped back down on the mattress and stared at the ceiling he'd covered with the glow-in-the-dark stars when he was a freshman in high school. It seemed like ages ago.

He drifted in and out of restless sleep, his thoughts shifting to his relationship with his brother and the continual competition between them. One of them would lose this time, ultimately hurting them both.

His thoughts strayed back to his dream. He had picked Annie up for a date the night before Tony's graduation from Teen Challenge. After dinner she'd invited him to her house to play pool.

Holding the cue stick, she'd teased him . "Can you help me? I can't line this up right."

His heart had fluttered. "Sure."

He put his arms around her, assisting her with the shot. When she hit the eight ball into the pocket to win the game, she dropped her cue stick on the table. In her elation she placed her arms around his neck and drew his head down until his lips met hers. He could still feel the heady sensation that had swept over him as he drank in the sweetness of her mouth.

Then she eased back on the table until he pinned her under him. She hungrily kissed his neck and face, heating his blood to a fevered pitch. He slid his hand across her blouse and played with the buttons, undoing them one at a time. Rather than resisting, she began to unbutton his shirt.

"Make love to me," she whispered in his ear.

He shivered with anticipation. His wildest dreams were coming true.

"Are you sure it's what you want?"

"Yes, Tony. I want you so much. I love you. I'll always love you . . ."

That's when he'd bolted upright still excited by their kisses, yet feeling crushed that she had called him by his brother's name. Was it really Tony she loved, not him? Instantly he started plotting ways to keep them apart.

Put away childish things.

He lay motionless, not wanting to hear the Spirit's quiet prompting.

Put away childish things.

He couldn't ignore the command that whispered in his heart. The competition between him and Tony for Annie's love *was* childish. More than that, it hurt all of them. Especially Annie.

His rigid posture relaxed, and he groaned. "But Lord, I don't want to lose her. I can't just let Tony waltz back into her life and steal her from me."

She was never yours.

"I know, Lord. I know her heart belongs to Tony. It always has. Is that what you're trying to show me? Are you trying to prepare my heart to lose her?"

She's Mine. She gave her heart to Me.

For a moment, he felt strangely comforted. "I don't mind sharing her with You, Jesus. I just don't want to share her with Tony. Please, don't let it happen. It'll totally crush my heart."

One of the Ten Commandments flashed through his mind. *You're putting another god before Me.*

"But I don't put her before You. I just love her a lot."

You deceived her.

Dan groaned and reflected on how he'd failed Tony too. He hated to admit his sin, but what God pointed out was true.

"Yes, Lord. I did."

He remained still. *Don't covet her. She's My daughter, like you're My son.*

The truth of it really hurt.

"I know. But, Lord—"

We can't share the throne of your heart. One of us will have to go.

Tears formed and he swallowed hard. "You win, Lord. I'm sorry I doubted You. Forgive me for my lack of faith."

Lean not on your own understanding. I hold your future in My righteous right hand.

Tears spilled onto his pillow. "It hurts, Lord, but You're right. I'll trust You.

Annie struggled with her feelings about how to handle Tony's graduation. His parents weren't sure of the exact nature of her relationship with Dan, at least as far as she could tell. But her parents obviously preferred Dan over Tony.

For the past few nights their conversations revolved around Tony, which bothered her. She was still unsure of how she'd feel when she saw him after more than a month apart.

When the phone rang she peeked at the caller ID, then lifted the receiver. "Hey, Dan."

"You want to go to dinner tonight?"

He sounds unusually perky, but I like it.

"Sure, but what's the special occasion?" She eased herself into her mother's plush easy chair.

"Besides you? I got the job at the hospital. I start the week after next."

"That's great!" Squealing with delight, she leaned back in the chair and crossed her ankles. "I'm thrilled you got the position you wanted."

"Thanks. The sooner I start earning a salary, the sooner I can move out of my parents' home."

She chuckled. "Having your own place could be dangerous, you know."

"Um, yeah." He cleared his throat. "Let's not go there. How about I pick you up in an hour?"

"I'll be ready."

She hung up the phone, her chest tightening. That was the third time this week he had deflected any reference to her affection for him.

She wondered why he didn't play along and tease her back. Did he think she would dump him as soon as Tony arrived back home? How could she convince Dan that her heart belonged to him, not to his brother?

While she got ready, she paced and worried. At last she realized that what she really needed to do was to pray, so while she waited for Dan to arrive, she talked to God.

Before she had never been able to think of anything to say to the Lord, but now she rambled on and on, sharing everything that weighed on her heart. She had the comforting feeling that God didn't mind at all. By the time Dan knocked on the door, she felt much less tense.

He brought her to her favorite Mexican restaurant, Juan and Chiquita's. At his insistence, she splurged a little more than usual. She loved how he spoiled her, and when they got up to leave, she wasn't ready for their evening together to end.

"I'm not ready to call it a night yet, are you?"

He shook his head. "Uh-uh."

With a playful grin she suggested, "Let's go to my house. We can watch a movie or something."

He grinned back. "Why not? I haven't been inside since we messed up the kitchen."

She laughed and poked him in the chest. "You mean since you messed up the kitchen?"

"You know what I meant."

He opened his truck door and helped her in, then walked around to the driver's side. When they pulled into the driveway he killed the engine and a suspicious look flared in his eyes.

"Where are your parents?"

"They probably just went to the store or something. I'm sure they'll be back soon."

Frowning, he studied her. She could feel his uneasiness.

When she thought of being alone with him her heart pounded. Maybe tonight she could show him she really did love him more than she loved Tony, and do so in a tangible way.

And maybe she would convince herself that Dan was the one she wanted.

Quickly she pushed the thought away. *Of course he's the one I want!*

Dan pulled out his new cell phone. "What's their cell phone number? I want to find out when they're coming back."

"Why? We're not doing anything wrong."

Pouting, she folded her arms and slid down in the seat. "Oh, go ahead and call. But I think it's stupid. They trust us."

He hesitated, and then returned the phone to his pocket. "You're right. I won't worry about it."

She pushed herself upright and reached for the door handle, grinning. "Great."

Fumbling with her keys in the dark, she found the one to the front door. He followed her inside and she flicked on the light switch, illuminating the room and startling Persnickety right out of her father's chair. The ornery cat didn't even stop to look at them but zipped out of the room without a glance back.

Dan stuffed his hands in his pockets. "Hey, you have a cat."

Annie cocked her head to the side. "I could swear I told you. Remember you got me a stuffed cat while I was in the hospital?"

He removed one hand from his pocket and rubbed his forehead. "Yeah. I feel stupid."

He acted fidgety and nervous, and she wanted him to relax. "Let's go to the game room."

He followed her down the stairs. "What do you want to do?"

"I don't know. Maybe play some pool?"

He flushed and shifted on his feet. Stuffing both hands in his pockets again, he mumbled, "I—that's not such a good idea."

She couldn't imagine why not, so she did her best to persuade him. "Come on sweetie, just one game. Or are you afraid I might beat you?" Batting her lashes at him, she feigned smugness.

His gaze darted down to her mouth before returning to her eyes. The darkening of his pupils made her heart flutter. Maybe a game of pool would be more fun than she imagined.

She grabbed a cue stick and handed it to him. "I'll try not to beat you straight up."

Dan's obvious discomfort flattered her, but she didn't know why. As she took each turn, she observed him. Several times he seemed short of breath when she slid the stick through her fingers and chewed her lower lip before striking the ball.

They were down to the last shot and the eight ball had wedged near the corner at an odd angle. She twisted as she tried to aim for it but the pins in her damaged hand were stiff and made it hard to grip the cue stick and get the right angle at the same time.

"My hand is too stiff. Can you help me with my last shot, pretty please?"

"Um . . . sure."

The electricity she sensed around him caused her pulse to race. He pressed his arms against hers and covered her hands as he helped her take the shot. The ball eased in.

"I won!"

She dropped the cue stick on the table and turned around to share her joy. Dan hadn't moved, so her body pressed against his. Gazing into his eyes, she felt her knees weaken. She touched his hair, brushing several strands away from his face, admiring its thickness and glossy sheen.

From that moment everything transpired in slow motion. She thought she'd die from the delightful sensations zinging through her when he whispered her name and covered her neck with kisses. The pleasure intensifying every second, she tugged him closer, crushing him against her.

They fell back onto the pool table together. Rather than feeling smothered, she reveled in their closeness. The back of his shirt had escaped from his jeans, exposing his back. She slipped her hand under his shirt.

"I love you, Dan. I love you so much."

He jumped back. "I have to go," he sputtered.

His eyes had widened in horror—just like a kid caught with his pants down. He rubbed his face and groaned.

"I'm sorry. We'll talk about this later." He disappeared before she had a chance to ask why he'd freaked out.

At first she was hurt, but then it occurred to her that he might have wanted her so badly he had to force himself to leave to keep them safe. What a stark contrast to his brother. Her heart warmed at Dan's chivalry.

She picked up the phone and dialed his cell number. He didn't answer. Maybe he had his radio cranked up too loud to hear it ring. With a sigh, she set the phone down and went to get ready for bed.

Snicky hopped up on the bed and joined her. The cat stared deeply into Annie's eyes before she plopped down and got comfortable.

It had been a while since they'd had a chat. "Snick, I have a question for you," Annie murmured. "If you were a female person, who would you want . . . the guy who had a relationship the Lord and respected you enough to leave when things got too hot? Or the one you've loved for years . . . only he always wanted to rub on you?"

Snicky stared into space as Annie scratched her behind the ears. "You'd be lost too, huh?"

Her cat fixed her cross-eyed gaze on Annie's face as though the answer was as simple as the nose on her face. She kissed Snicky between the ears.

"I thought so."

Her cat pressed her warm fur against Annie's neck and yawned. Annie rubbed her face against Snicky's plush fur. "Bet you're glad you don't have to decide. You can hide out in the house to avoid the male cats. I just wish I didn't have a choice."

Dan dreamed of Annie all night long. He couldn't explain it, but he sensed he was losing her. It was as if she was about to slip through his fingers and he couldn't bring her back.

When they played pool last night the similarity to his dream had been downright eerie. But in reality she confessed wanting him, not Tony. That's why he'd had to leave. Before his hormones controlled him and took over completely. He loved her too much to do something they'd both regret later.

He couldn't eradicate her beauty from his mind. And he didn't want to. He savored every thought, every portion of his dream. After tomorrow, when they both saw Tony again, it might be all he'd have to remember her by.

The thought made his throat ache. He couldn't breathe when he thought about losing her. Why did love have to hurt so much?

The constricting ache in his chest intensified throughout his morning routine. It hovered after he'd gotten into his pickup to drive to the graduation ceremony. Now he felt a bit strangled as well, like his throat had started to close from an allergic reaction.

This must be what people meant by all choked up. He'd never experienced such agony before, and he wasn't sure he even had a reason to grieve yet. But just in case, he'd asked Annie to get a ride with her parents. She had enough on her mind already. He didn't want to unduly influence her by his presence.

As he drove, he decided he'd slip into a seat near the back of the room. He'd make sure to be as far away from Annie and everyone else as possible. So he purposely arrived five minutes late. He scanned the group and found Annie sitting in a folding chair in the front row next to her parents. His parents had settled on the other side.

Annie kept dabbing at her eyes. She was already crying, and Tony hadn't even entered the room yet.

A lump formed in Dan's throat and he had to look away. He focused on the cross that hung on the wall behind the stage and recited his favorite scripture to help him remain calm.

"Keeping our eyes fixed on Jesus . . . For the joy set out for him he endured the cross, disregarding its shame, and has taken his seat at the right hand of the throne of God."

With the verse still echoing in his mind, his gaze strayed back to Annie. He longed to hold and comfort her, but he didn't want to pressure her in any way. She needed to see Tony and talk to him. Otherwise she might never heal from the emotional damage his abandonment had caused.

Dan had to trust the Lord to keep him from trying to wedge himself between Annie and Tony. If he allowed God to be his fortress, he'd find a way to survive. God would make a way.

Less than a minute after he slid into his seat, the graduates entered the small cafeteria. Footsteps echoed through the room until the crowd stood and their applause drowned out all other sounds.

Tony pranced in with a satisfied grin on his face. Physically he looked great and proud of his accomplishment. In fact, he radiated joy when he smiled.

Fear seized Dan's chest, making it difficult for him to breathe. His brother had changed. It was so evident, there was no way anyone could miss it, especially not Annie. He closed his eyes and tried not to hyperventilate.

She's going to forget me and go back to Tony.

Tears pooled in his eyes. He rubbed his face and tried to concentrate on what the leader was saying.

"Thank you all for coming out today in support of your loved ones. After our graduates share their testimonies and I say a closing prayer, we'll break for the reception. Let's begin.

"We thank You, Lord, that Your love is better than life, and You fulfill our every need. We praise You for being our all in all, for You alone are worthy to be praised. Thank You, Lord, for all You have done in these young men's lives and for what You will continue to do. Bless this ceremony. We pray it will honor and glorify You. In Jesus' name we pray. Amen."

"Amen." Dan whispered, agreeing with every word. "Help me to trust, Lord, and not look back. I thank You for what You're doing in my life and what You are going to do."

"We'll start with the graduates to my left," the leader continued. "Tony Lane. Why don't you take a minute to share what the Lord has done in your life?"

"Okay." Tony stared directly at Annie. "When I admitted myself into the program for the second time, I did it for a very special person. But then the Lord convicted me. He showed me I needed to change because I love Him and not just to win my girlfriend back."

Dan cringed. He wanted to slink out of the room before his brother noticed him. Before he could follow up on the impulse, Tony searched the back of the room and found him.

"And I want to thank my brother, Dan, for sticking with me even when I was a jerk. I love you, Danno. If you hadn't brought me back that night, I might not be here today."

Dan's eyes burned. He coughed, trying to hold back tears.

Tony continued, "You see, I'd thought about killing myself that night. I wanted to make the pain stop, yet I refused to let it go. After checking back in to the program, I sank into a deep depression. But after speaking with the pastor, I came to realize that when Jesus died, He bore my pain."

Their mother sobbed quietly and blew her nose. Tony glanced at her.

"I—I realized when Jesus died on the cross for me, He bore all of my pain on His shoulders so I could walk in faith and not wallow in sin anymore. Before that night I never fully understood what Jesus did for me. The next morning, I asked to be baptized."

Tony wiped his eyes with the back of his hand. "I want to thank my parents for visiting me and praying for me every day. I'll be going off to college next week, and I know I'll need continued prayer. Thank you."

Tony smiled at Annie and eased onto his seat. She covered her face with her hands, and Dan could hear her muffled sobs.

Lord, help us all.

Chapter 15

After Tony shared about his conversion, Annie had trouble concentrating. He used to insist he knew the Lord, just like she had. They were so much alike that way. Stubborn.

If she judged the truth of his statement based on the look of joy on his face, she'd have to agree that his conversion appeared genuine. But why did he have to change now? And why did Dan sit in the back when they had both agreed to be honest with Tony?

What should she do? Dan was too far away to ask.

Tony didn't give her a chance to check. The second the program ended he hurried over and caught her in his arms.

"I missed you so much." He buried his face in her hair and inhaled deeply as he clutched her. "You smell so good."

Annie tried to ignore his masculine scent and his touch, but found him difficult to resist. She stiffened, but he didn't seem to notice. The longer he clung to her, the more worried she became. Her throat ached as she forced back tears.

"We need to talk."

"I agree one hundred percent." He tugged on her arm. "Come on, let's go out back."

She searched for Dan, but couldn't spot him anywhere. Had he left her? Maybe he'd seen Tony pull her into his arms. She hoped not, but it would explain his sudden absence.

Weaving through the crowd, Tony led her across the room. He kicked open the side door and ushered her outside. *The alley?*

"Come on. I really want to talk to you . . . alone."

His puppy dog eyes were hard to resist, and he seemed harmless. He *had* just given his testimony so she decided to trust him.

"All right, but only for a minute." She glanced back into the room one last time before the door shut.

"I'll try to make this quick." He wrapped his arms around her, and she couldn't breathe.

The scent of rotting garbage assaulted her senses and she wrinkled her nose. "Ew, gross, Tony! It stinks back here. Can we talk somewhere else?" She stepped away from him.

He folded his arms over his chest, his well-defined muscles bulging under his shirt. "You're not worrying about what people will think, are you?"

She poked his chest. "No, I just want to breathe without gagging."

"Good."

His eyes slid to the scar on her cheek. He clasped her hand and led her down the alley toward the parking lot.

She exhaled with relief. "This is so much better."

He tilted his head and gazed into her eyes, making her stomach flutter. "So why don't you worry about what others think anymore?"

"I don't know. Maybe I'd rather worry about what Jesus thinks. At least that's my goal." Her mouth curved into a grin.

He blinked. "You accepted Jesus? How übercool!"

His genuine enthusiasm warmed her heart.

"And to think all these years I thought I already knew Jesus as my personal Savior. Doesn't it just flip you out when you think about it?"

"I don't think about it. All I think about is you."

His sly grin made her nervous. He caught several strand of her hair and rubbed it between his fingers, a habit of his she used to love. She shuddered with pleasure until reality screamed in her face.

Tony didn't know about her relationship with Dan. But this was not the best time or place to tell him. Not in an alley on the day of his graduation from rehab.

Lord, help me!

"Tony, I—"

"Shhh." He touched her lips. "Don't say anything. Just let me look at you."

She closed her eyes, trying to decide what to do. When she opened them, her courage waned. The tender expression on his face tugged at her heart and made her want to weep.

"You're still the most beautiful woman in the world to me. The doctors did a great job, you can hardly tell . . ." He caught his breath. "I've missed you, Annie."

He tipped his head and kissed her. For a moment she allowed herself to relish the familiar taste of him. But the love she once felt for him paled against what she enjoyed with Dan. Tony's kiss—though warm and tender—confirmed it.

She pressed her palm to his chest. "Wait. This isn't right."

He straightened and combed his fingers through his spiked hair. "What do you mean this isn't right? What could be wrong with my—with our kiss?"

She had to tell him the truth. It wasn't fair to string him along.

"It's not that. You're a good kisser, really."

"So why do you look sad? Something bothering you?"

Now would be a great time for the Rapture, Lord . . . I don't want to hurt him. I feel so bad.

She swallowed hard. "I—"

"What? Don't you love me anymore?"

His eyes shone with pain, unleashing her tears. "Of course I love you, Tony. I'll always love you, but . . ."

His eyes narrowed and several tears rolled down his cheeks. Wiping them away, he sucked in a shaky breath and cleared his throat.

"But what?"

She wanted to die for the pain she knew her words would cause him. Anything would be easier than telling him the truth. It sounded so much like betrayal. And maybe it was.

But her relationship with Dan felt so right. With Tony it was more of an intense crush, like puppy love. Until she got to know Dan's heart, she'd never understood the difference.

Dan's love for her was more mature. He'd stuck with her through hard times. He hadn't run out on her.

He would never pressure her. Not even now.

"This is so hard to say."

She tried focusing on Tony's eyes, but tears blurred her vision. When she blinked them away, her heart wrenched at the emotion she glimpsed in his eyes. She preferred blindness. Covering her mouth with her hand, she hunched over and sobbed.

Tony drew her into his arms and stroked her back as if he were comforting a child. "Shhh, Annie, it'll be okay. Just tell me. No matter what, I'll still love you, I promise."

His words only made her cry harder.

It was several minutes until she calmed enough to speak. Taking a deep breath, she stepped out of his arms and cast her gaze down.

"I'm going to say this quickly, because if I don't, I won't be able to say it at all. I . . . can't see you anymore."

"I don't understand. What happened to us?" He reached for her hand. "What about getting married?"

"Things changed. I didn't mean for this to happen."

"For what to happen?"

She couldn't answer. Her throat felt stuffed with rocks.

He rubbed his face and heaved a sigh. "I still want to marry you. I was wrong to act the way I did. I'm so sorry."

"Trust me. You don't want to marry me."

"You're talking crazy."

"Listen. When you were in rehab I—I fell in love with Dan."

Tony choked. "Dan? You mean my brother? You—and he—"

"We never meant to hurt you."

A caustic laugh erupted from him. "What a bunch of crap! How could it not hurt me?" His voice shook. "How could you do that to me? And behind my back! My own brother—"

"I'm sorry." She sobbed into her hands.

His face contorted and he balled his fists. "That back-stabbing, no-good, lying scumbag! I'm gonna rip his face off!"

The rage in his eyes frightened her. "Please, don't do anything crazy. Please—"

She grabbed his shirtsleeve, but he thrust past her, ripping his arm free.

"I know it wasn't you. My brother deceived you. He took advantage of you when you were down."

"No, it wasn't like that, I swear."

Leaning his forehead against the closed door, he groaned. "He manipulated your emotions. I'm not letting him get away with it."

With determination he whipped the door open, then rushed inside. When it struck her that there was going to be a fistfight, she burst for the door. Her shoes hit a slick spot on the ground and she slipped to the ground, scraping the side of her leg and shredding the skin on her forearm.

She ignored the pain and propelled herself back up, praying as she limped to the door and yanked it open. "Please, God, help Tony calm down. Please!"

What she saw made her stomach lurch. Tony was cursing like a madman, holding Dan on the ground as he punched his brother's face. While Dan surpassed Tony in height, Tony had more bulk and was clearly the stronger of the two.

Annie shrieked. As she watched, several men pounced on Tony and wrenched him off his brother, now writhing on the floor with blood gushing from his face.

Tony fought the men holding him. "You freaking wuss!" he screamed at Dan. "You should've fought back, but you didn't, because you're guilty! I can't believe I trusted you, you backstabbing lousy excuse for a brother! I would never do that to you! Never!"

Dan propped himself up and tried to mop his face with his shirt. "I'm sorry. I love you, bro. I swear, we didn't mean to hurt you."

Tony snorted and rubbed his knuckles. "Shut up! There is no we. It's all in your freaking mind. You can be sorry all you want, but I'm not gonna forgive you. You can rot in hell!"

He wrestled out of the hold the men had on him and ran out of the room, leaving his parents standing with their mouths open. Their eyes darted from Dan to Tony, then settled on Dan.

After a moment, Mrs. Lane caught Annie's gaze. She could swear the woman shot daggers at her as she glared across the room. Annie held in her tears and cautiously made her way over to Dan.

The guilt she glimpsed in his eyes made her heart squeeze. She turned away, not knowing what to believe. Had he deliberately deceived her? Unsure of how to handle such intense emotions, she walked out the door. Her parents followed close behind.

When she reached her parents' car, she broke down. "What am I going to do?"

Her mother embraced her. "I don't know, honey. This is all so tragic. All we can do is pray for you. Let's go home."

Annie searched her father's eyes. "Dad?'

His brow furrowed. "I think you should give yourself some space . . . from them both. You need time to sort things through. Then when you're ready, make a decision and stick with it. It's not fair to either of them if you leave them hanging."

"Okay, Dad." Annie glanced back at the building. "Let's go home."

The first thing Dan remembered was a blinding flash of stars. Then he was pinned to the floor, his brother looming above him, swearing and punching him in the face. Dan tried to speak, but Tony refused to listen. He raged as he cried, punching him, screaming in Dan's face. If the nearby men hadn't pried Tony off, his brother might have killed him with his bare hands.

Annie had stood at a distance, gazing at Dan with tears in her eyes, the confusion on her face tearing at his heart. He'd wiped his face on his shirt to stop the flow of blood, but his actions had little effect. His overwhelming guilt kept him from defending himself, which seemed to infuriate Tony even more.

Pain shot through his head when he tried to sit, so he lay back down. He watched Annie sobbing as she walked out, her parents following close behind. She must have told Tony. Nothing else made sense.

Earlier he'd thought he'd die from heartache when he saw Tony pull her through the side door and into the alley. But he refused to interfere. She needed to sort through her feelings.

Knowing she had told Tony the truth should have pleased him. But he hated himself for hurting his brother so much Tony flew into a blind rage. The ache in his chest even surpassed the pain in his head.

Someone tapped him on the shoulder. "You going to be okay?"

Dan shrugged his hand off. His left eye was swollen almost shut and blurred his vision. Looking up, he made out an elderly man who held out a handkerchief.

"Here. Use this. It's clean."

Dan mumbled thanks as he covered his nose and mouth with the cloth to stop the bleeding. He'd never felt more miserable in his life.

How did things get so out of control?

No response.

Don't you care that I'm hurting, Lord?

Nothing.

He hated it when the Lord seemed to pull back. But he understood it was his own sin separating him from God that made him feel that way. Regardless of the reason, the distance between them still hurt.

Whispering a prayer, he groaned. "Jesus, forgive my sin. I know I did wrong. Help Tony find it in his heart to forgive me someday."

Peace poured over his soul like a healing balm. He would survive, but he would still have to face the consequences of his actions.

"Lord, be with Annie today," he added. "Help her to forgive me too. Amen."

His father appeared in his line of vision and offered his hand. Dan accepted his hand and allowed his father to pull until he stood on both feet. His face still throbbed, but the bleeding had eased.

"Thanks," he mumbled, afraid to look into his father's eyes. Would he see disappointment there?

When he glanced up, he found confusion and concern. Dan's chest tightened at the look on his mother's face. Her lips curved downward.

"I'm disappointed in you. How could you do that to your brother?"

"I'm sorry, Mom. I love her. I can't help it."

"Well, I hope it was worth it, though I can't imagine why it would be."

"Don't blame Annie. It's between Tony and me. She never wanted to come between us."

His mother sniffed in disgust and turned away. "Take me home," she said to Dan's dad.

After casting Dan an apologetic look, his father ushered her away. Thankfully the spectators had dispersed. All except one.

"Anything I can do to help?" a sweet voice asked.

At first his vision was so blurred he didn't recognize her. Then he realized it was Susie Ziglar . . . from church.

Chapter 16

"**I** brought you some ice." Susie handed him an ice bag wrapped inside a towel.

He started to smile in gratitude, but his bruised cheek hurt too much. "Thanks."

"What a shame Tony beat you up on his graduation day, huh?"

She clasped her hands behind her back and shifted her feet like a schoolgirl with a crush. Though her expression was innocent, he hadn't forgotten how she had treated Annie on her first Sunday back in church.

He chose not to comment. Instead he turned away and faced the door.

She circled around him and caught his gaze. "Did I say something wrong?"

Dan shrugged, not sure if he could talk about it without getting angry.

"You're mad at me." Her lower lip curled in a slight pout.

He snorted. "You're loving this whole thing, aren't you?"

Susie stepped back. "What are you talking about?"

"Come on. Don't play dumb with me. Talking about Annie behind her back. Telling your friends she's two timing Tony. Need I go on?"

Susie cast her gaze down. "I guess I should apologize."

He pressed his lips together and held the ice against his face determined to keep his sarcasm in check. But he refused to let her play her coy games with him.

"You think?" She peered up, her eyes holding a measure of guilt.

He had to give her credit for being honest. She could have denied it or tried to blame someone else.

"It would be a good place to start." Searching her eyes, he asked, "What I don't get is why you'd do that to her after all she's been through. I thought you were good friends."

"We . . . were." Tears pooled in her eyes. "I'm so sorry. What I did hurt you too."

"I forgive you. I can't answer for Annie though."

"Then I'll talk to her. Think she'd like that?"

The gleam in her gaze suggested she wanted more than friendship with Dan. If she wanted to please him, she was wasting her time.

Shifting the cold pack to cover his cheek, he hesitated, feeling suddenly uneasy with her rapt attention. She was attractive, but he had eyes for only Annie. Susie's flirting irritated him.

"Don't look at me like that."

Her lips curled into a seductive smile, and she touched the front of his shirt. "Like what?"

"I don't know. Like you want me, or something. You're a friend, and that's all you'll ever be. My love for Annie isn't going to change."

A defensive spark shot from her eyes. She scowled at him.

"Get over yourself, Dan. I don't find you the least bit attractive."

He burst out laughing. "You're kidding, right?"

She planted her hands on her hips and stuck her chin out in defiance, but her voice betrayed her. "You're reading too much into things. I was just being . . . nice."

He almost felt sorry for her. Almost.

The flustered look on her face confirmed she had lied, but he wasn't going to push the issue. "So why did you come here? You know one of the graduates?"

Her cheeks flushed and she shook her head. "Just Tony."

"You knew he was here?"

"My neighbor's brother was admitted a few weeks ago. Last Saturday I went with her to visit him, and I saw Tony in the rec room. We chatted for a little while. Mostly he talked about how much he missed Annie. I went to her house to tell her and found you guys all over each other."

Dan resented her implication but decided not to comment. "So why didn't you go back and tell him after you saw us?"

"I tried, but they said he couldn't have any visitors except for family. They wouldn't even let me slip him a note. Annie was wrong to see you behind your brother's back. You were both wrong."

"We never planned to hurt him. We were just friends."

"Yeah, well, I'd never do something like that to the man I loved."

"I would never tell everyone at church my friend is cheating on her boyfriend either, which was just as bad if you ask me."

She offered a cocky grin. "Maybe so, but she earned every bit of it."

"If that's the attitude you're going to have, then you shouldn't see her. She doesn't need any more grief right now."

"Not my problem. She got what she deserved."

"What she deserved?" He leaned into her face, livid. "Annie didn't deserve to be stabbed and left for dead. I just befriended her when Tony bailed. There's nothing more to the story and I resent your implication.

"You know what I think? I think you're jealous that she has two men who want her and you don't even have one."

Her face turned crimson, and he immediately regretted his outburst. *Next time keep your mouth shut.*

"I'm sorry. I didn't mean that," he blurted.

She popped the side of his face with her open palm.

His mouth dropped open. He'd never been slapped before. *I'm really screwing up today, Lord. Help me to set my agenda aside and treat her like You would.*

Crying, Susie turned and ran toward the door.

"Wait." He tried to catch up with her.

She pivoted to face him, tears streaming down. "Go away."

He removed the cold pack from the side of his face. "I didn't mean it. You're a beautiful girl. Annie and I both think so. It's not you. It's me."

"Is that supposed to make me feel better? That you don't like me because you're a jerk?"

He winced. "Okay, I deserved that."

Her eyes thinning into slits, she raked him from head to toe with her gaze as if she couldn't believe he'd agreed with her. "Why apologize if you can't stand me?"

"I don't hate you. I just don't like you the way you want me to."

"Why should I care what you think?"

"Because Christians are supposed to love one another, and it was wrong for me to treat you like I did. Forgive me."

A slow grin covered her face. "I suppose I could. Why don't you give me a chance? I could make you forget all about her."

Dan cleared his throat. "Uh . . . see you in church."

"You know it." She sashayed out with a distinct sway in her hips.

The pastor of Teen Challenge appeared in the doorway. Seeing Dan still there, he approached.

"I'm sorry I messed up the reception. I'd hoped to talk to Tony but didn't have a chance." Dan sighed. "I don't blame him. I just pray he doesn't fall off the wagon because of me."

"Tony has the tools he needs to fight the craving for alcohol and to stay sober," Pastor Jim pointed out. "If he starts drinking again, he may try to blame you to justify his behavior, but that doesn't make it your fault. Anyone wanting an excuse to drink can find one. Don't blame yourself. Pray for him instead. He has a hard road ahead of him."

Dan nodded. "I will. And pray for me too. I've gotten myself into a real mess."

❧❧❧

Annie's chest ached. The whole way home, she wished she had access to an IV drip so she could shoot morphine straight to her heart to numb the pain and help her forget her troubles. First she prayed for Dan and Tony, and then she prayed for herself.

You know I care about them both, Lord. Show me what to do.

"What in the world is he doing here?" her father grumbled.

Annie opened her eyes and glanced out the window. As their car pulled into the driveway, Tony appeared in front of the house. He wore a long-sleeved Tommy Hilfiger shirt and matching jeans. He must have changed out of the polo shirt he'd worn earlier because of the blood he'd splattered on it.

When Tony stepped toward the car and offered her a tentative smile, Annie's mother turned to look at her. "I don't think you should talk to him."

"I agree with your mother," said her father.

She thought about what her parents wanted and debated talking to him anyway. But how could she face him after he'd viciously attacked his own brother? Though Tony believed her innocent, Dan hadn't manipulated her. She'd fallen in love with Dan of her own accord.

"I need to find out what he wants. Please give us a few minutes to talk things through."

With obvious reluctance, her father nodded. "All right. But no more than a half hour. Then he has to leave. Understood?"

"Yes. Please, just trust me."

Her mother reached for her hand. "We want to, Annie. We do."

"But?" Annie's gaze darted between her parents.

"We don't want you to get sucked into feeling sorry for him, honey."

"Your mother is right." Her father parked in the garage. "Tony is a master at making you feel guilty. Don't let him. Stand your ground."

"I will, Dad. First I need to figure out where I stand. Pray that I do the right thing."

"You're a smart girl. We'll pray and trust you."

Her father reached over to the backseat and patted her hand. Although her mother didn't say a word, Annie sensed her disappointment. With obvious reluctance, her parents got out of the car and went into the house.

Annie uttered a quick prayer. "Give me the words to say, Lord."

Tony's shadow appeared outside the car. She could feel his distress.

He tapped on the car window. "Can we talk?"

Her throat swelled with emotion. "Sure."

As soon as she opened the car door, he reached to help her climb out. She pulled her hand from his as soon as she stood up, and he ducked his head to stare at the concrete floor.

"I'm sorry I lost it. I didn't mean to embarrass you and cause such a scene."

When he looked up, the emotion in his eyes created havoc in her thoughts. The pounding of her heart confused her. She was in love with Dan, so why did Tony stir such emotion in her heart with his repentant gaze?

She steeled her heart against him. "And Dan? What about what you did to him?"

Tony glanced down at his hand, swollen from the beating he'd given his brother. A tear trickled down his cheek.

"I wanted him to fight back, but he wouldn't. He just kept telling me he was sorry and that he loved me."

His eyes took on a haunted look. "I couldn't stop. If we'd been alone I might've killed him. That scares me."

"I've never seen you so . . . violent. You scared me too. I— I can't believe you did that to him. You guys used to be so close." Her voice hitched. "I've ruined your relationship."

"We did it to ourselves. It isn't your fault."

"Thanks for saying that, but I still feel so guilty. I can't stand to see you angry with each other. I never wanted this to happen."

"We can't help it that we both love you. You're so easy to love." He reached out and caressed her cheek.

"You mean that?"

"Of course I do," he whispered. "Come here."

He opened his arms. She stepped into his embrace and sighed.

"I'll never stop loving you. And I forgive you for seeing Dan behind my back. I just want us to be together again."

His words caught her off guard. Even after all that had happened, he wanted her?

She tipped her head to search his eyes. At the same time he lowered his mouth to meet her lips. Quickly she shoved him away.

"Don't manipulate me! I can't deal with this right now. I'm still trying to figure things out."

"But I want you, Annie. Even though you kissed my brother." He ran his fingers through his hair and exhaled. "I still can't believe he did that."

"It wasn't like you think. It just happened."

"But we were so close . . . and you wanted to marry me. What went wrong?"

No, Tony. I agreed to marry you to make you happy.

"Please don't pressure me. I'm not making a commitment to you or anyone else right now."

Tony raised his eyebrows. "Not even Dan?"

Her chest tightened and she shook her head. "I don't know what I'm going to do. . . ."

"Come to college with me." He offered a seductive grin. "We don't have to get married right away. We can go for a semester or two and then decide."

"No! I'm taking a year off. Everything in my life has changed so much. You'll have to go to college without me."

Sadness and resignation filled his eyes. "It won't be the same without you, babe."

"You're going to have to handle going to school alone. I need time to figure out what I'm going to do with my life."

His eyes lit up. A broad smile spread across his face. "Sure, I'll wait for you to decide. I'll e-mail you every chance I get."

"That'll be nice, but please hear me out. I'm not talking about getting married, just attending college. I really hope you enjoy your first semester of school."

A sly grin tugged at his mouth. "I'd enjoy it more if you were with me."

She heaved an exasperated sigh. "Tony, you need to chill. When do you leave?"

"Next week. I plan to go to church and see my friends Sunday, and then next Thursday Dad's gonna drive me there. It's pretty far so he'll stay a couple of days to help me settle in."

Annie relaxed at the change in conversation. "I hope you have a great time. I really do."

He touched her scarred cheek, lightly tracing the line with his finger. Her throat tightened. She wished he'd keep his hands to himself but couldn't find her voice. She missed being with him, and it hurt to break things off, but she couldn't admit that to him.

"I'm sorry I wasn't man enough to stick around when you needed me," he whispered. "Can you forgive me for deserting you? I'd sure appreciate knowing you've forgiven me before I leave for school."

"I forgive you." The tender look in his eyes caused her knees to weaken. "I'll always care about you, Tony. But I love Dan."

He traced her jaw as if he hadn't heard a word she uttered. He focused on the scarf she wore on her neck.

"Can you take that off? I want to see how you healed."

Her eyes fixed on his as she untied the scarf and tilted her head. Sucking in a breath, he examined her neck with the gentle caress of his fingertips.

"I don't know how you survived."

A shudder racked her spine. His touch stirred up a longing she'd tried so hard to forget. She backed away from him before he confused her more.

"I've gotta go. I can't stay out here with you. It's too hard for me."

Tony nodded. "Okay, I'll leave. I just wanted you to know I still love you. I hope you'll wait for me. Pray about it, Annie. That's all I ask."

She headed inside before she broke down. He still didn't understand he'd never be right for her, not like he wanted. Her heart belonged to Dan, and though she wondered if he'd still want her after what had happened today, she could only pray and let God do the restoring.

Her parents greeted her on the other side of the door. She wondered how long they had stood there listening, but decided it didn't really matter.

Her mother enveloped her in her arms.

"Oh, Mom, what am I going to do?" Annie sobbed.

Chapter 17

Dan arrived home and found his parents waiting for him at the kitchen table. He opened his mouth, but his father raised his hand to stop him.

"Don't say a word. I want to talk first. Have a seat."

His father nodded toward one of the kitchen chairs. Dan plopped down and laid his arms on the table. He reached for a saltshaker and rolled it on his palm, staring at it while he waited for the lecture to begin.

After several minutes of silence he glanced up. His mother pointed at the condiment holder, and Dan set the shaker back on the tray.

With a sigh, his father began. "I'm so shocked I don't even know where to begin."

Dan's mother grabbed a napkin and wiped her nose. "Just look at you, Daniel. What has gotten into you boys? I warned you about spending time with Annie, didn't I?"

Dan nodded, casting his gaze down at his hands.

"Look at your mother when she's talking to you."

He glanced up, his chest tight from the stress of knowing he'd hurt everyone in his family. But it didn't change the fact that he loved Annie. No one could make him stop loving her.

"We want you to stay away from Annie. She's your brother's girlfriend. How could you do that to him? How?" His mother's eyes filled and she dabbed them with the corner of the napkin.

He hated to see his mother crying. In fact, he couldn't remember the last time she'd cried. He wanted to slink away. The strained look on his father's face made him feel even worse.

"I agree with your mother, Daniel. You need to stay away from Annie. Let it go. There are many, many women in this world to choose from, so why pick her?"

Dan shrugged. "I don't know. I never wanted this to happen. I love Tony and it really bothers me that he can't stand me right now."

His mother huffed, "Well, can you blame him?"

He shook his head. "I'd feel the same way if I were him."

"Good. Now that we have that settled, we want you to go stay with a friend until your brother leaves for college next weekend."

His head snapped up. "What? You want me to leave?"

"Yes. The tension will be unbearable with you both here, and I want Tony to go to college as planned. When he's gone you can come back home." His father glanced over at his mother, and she imparted a nod of approval. "You'll be moving out soon anyway, right, Son?"

Dan stared with his mouth open. His parents were kicking him out of his home. Could things get any worse? He nodded and then stood.

"I'll call a friend and go get my things."

While he packed his bags he could overhear his parents talking.

"Do you think we were too hard on him?"

"No, he needs to think about what he's done. This will do him some good."

"Well, if you're sure . . ."

He returned to the kitchen with two full suitcases and reached into his pocket for his cell phone. "I'm going to stay with my friend Jeff if he'll let me crash there. He has a two-bedroom apartment and no roommate."

His parents nodded without speaking.

Dan flipped open the phone and dialed. Jeff answered. "Hey."

"Hello, Jeff? It's me, Dan Lane. Can I stay with you for a week? I'm having some problems at home. I need to move out until my brother leaves for college next weekend."

"Um, sure. I don't see why that won't work. When do you start your new job?"

"The week after next. At least by then my face won't be so messed up."

"Hey, I heard about that. Did Tony bust your lip?"

"Who told you about our fight?"

"Susie, from church."

"When did you see her?"

"We live in the same apartment complex. But don't worry, she lives in the building on the other side of the block, so there's plenty of space between us."

Dan gave a short laugh. "Why would I be worried? I don't care where she lives."

"Good. When are you coming?"

"Now works for me."

"Okay, see you in a few."

"Thanks."

Dan touched the off button and snapped his cell phone shut before shoving it into the back pocket of his jeans. He grabbed a suitcase in each hand.

"See you in about a week."

His parents didn't respond as they watched him cross to the garage door. For a second he considered asking them where Tony was, but decided against it. They'd clearly demonstrated which son they supported when they asked him to leave.

Usually his father was more supportive, but he'd backed down. Dan hated it when his father let his mother make the decisions. He didn't do it often, so this thing with Tony must be a huge issue for her.

Dan hesitated for a moment, playing with the doorknob, but finally kicked open the door and went out to toss his bags into the back of his pickup truck. He glanced back at the house to see if they'd watch him leave or come outside to say good-bye. They weren't at the window or the door.

"Fine," he mumbled, a lump forming in his throat. "I can do this without your support if I have to."

Climbing into his truck, he slammed the door and drove off without looking back.

❧❧❧❧

Dan circled the parking lot twice before he found the right building. He parked and grabbed his suitcases. With a sigh of relief, he noted that Jeff's apartment was on the first floor, so he wouldn't have to drag his luggage up any stairs.

At the door he plopped the bags down and knocked. Someone inside yelled, "Give me a sec."

Jeff, a blond-haired, hazel-eyed ladies' man from the church choir, whisked the door open. Staring at Dan's face, he quipped, "Man, he got you good. You look like Rocky after the last round."

Dan grimaced. Just what he needed—wisecracks.

Jeff glanced down. "Is that all you brought?"

"That's all I need. I'm supposed to move back home next week, but I'm starting to think I don't want to. Not the way things are now anyway."

Jeff offered a sympathetic smile. "That bad, huh?"

Dan sighed. "I sure didn't expect my parents to tell me to go stay somewhere else. I mean, I never broke any rules. All I did was fall in love with 'the wrong girl'—not because she's bad or anything, only because my brother loved her first."

"Sounds like you got a bum deal." Jeff grabbed one of the suitcases and led the way into the spare bedroom, where he dropped it on the futon.

"It's probably for the best," Dan conceded. "Until Tony leaves for school it's going to be tense at home anyway. I really don't want to deal with it, so this just makes it easier on everyone. I can see where my parents are coming from, I guess. They want Tony to succeed and see me as being in the way. I've already finished college, and little bro is just now starting."

His friend chuckled. "Sounds like Tony is the prodigal son and you're the older brother who followed all the rules and never squandered a thing. Don't you feel kind of like that? You know—wondering why they're killing the fatted calf for him when he's blown things big time?"

"I try not to think about it. I know our parents love us both. Mom is just struggling with this whole alcoholism thing and Dad is trying to be supportive of her. I refuse to take it personally."

Jeff's eyebrows rose. "Well, you're a saint, then."

"Not really," Dan sighed. "It bugged me when I drove off and they didn't even say good-bye. I'm trying to be cool about it, but it hurts. Maybe I'm explaining it to myself to keep it from bothering me so much."

Jeff placed his hand on Dan's back. "How are you dealing with the girlfriend issue?"

Dan gingerly rubbed his swollen face, and his voice escaped in a throaty whisper. "That's still hard. I'll let you know when I'm ready to talk about it. Right now I'm just trying to survive."

"Man, you really do love her, don't you?"

"I can't help it."

Jeff punched him lightly on the shoulder. "Well, I sure hope this turns out better than *Romeo and Juliet*. I want to see a happy ending here. Think there'll be one?"

He peered at Jeff and frowned. "You're not getting anything out of me right now, so stop fishing. I told you I don't want to talk about it."

Jeff lifted his hands in surrender. "All right, man. Be cool. I didn't mean to set you off."

Dan couldn't help but quirk a grin. "You don't have to worry about me beating you up. That's not my style."

"I can tell. It looks painful, buddy. I still can't believe he got you so good. I mean, Tony is tough, but didn't you even *try* to defend yourself?"

"Nope." Dan rubbed his forehead. "I didn't do anything except apologize."

"While he pounded on your face you were telling him you were sorry? What are you, nuts?" Jeff's eyes widened and his mouth hung open. "I thought you were tougher than that. At least you were in high school."

A wry grin tugged at Dan's mouth, making him wince as his split lip stretched. "It's harder to not fight back, believe me. Especially when surrounded by spectators rooting for you to nail your opponent. I sort of feel like I know what Jesus went through when he let the soldiers beat him and he just stood there. But Jesus didn't deserve it. I did."

"I know you don't want to talk about this, but tell me you're not going to sit back and let your brother waltz in and take Annie back without a fight."

Dan stared at Jeff for a moment. "I have more faith in Annie than that. She's confused right now, but I really do believe she loves me. And I refuse to manipulate her to make her choose me over Tony. She needs to follow her heart or she'll never know if she chose the right thing. Know what I mean?"

"You really are a saint. If she were mine, I couldn't do that. I'd want to be right in the thick of things. Annie's hot, so you know for me . . . it would be harder."

Dan angled his head and studied his friend. "What are you saying?"

"If she were my piece I wouldn't allow the other guy to get a taste of the action." Jeff snorted. "Especially my brother."

Dan's face heated. "Who said she's anyone's piece?"

"Aw, come on. Tony's *your* brother. He's not gonna wait forever for a girl. She's been his steady woman for almost four years. I'm sure she gave him something."

Dan straightened. "No she didn't. How dare you assume she would?"

A wide grin covered Jeff's face. "Don't tell me you asked about what she did with your brother. No way! For Pete's sake, that's cheesy."

Dan scowled. "Just shut up. I'm through talking to you tonight."

"All right, that's fine. But the fat lady hasn't started singing yet, and this subject isn't over. Not by a long shot." Jeff offered a wicked grin on his way out of the room. "Be back soon."

Annie stared at her silent phone. Two days had passed since the fiasco at the Teen Challenge graduation, and Dan still hadn't called her. When she couldn't stand it anymore she called the Lanes' house and prayed that Dan would answer the phone.

"Lane residence."

"Dan?"

The man cleared his throat. "No, Dan isn't living here right now. Is this Annie? Do you want to talk to Tony?"

"No. I want to talk to Dan. How can I reach him? His voicemail says his mailbox isn't set up to take messages yet."

"He's staying with his friend Jeff until Tony goes to college. You know the Jeff I'm talking about?"

"From choir?"

"That's the one."

"Thanks, Pastor. I think I have his number. Please don't tell Tony I called for Dan."

"All right, I won't. But, Annie, please decide what you're going to do. And make it soon."

"I'm trying, Pastor Lane. I really am. Pray for me."

Pastor sighed into the phone. "I haven't stopped since the day you were hurt, and no matter which son of mine you choose, I'll keep praying for you."

A lump clogged Annie's throat. "Thank you. That's all I ask."

After she hung up the phone, she glanced at her reflection in the mirror. Her hair looked better than usual today. She'd gotten used to wearing it hanging over one side of her face. Her parents said it made her look like the seductive woman from the Roger Rabbit cartoon. With the right amount of foundation and perfect weather conditions, she could almost make the scars on her cheek disappear.

She grabbed her purse and searched inside for her little phone book. She found Jeff's phone number and dialed.

Her heart pounded. She hadn't spoken to Dan since Tony found out about them. She needed to know whether Dan still loved her. Was his guilt so great he wouldn't see her anymore?

Did he love his brother more? All the unanswered questions almost made her dizzy.

A woman answered. "Hello?"

Susie.

Annie choked and hung up. Dan was with Susie? She couldn't believe it. But that would explain why he hadn't called her, wouldn't it?

A million scenarios zipped through her mind. She'd waited too long and now Susie had moved in on Dan when she thought the coast was clear.

Tears brimmed on Annie's lashes. *Should I tell him how I feel?*

Quickly.

The answer was so clear it startled her. *But why quickly?* she questioned.

I'll be with you.

Ten minutes later she stood in front of Jeff's apartment, her hands sweating so much she had to repeatedly wipe her palms on her jeans. After taking a deep breath and exhaling slowly, she rapped on the door.

No one answered. She glanced back at Dan's truck in the parking lot before knocking again.

This time the door swung open, and she stood face-to-face with Susie. "Well, look who's here," her former friend said with a smirk.

Annie forced back the powerful urge to slap her.

A short distance down the hall, Dan stepped out of a door, barefoot and wearing only sweatpants. Stretching, he yawned.

"Who is it?"

Annie could see him from where she stood, but he couldn't see her. Her feet froze in place. The shock from finding him at Jeff's apartment apparently alone with Susie rendered her speechless.

"I said who's there?"

Susie glanced back at him. "Nobody important. Just some kid selling cookies."

Dan came to the door. "Annie?" His face split into a broad grin. "I'm so glad you're here."

Her eyes charged with fresh tears, and she bolted for the parking lot.

"Wait!"

Refusing to look back, she darted around the corner of the building. Reaching her car, she fumbled with her keys. Her hands were shaking so badly that as as she tried to insert the key into the lock, she dropped the set. With a sob she bent over, scooped them up, and tried again.

"Oooh, ow, ooh, ouch." Dan hopped from one bare foot to the other across the gravel parking lot. When he reached her he demanded, "Why did you come here?"

She swung around, tears streaming down her face. "I certainly didn't expect to find you with *her*, that's for sure."

He caught his breath, then laughed. "You think I'm with . . . ? No way! She and Jeff are friends. I was in my room sleeping and didn't even know she was still here—"

"Then why would she say I was a kid selling cookies so you wouldn't know it was me?"

Dan bent to pluck a pebble off the bottom of his bare foot. "I think she's still bugged that I won't go out with her."

Staggering, he steadied himself against the car with one hand and rubbed his foot with the other. "Man, those rocks are sharp."

He exuded the faint scent of perspiration, and he looked so buff. Her cheeks warmed when she realized how close they stood. She drank in his nearness.

"Your face . . ." she murmured, wincing.

He touched his swollen eye. "Yeah, I'm a mess. I was hoping to look a little better the next time you saw me."

A grin tugged at her mouth. "Is that why you haven't called? You wanted to look handsome for me?"

He chuckled. "Maybe."

"I was starting to think you didn't love me anymore."

He laid his palm against her cheek. "I just didn't want to pressure you. I want you to be sure. I don't want to manipulate you in any way. You need to decide for yourself . . ."

A lump formed in her throat. Unlike Tony, Dan never made her feel cornered. He allowed her the freedom to choose. That gave her confidence in their relationship.

For several minutes she peered into his eyes, not moving. *What should I do, Lord? I love him so much. I want him to know that. I want him to trust me.*

Be honest.

Gently she ran her fingers through his bangs, pushing the hair back off his forehead. His hair was always so shiny and soft. She loved touching it.

He closed his eyes as she stroked his hair. His injured face evoked guilt, and she cupped his bruised jaw.

When he opened his eyes, she said in a hoarse whisper, "I've missed you, Dan."

His eyes darkened. "I've missed you too."

She bit her lower lip. "You still love me?"

"Of course. Why wouldn't I?"

With her mouth slightly open, she stood on tiptoe. "I love you. I never stopped."

He gathered her into his arms and kissed her with such tenderness her pulse hammered. "I love you so much, Annie," he whispered against her lips.

When she got her breath back, she noticed moisture in his eyes. Her throat clogged, and she drew his head down and kissed his lips, one at a time. His arms tightened around her until she could hardly breathe.

He released her and stepped back. "Let's go inside."

She glanced over his shoulder, glad her parking space wasn't visible from the apartment. "Not with Susie hanging out there. I'd rather go somewhere else."

"All right. Give me a few minutes to clean up. I'll meet you at the park. Will that work? We can talk a little?"

"Sure." A slow smile spread over her face. "I'd love to talk about us. But please don't tell Susie anything. I don't trust her. I want Tony to leave for college in peace. If he knows I saw you, it'll be a mess all over again."

"I understand completely." He winked. "If Susie asks me anything, I'll just tell her to take a hike."

Annie grinned. "As long as she doesn't take a hike in the same park, I think we'll be fine." Glancing at his bare chest, she placed her flattened palms on him and ran her hands up to his shoulders. "You're tense."

He grinned. "Not so much anymore."

"I feel so blessed that we're together."

He tilted his head. "You're joking, right?"

"No. I still can't believe after all that's happened that you still love me. Especially after all the trouble I've caused your family."

"I could never stop loving you."

The sound of his deep voice warmed her insides. "What did I do to deserve you?"

"It's not about anything you've done. You don't have to earn my love. I love you because of who you are, and someday I want you to be my wife." He leaned over to kiss her scarred cheek. "I want to love you forever."

The heat of his mouth against her skin caused her to tremble. She could imagine being with Dan forever.

But was it possible that everything she enjoyed with him was only a twisted fantasy brought about by the horrible circumstances that knit their hearts together in the first place? She started to cry.

"You don't have to say anything. I know it's too soon to ask. I just want you to know that for me this isn't a fling or a summer romance. What I feel for you is real."

His bruised face blurred through her tears as emotion suffused her heart. "It's real for me too," she whispered.

He kissed the tears from her cheek and buried his face in her hair. As she nuzzled his neck, reveling in the feeling of his skin under her hands, she caught a blur of movement over his bare shoulder.

A woman with long brown hair darted around the corner of the building.

Her body stiffened, and groaning, she slid out of Dan's arms. It seemed as if every time she shared an intimate moment with Dan, Susie lurked nearby.

"What is it? What's wrong?"

"Susie was watching us. I have this terrible feeling she's going to tell Tony and this whole nightmare will start all over."

"This time we'll deal with it together. Just say the word and I'll stick by you."

Like you did at Tony's graduation?

As though he sensed her hesitation, he asked, "Don't you believe me?"

"I want to. I do. It's just . . ."

He tipped her chin up with his fingers. "It's just what?"

"You left me up front with Tony at the rehab. I searched for you and couldn't find you anywhere. It was so awful, Dan. I don't want to go through that again."

He nodded. "I understand."

But do you really? Will you help me through this?

"I can't be alone with him," she explained. "He tries to wear me down. He's so persuasive."

A concerned look etched his face. "What do you mean? What did he do?"

"He . . . he kissed me."

Dan's body stiffened. "He what?"

She nodded and cast her gaze down. "That was before I told him . . . about us."

Dan relaxed. "Well, as long as that was the only time. It was the only time, right?"

"No. He showed up at my house later to tell me he was sorry he upset me."

"Did you kiss him back?" Dan's voice sounded tight.

She scrunched her face and tried not to cry. "I stopped him right away."

"You . . . stopped him?" he whispered.

Annie nodded. "I don't want to be alone with him. He makes me uncomfortable."

"Do you still love him?"

She nodded and gazed into his eyes. "But it's different. With him it's more like a crush." Her voice lowered, "With you, it's a whole lot more."

He pulled her against him. "I'm so happy to hear you say that. You don't know how much it means to me."

Burying her face in his neck, she inhaled his scent. "I think I do."

A chirping sound trilled from Dan's pocket. He stepped back and pulled out his phone.

"Hello?"

His face dragged into a frown, and he offered her the phone. "It's for you. Tony."

"Annie?" Tony's voice rasped in her ear. "What are you doing with Dan? I thought we worked this out."

Annie felt sick and angry at the same time. "You heard what you wanted to hear. I never promised you anything."

Tony cursed and hung up.

Flinching, she handed the phone back to Dan. "He hung up on me."

Dropping his phone in his pocket, Dan said, "Might as well go to Jeff's place now."

"There's no point in trying to keep it quiet, is there?" she agreed, on the verge of tears.

Dan drew her close and said nothing.

"Why does everything have to be so complicated?" she mumbled against his shirt.

"I don't know. I wish I could fix it, but all we can do is pray it doesn't get any worse."

Chapter 18

Dan clasped Annie's hand and they walked back to Jeff's apartment. He shoved the door open. Susie stood on the other side.

When she saw them together, her smug grin fell flat. She obviously hadn't expected him to return with Annie in tow.

Jeff strolled into the living room. His brows rose when he saw that Dan held Annie's hand.

"So you haven't tossed in the towel. Is that a good thing?"

"We think so." Dan gave Annie's hand a gentle squeeze and let go.

An awkward silence filled the room.

Dan cleared his throat. "Excuse me. I'm going to clean up. Be right back."

He tipped his head down and kissed Annie's cheek. "I love you," he whispered in her ear, then hustled into his room.

He showered quickly but decided to skip shaving because his jaw was still sore. In less than ten minutes he emerged from his room fully dressed in jeans and a green short-sleeved shirt, carrying his sneakers. He found Annie on the couch in tears.

The smirk lingered on Susie's face. He wondered what had happened to make Annie look so miserable and shot Susie a stern glance.

He was still annoyed with her for coming into his room late last night. She'd woken him to get him to watch a movie with her, and he'd refused. After she'd left, he had trouble falling back asleep. He wondered if she'd spent the rest of the night on the couch, but decided he would rather not know.

He scooted next to Annie on Jeff's tan, overstuffed couch and plopped his sneakers in front of him. While he loosened the laces and shoved his feet into the shoes, he stole quick glances at her. Tears had collected on her lashes and threatened to roll down her cheeks as she blinked.

Finished tying his sneakers, he draped his arm over Annie's shoulders. Leaning close, he asked, "Want to go somewhere else?"

Annie nodded. She clamped her mouth shut like she was trying hard not to cry.

He helped Annie off he couch and accompanied her outside. He could confront Susie later, if at all. Better yet, he might just find another place to spend the rest of the week. He could ask his friend Dave from the men's group he'd joined last month. Dave lived about a thirty-minute drive from Boise.

Susie had made a habit of hanging out at Jeff's place every day since Dan arrived, and since he was only staying a week, he didn't feel right asking her to leave. Though Jeff had mentioned liking Susie, Dan had the impression she didn't reciprocate his feelings. Apparently she wasn't beyond using Jeff to get to Dan, however, and that really bugged him.

He thanked God that Annie wasn't manipulative like many of the women he'd met at college. If anything, he'd fault her for being too honest. But her honesty was one of the things he loved most about her.

He helped her into his truck, and after climbing inside, turned to face her. "What's bothering you?"

The tears, which had threatened to overflow, now slid down her cheeks. She squeaked, "I'd rather not talk about it."

"Did Susie say something mean to you in front of Jeff?"

Annie shook her head. "She waited until he left the room."

The look in Annie's eyes concerned him. "What did she say? Please tell me."

She reached over and touched the two-day-old stubble on his face with her fingertips. Leaning closer, she kissed his rough cheek, allowing her lips to linger on the scratchy surface. She inhaled and sighed.

"I love the way you smell."

"Tell me what she said to hurt you."

She swallowed and stared at him wide-eyed. "She . . . told me she slept at Jeff's apartment last night and she went into your room and got in bed with you."

Dan burst out laughing, "Ha! She told you that? Did she mention the fact that I told her to get lost and kicked her out of the room?"

"That's not all." Her voice wavered. "She said you told her you never wanted to fall in love with me but you felt sorry for me and that's the only reason you spent so much time with me. She said you wouldn't be with me now if I hadn't been stabbed."

His smile transformed into a scowl. "You don't believe that crap, do you?"

Annie averted her gaze.

"I can't believe you listened to her! I told you I've loved you since the first time we met."

"I know, but . . ." Her head tipped down and he couldn't read her expression.

"But what?" He fought to remain calm but anger constricted his lungs.

She raised her gaze to meet his. "Part of what she said is true."

His mouth went dry. "What part is that?"

"If I hadn't been attacked I never would have gotten to know you. I wouldn't know Christ like I do now either, which is pretty cool." Her lips curved into a slight grin.

His tension eased. "God works things out for the good, doesn't He? But that's not really what's bothering you, is it?" He lifted her chin.

"No. It's just . . . when I look in the mirror . . . and every time I try to use my left hand, I'm reminded of what happened. I still don't understand it." With trembling hands she untied her silk scarf and exposed her neck. "Look at me. I'm hideous."

True, her neck was irrevocably scarred. But underneath her skin was the same beautiful Annie he'd always loved.

"Hideous is the last word I would use to describe you."

He lowered his head and kissed her neck with a playful growl. She erupted into a fit of giggles and playfully swung her hand at him.

"Stop! I'm trying to be serious." She laughed, tears rolling down her cheeks.

"Come here."

He wrapped his arms around her and pressed her silky head against his chest. Stroking her hair, he snuggled her close.

"Go ahead and cry. I'm here for you. I'm not going any-where."

She sobbed, soaking his shirt with her tears. "Why? Why did this happen to me?"

When her crying eased, he placed his hand on her scarred neck and tipped her head up. "I don't know why it happened, but I'm thankful you're alive. When I found you like—"

He stopped and pinched the bridge of his nose. "When I thought you were dead it tore my heart out. I'd rather have you with scars than not have you at all. You're still gorgeous to me. Can't you see that when you look in the mirror?"

She shook her head. "All I see are the scars."

"Well, I see the beauty." He gazed into her blue-green eyes, unwavering.

"Why do you love me?"

His heart lodged in his throat, and he wanted to hurt the man who'd so viciously attacked her. "Words can't describe what I feel when I look at you. You make my heart sing. I feel like I can fly when you smile at me. I want to hold you in my arms forever. I—"

She muffled his words with a heart-pounding kiss, wrenching every thought from his mind. He treasured her with everything he had in him and marveled that she cared for him too.

The taste of her mouth was sweeter than the finest chocolate, and he wanted to indulge forever without restraint. But instead he broke off the kiss and pulled away to turn the key in the ignition.

"I better take you home. All this kissing is making me nuts."

"Wait! I drove my parents' car, remember?"

He killed the engine. "That's right. I feel stupid."

"Not any more stupid than me." She winked.

His heart lifted to see the sparkle return to her eyes. As they walked to her car, he said, "Why don't we take your car? We can drive back here later." Remembering he'd be moving again, he added, "I'm going to talk to Dave about moving in with him. Maybe we can drive out there after I get settled in."

"Sure."

She unlocked the car door with her electronic key. Before she could get in, someone pull up behind them. They turned at the same time to find Tony parked behind them in his parents' car.

He looked furious. And he'd blocked them in so Annie couldn't leave.

She groaned. "Please, not again. This constant fighting—it's not about me. You need to work things out between you. Leave me out of it."

Dan winced. He didn't want to see Tony start another confrontation in front of Annie any more than she did. When Tony got out of the car, Dan handed Annie his cell phone.

"I'll talk to him. Call your parents if things get out of hand."

"I may just call them anyway. I don't want to deal with this."

Dan exhaled and whispered, "Lord, give me strength and wisdom. I want to do what's right."

He approached his brother. "Hey, Tone. Let's go somewhere we can talk alone."

Tony glared and spoke through clenched teeth. "We can talk right here. In fact, I'll get straight to the point. Susie told me you were making the moves on Annie again, that you went to Jeff's place so you could be alone with her."

The blatant lie rendered Dan speechless.

"Well, aren't you going to say something?"

"I can't believe Susie would lie like that."

Tony's eyes narrowed. "Why should I believe you? Annie's here, right?"

Annie stepped between them. "Dan didn't call me. I wanted to know how he was doing, and your dad told me he was staying here. He didn't know I was coming."

Tony's gaze skittered between Annie and Dan. "Why would Susie make something like that up?"

Dan rolled his eyes. "Because she wants me."

"Oh, get over yourself! You are *not* God's gift to women, contrary to what you believe."

"That's not what I meant."

His brother snickered. "Maybe you meant that's why Susie was in your bed last night, right bro?"

Dan's face heated.

"I can tell by the look on your face that she wasn't lying. Am I right?"

The intensity of his rage clipped Dan's words. "I was sleeping. When I woke up and found her in my bed, I told her to *get away from me*. How dare you imply I wanted her there? You're the guy with the porn habit, not me."

Tony clenched his fists. "Shut up!"

Dan's gaze followed Tony's. His heart squeezed at the sight of Annie's pain.

"Stop fighting, both of you!" She dialed Dan's cell phone.

"Mom?" She slid her fingers through her long hair and drew it back. "Can you come here and get me?" She gave the address.

She paced back and forth. "Yes, I have the car but Tony has me blocked in."

She stopped and heaved an exasperated sigh. "He's fighting with Dan again, and I can't deal with it . . . . Okay . . . No, I haven't heard back yet. . . . No, I didn't get a call from them today. What did they say? When is it?"

While Dan listened to her conversation, Tony joined him and whispered under his breath, "Just back off, and everything will be cool."

"I'm not going anywhere. I promised Annie I'd stick with her, so stop threatening me."

"Find another girl. Leave Annie alone."

"Stuff it. I'm not—"

Annie hung up the phone. "Stop fighting, both of you," she sobbed. "I need your support. The county prosecutor called. For some reason he had the wrong number and couldn't reach me before. He said I have to go to court tomorrow. They want me to get there early so he can go over what I need to do. They're sentencing that . . . that . . . I can't even say it! You know who I mean."

Tony's brows rose. "He's going to be sentenced? I didn't even know he was convicted. That sure happened fast. But what do they need you for?"

She choked out, "He confessed and waived his right to a trial. The evidence against him was enough to convict him without one."

"That's great," Dan said. "But I still don't see why they need you there. Are you sure you want to go?"

Annie shrugged. "He said he thinks if the judge meets me and sees my scars, he'll give him a stiffer sentence."

"But will it be worth it?"

She bit her lip and blinked back tears. "I don't want to be on the same block with him, let alone in the same room. But I feel like I need to be there."

Dan pulled her into his arms. "It's okay. I'll go along and sit by you."

She squeaked out, "Really?"

"Yes, really."

He pressed her head against his chest and she clung to him. Tony scowled at them.

"I want to go too, Annie. I want to see the man who hurt you sentenced for a long time."

She straightened and considered Tony for a moment. "I don't know. What if you get angry and say something that makes things worse? I know how mad you are about all this."

"Do you really think I'd say something to upset you on purpose?"

"I don't know anymore. You're different now."

Wearily he rubbed his hand over his face. "I'm sorry. I don't know what's going on with me. I just want to know that you're okay. Can I spend some time with you before I go? Maybe take you out to dinner or something? Please?"

Dan tensed. When his brother poured on the charm, people had trouble saying no to him. He studied Annie. Her blue-green eyes fixed on him, and she looked torn.

Did she want him to help her say no? Or was the look in her eyes a request for him to say it was all right with him? He wished he could read her mind.

Instead, he leaned over and whispered in her ear, "What do you want me to do?"

"I need to make it through tomorrow first," she murmured.

Dan turned to his brother. "Let's help Annie survive court tomorrow. Then she can deal with saying good-bye. What do you say?"

Tony smiled at Annie, ignoring Dan. "Is that what you want?"

Nodding, she drew herself against Dan.

Tony eyed Annie so wistfully that Dan's heart went out to his brother. He'd lost so much. Dan had to admit he'd be devastated if he stood in Tony's shoes.

"See you tomorrow then?"

Tony nodded and with obvious reluctance. He got into his parents' car, peered one last time at Annie, and then drove off.

A minute later Annie's mother arrived in the parking lot. Her father was in the passenger's seat.

"Still need a ride?" Annie's mother called.

"Not anymore, but thanks for coming. Can Dad drive my car back? Dan's going to bring me home so I won't have to drive after dark."

"Sure," her parents responded in unison.

"Thanks for coming by." Dan nodded at them. "Sorry about the inconvenience."

"No problem, Son. I'm just glad to see you taking such good care of my girl."

Annie handed her father the keys. "Thanks."

"Don't worry about it, honey. We'll see you tonight when you come home. "

Her father got into Annie's car, and they both drove off.

"Ready to go visit Dave?" Dan asked. "I'm itchin' to make a move."

"That sounds like a great plan," Annie agreed.

He kissed her cheek and slowly moved his mouth over the scar on her face until his lips locked onto hers.

She finally drew back, giggling. "You're so good for me. And I think my parents really like you."

A broad smile tugged at Dan's lips. "I like them too."

That evening Dan returned to Jeff's apartment with his friend Dave. Within minutes they'd collected Dan's belongings, thanked Jeff for his hospitality, and left.

Dan hoisted the suitcases into the bed of his truck. "You picking up Joey on the way to your house or after we drop my stuff off?" He wondered briefly what it would be like to have a son with Annie, even if they had to adopt as Dave had.

"Let's run by the house first. You need time to settle in, and I can pick Joey up later."

"All right. Thanks so much for offering me a room until I find my own place."

"No problem. I was once right where you are, trying to make it on my own with tight finances, wondering when I'd be able to make enough money to support a family."

"You sure this is gonna be okay? I don't want to be in the way with your wedding coming up soon."

"No problem," Dave insisted. "Man, I can hardly wait for the big day! Maybe you can house sit for us when we go on our honeymoon. Interested?"

Dan grinned. "I'll think about it, but I don't see why not. And I really understand about having trouble waiting. When I kiss Annie I feel like I'm in another world. I don't care if I eat or sleep. I only want to delve deeper. Know what I mean?"

Dave's eyes twinkled. "Sounds like you're in love."

"I've got it bad," Dan confessed.

"How's Tony handling everything?"

Dan shrugged. "Okay, I guess. With him, you never know what he'll do."

"Think you two will ever be close again?"

Dan's eyes pricked with tears. "I don't know. I miss how it used to be between us. I just wish I could fix it. My parents are mad at me, too, though my dad has called a few times. I think it's weird Dad has to be sneaky to call me, don't you?"

"I'll give you that. Do you think your mom will come around?"

Dan leaned on the tailgate and stared, unseeing, at his suitcases. "I hope so. I never meant to hurt anyone. I just want to love Annie. She wants that too."

"Then I'll pray that your mother calls and you work things out."

"Thanks, Dave. I appreciate it. You're a good friend."

When they arrived at Dave's place, Dave helped Dan haul his suitcases inside. Although he'd never had a full tour of the expansive house before, Dan decided to check everything out later. Right now, he just wanted to lie down and pray for Annie.

Tomorrow would be a trying day. His stomach twisted at the thought of seeing the man who had cut Annie and almost ruined her life. How could he be in the same room with him and not want to kill him?

Chapter 19

Annie called Dan early the next morning. "Can you just meet me at the courthouse?"

What time is the hearing?"

"It starts at nine. I'm meeting with the prosecutor at eight thirty, so if you can be there then, I'd appreciate it."

Dan glanced at his watch. "That doesn't give me much time, but I'll be there."

"See you soon. And thank you so much for sticking with me through this nightmare."

"No need to thank me, Annie. I want to be there for you all the time."

You're an amazing man, Daniel Lane," she whispered in a husky voice.

"I love it when you say my name. See you soon."

"Annie, we're leaving in twenty minutes," her mother called from the kitchen as Annie hung up the phone.

Her heart pounded. In less than two hours she would see her attacker up close—for the first time since that horrible night. She shuddered at the thought.

During the drive to the courthouse, she struggled to appear calm. But her pulse throbbed and she had to wipe her sweaty palms on her slacks repeatedly.

When they arrived, she anxiously searched the hall. To her relief, Dan was leaning against the wall near the courtroom door.

Except for his bruised face, he looked like a male model in his navy blue slacks and dress shirt. The poor guy had to be embarrassed to be seen in public with black-and-blue marks all over his face. She loved him even more for putting her needs above his own. It was so typical of him.

As soon as she made it through the metal detector, she headed straight for him. Her parents followed close behind. Running as fast as her black pumps would allow, Annie didn't stop until he wrapped his strong arms around her.

He kissed the top of her head, and she reveled in his wonderful, fresh scent. Everything about Dan exuded strength and stability.

Annie's father patted him on the back. "Glad to see you, Dan. Your support means a lot to Annie, and to us."

"Yes, thanks so much," Annie's mom echoed."We appreciate all you've done."

An older gentleman approached Dan from behind and tapped him on the shoulder. "Excuse me. Are you here for the sentencing of Wilhelm Moniker?"

Dan turned. "We are."

The man eyed Dan. "I'm Jack Farmer, the prosecuting attorney for this case. And you are—?"

Dan shook the hand Farmer extended. "Daniel Lane. Annie's boyfriend."

"Nice to meet you. I'd like to talk to you for a few minutes, alone—if you don't mind."

Annie gave him a reassuring smile.

Dan squeezed her hand. "I'll be back in a minute."

He disappeared around the corner with the lawyer. Annie's mother nodded toward a cluster of brown plastic chairs.

"Let's sit over there."

She followed her parents. When she turned to sit down, she saw Tony coming toward them.

"Hey." He nodded at her parents, then laid his hand on Annie's shoulder. "You doing okay?"

He looked incredibly handsome in his suit and tie. She had forgotten how gorgeous he was. But the truth was that looks didn't mean as much to her anymore as they once had.

A scripture passage floated into her mind: *Man looks on the outward appearance, but God looks on the heart.* Suddenly she realized she wanted to see things the way God did.

Annie's parents cast Tony disapproving glances. Apparently he noticed, because he stuffed his hands in his pockets and shifted his feet.

"I'm doing fine . . . for the moment anyway," she said. "Once I'm inside the courtroom that might change. I'm not sure how I'll handle any of this."

Tony placed a hand on each of her shoulders. The affection she glimpsed in his eyes caused her throat to constrict. She hated that she'd hurt him. She wished she could make it go away, and yet she still wanted to keep her relationship with Dan. Why did love have to be so complicated?

Heat rose into her cheeks as a flash of recognition passed over Tony's gaze. He knew he'd gotten past her defenses.

"Come here."

He pulled her up into his arms. And to her disbelief, she let him.

At that moment Dan turned the corner, walking beside the prosecutor. His bruised face wilted from a grin to a frown when he observed her in his brother's arms. He picked up his pace as Annie drew away from Tony.

"Thanks for coming," she mumbled before turning to Dan. "Hi, Dan," she blurted out.

Tony startled and swung to face his brother. "Hey, bro."

"Hey, Tone." Dan's voice was cool.

The prosecutor cleared his throat. "I need to talk to Annie for a minute."

He guided her to a bench around the corner. When she settled on it, he took a sheet of paper out of his folder and handed it to her.

"These are some of the questions I may ask in the courtroom. Do you have a problem with any of them?"

Annie studied the list scribbled on the page, and then shook her head. "These look all right."

"Great." Farmer smiled and stood. "Well, that's it then. This shouldn't take long at all." He glanced at his watch. "In a few minutes this will be all over."

He escorted her back to the others. Chewing her lip, she watched as the bailiff assembled the hearing's participants in the hallway. He disappeared inside the courtroom for several minutes, and then approached the group again.

"Okay, folks, we're ready to begin. Everyone follow me."

The bailiff showed people their respective seats. Tony slid next to Annie on one side while her parents and Dan settled on the other, with Dan sitting closest to her. Once they were settled, Annie found it difficult to breathe. She searched her purse for a lifesaver and popped it into her mouth.

The bailiff pounded the gavel. "All rise. The Honorable Judge Dessings is presiding."

The judge entered, and a rustle of movement filled the courtroom. Annie sprang to her feet with the others.

Her purse slipped out of her sweaty hand and landed on the floor with a clatter. Everyone in the vicinity craned their heads to see what had created the disturbance. Annie could feel the heat climbing from her neck to her forehead.

Both Dan and Tony bent to retrieve the purse. Snatching it out of Tony's reach, Dan straightened and laid it on the seat beside Annie. Tony scowled at him, his jaw tightening.

"You may be seated." Judge Dessings directed a sharp look at the three of them as he took his seat on the bench.

Everyone sat. Annie slid down in her seat, wishing the floor would open up and swallow her.

While the court transcriber set up her machine, motion and sound slowly quieted. Suddenly the rattle of a chain grabbed Annie's attention. She turned her head and nearly choked on the lifesaver.

The man who'd assaulted her was being led into the room. Although he wore leg irons, he was dressed in a new suit. His hair had been shorn and his beard trimmed. If she hadn't known better, she would have thought the judge was sentencing a sweet old grandfather instead of an aggressive, knife-wielding robber.

The hearing proceeded, Annie focused everywhere except on the madman who had stabbed her and left her for dead. When it was time for her to be interviewed, she whispered a prayer and approached the bench, her knees trembling.

"This is a sentencing hearing. I need to remind you that the accused has already been proven guilty based on physical evidence found at the crime scene and his corroborating confession. All the hearing will do today is to establish the length of the defendant's sentence." The judge turned his gaze from the spectators to Annie. "Is that understood?"

"Yes, Your Honor." Her voice came out in a squeak.

Gathering her courage, she answered the prosecutor's questions as calmly as she could. But when he asked her to describe her injuries, she couldn't stop tears from streaming down her face. She fumbled with the scarf around her throat until she finally got it untied.

Several spectators in the area behind the railing gasped at the sight of the livid scars that marred her neck. She lifted her long bangs so they could see the full length of the scar along her cheek that she hid by parting her hair on the side. Then she raised her hand. Though small, the protruding pins that held her finger together were noticeable even from a distance.

The pins were scheduled to be removed by the hand surgeon on Friday, she explained. She couldn't wait to finally have her hand back to as near normal as it would ever get.

The bailiff approached the bench and offered Annie a box off tissues. She wiped her eyes, then glanced over at Dan.

His eyes shimmered. So did Tony's. Both men clearly had been affected by her testimony.

"Now please tell us about the psychological damage you've experienced," Farmer prompted. "How has the attack by Mr. Moniker negatively affected your life?"

Annie fought to hold back a sob. "I planned to go to college this fall." She dabbed her eyes with the tissue. "Now I have to put it off for a little while until I make it through this."

"Have you received any counseling?"

She clenched her hands on her lap. "Formally, no. But I talk things through with my friends and family. They've helped me a lot."

Everyone except Tony offered her a reassuring smile. His head tipped down and he rubbed his eyes. Her heart pricked.

When she finished her testimony, Farmer called Dan up front. "Tell us what you saw the night of the attack."

"I . . . I found her in a . . ." Dan cleared his throat. "In a pool of blood."

Annie shut out Dan's voice, unable to listen to his description. She noticed Tony blinking. She fixed her attention on the tears that fell from his eyes. It was clear both brothers loved her deeply. How she wished there didn't have to be a winner and a loser in the contest for her heart.

When Dan's voice grew hoarse she glanced up. As he described the condition he found her in that night, she understood for the first time how truly horrific discovering her lying in a pool of her own blood really had been for him. She could almost understand Tony's abandonment of her under such cruel circumstances.

Tony reached over and placed his hand over her injured one. She pulled it away and a shadow passed over his gaze.

She mouthed, "My hand still bothers me. Sorry."

A relieved grin tugged at his mouth. Distracted, she missed the last part of Dan's testimony.

Dan returned to his seat. He draped his arm over her shoulders and gave them a gentle squeeze.

While Judge Dessings explained the laws that govern sentencing, Annie braced herself for the verdict.

"Wilhelm Moniker will forthwith be sentenced to a minimum of ten years in a maximum security prison." The judge pounded the gavel, then nodded at Annie and her family. "Thank you for your time. You may be dismissed."

Annie directed a fearful glance at her attacker and found him scowling at her. A chill raced up her spine and she thanked God he couldn't hurt anyone else.

Farmer approached them as they gathered to leave. "You'll now be able to pick up the personal effects that were used in this case from the police station.

Tony's brows shot up. "You mean I can have my grandmother's ring back?" When the prosecutor nodded, he swung to face Annie. "It's still yours if you want it."

Annie's chest constricted, and she shook her head. "That wouldn't feel right since we're not going to get married. Save it for your future wife."

He turned away for a moment, then caught her gaze again. "If that's what you want. I won't push you, but I'm going to keep praying you'll change your mind. I'll always love you."

The sight of his tears stirred up more guilt and pity. He seemed to have matured overnight. She thanked God for helping her make it through the morning without completely falling apart. Tony's civil behavior had helped tremendously.

Later that evening Dan and Dave lounged on the couch at Dave's house and watched the news. The large screen television made everything look larger than life. It was like being in a movie theater. All they lacked was popcorn and drinks.

Dan's phone chirped, and with an apologetic glance at Dave, he snatched it from his belt. "Hello?"

"Dan? This is Susie. We need to talk."

He stiffened. "I don't think so. You've caused me enough grief already."

"Wait!" she sobbed. "Don't hang up. Please."

He hesitated, on the verge of flipping the phone shut. But she sounded distraught. He groaned under his breath.

"What is it?"

"I . . . I think I might be pregnant."

More sobs and a whimper followed. He grew concerned.

"I don't understand why you want me involved. What can I do?"

"I'm really scared. I hate to even say it . . . but I think Tony's the father."

The room started spinning. His first thought was that she had to be lying. Surely Tony hadn't been sexually involved with her. Had he?

"Why should I believe you? You've lied to me before."

"I know I have, and I'm sorry about that. But I wouldn't lie about something like this, I swear. My father will kick me out if he finds out I'm pregnant. Then I'll have nowhere to go, unless I move in with Jeff. I don't want to do that."

More sobs gave way to hiccups. She sounded miserable.

Meeting Dave's concerned gaze, Dan covered the receiver with his hand. "Susie, from church."

Dave nodded, frowning.

Dan closed his eyes. *Lord, what should I do?*

He waited for several seconds.

She's hurting.

Dan recognized the Lord's prompting. Of course He would want him to minister to Susie's needs. Dan chided himself for even asking.

But, Lord, why me?

A phrase from a worship song echoed in his mind. *Be My hands and feet.*

"Dan? Are you listening? I'm thinking about getting an abortion. I don't know what else to do. I don't want to kill this baby, but I can't have it either. Oh, Tony is going to hate me."

"How do you know if it's even his?"

"Remember the night before he got so drunk he ended up in the ER?"

Dan reflected on how Tony got intoxicated three days in a row and nearly died. He'd told Dan he didn't remember what he'd done or how he ended up in the hospital.

Dan's gut tightened. "Yeah, what about it?"

"Sam dropped Tony off at Jeff's apartment with a bottle of whiskey. He went out with Jeff to buy some pot, so Tony and I were alone in the apartment. Tony was crying over what happened to Annie, and I tried to make him feel better. We started kissing, and the next thing I remember is we'd had sex. I was pretty drunk, too, but not so drunk I'd forget that."

"Wait a sec. I thought you were in Mexico on a mission trip with a singles group from another church."

"I was, but I came back early. Tony doesn't even remember being with me. A couple of times I asked him questions to trigger his memory, but he doesn't remember going to Jeff's at all.

"This is so embarrassing," she whined. "I just want to die. I need someone to help me and if you won't, I don't know what I'll do."

"You have no one who can help? No girlfriends or family?"

"My mother is dead. I have no brothers or sisters, and my dad is an alcoholic with a mean temper. That's why I spend so much time at Jeff's. To be away from my dad, you know?"

Dan couldn't help feeling sorry for her. No wonder she was so screwed up. She was looking for love and acceptance in all the wrong places, and now it had gotten her in serious trouble.

"Aren't there any women from church you're comfortable with?" *Please, God, let there be someone. Anyone but me.*

"No. Annie was my only real friend, and I royally screwed that up. Your mom is the only other woman I really know, but I'm just so afraid to tell her. She'll think I've ruined Tony's life forever. That's why I need an abortion. Say you'll help me. I don't have any money and I heard it costs over three hundred dollars. I'll pay you back, I swear—"

"Whoa. Hold on, Susie. I won't pay for you to abort your baby."

Dave gaped. Dan had almost forgotten he was sitting next to him.

Hastily Dan shook his head and mouthed, "Not mine. My brother's."

Understanding and sympathy passed over Dave's face.

"I'll take you to the crisis pregnancy center for counseling, but that's all I can do. Will that work for you?"

Susie groaned. "Do I have a choice?"

Chapter 20

As Dan drove to Susie's apartment the next morning, he struggled with where he should draw the line in helping her. He supposed if she'd told him the truth, he'd know within minutes of her taking the pregnancy test. Then he'd worry about figuring out the rest.

Dave had offered a possible solution. His fiancée, Diane, had begun volunteering at the crisis pregnancy center last month. Maybe she'd be there when he brought Susie to the clinic. He prayed the Lord would allow him to pass the baton to Diane and get out of the loop.

Susie was waiting in the parking lot, glancing around as if worried someone might see her. The moment he arrived, she hopped into his truck.

"Please hurry. My dad will be home any minute, and I don't want him to see me with you."

Dan drove with a silent prayer on his lips. *Please, Lord, let Diane be there today.*

From time to time he glanced at Susie. She clenched her hands on her lap, her knuckles white. His heart flooded with compassion for her. He'd hate to be in her situation. And what about his brother? Could Tony screw his life up any worse?

Susie met his gaze. "You look worried."

He took a deep breath, then blew it out slowly. "I'm stressed out about this whole thing. Tony is a brand-new Christian. He still hasn't figured out how to crawl, let alone stand in Christ. What if you really are pregnant?"

Her face crumpled. "You don't believe me? Why would I make something this horrible up? Would you?"

His chest tightened. He hadn't meant to upset her.

"It's not that I don't believe you about what happened with Tony. I do. I'm just hoping the test will come back negative and this will all just be some horrible mistake."

She wiped the tears from her face with a tissue she extracted from her purse. "You and me both. I hope I'm just late. But I've never been late before. I should have started over two weeks ago. I'm really scared, Dan . . ." She started crying again.

"It'll be okay. We'll find a counselor who can walk you through this."

"Thanks. I didn't know who else to call. I know you don't like me, and I don't blame you after what I did the other day, but I tried to put it out of my mind, you know? Then when I started throwing up in the morning, I freaked out."

"Do you plan on telling him?" He watched her from the corner of his eye.

She shook her head. "Not unless I have to, and Lord knows I don't want to. This is so awful. I still can't believe it."

"Have you been with anyone other than Tony?"

A frown formed on her face. "What are you trying to say?"

"Just wondering if there are any other possibilities."

She bit her lower lip. "Honestly? I don't know. I was pretty drunk. I remember kissing Tony, and you know . . . then the next thing I knew I woke up in Jeff's guest room, but Jeff was gone. I don't remember seeing him at all. Tony's the first guy I've actually done that with." She ran her fingers through her hair and stared out the window. "You know what's so pathetic?"

Dan shook his head. "Haven't a clue."

Her voice broke. "I don't remember a thing. I wanted my first time to be with you, not your brother." She hunched over and sobbed into her hands. "I feel like such a slut."

Now he felt even sorrier for her. She had guts to admit the truth, especially when it made her look cheap.

"I don't think that about you."

A derisive snort erupted from her. "You'll be the only one. And my dad is gonna kill me. I'm afraid to go home." Her voice shook. "You think Jeff will take me in?"

He cleared his throat. "I don't think that's a good idea. People might get the wrong idea about you and Jeff."

She sighed. "I suppose you're right. I really don't like Jeff that much anyway. He's always trying to get me drunk. As if I don't have enough problems in my own house."

"Isn't Jeff in choir?"

"Yeah, but what does that have to do with anything?"

"I just figured Jeff was a Christian. Otherwise, why bother to go to church?"

Susie clucked her tongue. "You are so naive, Dan. Who really cares if Jeff is a Christian. He goes to church to meet 'wholesome women.' You know, less risk of STD and all that. At least that's what he told me."

He stared. "You're kidding. That's so lame."

"Not if you don't fit in anywhere else. If no one accepts you."

He suspected she was referring to herself. They arrived at the crisis pregnancy center, and he turned off the engine. After unclipping his seat belt, he faced her.

"What about you? Why do you go to church?"

Her cheeks reddened. "At first I went because I knew you'd be there. Then I started to make friends, like with Annie. I never had many friends in school. I guess I felt more accepted at your church."

"But what about Jesus? Doesn't He mean anything to you?"

Susie closed her eyes and tipped her head down. When she looked up again, she whispered, "I've prayed. God just doesn't want to listen."

"What? He always hears when we pray from our hearts. He may not answer our prayers the way we want, but that doesn't mean He isn't listening."

She stiffened. "Glad you think you have all the answers, 'cause I sure don't."

Her comment startled him. Climbing out of his truck, he thought about what she'd said as he open her door. With a sly grin on her face, she slid from her seat and pressed against him.

"Ah . . . keep your distance, okay? I don't want to be angry with you, so don't push it."

She glanced over his shoulder, then back at him, and a calculating look came into her eyes. He turned to see what she had been looking at, but all he saw was the grocery store across the street.

When he swung back, she wrapped her arms around his neck, her eyes lowering seductively. "Can you just give me a hug?" Before he could answer, she drew his head down.

He shoved her away. "Do that again and you can find yourself another ride."

Her lips curled into a coy pout. "I'm sorry. I promise I won't do it again."

He felt about as safe as a man standing next to a rattler. He didn't believe her for a second.

"You won't because I'm not sticking around. I'll set you up inside, but don't expect anything more."

Susie raised her hands in surrender. "I didn't mean to offend you. I just needed a little hug."

The tension in his neck refused to ease. He had a bad feeling that her sudden desire for closeness had an evil purpose.

Lord, give me strength.

He grabbed the door handle to the crisis pregnancy center but couldn't yank it open. The sign in the window said they were open, so he knocked. Dave's fiancé from church, Diane, appeared inside and ripped the door open with both hands.

"Sorry, this door sticks," she apololgized.

"No problem. Dave told me you volunteered here, and I really need your help." Dan cleared his throat. "Um, can we come in and talk for a few minutes?"

"Sure, come in. Don't be shy." Diane ushered them inside.

He sat on a vinyl couch across from Susie and peered around the room. His gaze fell on a poster of a shirtless man holding a newborn baby. A lump formed in his throat.

"Tell me." Diane sat beside Susie and folded her hands on her lap. "What's going on?"

❧❧❧❧

The air rushed from Annie's lungs when she observed Susie heading into the crisis pregnancy center with Dan. She had to lean on the vehicle to keep from falling over. "Mom? Did you see what I think I did?"

"Yes, but I don't believe it for a second." Her mother's voice sounded tight. "What reason could Dan possibly have to be with Susie?"

"There has to be an explanation, right?"

Had Dan lied to her? She believed him when he told her he'd never kissed a girl before. Not that she could tell. He was so wonderful at it.

Maybe he'd lied about that too. Maybe the reason he acted like he disliked Susie so much was because he had something to hide. Susie had been in love with Dan for years. Could she be scheming to break them up?

Her mother took her arm and guided her to the car. "We need to bring these frozen groceries home before they thaw. Then we need to pray."

By the time they reached her house, Annie was certain she would get sick from the stress burning in her stomach. "Mom, I need to lie down. I feel queasy."

"Sure, you go lie down, honey. I'll get these."

Without another word Annie trudged down the hall to her room. No matter what the explanation was, Dan had been with Susie at the crisis pregnancy center. That fact alone meant they were closer than he'd let on.

The second she lay on her bed she burst into tears. "How could you, Dan? How? I thought you loved me!"

After crying until her energy was spent, she finally dozed off.

She woke to the sound of the phone ringing. Her pillow was drenched with tears. She propped her elbow on the satiny pillowcase and reached for the phone on the table.

"Hello?"

"I'm so glad you're home. You want to go get something to eat?"

The sound of Dan's voice stirred her anger. She hung up on him.

Seconds later, the phone rang again. "Annie? Why'd you hang up? What's wrong?"

She decided to confront him and asked hoarsely, "Where were you earlier today?"

Silence lingered between them.

"I . . . I had a personal errand to run."

Okay, so he's not a complete liar.

"How personal?" She clamped her lips together to keep from crying.

"I had to take someone to an appointment. Why are you asking me questions?"

"Because I saw you with Susie at the crisis pregnancy center, you lying jerk!" She slammed the phone down and sobbed, "Why is this happening to me? Haven't I gone through enough?"

As she cried, the Holy Spirit spoke to her heart.

Be still.

It sounded a lot easier than it was.

Beads of sweat formed on Dan's upper lip. He dropped his cell phone and ran his fingers through his bangs.

Annie saw me with Susie?

Then he remembered how Susie had pressed against him and peeked over his shoulder. She must have seen Annie and tried to compromise him again so Annie wouldn't want him anymore. How disgusting and devious.

Instant regret for his empathy toward Susie pricked his heart. He wanted to pound his skull into the dashboard of his truck. Would he always be such a sucker?

For all he knew the whole pregnancy story could have been a lie concocted just to make him go there with her. Then he remembered how Annie and her mom always shopped at Safeway on Saturdays. The crisis pregnancy center was right across the street. Did Susie know that? Had she plotted all along?

He groaned. Since he'd left right after dropping her off, there was no way for him to find out if Susie's pregnancy test was positive or not. He could kick himself for being so stupid.

Though he and Diane were friends because they attended the same Bible study, she couldn't breach confidentiality. What was he going to do?

Go to Annie.

"But Lord," he prayed aloud, "she's mad. She'll just turn me away."

Go.

"All right. It doesn't make any sense, but I'll do it."

Within minutes Dan arrived at Annie's house. The garage door was open, but no one appeared to be home.

"See, Lord? She's not here. I've wasted my time." He considered leaving, but a still, small voice urged him to knock.

He prayed, "Help me explain. Susie will just have to deal with Annie knowing. I'm not keeping this from her."

He knocked on the front door and waited.

Inside, he heard her sweet voice. "Just a minute."

She swung the door open, and her eyes widened. Before she could swing it shut, Dan wedged his foot inside the opening so it wouldn't close completely.

"Hold up, Annie. We need to talk. I need to explain. Please, just hear me out."

Annie crossed her arms and snapped, "I'm not stupid. I know what pregnancy is and how you get that way."

The hurt in her eyes stung like a slap. She believed he'd lied.

Her assumption stole the air from his lungs. She thought he'd slept with Susie?

"You don't think—no way! But I told you I've never even kissed anyone else. How could you think such a thing?"

Annie blinked. "I just—I don't—I'm not sure why I believed that." She shrugged and stared at her shoes. "My mother couldn't believe it either, but we know what we saw."

He stepped closer. "Don't you trust me?"

She hesitated, then gestured for him to come into the house. "I want to. I thought I did."

Dan followed her into the kitchen. "I would never betray you."

Her shoulders shook. "I'm sorry."

Pulling her into his arms, Dan stroked her hair. "I forgive you. I'll tell you why I was there with Susie, but you're not going to like it."

She nudged away from him. "Just tell me the baby isn't yours. That's all I need to know."

Peering into her eyes, he caressed her with his gaze. "I'm saving myself for you. I wouldn't squander something so precious for a fling. The baby isn't mine. I was trying to prevent Susie from getting an abortion."

Moistening her lips, Annie stared at him. "Wow! I'm really sorry. I thought—"

He stopped her with a kiss. When he stepped away from her and gazed upon her sweet face, he wanted to kiss her again and never stop.

She opened her eyes. She stared past him for a moment, then clapped her hand over her mouth and burst out laughing. His face heated. Was she laughing at him?

She clutched her stomach with one hand and pointed at the wall with the other. He turned to see what she found so amusing.

A chunk of banana stuck on the corner of the kitchen cabinet over the sink. He had to laugh. Obviously he'd missed a spot when he cleaned the kitchen after their milk shake mishap.

When he pondered their first kiss he tingled all over, until he remembered how he'd kept Tony's request from her. He'd vowed never to keep anything from her again. Dread weighed heavy on his chest.

Help, Lord. This is going to hurt her.

"I have to tell you something. I promised myself I wouldn't keep secrets from you."

Worry clouded her gaze. "What is it?"

"She claims Tony is the baby's father."

Annie laughed. "And you believe her? Her lies are getting more creative all the time."

He clutched her arms and gazed into her eyes. "Maybe she isn't lying. Remember when I told you about the night Tony got so drunk he had to have his stomach pumped?"

She and nodded, her gaze never leaving his.

"Susie said Tony was upset about what happened to you and went to Jeff's house with Sam. They both drank way too much. One thing led to another—"

She cut him off. "No! I don't believe her. Tony wouldn't hurt me like that."

"Maybe he blacked out and she comforted him. He doesn't remember anything about that night. It's possible. Sometimes people do crazy things when they're drunk."

Running her fingers through her long bangs, Annie sighed. "You're right. Do you think she'll tell him?"

"No, she doesn't want him to know anything about her pregnancy. That's why she wanted an abortion, to make the problem go away."

"You know what? I don't believe her. I'm telling you, the girl is a sociopath and a chronic liar. I'm sorry I was friends with her."

"Maybe so, Annie, but I didn't want to take a chance. If my brother did get her pregnant, I sure didn't want her having an abortion. No matter who the father is, I couldn't let her kill her unborn child. Can you see that?"

Her shoulders sagged. "Yes. I suppose I don't see any reason to tell him either. We should let him go to college. In a few months we'll know if this was all just another crazy scheme of hers or if it's really true."

"I agree. Then that's what we'll do."

Chapter 21

Weird dreams plagued Annie all night long. When she finally awoke, she lay staring at the ceiling, reviewing the dream one scene at a time.

First, she married Tony. But he cheated on her with Susie, so Annie dumped him. Dan came to her rescue and swept her off her feet, but then he chose Susie as well.

In her dream Susie looked even more attractive than she did in real life with her long, chestnut brown hair and light brown eyes. Susie had kissed Dan while Annie watched and wept.

Even her sleep reflected the soap opera of her life.

The most frightening part of her dream came when the man who assaulted her appeared, looking ghoulish and angry as he swore in her face. He repeatedly stabbed her in the neck while Dan, Tony, and Susie stood outside the door and watched but did nothing to stop him.

Annie knew it was just a dream, but it still hurt to imagine them abandoning her like that. She had to force the thoughts from her mind before she obsessed on them. It was bad enough that she still woke up in a cold sweat from occasional night terrors about the attack.

Before she could ponder things further, Tony called. "Have you thought any more about getting together to say good-bye?"

Her heart constricted. She wanted to send him off with a blessing, but she didn't want to jeopardize her relationship with Dan.

"Annie, are you there?"

She rubbed her forehead. "Yeah, I'm just a little sleepy. The phone woke me up."

"I'm sorry. It's nine, so I didn't expect you to be sleeping. Are you going to church tomorrow night?"

"I was thinking about it. Ever since Susie gossiped about me I've been nervous about going back."

"Then let's go out and grab a bite to eat, just you and me. I won't do anything you don't want me to do, Annie. I just want to talk to you."

"Can Dan come?" She flinched and waited for a nasty reply.

"Sure." Some of the enthusiasm faded from his voice. "If that's what you want."

"Okay, I'll call him, and we'll meet about seven o'clock. Will that work?"

"That's fine. Let's go to Mama Mia's off of Interstate 84. Have you eaten there yet?"

"No, but I love Italian food." She laughed, then sobered. "Thanks for understanding, Tony. I know this has been hard for you."

"I'd do anything for you. I've been such a jerk. I hope you'll forgive me."

"I already told you I forgive you, Dan. Don't worry about it, okay?"

"You called me Dan."

She gasped. "I'm so sorry. I don't mean to mix up your names. It's not like they sound anything alike. I've done it to Dan too. I don't know why I do that."

"Sometimes you call Dan by my name?" His tone sounded lighthearted again.

Giggling, Annie held the phone between her shoulder and her neck and reached for a tissue on the bedside table. "Yeah, and he noticed, believe me."

Tony snorted. "I'll bet it doesn't go over too well."

"Come on, Dan loves you. This is tearing him up inside. He talks about wanting to make things right between you all the time."

"He does?" Tony's voice hitched.

"Yes, and I wish none of this had happened. I never meant to come between the two of you."

"You can always change your mind." Tony whispered into the receiver, "I'll always love you, Annie. I'll even wait for you if I have to."

A walnut-sized lump expanded in her throat, robbing her of speech. After waiting for him to say something, she finally broke the silence.

"I'll see you at seven. Will that be all right?"

"Sure. See you then." His voice sounded thick, as if he'd been crying.

She called Dan right away.

"Annie? Hey, how are you this morning? I was wondering what plans you have for later this week. I wanted to make sure we went out to celebrate, especially since we couldn't go when you had your pins removed last Friday like we planned."

"Don't worry about it. Dan?"

"Hmm?"

"I spoke with Tony. Since he leaves the day after tomorrow for college, he wants to take me out tomorrow night instead of going to Wednesday evening service."

"What did you tell him?"

"I said I'd go . . . but only if you came along."

"Thanks for including me. Of course I'd love to join you. I want to say good-bye to my brother too."

"I thought so. Maybe you can mend the rift between you before he leaves."

"I wish. But I'm afraid Tony will never be comfortable with me as long as I'm with you."

"Keep praying for him. He'll come around."

"Are you praying for him?"

"Every day."

"Well then, since he's being prayed for by so many people he has to be getting something out of it, right?"

"Right." She chuckled. "If you say so."

❧❧❧

He prayed while getting ready for dinner. *Please Lord, heal the rift between me and Tony.*

After he picked Annie up, they headed over to the restaurant. Tony waited by the front door of Mama Mia's holding a blinking pager. He glanced down at their linked hands for a second, but then pasted on a cheery smile.

"Hey there." Annie greeted Tony without letting go of Dan's hand.

"Just in time, guys." Tony held up the flashing square. "We're up next."

They followed the hostess inside. Dan pulled out Annie's chair for her to sit down. She giggled and offered him a flirty smile.

"Thanks. You're such a gentleman."

Tony rolled his eyes. Dan couldn't help but laugh. Thankfully, Annie hadn't seen Tony's expression.

His brother's eyes locked on his, and though he still bore a look of sadness in them, Dan sensed a new willingness to let go and forgive. He offered his hand. Tony stood to receive it, then threw his arms around Dan and hauled him into a bear hug.

Clapping him on the back, Tony chuckled. "I wanted to leave on good terms. I'm willing to forgive you for Annie's sake, and because I still love you."

Tony's sincerity rendered Dan speechless. Either Tony was trying to win an academy award or he meant every word.

"Thanks." Dan's voice caught. "Same here, little brother." He cleared his throat and blinked the moisture from his eyes.

Annie smiled and her eyes shone as well. She reached across the table and clutched both their hands. "I'm glad the Lord is healing your hearts toward each other."

Dan gently squeezed Annie's fingers. "Thanks to your prayers."

Tony's brow rose. "You've been praying for us?"

She smiled and unfolded the dark red cloth napkin over her lap. Smoothing it out, she nodded shyly. "Yeah."

Dan drew a smile in the condensation on his glass of water. He lifted it and took a long drink. He had no idea he was so parched.

"You ready to order now?" The server asked, flipping her long, black ponytail over her shoulder.

Tony grinned. "Sure. We'll have the house salad with crumbly blue cheese dressing." He exchanged a knowing look with Annie.

Dan stared at his brother, unsure how to respond to their interplay. "I'll have the Caesar salad," he said, frowning.

"Drinks?" Their server chewed on the end of her pencil.

"Water's fine," Dan replied.

Tony and Annie nodded in unison.

The server scribbled down their orders and collected the menus. "Let me know if I can bring you anything else. I'll be right back with your salads and garlic bread."

"Thanks." Dan turned to Tony, "How did you know what to order for Annie?"

Smiling, Tony captured Annie's gaze. "You don't date someone for four years and not know what she likes."

Dan's chest tightened. He didn't know if he could handle losing Annie and cope as well as it appeared Tony was. For that, he admired his brother, who was amazing him with his gracious attitude.

When the garlic bread arrived, Tony grabbed the knife and started slicing the steaming loaf.

"Wait. Let's pray first," Dan suggested.

Tony quickly laid down the knife and bent his head. Dan saw Annie glance at his brother with a look of awe.

Pushing jealous thoughts out of his mind, he prayed, "Thank You, Lord for bringing us together this evening and for giving us Your peace. Knit our hearts together, Lord, and bless this food. In Jesus' name. Amen."

"Amen." Tony echoed. He resumed slicing the bread and distributed it to Dan and Annie.

The server returned with their salads just as they cleaned up the last garlicky slice. By the time their entrees arrived via another server, Dan was wondering when their conversation would turn to Tony's departure the next day. He decided to initiate the discussion and get it over with.

"Have you decided what you're going to major in?"

His brother shrugged. "I thought maybe biblical studies."

Dan's brows shot up. "Really? You're considering the ministry?"

Tony winked at Annie. "Maybe. Never would have guessed that before, huh?"

Annie shook her head. "You really have changed. Wow, I can't believe how far you've come in such a short time."

Dan became aware that his stomach was cramping. Sweat beaded on his forehead, and he felt faint.

At first he thought the topic and the admiring glances Annie kept casting at Tony had instigated his nausea. But when his mouth filled with saliva that had a familiar flu-like sour taste, he covered his mouth and pushed back his chair.

"Excuse me. I think I'm going to be sick. Tony, can you take Annie home?"

Tony's eyes widened. "Sure, bro. You gonna be okay?"

Annie started to rise.

"No, Annie, don't leave on account of me. I'd rather not drive with you when I'm feeling this way. It might not be safe. Please, stay."

Afraid to give her a hug, Dan nodded at both of them, and then took off running. He dodged a server carrying a heavy tray and hit the bathroom stall just in time to lose his salad in the toilet without making a huge mess.

His eyes watered and a chill raced up his spine. He needed to go home immediately and lie down. He didn't want to risk spreading his germs. Thankfully he hadn't kissed Annie earlier that day.

Annie and Tony studied him with concern when he returned. "Talk to you guys later," he told them hastily. "Best wishes, Tony. I pray you and Dad have a safe trip."

His stomach churned again, and this time it released a strange noise. "I'm sorry. I've gotta go."

He rushed out of the restaurant and dashed to his truck, sweating all the way. "Lord, help me make it home in one piece."

Annie turned to Tony. "I hope he's going to be all right. You don't mind taking me home, do you?"

"Are you kidding?" His smile brightened. "I'd love to have time with just the two of us."

She looked down and nibbled on her lip.

"Of course, I feel bad that Dan's sick." He touched her hand. "But I'm glad he trusts me with you."

With his hand covering hers, a strange tightness gripped Annie's lungs. She withdrew her hand from under his.

"Tony, please—"

"I won't do that again. I don't want to upset you."

She peered into his eyes, searching for the truth. What she read there made her believe he meant what he said.

"Thank you."

An awkward silence ensued while they finished their meal. Conversation and laughter buzzed around them. The clink of dishes and silverware sounded louder than usual in their silent company. What could they discuss on neutral ground? Annie wondered.

Tony finally broke the silence. "Will you care about me even if you marry Dan?"

Her eyes met his. Without blinking, she nodded and held his gaze.

Tony exhaled and his shoulders relaxed. "That's all I ask. Just don't forget about us and how much we once loved each other, okay?"

She didn't know what to say.

His eyes glistened and he rubbed his face. "Man, I didn't think I'd get that out without bawling. What is it about you that gets me so emotional? I feel like a girl."

A tear ran down her cheek. "You did fine."

He offered her a wistful smile. "Ready to go?"

"Sure."

Annie accepted Tony's offered hand as she slid from the booth. He laid three twenties on the table, then escorted her outside. They walked to the parking lot in silence. Unlocking his parents' Suburban, he helped her inside.

After he climbed in and started the engine, she asked, "You all packed?"

He turned to look around while backing the car out of the parking space, his hand braced on the seat behind her head. "Yep."

For a moment she stared at his handsome face. In her heart of hearts she knew she was doing the right thing by cutting him loose. Someday he would find a woman who would make him very happy. It just wouldn't be her. Their conversation tonight had settled the issue for her, and she was grateful.

While they drove, Tony quipped, "What are you smiling about?"

"I was just thinking about how wonderful you are."

He turned and stared, then quickly resumed watching the road. "You're not saying what I think you are—or are you?"

"No. I mean you're a wonderful guy and I'm praying you find the right woman so you'll know what I mean. I'm not the one for you, Tony. I know you believe I am, but when you fall in love again you'll see our breakup was meant to be. It hurts, but you know it's right."

Tony's brow contracted into a slight frown, but he nodded. When they arrived in her driveway, he remained rigid, facing forward.

He hadn't glanced at her or spoken since she told him it was over. He knew she wasn't going to change her mind, and she ached for him.

When he turned to say good-bye, he opened his mouth, but nothing came out. Instead, he closed tear-soaked eyes. She leaned over and kissed his cheek.

"Good-bye, Tony," she whispered. "I'll be praying for you."

He avoided eye contact. Feeling sad and free at the same time, she slipped out of the vehicle and walked up the sidewalk to the front door.

She could see her parents through the open window, nestled together on the couch in the living room watching television. Her mother had her head on her father's shoulder. Annie pictured herself with Dan twenty years from now and smiled.

Turning, she waved at Tony one last time. He raised a hand and offered a brusque wave in return, his face etched in granite.

Lord, be with Tony and let this horrible situation with Susie not be true. He'll be devastated if he learns he fathered a child by a woman he doesn't even like.

She slipped her key into the lock and went inside.

"There's a letter for you by the phone, sweetheart," her mother called.

Annie went to the small table in the foyer and stared at the envelope. She recognized the handwriting on it, and bile rise from the pit of her stomach into her throat. She wanted to run far, far away from everything rather than deal with what a sinking feeling told her was inside.

Chapter 22

Annie ran her finger over the return address. It gave the street and apartment number, but no name.

Susie had sent her a letter. But why? Hadn't she tortured Annie enough between the gossip at church, trying to steal Dan, and haunting her dreams at night?

"Annie? I asked you if you're all right. Are you?"

"Um, yeah. I'm fine. I'm going to my room, okay?"

"Sure, honey. I'll call you when it's time to watch the movie we rented."

She entered her bedroom and found Snicky snoozing on her pillow. Her cat looked so adorable with her head tipped back and mouth slightly open. Tiptoeing past so she wouldn't wake her, Annie eased into the mauve recliner on the other side of the room. She flicked on the reading lamp and lay back in her easy chair.

Feeling sick with dread, she ran her finger inside the flap of the envelope to tear it open, holding her breath while she extracted the note.

Dear Annie,

I'm sorry I haven't been a very good friend. I hope some-day you will forgive me for getting involved with Dan and Tony. I know you love them both and I was horribly jealous. So when they were feeling down and wanted some comfort I gave it to them.

I know you probably think I'm a slut. I don't blame you. But the worst part is I'm pregnant, and I don't know which brother is the baby's father. I feel bad telling you this, but I need the money to pay for an abortion and Dan won't help me. I tried to ask Tony, but he was so drunk the night we were together than he doesn't remember a thing. I'm not ready to be a mother yet.

Please do me this favor. I will be forever grateful. Again, I'm sorry. If you don't believe my claim, then check their bodies. Dan has a tiny mole on the back of his upper left thigh and another behind his right knee. Tony has three moles on his chest and one below the belt.

I hate to break the news to you and shatter your love for them, but at least now you'll know the truth. You can't trust either of them. So please consider getting me the money. If you do this, I won't tell a soul, I swear. I just don't want anyone to know I had an abortion. I can make this all go away if you'll help me out. The proof of my pregnancy is enclosed.

Please forgive me,
Susie

With distaste, Annie peered into the envelope. A narrow strip of cardboard lay in the fold at the bottom. Two blue lines glared across the end of the strip.

She'd seen enough TV commercials to know she was look-ing at a positive result on a home pregnancy test, and her tears dripped onto the note.

Why would Susie do something so cruel? Annie didn't want to believe her allegations, but curiosity about her description of the brothers' bodies attacked her resolve. She wanted answers.

She decided to call Tony first. She needed to know the truth—tonight.

Poor Dan was too sick. If he still felt bad in the morning, she'd wait until he was feeling better to talk to him. He didn't concern her nearly as much as Tony did. Hadn't Dan told her about Susie wanting an abortion? If Dan suspected he might be the father, he wouldn't tell her something like that. She was sure of it.

Reaching for the phone, she offered a quick prayer. "Lord, help me to talk to Tony without him getting the wrong idea. I can't stand the idea of his being caught up in this mess Susie created. I have to prove she's lying so I can stop her from hurting Tony, so he can go to school in peace."

No you don't. You can pray for him.

"But I have to know. It'll make me crazy until I know for sure."

Where is your faith?

She bit her lip and stuffed the letter into the drawer of the end table. Snicky jumped on her lap and rubbed her nose on Annie's face and neck, reminding her again of all she had been through with the brothers. Susie had to be lying.

"I'm just going to ask Tony a few questions, okay, Lord?"

She glanced at the incandescent clock by her bed. Tony would be home any minute since he lived only a few miles from her house. She waited as the next minute dragged by, then lifted the phone from the table.

A husky voice greeted her. "Hello?"

"Tony?"

His voice perked up. "Annie? Did you change your mind about us?"

Her throat swelled with guilt. He sounded so hopeful. She didn't want to let him down, but she had to be straight with him.

"That's not why I'm calling, Tony. I wanted to ask you a crazy question. Don't take this the wrong way, okay?"

He cleared his throat. "Okay, shoot."

"Do you have three tiny moles on your chest?"

Tony burst out laughing. "Why do you want to know that?"

Her voice wobbled. "It's not funny. I'm serious."

His voice sounded husky. "I'd love to show them to you."

"Tony—" *He just admitted it. Susie was right. But how would she know that, unless—*

Her blood boiled. Susie must have been awfully close to Tony to notice something so intimate. Even she didn't know that about him.

Maybe she should take him up on his offer and make sure. Quickly she shoved the thought from her mind. Dan wouldn't understand.

"Why do you care about my moles?"

"Someone told me they saw them. A female someone. Tell me. Is one of them below your belt?"

"Hey. Now that's getting even more personal. Who would tell you something like that about me? Or even know that?"

Someone who is obviously set on hurting us.

"Susie said she slept with you. She said I'd know she was telling the truth if I saw your moles. How else would she know about them?"

Tony muttered something under his breath.

"What are you saying?" Annie clutched her throat with her free hand.

"I can't believe she has you thinking that about me. She tried to convince me too. I think that girl is out of her mind. I might have gone over there when I was drunk, but I'm sure I'd remember something so major, believe me."

"Do you remember much at all?"

He coughed. "No, but I know Susie is lying. I wouldn't do that with her. I love *you*, Annie, not her. I waited for you."

"Yeah, but if you were drunk enough—"

His voice softened. "Why do you care so much? Do you still have feelings for me?"

"Yes. I mean, I told you I'll always care about you. I just don't want to see you hurt, and that girl is trouble."

Tony snorted. "Tell me something I don't already know."

"Just answer me one thing. How would she know about your moles if you never showed them to her?" Nausea washed over her and the room spun for a moment.

"I don't have a clue. But I'm tired, Annie. And I don't feel very well. I hope I didn't catch what Dan has."

"I hope not too, or you'll be sick on your way to school."

"Yeah. Well, I better head on to bed. We can talk about this later if we need to. Remember, I still plan to e-mail you as often as you want me to . . . as a friend."

"I'm looking forward to it, and I'll be praying for you. Have a great trip."

She hung up, her stomach churning. Sweat beaded on her forehead and a sharp pain reverberated through her skull. She stood and ran toward the bathroom but didn't make it in time. Vomit spewed all over the tile floor.

A pitiful wail erupted from her as she retched again. The cramps came so hard and fast she could barely catch her breath. Her mother ran into the bathroom.

"My heavens, Annie. What's going on?"

Exhausted, she collapsed on the floor. Never in her life had she gotten so violently ill so fast. It must be food poisoning. Nothing else made sense.

"John! Come here and help me. Annie just got sick all over the floor."

Annie's eyes drifted shut as she tried not to move her head. Her skull pounded with every movement. Strong arms gathered her up and lifted her from the floor.

"Oh, dear Lord. What are we going to do, John? She looks so pale and sweaty. What do you think is wrong?"

"I don't know. Annie?" Someone tapped her cheek but she was too weak to respond.

"Honey? Do you think it was something you ate?"

Annie managed a slight nod but kept her eyes pressed shut. Her stomach churned again and she moaned.

Before she could warn her father, she got ill again. She was convinced she was going to die any moment. Chills and sweats intermingled as shivers racked her body.

"I'm calling the doctor. This is bad."

Minutes later, her mother returned to the room. Annie's eyes cracked open and she glimpsed a panicked look on her mother's face.

"They think it could be food poisoning. We need to make sure she doesn't become dehydrated. There's nothing we can do except make her comfortable. Oh, dear. I'm worried. This is so awful."

The sounds around Annie muffled as she drifted in and out of sleep. She wondered if Tony and Dan were as sick as she was. Somebody needed to call the health department.

As if she'd read her mind, she heard her mother say, "I'm calling the department of health services. This is criminal."

The next morning Annie woke in the same condition. Food sounded horrible, she shook from the chills, and she prayed for death. Anything would be better than the wicked headache and nausea she suffered from. The rest of the day went by in a blur. She spent most of the time sleeping, and by the time she woke again, she had recovered some strength.

"Mom?"

Annie's mother entered her room. "Are you feeling any better, hon?"

Annie squinted as her eyes adjusted to the lighting in the room. "What day is it?"

"It's Friday afternoon. Do you want something to drink?"

Her stomach protested. "Not yet. I'm afraid if I eat anything, it will just come back up."

Her mother nodded. "I understand."

Annie opened her mouth to speak, but couldn't remember her question.

"Tony stopped by this morning on his way out of town," her mother said brightly. "They left late because he had food poisoning too. He brought you some flowers."

Annie glanced in the direction her mother indicated. A gorgeous bouquet of yellow roses in a tall crystal vase perched on her dresser.

Tears formed in her eyes when she realized Tony offered friendship with the yellow roses. How could she refuse?

"They're beautiful, Mom. Did you tell him thank you for me?"

"I sure did, honey. He wanted to see you, but I told him you were too sick. So he left the flowers with a note."

Her mom plucked it off the bouquet and handed it to Annie. Opening the envelope slowly, she removed the card.

Get well soon, Annie. I'll miss you and I'll always love you. Your friend forever, Tony.

Annie wept.

Her mother snatched the note from Annie's hand and read it. Her face softened.

"Oh, how sweet of him. That was really nice, don't you think?"

Annie couldn't speak. She kept swallowing and taking small gulps of air. Guilt threatened to suffocate her.

"I'm so sorry I hurt him. I wish I could have at least said good-bye on a good note."

"Relax, honey. I believe he's forgiven you. Now you just need to forgive yourself. The Lord doesn't want you stuck here. Move on, sweetheart. I think this is Tony's way of saying it's okay for you to move on too."

Annie squeaked out, "You think so?"

"I think Tony wants you to be happy." Her mother squeezed her hand. "Dan called earlier. Seems he was deathly ill for a while there too. He wants to see you."

Annie's mouth fell open. "Today?"

"It's up to you. Why don't you try a shower and see how you feel."

"Okay. I need to talk to him. But I need to shower first. But—" she sputtered. "Can you please call him on his cell? If he answers, tell him I want to see him after five if he doesn't mind coming over here."

Her mother grinned. "I don't think wild horses could keep him away. He seemed pretty worried about you. I tried to reassure him, but he still keeps calling." She handed Annie the phone. "Maybe it would work better if you called him back yourself.

{⚉{⚉

Dan grabbed his cell phone and flipped it open, cutting off the ring tone's jazz rhythm.

"Dan?"

He relaxed and lay back in bed of the guest room at Dave's house, the phone pressed to his ear. "Are you finally feeling better? Man, wasn't that food poisoning awful?"

"I don't think I've ever been so sick in my life."

Delicious chills pebbled his skin at the sound of her voice. "I'm sorry we ate there. I think it was the salad."

"Definitely the salad. Isn't it weird that we all got sick at different times?"

"We all got sick not long after we ate our salads. That's how you know it was food poisoning. I couldn't move for over twenty-four hours after I lay down."

"Did you make it back to Dave's okay?"

"I had to pull off the road a few times, so I was pretty much done by the time I got there."

"Poor guy."

Her voice sounded coy. He imagined her full lips in a slight pout, and warmth washed over him.

"Yeah," he chuckled, "poor me."

"You looked so awful when you left. I felt bad for you."

"Gee, thanks for the compliment."

Dan's grin widened as he imagined Annie caring for him once they were married. No doubt she'd spoil him. He'd certainly lavish her with attention.

"Do you feel well enough to come over later today? I need to ask you something."

"Sure. I can be there in an hour."

"Make it two. I look disgusting. My hair is all stringy and I stink. I really need a shower."

"Two hours it is. And you could never look disgusting, so stop putting yourself down."

Annie giggled. "You know what I meant."

Two hours later Dan rang the doorbell. The garage door was open, and her parents' car was gone. He tried not to focus on the fact that they might be alone again, but his thoughts still strayed.

She answered the door wearing a sweet smile. The glow in her eyes evoked the desire in him to kiss her soundly, though he didn't dare if she didn't feel well.

"It's hard to believe you've been sick. You look great."

She blushed. "Thanks. Come on in."

As he passed by, he caught the sensual scent of her perfume. It stirred him, and suddenly he wanted to hold her, to touch her silky hair, to press his lips against hers.

Giggling, she peered into his eyes. "What's with the funny look, lover boy?"

He didn't care if his expression gave his feelings away. He just wanted to drink in her presence.

"Can I just hold you a minute?"

Fluttering her eyelids, she walked into his arms. He drew her against him, inhaling her fresh scent as he buried his face in her luxurious fox-red hair. She nuzzled his neck, and he reveled in their closeness.

A shiver went through him at the awareness of her body pressed against his. *Love* was an insufficient word to capture the depth and essence of his affection for her. She intoxicated him, overwhelmed him.

His feelings were intense and addicting. Yet even those words lacked precision.

If only she perceived how much he felt for her. He wished he could tell her in words.

When he straightened, her blue-green eyes lingered on his. As if drawn by a magnetic force, he tipped his face down and brushed her forehead with a feather-light kiss.

"Mmmm." She smiled.

He moved to step out of their embrace.

"Wait! I need ask you this question before we get any closer."

Closer?

"Ask me what?"

"I want to see your legs." Her cheeks reddened and she bit her lower lip.

His neck heated. "What?"

She touched his thigh, making fire shoot through him. "Please. I want you to put on a pair of shorts. I want to see . . . um . . . more of you."

The excitement coursing through his flesh scared him. He had to be misinterpreting something.

"Annie, I can't. I won't."

"Why not? Don't you trust me? I just need to see something."

"Of course I trust you," he said with a laugh. "I don't trust *me*."

"Don't be silly. I'll go find a pair of my dad's shorts. It'll only take a minute."

He couldn't imagine why she wanted to see his bare legs.

"Annie, I planned to wait . . . you know . . ." He stopped, feeling helpless. "I thought you said you wanted to . . . well, you know."

Her brows rose. "You think I *want* to do that? You've got to be kidding."

Her tone of voice wounded him. She made it sound repugnant. Hardly what he thought of when he considered her request.

"If not that, then why do you want me to change my pants?"

"It's always about sex with you guys, isn't it?" Her expression had turned from amusement to irritation. "Susie sent me a letter. She says you have a mole behind your right knee and one on your upper left thigh. I want to know if she's right. I want to see for myself."

"Whoa. You think I showed her my body? I can't believe you."

"Well, do you have two moles?" She placed her hands on her hips, and her eyes narrowed. "You wouldn't lie to me, would you?"

"How would I know if I have moles behind my legs? I can't see back there. This is ridiculous."

"So show me, then."

"You should take my word for it. Susie can say whatever she wants, but I don't have any obligation to prove I'm telling the truth. And I sure don't plan to change my pants so you can inspect me. That's the stupidest thing anyone's ever asked me to do."

She reached for him. "Come on. It'll only take a second. I just want a teeny peek. Please?"

"No."

A wounded expression covered her face. Her eyes glistened as she asked in a tiny voice, "Dan, please—"

He shook his head and backed away from her when she reached for him. "I'm leaving before this gets out of hand."

She inched closer with her eyes pleading. She clutched him and grabbed his pants.

Dan wrenched away. "I've gotta go. Call me when you aren't so desperate to believe the psycho woman."

"Please." Her voice wavered.

He walked to the door and opened it. He had to leave before he changed his mind and got into a compromising position with her. It would be so easy to do what she asked, but then how would he stop? She had no idea what went through his mind, and he wasn't about to tell her. Better to flee like Joseph.

"Fine, then. Leave! Just go away!"

He could still hear her yelling through the door as he marched to his truck. His heart squeezed as her words were followed by gut-wrenching sobs. The whole situation was crazy. But how could he fix it without getting half naked before her . . . knowing what that could lead to? And why should he have to prove himself? Maybe giving her a little space would work. He'd call her in the morning. Meanwhile he'd pray, because she didn't believe him, and he didn't know why.

Chapter 23

Annie sobbed into her hands. He wanted her to believe him on his word. She wanted it too. But she'd seen the proof that Susie was pregnant, and someone had to be the father. Although she hated herself for her lack of trust, like doubting Thomas she needed to see Dan's legs before she could believe him.

Of course her behavior didn't make any sense. But the doubt in her mind had driven her to the edge. Why did she doubt his word? He had given her very little reason to not trust him. Other than keeping Tony's message from her, he'd been the perfect boyfriend.

Snicky rubbed against her leg and gazed up at her with pleading crossed eyes. She nickered like she always did when hungry, reminding Annie of a tiny horse. She bent down and scooped up her cat.

Holding her close, she kissed Snicky between the ears and mumbled, "I wish I had your life."

After feeding her cat, she went into the game room and plopped on the couch. She grabbed the remote and turned on the large flat-screen television. A movie scene portrayed a woman arguing with a man. Seconds later they dove on each other and exchanged heated kisses as they begged each other for forgiveness. How pathetic.

Like your behavior?

Annie ignored the thought as she pressed the off button. She tossed the remote on the coffee table. The last thing she wanted to do was dwell on her own faults and soften toward Dan. She wanted to stew awhile, to make him worry before she talked to him again so he'd see how stupid he was to ignore her simple request. All she wanted to do was to see his moles, for goodness' sake!

Her cheeks heated at the memory of his discomfort. How he had trembled when she touched his pants. The desire in his eyes had caused her knees to weaken, and she'd relished the warmth filling every nerve ending.

Why did he refuse if he loved her so much? Was he afraid he'd lose control?

She supposed the thought should flatter her, but instead it ticked her off. Grumbling, she fell back on the sofa. Exhaustion from her recent illness had sapped her energy and made her moody. Crying for the last ten minutes straight hadn't helped things either.

Laying her head on one of the large, white throw pillows, Annie curled into a ball and fell into a deep sleep. Dreams permeated her mind and visions of her life before the attack flashed before her eyes.

Dan is watching her during church. He follows her across the sanctuary. Shadows her in the stairwell. Once behind closed doors he kisses her neck, her cheeks, and then travels across her face. Where's Tony?

"Marry me, Annie. I want to be with you forever."

"I don't know, Dan. We're awfully young."

Giving her a sly smile, he winks. "Maybe for some things, but not for what I have in mind."

Moving his lips over her mouth with precision, he indulges for a moment, then covers each eyelid with a breathy kiss and whispers, "I love you, Annie. Let me come over tonight."

She pushes away from him. "W-what do you mean?"

He quirks a grin and kisses the tip of her nose. "What do you think I mean? I want to ask your parents if I can marry you."

"Marry me? But I'm going to college. We can't marry for at least four years."

"I'll wait for you. Just think about it."

Tears form in her eyes and she bites her lower lip. "You mean it? You'll wait for me? No fooling around?"

"Yep." His warm smile makes her knees mushy.

"I don't care about anyone else. Never have and never will. I only have eyes for you."

A tear rolls down her cheek. Dan kisses it away. He straightens to full height. Smiling down at her, he cradles her face and brushes her cheekbones with the pads of his thumbs. The love she glimpses in the depths of his eyes makes her tremble.

Laying her head on his chest, she wraps her arms around him and hugs him tightly , "Love me," she whispers. "Touch me."

"Don't tease me. You know I won't do that before we marry." He steps out of her embrace. "I can't believe you're even suggesting it. And with your parents upstairs . . ."

His incredulous gaze makes her want him even more. "Come on, let me see you."

He stares at her with pursed lips. "What?"

"Okay, to be honest, I just wanted to see the moles on the back of your legs. Show me."

Dan's eyelids droop and he nods. "All right."

"Thanks, sweetie."

She smiles. Pushing up on her tiptoes, she kisses him, running her tongue over his lower lip as she draws him close.

He presses her against the wall. "Oh, Annie . . . Forget what I said. It's too hard to wait."

Struggling to push him off, she cries. "Wait, what about your moles? I want to see them first. Then we can do whatever you want."

"Sure." He winks and steps back. His pants fall around his ankles.

She bends down and checks behind his legs. The telltale marks are as Susie described.

Her breath expels in a horrified whoosh. "Susie was right! You are her baby's father."

Growling, she punches him, pummeling his chest with all her might. Beating him senseless like she should have beaten that horrible man who stabbed her.

Tears stream down her cheeks. With a hearty slap, she cracks Dan across the face.

Dan laughs and his face contorts. "Ha-ha. Got you now. You know you love me."

Her fists shake as she clutches them at her sides. "You're such a jerk."

"And you're so cute when you're mad." Dan whistles. "But I love it when you're angry."

She raises her fist.

He raises his hands in surrender. "Chill out. Susie can still be the mother of my baby even though you're my girlfriend. You'll be the one I love, not her."

"Are you nuts?"

He tips his head down to kiss her, nipping at her lower lip. "Yeah, I'm nuts about you. So I made a mistake. I'm sorry."

"*Sorry isn't good enough.*" Her voice wavers. "*I can't see you anymore.*"

"*Come on, loosen up. You can have your cake and eat it too. I won't mind.*" He places his finger under her chin. With an amused grin, he adds, "*But don't expect too much from me. Men can't be faithful. It's not in our nature.*"

The telephone rang, jarring Annie from her twisted dream. She glanced around, dazed. Dan's final comment in her dream really bothered her, and for several seconds she thought the conversation might have actually taken place. Stretching, she yawned.

The ringing persisted, and she scrambled for the phone. "Hello?"

"Annie? It's Dan."

Anger welled in her chest. She closed her eyes and exhaled, reminding herself it had only been a dream.

"What do you want?"

"We need to talk about what happened a little while ago."

"What's there to talk about? You refused to show me proof. Has that changed?"

"No. But Annie, you don't understand—"

"Why not? Got something to hide?"

He groaned into the phone. "No, Annie, listen to me. This is important."

"Okay, fine. I'm listening."

"All right . . . Um, well, first off . . ." He cleared his throat. "I'm not sure how to begin, so I'll just say it. Men are different from women, Annie. We feel things differently."

"Huh?" Running her fingers through her hair, she eased back on the pillow.

"When a man loves a woman as much as I love you, well, he starts thinking of her in more intimate ways. Are you understanding me?"

Annie stared at the blank TV screen, recalling the scene from the movie. "I'm not sure."

"When I'm thinking about loving you, I'm also thinking about touching you, Annie. I want to do everything with you. . . ." His voice faded and he heaved a shaky sigh.

"So, how is it different from the way things are now?" Tucking loose strands of hair behind her ear, she chuckled. "You kiss me and we do things together all the time."

"Annie, I don't mean just regular activities, I mean intimate things. . . ."

Her flesh tingled at the thought. "Oh, like you want to touch me all over?"

"Yes . . . of course I do. That's why I left. I didn't want to lose control. I was afraid if I showed you my legs it would turn me on even more. I already ache enough as it is."

A shiver went up her spine when she thought about him feeling that way about her. "You ache for me? Really?" Her voice sounded breathless to her own ears.

Clearing his throat, he whispered, "Yeah, I do."

"Wow." She pressed her fingers on her mouth as a grin crept over her face.

"Now do you understand where I'm coming from?"

"Sure. I think so. How about you show your mom or dad the back of your legs? Then they can tell me if you have two moles—"

"Annie! I can't believe you. I don't intend to prove my innocence. If you don't believe me, then I don't know what to tell you—"

"Just say you'll do it. If you love me, you will."

"That's a bunch of crap. You know I still love you even if I won't do what you ask. You need to decide what's more important, believing me or having me prove my innocence to you."

"Why can't it be both? I *do* believe you, Dan. But I also know I can't fully accept your innocence until I see the proof."

"But why do you need proof?"

"I just do, please—" The whiny sound of her voice made her cringe.

"I won't. That's not going to change."

"You've got something to hide, don't you?"

"Why can't you just believe me?"

"I don't know. But I just can't. I'll pray for the Lord to give me peace about it."

"While you're at it have the Lord show you I'm innocent, will you? This whole thing is so aggravating." His voice sounded strained.

"I already had a dream about you. Maybe that's my answer." Her shoulders sagged. "I don't know what to think."

A joyous lilt appeared in Dan's voice. "You dreamed about me?"

"Yes, and you asked me to marry you. I asked you to take your pants off and you did and I peeked behind your legs and—"

"And what?"

"I found the moles right where she said they would be."

"What did you do about it—in your dream?"

"I punched you. Slapped your face. Told you I didn't want to see you anymore."

"You smacked me in your dream?"

"Yeah. You tried to convince me I should let you keep Susie too, since she was pregnant with your child. You told me I should be happy because I was the woman you loved, not her."

"Well, that's obviously not true. She can't be the mother of my child if I've never touched her. I already told you I'm waiting until I get married."

"I know what you said, Dan. But—"

"But what?" His words were clipped.

"In my dream you said men lie and they can't be faithful. It's in their nature to cheat."

"Then that's the most off-the-wall dream I ever heard. I'd *never* say that."

"Yeah, I know. But still—"

"Now you're starting to tick me off. Either you believe me without proof, or you don't trust me. And I can't be in a relationship with you if you don't trust me."

"You're right. I can't either. Maybe we should give each other some space. Give me a few days to figure this out."

"No problem. I really need to pray about this . . . this whole thing. I won't call you till Sunday. Maybe we'll come to a resolution by then."

"Maybe."

But something deep in her gut told her things would get worse before they got any better.

❧❧❧

Dan missed Annie terribly, but she couldn't see past her desire for proof. Why couldn't she just trust him?

He left Dave's home and stopped early Sunday morning to visit his parents. The side door was unlocked. He went in and sat astride a chair at the kitchen table while he sought wisdom from the Lord.

His father entered the kitchen in his bathrobe and startled when he saw Dan. "How did you get in?"

"No one locked the side door. That's dangerous."

His father sat down and opened the Sunday paper. "What brings you by?"

He swiped his face. "I have a goofy question. Don't take this the wrong way, but . . ."

His father refolded the paper and set it back down. "But what?"

"I need you to check something. Can you tell me if I have a mole behind my one knee and another one on the back of my upper thigh?"

Sticking his finger in his ear and jiggling it around, his father chuckled. "Am I hearing things or did you just ask me to look at your legs?"

"You heard right." Dan rubbed his sweaty palms on his pants.

"Why?" An amused grin tugged on his father's lips.

"Look first, and then I'll explain."

"All right. Go ahead."

Dan unbuckled his pants and turned around, then dropped them. He could hear his father's chair squeak as he leaned forward.

After a moment he said, "Yep. You have them right where you said. Why does it matter?"

His mother entered the kitchen wrapped in her terrycloth robe. Her eyes widened as she took in Dan's bare legs.

"What are you boys doing?"

Susie came in right behind her, also wearing a robe.

Dan scrambled to pull his pants back up over his briefs. His face burned as he glanced at Susie. She watched him with a wicked grin playing across her mouth.

"What's she doing here?" he demanded.

Before his parents could answer, he rounded on Susie. "My brother is only gone a few days and you zoom in on my family? Haven't you screwed with our lives enough?"

"Dan, apologize this minute!" His mother frowned. "She's a guest here. Her father kicked her out of the house and she had nowhere to go. Have some compassion."

Dan snorted. "Yeah, right. Like the kind she showed me when she told Annie she wasn't sure which one of us fathered her baby?"

Susie gasped and covered her mouth with her hands.

His parents stared at him as if he'd spoken Chinese.

"You heard me right," he said through clenched teeth. "Susie wrote Annie and said she'd slept with both me and Tony. Can you believe that bull crap?"

His father turned his attention from Dan to Susie, now sobbing. "Is that true?"

"Did you?" his mother echoed.

"No!" Susie sobbed. "He's just saying that to cover for Annie. She wants to hurt me because I've liked Dan for years, and she's jealous."

"I'm not covering for anybody. Why don't you tell them the truth, Susie? Tell them how you called me asking to help you pay for an abortion, and how I refused."

Susie cried harder and shook her head. "No, that's not true!"

"Tell them how you slept with Tony the night before he got so drunk he ended up in the hospital. Tell them how you got pregnant, and why I took you to the crisis pregnancy center."

"Is that why your father kicked you out of the house?"

The tenderness in his mother's voice irritated Dan. He wanted to stick his finger down his throat so she'd see how much Susie's manipulation nauseated him.

Somehow she'd burrowed her way into their family through his mother. He needed to snap her off like a tick before she worked herself in so deep she sucked the life's blood from his family.

His hands shook as adrenaline pumped fury through his veins. The tempo of his pulse doubled as he glared at Susie. The conniving, manipulative woman was not going to destroy his family if he could help it.

"Well? Go ahead. Tell them the truth."

She sank onto one of the kitchen chairs and slumped over. "It's true," she sobbed. "I'm pregnant and Tony *is* the baby's father. I'm sorry."

Dan's mother moaned, "No, please Lord, let this be wrong!" She approached his father and laid her hands on his shoulders. "What are we going to do? Tony can't deal with that kind of responsibility. He needs to finish college."

His father answered in a gruff tone, "Well, I can tell you one thing we *aren't* going to do, and that is pay for an abortion. But, we also can't put Susie out on the street. Does Tony know anything about this?" He peered at Susie.

Dan followed his father's gaze, still stunned by his mother's comment. Susie was going to stay with his parents? *No way.*

Susie shrugged. "I tried to tell him but he doesn't believe me. He was really drunk and so was I. Please understand. I didn't want it to happen." She sobbed into her hands. "Please forgive me. I don't have anywhere to go."

Dan's mother went to drape her arm around Susie's shoulders. "No one is going to put you out on the street, honey. Don't worry. We'll take care of you."

Dan choked. "She can't live here."

Both of his parents stared at him. That was obviously the wrong thing to say.

His mother snapped, "Yes she can, Daniel. If she's carrying your brother's child, she isn't leaving."

"Well, then I'm not coming back home. I won't sleep under the same roof with that lying, scheming—" Dan growled out his frustration. "Why are you letting her live here? I'm your own son, for Pete's sake. Can't she go stay with someone else? Like maybe Diane?"

His mother scowled. "Diane's getting married soon."

"I don't believe her, Mom. Please just think about it first."

"I have. If Tony is this baby's father, then it's our grandchild. We need to help Susie while she's pregnant for the baby's sake. Can't you see that?"

Dan stole a glance at Susie and noted her pinching her lips together, as if trying to hold back a smile. She'd won and she knew it.

"I can't believe this," he muttered. "Just when I thought things were settling down."

He clenched his fist again, wanting to hit something. Instead, he pressed his mouth shut before he said something he'd regret.

Without another word, he stormed out of the house, slamming the door behind him.

Chapter 24

A week passed before Annie returned to church. She refused to stay away any longer just to avoid Susie. Besides, she wanted to talk to Dan, and he hadn't returned her calls. Maybe she could find out what was going on if she met him there.

"Are you ready?" her mother called from the other room. "It's time to leave."

"Yeah, I'm coming." She walked into the living room and her father whistled. "You look stunning in that dress. And the scarf matches perfectly."

She felt the color climb into her cheeks. "Thanks, Dad. I know you're trying to make me feel comfortable, and I appreciate it. I really do."

"No, I mean it. I don't have any reason to lie to you. Honestly, honey, you look fantastic. Doesn't she, dear?"

Her mom nodded her approval. "You look gorgeous. The guys will be drooling when they see you coming."

Annie rolled her eyes and flipped her bangs. "Slight exaggeration."

"Not at all. No wonder the Lane boys were smitten." Her father grinned wide. "You look like your mother did at your age. And believe me, she was the best-looking girl in town."

Chuckling, Annie grabbed her father's arm. "Come on, Dad, let's go."

The drive to church was uneventful until Annie spied Dan's truck. Her heart pounded, and she whispered a prayer.

"Help me, Lord. Give me courage to talk to Dan about what You put on my heart."

She grabbed her purse and followed her parents toward the front steps of the church. When they approached Dan's truck, she could see through the back window. He was sitting inside, having an animated discussion with someone.

"I'll be there in a minute," she told her parents. "I want to talk to Dan."

Her father winked. "All right, princess. See you after church."

The muffled voices drew her closer. She couldn't make out the words until she stood behind the door, but far enough from the window they couldn't see her standing there.

"I just wish I knew what to do, Dave. I mean, I love her so much, but I can't be with someone who doesn't trust me. I tried to work this out in my own strength, but the Lord keeps telling me to step back and wait on Him. I'm trying. It's just so hard."

Wow, Dan misses me that much? He has such strong faith. I want to trust in You as much as he does. To have unwavering faith . . .

"I know what you mean. There was a time when I thought Diane would never trust me, but the Lord worked on her heart. Now we'll be married in just a few weeks. I still can't believe it's coming up so soon. She's been out of town for a few days, and I can't wait for her to get back."

A sharp yelp from backseat of Dan's extended cab truck startled Annie. She had forgotten Dave's little boy, Joey, would be with his father.

"Daddy, I hot."

"All right, Son. We'll be going inside in a minute."

Dan opened his door and hopped out of the truck. He stepped back when he noticed Annie.

"Man, you startled me. I didn't see you standing there."

"Sorry. I didn't mean to scare you." She played with the end of her scarf, twirling it around her finger as she stared at him.

"Did you want to talk?" His warm blue eyes fixed on hers.

"Hey, see you later, Dan, Annie." Dave grinned and lifted Joey into his arms. He headed toward the church, the three year-old balanced on his hip.

"Meet you in a few," Dan called after him before turning back to Annie. He whistled. "You look gorgeous."

She ducked her head and whispered, "Thanks."

"We still have a few minutes before the service starts. Want to talk inside my truck or out here?"

She chewed on her lower lip. The innocent look in his eyes tightened her chest. She had hurt him with her doubt by questioning his truthfulness, and he deserved an apology. If only she could force the words past the peach-pit-sized lump in her throat.

"You all right?" The concern in his eyes warmed her from the inside out. "What is it?"

His face blurred as her eyes flooded with tears. She didn't deserve him. Looking away for a moment, she shrugged.

"What's wrong?" He gestured toward the truck. "Here, climb in so we can talk privately."

After they were inside, he gently stroked her hair. "Talk to me. Tell me what's bothering you."

"I . . ." Tears ran down her cheeks. "I'm so sorry."

His eyes softened. "I've already forgiven you. I love you, Annie. That's not going to change."

"I don't deserve you," she sobbed.

He gently moved her hands away from her face and drew her against him. Rubbing her back, he sighed.

"It's me who doesn't deserve you."

"No." Her voice squeaked as she leaned into him and wrapped her arms around his waist. "I doubted you, but you've never doubted me. I don't know why I wanted to believe Susie. I believe you told the truth. I knew . . ."

He drew her closer. She could feel his heart beating against her cheek through his shirt. Reaching up, she ran her fingers along his jaw.

"I missed you. I don't care about your silly moles. Whether you have them or not, I still love you. I never should have doubted you."

He kissed the tips of her fingers. "Then let's put it behind us."

"Okay."

She snuggled into his arms and parted her lips to receive his kiss. Someone rapped on the truck window, and she bolted upright.

Dan tipped his head. "It's Jeff." He cracked the window. "What?"

Jeff peered inside. "Hey, you have a girl in there. Sweet."

"What do you want?" Dan snapped.

"I thought I'd let you know church started five minutes ago. I'm running late myself."

"Thanks. See you inside."

She watched him roll up the window. "The Lord showed me you're a man of integrity. When I prayed about what to do, the Lord told me I could trust you. He reminded me you love Him, and that you're His child too."

"I'd do anything for you, Annie."

A chuckle burst forth and she slapped her hand over her mouth. "I'm sorry. What you said isn't accurate. You still won't show me your legs."

"Picky, picky. You know what I meant, hon." Dan lightly flicked the tip of her nose. "Come on, let's go inside."

They walked across the parking lot and up the stairs side by side. Inside the foyer, the sweet sounds of a flute solo to the hymn "Old Rugged Cross" greeted her ears.

He led her into the sanctuary, and they slid into the back row. She scanned the crowd, and her gaze found Susie. She was settled next to Dan's mother.

Annie elbowed Dan in the ribs. "Why is she sitting next to your mother?"

He leaned over as he whispered in her ear, "My parents think Susie's baby is Tony's, so she's staying with them."

Her eyes widened. "You're kidding. She told them?"

"I guess I sort of helped things along without meaning to. I can hardly believe it myself, but it's true. And I won't move back home as long as she's living there."

"Good. Stay away from her."

"Believe me, I plan to. I feel for bad Tony. When he comes home for Diane and Dave's wedding, he's going to find Susie living at our house. We'd better start praying for him now."

Annie nodded, her thoughts running in ten different directions at once. *Poor Tony. He's going to be devastated.*

"When will they tell him?"

"About what? Her pregnancy?"

"Yeah."

"Not until he comes home. He's struggling in a few of his classes, and my parents don't want him to freak out in the middle of midterms."

"I'd hate to be around when he finds out."

Dan raked his bangs off his forehead and exhaled. "Me too."

❧·❧·❧·

Dan thought about the sermon while they sang the last hymn. When it was over he decided to apologize to his parents for his behavior that morning. He started to tell Annie and paused. His chest tightened as he spied the fear in her eyes.

"You look worried. Do you need to talk?"

She furrowed her brow. "I feel like God spoke to me during the sermon. I've been angry with Susie for lying and making me doubt you. I realized something was making me feel distant from God. It's because I haven't forgiven her."

"That's what I wanted to talk to you about. I was angry this morning when I left home. I said some mean things to Susie and to my parents, and I need to apologize to them."

"Maybe we could do it together. They say there's strength in numbers." She giggled. "Why are you staring at me? You make me self-conscious when your eyes get all mushy looking."

"It's because I'm in love," he whispered into her ear.

"Dan, Annie, we need to talk."

Dan turned to find his parents standing behind them. Susie was with them.

"Let's go to my office," his father said.

Reaching for Annie's hand, Dan complied. Once they were all seated in his father's office, Dan held up his hand.

"First, I just want to apologize to all of you." He paused and looked at Susie. "I forgive you, Susie. I know things are hard for you right now. You must be feeling pretty desperate. I don't hold it against you. I hope things work out for the best."

Susie's jaw dropped.

"I apologize too," Annie broke in. "I've been angry with you ever since I got the letter you sent. I know it's not true. I don't know what made you do it, but I forgive you regardless."

Susie appeared taken aback. "You do? But why? I don't understand."

Dan took Annie's hand. "We didn't realize until today that harboring anger against you has been holding us back from living in a way that pleases God."

From the corner of his eye, he noted his father's eyes welling with tears. "Well, now that we have that settled, we need to discuss what happened."

Dan's mother dabbed tears from the corners of her eyes. Her mouth still open, Susie had turned pale.

"I, um . . . ah . . ." She choked and grabbed a tissue. "Okay! I'm sorry I lied about you, Dan. Please don't hate me."

"I don't hate you. I feel for your situation, I really do." Looking over at his parents, Dan continued, "And I'm sorry for how I treated you this morning. Please forgive me."

His mother looked down at her clenched hands. "Thank you, Daniel," she murmured. "It means a lot that you care enough to apologize in front of everyone."

"I love you, Mom. I try to be a good son."

"I know. And you are. But I haven't been a very good mother." Her voice choked, and she dabbed the corners of her eyes again. "I haven't listened to you. Will you forgive me?"

She got up and came to stand in front of him. His throat squeezed and his eyes burned. He rose from his chair and drew her into a crushing hug. She patted his back.

"I love you, Daniel. You're the best son a mother could ask for. Please forgive me for not being there for you when you needed me."

He couldn't hold it in any longer. A sob burst forth.

For several minutes no one spoke. The sound of Annie's quiet grief touched him deeply. She understood his pain, and he loved her even more for it.

Glancing over at Susie, he noted a profound sadness in her eyes. She no longer seemed ominous and mean, but pathetic and small. He really did feel for her situation. Tony didn't love her. She might bear his child, but she would never have his heart.

Susie bit her lower lip and caught Annie's gaze. "I only knew about Dan's moles because when he stayed at Jeff's apartment he slept on his stomach in his boxers. That's how I saw them."

He swallowed hard. "But what about Tony? How did you know about his?"

She shrugged. "He started sweating when we were playing quarters, and he tossed his shirt on the couch. His pants hung low on his hips, and I saw his stomach when he put his shirt back on . . ." Her cheeks turned crimson.

"So you're saying you never slept with Tony?" Dan demanded. "Did you make that up too? How do we know you're even pregnant?"

Susie burst into tears. "I hate myself." Her shoulders shook with racking sobs.

Annie stood and walked over to her. "Don't say that. God loves you. No matter what you've done He'll forgive you if you ask Him to."

Susie peered up at Annie, tears streaming down her face. "I . . . don't . . . know . . . who . . . who . . ." She wailed louder, clutching her abdomen. "I don't know . . ."

A lump formed in Dan's throat as he watched Annie squat in front of Susie and offer her a hug. "It's going to be okay. We'll make it through this. I'll still be your friend."

Susie's head popped up. "But why? I've been so mean to you." She wiped her eyes with the tops of her hands. "How come you don't hate me?"

"Because I think I understand. You're scared, but we can help you through this."

Sobbing again, Susie cried, "No, you c-can't. I don't know who the . . . father even is."

Dan sucked in his breath. "You don't know?"

"I don't know how I got pregnant. I don't remember a thing."

Everyone waited for her to continue.

"I tried to make Tony kiss me, but he just laughed in my face, so I drank more. I remember flirting with some guys. Then Tony got up and stumbled out the door with Sam. The next morning I woke up, and I knew something happened because . . ." She stopped, flushing.

Staring with his mouth hanging open, Dan caught himself and closed his lips. Some dirtball had raped her when she passed out. No wonder she was desperate.

"Who else was there?"

"You mean besides Jeff?"

"Yeah, do you remember any of their names?"

She shook her head. "There were too many of them. Once Tony left with Sam, I only remember talking to Jeff. He tried to kiss me, but I shoved him away so he left me alone. Then next thing I remember was rolling over to sleep. I remember thinking I was dreaming when someone kept touching me. Maybe I was, but I was so drunk I couldn't lift my head. I never saw his face."

"How do you know it happened?"

Her face crumpled. "I woke up the next morning . . . without any clothes on, and . . . oh, I'm so ashamed."

Dan's father asked, "But you're sure you're pregnant?"

She nodded. "When Dan took me to the crisis pregnancy center for a test it came back positive. I wanted an abortion, but Dan wouldn't help me pay for one. I thought if I bribed someone I could get the money. When that didn't work I thought I could convince Tony he was the father, but he didn't believe me. Then I got mad."

She glanced at Annie. "I was jealous. She had two men who loved her and I had no one. I just wanted a family."

Annie whispered, "It's okay. I understand."

"I'm so sorry!" Susie cried. "You've never been anything but nice to me. I feel like such a horrible person."

"We're all bad," Annie said gently. "It's only because of Jesus that any of us can change."

"That's what Pastor always says. I've never understood it really."

Dan's mother returned to her seat beside Susie. "Do you know the Lord as your personal Savior?"

When Susie shook her head, Dan felt terrible. He hadn't loved her like the Lord had told him to the day of his fistfight with his brother.

"Do you want to accept Him into your heart?" Dan's father asked.

"I . . . I want what you all have, but I'm scared God won't want me," Susie admitted.

Dan's father laid his hand on her arm. "He longs to forgive you. Let's pray for you, okay?"

Susie nodded and hung her head. They surrounded her and laid their hands on her back and prayed for Susie to have peace and to know the Lord if she wanted to receive Him into her life.

When his mother asked Susie if she wanted to pray, Susie nodded again and repeated after his mother word for word, "Jesus, I need You in my life. Change my heart and make me more like You. Forgive me for my sins and live in me. Amen."

Dan didn't realized he was crying until a tear trickled down his cheek and dripped from his chin. He rubbed it and sighed.

Annie's eyes glistened as she walked into his arms. He kissed the top of her head, realizing how blessed he was to have her in his life.

"Isn't God awesome? Only He could take such a mess and work it out for good."

He watched Susie crying and hugging his parents. She clung to his mother and sobbed as his mother stroked her hair.

Susie's mother had died when she was only eight. Who was he to deny her a mother's love?

After a tearful good-bye, Dan drove Annie home. Pure joy radiated from her face. She talked about God's love and how much better it felt to love Susie than hate her.

He offered Annie a quick kiss good-bye, then drove to Jeff's apartment. He wanted answers and he was going to find them, some way, somehow.

Chapter 25

Annie changed out of her Sunday dress into a pair of loose-fitting jeans. She slipped on a hot pink T-shirt with a picture of Eeyore on the front and examined herself in the mirror.

So far she hadn't gone out in public without a silk scarf around her neck, which limited her wardrobe to dressy clothing. Even with makeup, there was no mistaking the scars. Ugly purple and pink lines zig-zagged up and down her neck in an erratic pattern. She cringed as she remembered the night the man assaulted her.

Someday she would have to show her neck in public without a scarf to conceal the scars. She still didn't feel ready to deal with the curious stares or empathetic looks. Someday the marks would represent an event in her past, but until then she would cover them up. Running her finger over the lines one more time, she extracted a pink scarf from her lingerie drawer and tied it snugly around her neck.

With a sigh she walked out into the living room, looking for her parents. She found them in the recreation room kissing.

She cleared her throat and grinned when they jumped up. Her mother smoothed her hair. "I didn't hear you."

Annie chuckled as her father pretended to be engrossed in the western playing on the large-screen TV. "At least I know you two still love each other. Go ahead. I didn't mean to disturb you." She turned to leave.

"Don't be silly. Sit down. You obviously had a reason to come looking for us."

She crossed to the comfy chair beside the overstuffed couch and perched on the armrest. "If you're sure I'm not interrupting, 'cause it sure looked like I was."

Her father winked. "Nothing we can't continue later, right dear?"

Her expression supremely innocent, her mother said, "What did you think of the sermon today?"

"It was pretty intense. In fact, I was convicted by it." Annie slid down the armrest onto the cushion. "Thanks for not waiting around for me, by the way."

"We knew Dan would bring you home."

"I wanted to talk to you about that. We met in the pastor's office after church. Susie really is pregnant, but she doesn't know who the dad is. It's not Tony's baby after all."

Her father's brows rose. "Not know the dad? How's that possible?"

Annie's mother elbowed him and rolled her eyes. "Really, honey."

Annie shrugged. "I guess when she passed out someone took advantage of her. She never saw who it was. She remembered Tony leaving before she fell asleep, so it couldn't be him. She just lied about it."

"Well that's a relief. I'll bet Tony's glad he's off the hook."

"He doesn't know. He never believed her claim anyway, so it doesn't matter. I just wish she knew the father so she could prosecute him for raping her and getting her pregnant."

Her mother sighed. "Poor Susie. I feel for her. What's she going to do?"

"She wanted an abortion to make the problem go away."

Her mother's sharp intake of breath caused Annie to pause. "Don't worry, she isn't going to follow through. Dan's parents are going to help her out for a while. Then maybe she can go to a shepherding home for pregnant women. And the crisis pregnancy center sometimes offers assistance."

Her mother tapped her lip. "You know, I think Diane signed up to be a shepherding home, but I wonder how she'll do it once she's married."

"I guess she could let Susie stay in her condo after the wedding."

"That's possible. Well, what are your plans for today?"

Annie ran her fingers through her bangs. "Dan said he'd call me after he ran an errand. We might go out for coffee or a hike or something. I just want to be with him."

"Sounds like fun."

Her mother reached for her father's hand and smiled. Annie figured it was her cue to scoot out of there.

"I think I'm going to write an e-mail to Tony. I haven't checked my inbox in about a week. I probably have tons of messages."

She climbed up the steps two at a time, smiling. Knowing her parents were still in love gave her a feeling of security she treasured. She'd always dreamed of having a marriage like her parents enjoyed. And Dan reminded her of her father in so many ways.

She slid into her desk chair and booted up her PC. When her e-mail finally opened she had about fifty messages. Twenty of them were from Tony.

Annie smiled. He hadn't been kidding when he promised to write her, though he'd never mentioned doing so more than once a day.

She went through his messages one at a time.

Hey, Annie. How's it going? I met my new roommate today. His name is George and he's pretty cool . . .

Hi, Annie. Thinking about you today. My mind drifted in class. All of my subjects are hard, and I think I got the worst hours possible. Must be a freshman thing to get all of the eight-o'clock-in-the-morning classes. Ugh . . .

Annie, how is Dan doing? Are you two still seeing each other? I've been thinking about you. Don't mention how much I'm writing you. He might not understand . . .

Hey, Annie. Did you like the roses I left for you? I really did meant it when I said I want to be forever friends . . .

Annie, were you fitted for your bridesmaid's gown yet? What color is it? You know I'm singing, right? It's the coolest song. I think you'll like it. Make sure you pay attention to the words, okay? I still think about you all the time . . .

Hey, Annie. I can't believe they gave us a quiz already . . . and in biblical studies of all things. Maybe they wanted to test us to see how Christian we really are. LOL! Thank the Lord I found Him in Teen Challenge. I don't know where I'd be right now if they hadn't helped me out. I'll always be grateful for their ministry. It saved my life . . .

Annie, I joined a group called the Navigators. They have a weekly Bible study. I'm excited about going. The only goofy thing is for every guy there are two girls. Several follow me around and I have one girl who always sits with me in the dining hall. She's kind of cute. Her name is Julie. She reminds me of you.

Love ya,
Tony.

The rest of his e-mails followed a similar pattern. She wasn't surprised girls were following him around. He was one of the most attractive men she had ever known. It wouldn't be long before he found another girlfriend. She wondered how long it would take him to fall in love with someone else.

The twinge in her chest caught her by surprise. She didn't want Tony to find another girl, yet she realized it was lame to expect him to pine away for her when she intended to marry his brother. If Tony was smart, he'd move on. And fast.

Choosing to reply to only three messages, she emphasized her desire for him to be happy and to find love again. She followed up with "I'll always love you and be your friend. Annie."

She hit send and the last reply zoomed off. Turning off the computer, she stood and stretched. She then sat at her vanity and brushed her hair. She adjusted it to cover as much of her facial scar as possible.

While applying lipstick to match the color of her Eeyore shirt, she decided to remove her scarf. Maybe she would try going without it today. If it didn't bother Dan too much, she might even try going somewhere without the scarf to see how she'd handle the curious stares.

She tucked the scarf back into the lingerie drawer of her dresser. She fingered the scars, then picked up a compact and powdered the area on her neck with the most visible marks. It helped conceal them more than she'd anticipated.

After blotting her lipstick, she rose and selected a pair of comfortable shoes to wear with her jeans. She slipped them on and went to the kitchen for a drink.

The phone rang before she had a chance to open the fridge.

"Hello?" Annie unclipped her earring and adjusted the phone over her ear.

"Hey, Annie. How's it going?" Tony sounded breathless.

"Are you okay? You sound winded."

He chuckled. "I am. I just ran up six flights of stairs to call you. I read your e-mails at the library and decided I had to hear your voice. I hope you don't mind."

Annie grinned. "No. Not at all. Thanks for writing. Some of your e-mails were hilarious."

"You liked them, huh? What do you think about my little fan club? Is that ridiculous, or what? I can't go anywhere without some girl trying to talk to me."

"Of course you can't believe it. You've been with me so long I think you forgot how attractive you are."

He laughed. "You really think I'm attractive?"

Annie snorted. "Of course, you weirdo. You're the best-looking man I know."

Tony stopped chuckling. "I am?"

"Yeah. Why do you sound surprised?"

His voice lowered in a conspiratorial manner. "You think I'm better looking than Dan?"

She giggled. "In your own way, yes. But you're brothers, so you look alike."

"Yeah, but I have brown eyes. Dan's are blue."

"I know. You both have nice eyes, even if they're different colors.

"Hmmm. . . . So what are you doing later?"

"Dan's taking me out after he finishes running an errand."

"Great. Well, I better go. Someone's knocking at my door. Probably another groupie."

"Probably. Talk to you later."

She hung up, her heart sinkng. As much as she wanted him to find true love, she'd been the object of his affection for so long it would still take some getting used to.

Lord, send a nice girl Tony's way who will warm his heart.

Dan stood in front of Jeff's apartment door rehearsing what he planned to say. He wondered if Jeff even had a clue. Well, he'd soon find out.

After knocking, Dan cracked his knuckles and waited. Finally Jeff opened the door.

"Hey, dude. What brings you here?"

All of the speeches Dan had prepared in advance flew out of his brain. "Uh . . ."

"Want to come inside? Have a beer?"

"Sure, I'll come in but I'll pass on the booze. Why do you drink so much?"

Jeff scowled. "I'm not an alcoholic if that's what you're implying."

"Never said you were. I just wondered about it because it seems like you're always downing one."

"Hey, that's nothing. You should've seen my old man pack it. He could kill a case and still stand. Why do you care anyway?"

Dan plopped down on the armchair. Placing his hands on his knees, he said, "I'm here about Susie."

"That chick? I haven't seen her in a while. What does she want?"

"Why do you refer to women as chicks?"

"Beats me. Why do you care what I call them?" He glared at Dan as if he had sprouted horns on his head.

"It doesn't matter. I'm here because Susie's in trouble."

"Tell me about it. Her old man showed up looking for her, and boy was he ticked off. Said if I see her to tell her she's not welcome back home."

"Man, that bites."

Jeff leaned forward. "What's up with her anyway?"

"Don't tell anyone. She doesn't want the world to know. I'm only telling you because I think you might be able to help me find out who hurt her."

Jeff's eyebrows shot up. "Hurt her? When?"

"At the party you had a few months back. Remember, the one where Tony ended up in the ER with alcohol poisoning?"

Jeff got up and went to the fridge. He cracked open a can of beer.

"Not my fault."

"What wasn't?" Dan stared as Jeff tipped his head back and took several long pulls from ~~from~~ the can.

Jeff burped. "Wasn't my fault he got drunk. When he left with Sam they were talking about buying more whiskey. They only had a few shots at my house. Ask anyone who was here."

"Do you remember who came to your party?"

Jeff took another few gulps. "About twenty or thirty guys came in and out. Some with girls, some without."

"Are you telling me you didn't know all of their names?"

"I recognized about five or six guys. The rest just kind of crashed. I think they were at another apartment and noticed the action at my place, so they joined us for a while."

Dan rubbed his forehead. "Man, this is way worse than I thought."

Jeff finished off the beer and wiped his upper lip with the top of his hand. "How so?"

"Susie's pregnant, and she doesn't know who the father is."

Jeff's mouth fell open. He stared at Dan with a dazed expression.

"No way."

"What do you mean, no way? What do you remember?"

"Not much. She was pretty sauced and kept walking in and out of the guest room. I tried to kiss her but she pushed me away. Didn't stop her from flirting with a bunch of the other guys." He grunted. "I never understood her, so I stopped try-ing to."

"What happened?"

Jeff scratched his head. "A couple of biker dudes and some other guys went into the room. I'm not sure what they did in there but I didn't hear any fuss, so I figured they went in there to make out. I didn't care what they did. Maybe Susie got laid by one of them."

Dan scowled. "She was too drunk to move and said she never even saw the guy's face. I can't believe you had such a loose party going on here. What's your trip, man?"

"Hey, I didn't think anything bad was going on, honest. I was pretty drunk myself, and by the time I started kicking peo-ple out I was about to pass out anyway."

Dan's eyes narrowed. "So where did you crash?"

Jeff chuckled. "I was going to crash with Susie but when I tried to wake her up, she just shooed me away. You know, she slapped her arm in the air like she was trying to hit me."

"Did you . . . touch her?"

Jeff's neck reddened. "I backed off when she started to cry."

"Did she have clothes on?"

"Never checked under the sheets, so I couldn't tell ya."

"So, where'd you end up?"

"In my own bed. Funny thing was this fat chick had passed out on my pillow. She tried to kiss me when I woke her up. I shoved her out the door real fast."

Dan stared at Jeff for a few moments. "Why do you bother to go to church?"

His friend shrugged. "I don't know. To pick up nice girls, I guess."

"You go to find women?" Dan rubbed his eyes. Unbe-lievable.

"Yep. I like to sing too, but unless I go to karaoke night at the pub I don't get a chance. I grew up in church. It's just something you do."

"So you don't go to church to actually worship Christ?"

Jeff grinned. "Oh, I love Jesus in my own way. He doesn't mind how I live my life."

Shifting in his seat, Dan said, "I can't agree with you there."

"Who said you had to? It's my life. I do my hour on Sunday and volunteer when I can. I've met some pretty nice girls on singles nights."

"I can't believe you've attended church your whole life and never heard the message."

Jeff gave a short laugh. "My old man thought he was a pretty good Christian. Wore out more belts on my backside than I can count. Never did fix me though. So much for sparing the rod, huh?"

"Your father beat you?"

"Nah, not really. Just whipped me real good when I needed it." Jeff snorted. "I just happened to need it every day."

"You're kidding." Dan stared at his friend, astounded.

"Nope." Jeff went to get another beer. "Sure you don't want one?"

"I'm sure. Thanks anyway." Clearing his throat, Dan asked, "So you have no idea who raped Susie while she slept?"

Jeff paled. "Raped? Wait a minute. Nobody raped anybody at my place."

"What do you call messing with an unconscious person then? It sure isn't mutual consent."

Jeff heaved a sigh. "Man, poor Susie. I feel bad for her."

"Not as bad as she feels. I wish we could at least identify the father so he could be prosecuted."

Jeff's eyes widened. "Does she think it was me?"

Dan shook his head. "She doesn't know what to think. If you remember anything that might help us figure this out, will you please tell me?"

Jeff rubbed his face. "I can't believe someone would do that here. It could have been anyone. I feel bad about it."

"Just keep thinking. Maybe someone will come to mind."

"Maybe."

Dan rose to leave. "I'd better go."

Jeff followed him to the door. "I used to like Susie, but it seemed she flirted with everyone but me. Maybe that's why I saw her as a challenge. I wanted her to like me. Not enough to use her, though. That's just sick."

Dan leaned against the doorjamb. "I won't argue there. But I'm concerned about your beliefs, Jeff. You aren't going to church for the right reasons."

"Yeah, well, I had the Bible beat into my brains so much as a kid I suppose that's why I rebel. I don't mind a cool Christian chick, though. You won't find nice girls hanging out in a bar."

Jeff needed a lot of prayer, Dan decided. Even more than Susie because at least she had accepted Christ.

He never would've guessed anyone in his father's congregation held such little regard for Jesus and didn't know Him personally. Was it different for people who didn't grow up with a minister for a father? Then again, Tony had the same dad, and he had rebelled too. Dan would never understand it.

He'd hung out at church with Jeff on and off for the past two years during school breaks, but he never would have guessed his friend was lost because Jeff never acted that way around him. He couldn't help wondering how many others mingled with the flock without knowing the Shepherd.

Chapter 26

Dan knocked on the door of his parents' house. He prayed his dad would hear what he had to say and not take it personally.

The familiar creak of the wooden steps told him someone was coming. But it was Susie who peeked through the curtains and unlocked the door.

"Hi." She blushed and stared down at her feet.

He stepped inside without answering. It felt weird having someone who wasn't even family open the door and let him in to his parents' home. If Susie hadn't admitted the truth about Tony, she might have become family through her deception.

He was thankful God touched her heart before she hurt even more people with her lies. Like Annie, he held no animosity toward Susie, just pity.

Following her inside, he was so lost in thought he bumped into her. She turned.

"Have you—"

He lifted his hands and backed away from her. "Whoa. Why'd you stop?"

"I had a question, but now I forgot what I was gonna say."

"Are my parents home?" His gaze darted around, checking for their presence.

"They'll be back in about ten minutes."

"Great, just great," he muttered as he walked into the living room and plopped down on the couch.

Susie parked next to him. "Why'd you stop by?"

"I wanted to talk to my dad. Can I ask you something?"

"Sure." She avoided eye contact.

"Did you know Jeff said he *only* comes to church to socialize?"

Susie bit her lower lip. "I noticed sometimes he drank too much, but I never asked. Did he tell you he's not a Christian?"

Dan rubbed his chin. "Not in so many words."

"I never liked Jeff like a boyfriend. He's fun to hang out with, but he reminds me too much of my father. Guys who drink are okay for friends, but that's it. I'd never marry a drinker. I don't usually drink. I guess now I know why."

"That's good you see it as a problem."

Susie just stared at him. He shifted and sank deeper into the cushions. The old couch always made his back hurt if he stayed on it too long. He usually had trouble getting out of it too, but he refused to ask Susie to help him up.

"Thanks for what you did today."

Susie's light brown eyes clouded as she gazed at him with a shyness he hadn't recalled seeing before. She looked feminine and even sweet, something he would never have predicted a week ago. God was softening her. He could see it in her eyes.

He rubbed his palms on his knees. "You deserved an apology."

Her lip trembled. "I still feel bad that I lied about you. I'm praying God will help me to be honest and not seek revenge when I feel like someone did me wrong."

"I'm glad to hear about your changed heart."

A tear rolled down her cheek. "Please don't hate me. You say you've forgiven me, but can you honestly look at me without getting mad?"

His heart warmed. "I can do that."

"Then I believe you." Susie stood. "Can I get you a drink?"

With an effort, he levered himself up off the couch. "Nah. Thanks though."

"Thanks for being my friend. Sometimes I feel so alone. Like nobody cares. I know Jesus does, but what about everyone else?"

"What do you mean?"

"Well, your parents, for one. Now that I told the truth, they have no obligation to let me stay. If I try to go back to my dad, he'll just put me out on the street."

Running his hands through his hair, Dan said, "My parents will figure something out."

Her chin quivered. "You think?"

"Absolutely." It made him sad to see the uncertainty and fear in her eyes. "You'll be taken care of, Susie. God won't abandon you. This will all work out."

As he spoke, he waved his arm. Susie stepped closer. Before he could stop her, she threw her arms around his waist and leaned into his chest.

"Thank you. I really appreciate it."

His gesture hadn't meant "come here," but apparently she thought so, because she latched on tight and mumbled into his shirt, "Annie's so lucky to have you."

He stiffened. She was way too close and he didn't like the way she clung to him. "Ah . . ."

Susie lifted her face until it was within inches of his.

He tried to catch his breath. She was a beautiful girl. Large, brown eyes bore into his gaze as she sighed wistfully.

"I wish I had someone who loved me. Someone like you."

She gazed up at him with obvious yearning. Though only mere seconds had passed, even one second was too long as far as he was concerned. He wrenched away from her before she got the wrong impression.

"I'd rather we didn't touch, if you don't mind."

Her cheeks reddened. "Why?"

"You're a gorgeous woman, Susie. I'm a man, but I'm taken. I don't want to give you the wrong idea."

Her head bowed. "It was nice for you to hold me. Even if it never happens again, I'm thankful."

The side door creaked, and heavy footsteps echoed as someone entered the house.

He walked into the kitchen to greet his parents. "Mom, Dad. Glad you're home."

His father tossed his keys on the table by the door and approached Dan.

"Dad, I need to talk to you in private. Can we talk in Mom's office, man to man?"

His father patted his back, and then led the way into the home office where his mother operated her accounting business. Dan entered behind him and closed the door.

"What's up?" His father settled behind his mother's desk and placed his hands behind his head.

"Something is bothering me you should know about. Did you know some people in our church don't know the Lord? When I saw Jeff today, he admitted that for him church is a social club. Annie didn't know Jesus until she was attacked.

"Tony didn't know Him until he ended up at Teen Challenge. And Susie didn't until she wound up pregnant. How many others are attending every Sunday but still missing the point?"

His father steepled his fingers under his chin. "Funny you should mention that. The Lord has been prodding me in a different direction for my sermons, but I've been resisting Him. So I asked for a sign. He just showed me one through you."

"He did?"

"Yes. I think we need to go back to some of the basics pertaining to salvation. Then I'll know the majority of the church has heard the gospel message in its entirety. I just pray they will hear the true gospel this time and not just what they want to hear."

"Why don't we pray about it right now?" Dan suggested.

Annie couldn't believe the morning of Dave and Diane's wedding was finally here. She and Tony had really enjoyed being part of their Bible study group during past year and getting to know them.

Dan had agreed to pick her up and was due to arrive at any minute. Later they would meet up with Tony at the church. She would finally hear the song he had been diligently practicing as a surprise for the happy couple.

She stared at her reflection in the mirror. The lavender sleeveless dress flattered her figure. Earlier that morning her mother had pinned her hair up on one side of Annie's head, revealing her high cheekbones and smooth skin. She had also curled Annie's long bangs so they adequately covered the scarred side of her face.

Clasping a satin scarf in her hand, she tied it around her neck. Last week she'd tried to go out without the scarf but couldn't do it. Her breathing had quickened, and she hyperventilated as soon as she arrived at the café. So they had gone back to her home and retrieved her scarf. She was grateful Dan was so patient and supported whatever decision she made.

The doorbell rang. Butterflies danced in her stomach as she took one last glance in the mirror. She definitely looked her very best. At rehearsal Diane had promised Annie she would walk down the aisle with Dan, while Tony would be paired up with Susie.

She thanked God the issue with Susie and Tony had been worked out. Otherwise the entire wedding might have been a disaster.

His smile wide, Dan appeared stunning in a black tux. For several seconds Annie just stared at him, drinking in his handsome features.

Then he drew her into his embrace. "You look great."

She breathed in the scent of his cologne. He had so many wonderful qualities, and they had so many common interests like cooking, and reading, and . . . kissing.

Warmth suffused her cheeks. "Thanks. I was just thinking the same thing, you hunk."

"You were, hmmm?" Stroking her chin with his thumb, he murmured, "You take my breath away."

She giggled. "Now you're stretching things."

As she headed for the door, he took her by the shoulders and turned her back around. "Wait a second. I want you to look at me. Come on."

Her gaze darted around everywhere except at him. "Look at me," he commanded.

Lifting her eyes to his, she hesitated, afraid he was annoyed with her for putting herself down again. He surprised her with a kiss instead, his lips covering hers with amazing tenderness.

A small gasp escaped her when he released her mouth. He stared into her eyes and growled deep in his throat.

"You always taste so good."

His affection warmed her to her toes.

"Now stop putting yourself down. Scars or no scars, you're the most beautiful woman in the world to me."

Tears blurred her vision and she nodded, choosing to accept the compliment rather than argue with him. Hand in hand, they went outside and climbed into his truck.

When they arrived at the church, the members of the wedding party were milling around, waiting to assemble for one last run-through. Dave's son, Joey, the little ring bearer, zipped around the reception hall where everyone had congregated. He chased another little boy in circles, dodging around people as he and his friend played tag. It was utter chaos. Dave finally caught them both in his arms and spoke firmly to them. Whatever he told them worked, because they sobered in an instant.

Annie glanced around, but didn't see Susie or Tony, which she thought was odd. Then she remembered how last night Tony had called her and asked for prayer. He'd felt weird having Susie in his home while he slept, even if she was a baby Christian. Annie agreed and prayed for him. Tony had mentioned something about Susie's moving into Diane's condo while she and Dave went on their honeymoon. That sounded best for Susie, so Annie had no complaints.

Five minutes before they were scheduled to go upstairs, Tony and Susie bounded down the stairs and into the fellowship hall together. Everyone breathed a sigh of relief as they waited for the music to begin.

Susie's dress complemented her skin tones. With her hair piled on her head, she looked stunning. They made a nice-looking couple, Annie mused, but then caught herself. She didn't want to even think about that. Not after what had happened.

Tony seemed cool with Susie, unflustered. He glanced at Annie and winked. Her mouth curved into a grin.

He came over to her. "Can a friend get a hug?"

"Sure."

Annie savored his embrace, relieved that Dan stood by and smiled. He seemed confident enough in Annie's love for him that a hug from his brother didn't stir up jealousy this time.

She took Tony's hand in hers. "I'll be praying for you when you sing."

"Cool," he chuckled. "It's been a while, so I am a little nervous. When are *you* going to sing again, Annie?"

Shrugging, she tried to ignore the tightness in her lungs. "I don't think I will. That part of my life is over."

He tipped her chin up until she met his gaze. "Then we need to talk later because you *will* sing again. I'll just keep praying until it happens. You have such a beautiful voice."

Dan came over to them and thrust out his hand. "Hey, little brother."

Tony bypassed Dan's hand and embraced him. "What's with the formality, you goon?" He rubbed his knuckles on Dan's head, mussing his hair. "What's this stiff stuff in your hair, pretty boy?"

Dan laughed and slapped Tony on the back. "I wanted to look as good as you. You'll never change, dawg, but I love ya anyway."

Music wafted on the breeze and drifted down the staircase. Everyone in the wedding party assembled. When they moved forward, Annie glanced at Dan, thinking how handsome he was. He winked, making her blush.

She slipped her hand into the crook of his arm, and they ascended the stairs in pairs of two, with Tony and Susie behind them. When they arrived at the front of the sanctuary, she strained to see Diane, but it was virtually impossible once everyone stood.

She finally caught sight of Diane, and her eyes flooded with tears. The look of sheer joy on her friend's face made Annie long for her own wedding day.

Dave's parents beamed at their son. Annie peered over at the bride's side and noted Diane's mother hadn't shown up.

From what little she had gathered from Diane, that wasn't necessarily a bad thing.

Diane had told her once how much she wanted to be close to her mother, but it just wasn't meant to be. So Dave's mother essentially adopted Diane, making her feel a part of the family long before she and Dave planned to wed.

The tender look on Dave's face as he watched his bride approach caused Annie's heart to beat faster. She glanced at Dan again. He stared back at her with longing, and it was that moment she knew without a doubt that he would be her husband someday. A slow smile spread over his face, as if he had read her thoughts and agreed with her.

Annie deflected her gaze to control her emotions and focused on admiring the lavender silk flowers arranged by the communion table. The quiet intimacy of the setting overwhelmed her.

She could literally sense Dave and Diane's love, like the sweet scent of lilacs, as the spirit of the Lord surrounded them. Even the children were subdued.

Annie had to blink back tears on and off throughout the ceremony. And by the time the bride and groom announced, "I do," she'd developed a major smile headache.

It was time for the special music. Everyone sat down as Tony grabbed the mike. When the music started playing, Annie immediately recognized the tune. The sound of Tony's voice, deep and mellow, drew her attention, and she watched him, mesmerized. He sang a love song to the bride and groom and poured so much feeling into his performance that she thought she saw Dave swipe a tear from his face.

Listening to the words, she thought about how much she had once loved Tony and how suddenly that had all changed. No longer saddened by the thought, she let peace envelope her.

Just then Tony turned and captured her gaze as he sang, "I've always loved you, my sweetheart, and I always will."

Her heart stuck in her throat. Dan's gaze darted from her to his brother. As Tony returned to his seat, Dan shot a questioning glance toward Annie.

After the ceremony, Tony intercepted Dan and guided him toward the cry room off to the side of the sanctuary. The expression on Dan's face appeared pretty intense, and Annie remembered the look she and Tony had shared as he sang. Had Dan misinterpreted it?

She prayed under her breath, "Please, Lord, don't let them fight today. I can't deal with it."

Dan's chest had tightened when Annie clapped for his brother, and a twinge of jealousy flared inside him. He knew there was no point in being jealous because Annie had clearly chosen him, but the way his brother smiled at Annie still bothered him.

The Lord had brought them together and would keep them together. He believed with all his heart. He just prayed that someway, somehow, Tony would finally let go and allow her and Dan to move forward without guilt.

Tony smiled and rubbed his hands together. "I'm feeling crazy today. But you can't be too happy, can you?" His eyebrows wiggled up and down, and he ducked into the cry room off to the side of the sanctuary.

Dan scratched his head and followed Tony. He closed the door behind them. His little brother was acting like he'd lost his mind.

"Now you've got me curious. Something's up. What is it?"

"I have a gift for you. I prayed about it for days and I just know giving you this gift is what God wants me to do."

Dan stared. "How do you know?"

"Well, I feel joy inside, for one thing. I never realized being a Christian could be so awesome and . . . freeing. I get chills just thinking about it. Now everywhere I go I get encouragement. I feel so close to God, you know?"

Dan's heart pounded. The light in Tony's eyes convinced him that his brother spoke from the bottom of his heart. A lump formed in his throat.

"You've already given me the best gift of all by accepting Jesus. You're a living miracle. I never thought I'd see this day, but I'm so glad I waited on God."

"Cut it out, Danno, or I'm gonna start bawling like a baby." Wiping his eyes with the back of his hand, Tony sputtered, "See what I mean." His shoulders shook as he laughed.

Dan wiped his eyes too. "I'm cool now. Tell me."

Tony removed a box from his pocket. Dan nearly choked when Tony smiled and lifted the lid.

"I want you to have this and I want you to give it to Annie."

Dan shook his head and backed away. "I can't. No way. Uh-uh."

"Yes."

"No. That's too much. I know how special Gram's ring is to you. I won't take it."

"Shut up and listen. You *will* take it, and I'll tell you why. It was never meant for me." His voice wavered. "It was never supposed to be mine. It was meant for you all along."

Dan rubbed his forehead. "What are you talking about?"

"It was supposed to be yours, but I talked Gram into giving it to me instead. I told her you didn't want it because you didn't have a girlfriend. I told her you wanted me to have it."

Tony offered Dan the ring. "She believed me." His voice cracked. "I just loved her so much I wanted something from her, you know?"

Dan pushed the box back into Tony's hand. "Which is why you're keeping it."

Shaking his head, Tony rasped, "No, I want you to have it. Didn't you hear me? It's rightfully yours."

"And I'm telling you to save it for your future wife. Someone with no history attached."

Tony peered at the box and grew quiet. "But I want Annie to have it. I want her to know I'm giving this to you so she'll know I'm supporting your relationship. I just want you guys to be happy."

Dan thought he was hearing things at first. Tony wanted them to be together? His brother really must have had a change of heart.

"Why are you doing this?" he asked hoarsely.

"I don't know. 'Cause I love you guys? 'Cause it feels right?"

"Did you meet someone at school? Is that why you're cutting Annie loose?"

"Nope. There's no other girl in my life." Tony's voice softened. "I just love Annie so much, and I know she loves you. You make her happy. That's all I want." He gave Dan a weak grin.

"But Tony . . ."

He shoved his hand out. "Take it. Tell her it's from you, but I offered it with my blessing."

Reluctantly Dan accepted the box, still unsure as he stared at the ring. His eyes welled with tears at his brother's sincerity.

"Thanks. And I mean it. I really do hope you find the right girl for you someday."

Tony laughed. "Right now I just want to pass my courses. The rest can come later."

Nodding, Dan swallowed hard. "Thanks. This means a lot to me."

"You're welcome. So are you going to ask her?"

"Maybe soon. I don't want to scare her by rushing things."

"Come on, you big dork. I saw how she was looking at you during the wedding. When I sang that song to her it was my way of saying good-bye. I think she understood that. I hope we'll always be friends."

"All is forgiven and forgotten."

"Same here, if you'll accept my apology."

"Of course."

As Tony enveloped him in a bear hug, Dan saw Annie watching them through the glass and waved. Her mouth curved in a broad grin as though she knew she'd just witnessed a miracle.

And she had.

Chapter 27

Annie noticed the puffiness around Dan's eyes and feared the worst, so she didn't ask. They drove several miles before he glanced over.

"Want to go someplace special, like maybe the park to see the geese?"

"Sure." Annie let out her breath, relieved that Dan didn't sound upset at all.

He veered toward the road leading to the park on the other side of town. She studied him from the corner of her eye.

His knuckles whitened as he clutched the steering wheel. Fear seized her chest. Maybe it wasn't a good sign that they were going somewhere quiet to talk.

She mulled over the possibilities. Tony might have told Dan about their e-mails. But he knew they kept in touch and she never wrote anything to be ashamed of. She even invited Dan to read their correspondence.

Reaching over, he covered her hand, and she reveled in the sensation of his large, warm palm caressing her knuckles. He stroked her fingers one at a time and offered a sad smile.

"You look bummed. What's up?"

He cleared his throat. "The surgeon did a pretty good job."

Not sure why he changed the subject, she decided to play along anyway. "I can't imagine what I would've done if the doctor hadn't been able to reattach it. I'd be an even bigger freak—"

"Don't put yourself down." He brushed his knuckles against her cheek, and his gaze traveled to her neck.

"Think you might be ready to go without a scarf?"

"I don't know. Maybe I could try it again." She peered out the truck window. The park was almost empty.

"Want to walk to the bridge over there?"

Dan's gaze clung to hers. "If you want to."

Her heartbeat sped up. She whispered, "Help me take it off?"

"If you want me to."

As he untied the scarf, his hands trembled. He tugged at the snug knot until it loosened, then slowly removed the scarf from her neck. Her gaze never wavered as he laid the scarf between them and lowered his head. His lips clung to hers.

She kissed him back until dizziness overwhelmed her and she had to stop and catch her breath. "Maybe we should go for a walk."

He exhaled, looking a bit flustered. He raked his hair with his fingers and got out of the truck. He opened the door for her and took her hand in his. They strolled to the little bridge built over a pond.

When they arrived at the center, Dan stopped and leaned over the railing as if deep in thought. "I thought I might trade my truck in for a car."

"Why would you do that? I like your truck."

He turned to face her and crossed his arms over his chest. "Now that I have a job with a good salary I'm thinking about settling down. My truck has a lot of miles on it."

"But it still runs."

"Yeah, but if you drove my truck and it broke down . . . I wouldn't want you stranded on the road." He studied her intently.

His words buzzed in her head. She stared at the pond. He loved his truck. But why would she drive it, unless . . . She glanced up and caught him grinning at her.

Her throat tightened. He reached to tuck loose strands of her hair around her ear. The wind pulled her locks free. With a chuckle he tucked them back again.

She rose on tiptoe and brushed her lips against his. "You're a good man. I feel safe when I'm with you."

His fingers grazed the scars on her neck when she eased back onto the soles of her feet. "Forget to worry?"

"I'm beginning to."

"Think you're healing on the inside?"

Biting her lower lip, she nodded. "Yeah, I do."

He lifted her hand and kissed her knuckles, lingering on the one the surgeon had reattached. "And what about this? Still bothered by what happened to your hand?"

"Not so much. I'm more thankful now. Yes, it hurt like crazy, and I'll never look or feel the same. But deep inside I believe God used what happened to bless me."

"How?"

"I have a new heart and a love for you that's so precious, I could just . . ." She struggled to finish. "I could just cry."

Several tears trickled down her cheeks. Dan kissed them away.

"It sounds so pathetic, but do you see what I mean?"

Little sobs interrupted spurts of laughter as she reflected on their love. It would have been impossible without Christ.

He nuzzled the scarred side of her neck. A shiver raced up her spine as his warm breath encountered her ear.

Overwhelmed with gratitude, she searched her heart for the usual guilt she experienced and found it strangely absent. Something had changed in her heart.

Maybe the song Tony shared at the wedding had finally released her.

"What's going on in your pretty head?"

Dan's husky voice evoked a shiver. She met his steady gaze. The love she glimpsed in the depths of his soul gave her goose bumps.

"I was thinking about us. I don't feel guilty about Tony anymore. I really think we can be friends."

He smiled and reached into his pocket. "I have something for you. I wasn't sure now was the right time, but I feel like you're ready. I know I am."

"Ready for what?"

"Before you see this I want to tell you something important, okay?"

"Sure." Annie swallowed hard. He sounded so serious.

He opened his palm and showed her a velvet box. "This contains a gift Tony offered me. We want you to have it."

He heart thumped as she examined the box. It couldn't be . . .

"Ready?"

"Okay."

He grinned. "Wait a second."

Anticipation made her shiver. Was Dan going to propose? He bent down.

At first she thought maybe he crouched to tie his shoe. Of course, how silly of her. He wasn't going to propose. He just needed to . . .

But he knelt and peered up at her. "Open it."

She cracked open the lid of the velvet box and gasped. Her hand flew to cover her mouth. Choking on sobs, she shook her head. No. It couldn't be.

Confusion slid over his face. "I want you to be my wife."

Forcing her voice to engage, she choked out, "It's that ring."

He sprang to his feet, his face stricken. "Oh, man. I made a mistake. I can buy a different ring. I'm sorry. I never meant to hurt you. I didn't think about—"

She sniffled. "No, no. I don't want a different ring. I'm just so . . . surprised. I can't believe Tony gave it up."

"Me either." He eyed her skeptically. "You sure you want it?"

"Yes. It's still the most beautiful setting I've ever seen."

She stared at the diamond ring, the cause of so much pain. But God had healed her, expanding joy in her heart, penetrating it.

Dan removed the ring from the box and carefully slid it over her damaged finger. The ring seemed looser than before. Her heart squeezed when she realized what that meant.

Dan must have had the ring enlarged to conceal her scar and make sure it would never be so tight she couldn't remove it. Gratitude over his thoughtfulness evoked a sob. She threw her arms around him and cried.

"Annie? You all right? You sure this doesn't bother you?"

She nodded against his shirt as tears coursed down her cheeks. When she let go and glanced up, his eyes softened and welled with tears. She basked in the love radiating from him.

"Tony met me after the wedding. He insisted I take the ring and give it to you. He said he knows you love me, and he just wants us to be happy."

Tony found someone else?

As if reading her thoughts, Dan added, "And before you start thinking Tony found a new girlfriend, he wanted you to know he hadn't. He said he still loves you, but Annie, he wants you to marry me."

"Tony said that?"

"Uh-huh."

Her heart stilled. "Are you asking me to marry you because he said you could, or because you really want to?"

His brow furrowed. "Because I want to, of course. I'm just thrilled he accepts us. And now my parents will be more approving. It's like a dream come true."

Annie tipped up her head. "Yeah, it is, isn't it? I know your family means a lot to you, and for a while it seemed like everyone was against us."

"Hmmm-hmmm." Dan scanned her face, her eyes, and lingered on her mouth. Cupping her cheeks, he murmured, "I've never loved anyone else and I never will. Say you'll be my wife."

"I want to marry you, Dan. I really do."

"Praise the Lord!"

He clasped her to him and pressed his face against her hair. She felt the beat of his heart against her cheek as he clung to her. She reveled in his scent and the feel of his body against hers, savoring the moment.

When he finally released her, contentment washed over her like a warm rain shower. Without speaking, they leaned against the side of the bridge, hip to hip, and watched the geese swimming.

When they started to leave, a boy who looked to be about six years old raced up and stopped in front of Annie. He pointed at her face.

"What happened to you?"

Annie had forgotten about her appearance. She reached to touch her scarf and remembered leaving it in the truck. Wondering how to explain such horror to a young child, she peered down.

After a moment she crouched down to his eye level. Twirling the engagement ring with her thumb, she answered, "Something bad happened. A man hurt me, but Jesus healed me, and I'm better now."

"But if Jesus healed you, how come you still have those marks?"

She glanced up at Dan with tears in her eyes, and then returned her gaze to the boy. "That's just some scars. Jesus healed me on the inside."

Once the words tumbled out, she realized she meant every one of them.

Dan's heart squeezed at the peaceful expression Annie wore. She'd changed so much since the attack, she seemed like a different girl. And he loved her with his whole being.

Reaching for her hand, Dan caressed her fingers as the boy ran off yelling, "Hey, Ma! You said Jesus didn't do no miracles no more, but this lady told me Jesus healed her."

Annie burst with joyous laughter. Dan joined her, marveling at the truth in the child's words as they strolled toward his truck.

He stopped outside the door and gazed at Annie. Her hair was now mussed and windblown. The chilly air had darkened her scars until they matched the purple in her clothes. But she still looked beautiful to him.

"You handled that very well."

Gazing up at him, she smiled. "God has blessed me so much. Sometimes it's hard to understand why bad things happen, but I see it now. I see His love for me. Even through my attack. He didn't want it to happen, but He knew it would. And because I would grow from the experience, He didn't intervene.

Dan stood silent, pondering her words. "You're amazing."

She giggled. "Yeah, I suppose. But you have to admit it makes sense."

Searching her eyes, Dan asked, "If you had a choice in the matter, knowing what you know now . . . would *you* have allowed it if you could have prevented it?"

Without hesitating she answered. "I wouldn't change a thing. I have your love and my relationship with the Lord. And

I still have Tony's friendship. I don't obsess over what people think anymore. I have a better life now."

Dan stroked her cheek and dipped his head to kiss her scar. She trembled as he cupped her face in his hands, then pressed her mouth against his, sealing their commitment with a tender kiss.

Suddenly Annie pulled back, chuckling. "You know what, Dan? We've enjoyed so many things together, like studying God's word and taking nature walks. I can't believe how much we have in common."

Wiggling his eyebrows, he started to speak, but she touched his lips with her finger, stopping the words.

"Shh—I just realized something cool." Her voice grew husky as she touched her scarred neck. "If this hadn't happened to me, I wouldn't have waited for you."

Her gaze turned serious, then teasing again as she fingered the collar of his shirt. "Isn't it cool how the Lord works things together for our good?"

He nodded. "For being a new Christian, you sure have a lot of spiritual insight," he said huskily.

She smiled into his eyes. "The Lord prevented me from making what could've been the biggest mistake of my life by marrying Tony. Now I'll have no regrets. You'll be my first and my only."

Dan trembled as he gazed into her eyes. He tipped his head to hers once more.

"And you'll be mine."

Epilogue

People often view physical healing and amazing feats as miracles, but to me the greatest miracle of all is a changed heart. God has done so much for us.

For love spurns our former animosity.

Peace moves us beyond the controversy.

Joy overtakes our discouragement.

And healing through Christ bonds us together for all eternity.

Discussion Guide

1. Annie is a good daughter and tries to live a moral life, but she has difficulty saying no because she doesn't want to hurt others. How can this be a bad thing in relationships? How does it influence the choices she makes? Is Annie in love with Tony, or more the idea of being in love?

2. Tony has a problem with pornography and it has changed the dynamics of his relationship with Annie. How would you feel if you found out your relationship was affected by pornography or another addiction? What would you do about it?

3. Dan steps in and befriends Annie when his brother abandons her. Was this the right things for him to do? Can you really be "just friends" with someone you are very attracted to?

4. After the attack, Annie discovers her faith was not only weak, but had no foundation. Do you think Dan did the right thing by gently confronting her with this concern? Did you agree with his mother's statement about not judging, or are you more inclined to agree with Dan's perspective on how to deal with friends you think may be "lost?"

5. Tony realizes he has a problem with alcohol and needs help. Do you have anyone in your life right now who is out of control and needs treatment for an addiction? How do you think you could go about encouraging him or her to consider getting professional help?

6. At graduation from Teen Challenge Tony finds out his brother became emotionally and physically involved with his girlfriend. Do you agree with how he handled it? Were his anger and his actions toward Dan justified?

7. Susie comes up with some significant lies in an effort to break up Annie and Dan's relationship, including trying to make Annie believe Susie had a relationship with him. Did Dan do the right thing by trying to help Susie despite the risk to his relationship with Annie? Why or why not?

8. Annie has to go court and testify at her attacker's sentencing hearing. Tony and Dan rally to support her. How did this play a role in the healing of the brothers' relationship?

9. Tony agrees to give Annie some space when he goes to college. Do you think it was right for them to keep in touch by e-mail? Do you think Annie did the right thing by letting him go?

10. The ring plays a significant role in this story as a symbol of healing. Should Dan have given her a different ring when he proposed? Why or why not?

it's NOT about Him

A Second Glances Novel
2

Michelle Sutton

September 2009

Prologue

Ever had a decision to make that was so awful you wished it would go away? I did. But I couldn't ignore the problem. It had a time limit. So not making a decision was still making one.

It was the hardest thing I've ever gone through.

But I learned some things from my experience. For one, I found out there are plenty of people willing to give advice, most of which is not at all helpful.

The thing is . . . not many people understand how hard a decision is to make when no matter what you do someone gets hurt. I'm not talking easy stuff like what you want to order at a restaurant. I'm talking about dishing up someone's future. Deciding who will take care of the most precious gift you have ever received.

Honestly, I was so out of it I don't remember much about the night my life was forever changed. Yet I still had the consequences to deal with. And I had to grow up fast.

Jeff, God bless him, tried to help me. But he made it harder, because it's not about him. It's not about doing what someone else thinks is best. It's about learning to make the right decision for my child.

The pain of that decision was excruciating. But it taught me that my pain doesn't have to define me, nor does a mistake. I am *not* what I did.

In the end, what matters most is love, because only love will get you through the most impossible situations. And while that doesn't make everything better, it does make sense of something that makes no sense.

In the end, all I had left was God. But He was enough.

Chapter 1

Susie Ziglar groaned as she leaned against the grocery cart and sipped from her cup. The ache in her back seemed to be getting worse. She needed to hurry up and finish shopping so she could sit and rest a minute. Pressing her hand into her lower spine, she set her drink down and straightened, then bent her shoulders back.

"My back is killing me."

Jeff Rhodes, her constant companion and best friend for the past six months, eyed her with brows raised. "You think it's time?"

Susie grimaced. "How should I know? I've never been through this before."

He rubbed his forehead. "Oh, man. What if it is?"

"I doubt it. I'm not due for two more weeks. Anyway, my back has been aching like this for days. I can hardly sleep!" She sighed as the ache eased a bit. A tiny kick told her the baby probably didn't like it either.

They resumed shopping and turned into another aisle. She was suddenly surrounded by baby products—pictures of babies on boxes and diapers. Before she could take her next breath, her eyes flooded with tears. Her muscles tensed and she turned around.

"Sorry, I didn't realize . . . " Jeff sounded contrite as he tried to keep up.

She sped around the corner and marched away from him so he wouldn't see her cry. What she was going through was hard enough, but did she have to be reminded of it everywhere she went? What did women do when they had miscarriages? She couldn't imagine.

Her chest tightened, and she felt a tear slide down her cheek. Angrily she brushed it away. Pregnancy hadn't been so bad. She never even got sick. But how she would miss that little person who had been inside her for so long.

"I said I'm sorry. I should've paid attention. Can I help?"

"Nah. Besides, I can't stop it once it—Ooof!" Her shirt suddenly popped up, like someone punched from the inside. The material floated down like a parachute.

Jeff's gaze fixed on her belly, and his mouth pulled into a sly grin. He spoke to her tummy in a funny voice. "Is my little girl doing jumping jacks again?" He patted her stomach.

Gently she moved his hand away. "Don't."

How she wished Jeff wouldn't refer to the baby as if he knew it was a girl. When she had the ultrasound, Susie had told the doctor she didn't want to know what the baby's sex was. She wanted it to be a surprise. Now, the more Jeff talked about her child with such delight, the more she questioned her decision. But she couldn't go back no matter what he said to try to change her mind.

Jeff rubbed the back of his hand across his lips. He had a faraway look in his eyes.

She stopped pushing the cart. "What?"

He shook his head as if he was trying to snap out of whatever had pulled him away from her. "Nothing. Let's get this over with. So what else do you need? Cheese? Bread?"

Releasing an exasperated sigh, Susie grunted. "Don't give me that. You were thinking about something. I'm not stupid."

Jeff's attention settled on her eyes, and his voice lowered. "I know that. I just can't help wondering . . . are you sure you're doing the right thing?"

She squinted at him. "Of course, I'm sure. I want this couple to adopt my baby. I can't see myself raising a child alone."

"I've already told you a hundred times. You don't have to—"

"That's not reality, Jeff," she snapped. "I don't have any way to care for this baby. The last thing this innocent child needs is to live with a struggling single mother when there are two wonderful people who can raise it in the love and security of a Christian home."

A flash of memory from the night of the party zipped through her mind. But as usual, she didn't see any faces. Everything was a one huge blur.

She sighed. "I can't even collect child support since I'll never know who the baby's father is."

"I know. But won't you at least consider my offer?"

Susie chewed her lip and avoided looking into his eyes. "I love you as a friend, Jeff. But you know we can never be more than that."

His hand touched her shoulder. "But, I still think we—"

She shrugged him off. "I refuse to be a charity case. I won't marry you just so you can help me raise another man's child. It wouldn't be fair to either of us. Marriage is forever. Why can't you see that?"

"I know what you're saying, but it doesn't seem right. I'm glad I wasn't aborted, and I still wonder if my real parents are out there somewhere wishing they could find me."

"Which is why I'm doing an open adoption. I'll know who they are, and they'll know me." She grimaced as another ache started in her lower back.

He pushed back her long bangs and tucked them behind her ear. "Susie . . ."

"No! We've discussed this a thousand times—" She stopped and cast her gaze down.

"I can't help wondering if my real parents would have done a better job, you know? Especially since my dad never seemed to like me."

"But this isn't about you. I can't fix what your parents did wrong. Neither can you."

"Just think about it. Please."

Something in his rough tone made her glance up. Her eyes stung as she glimpsed the pain in his.

"I don't want to talk about this. I'm signing my baby over to them, and you can't change my mind. My child will always know who I am. It won't be anything like your experience—I'm sure of it."

"Please?" He tipped up her chin and brushed her cheek with his thumb.

She stepped back, eyes wide. The gesture seemed too intimate for mere friendship. He'd been touching her a lot lately. His tenderness stirred feelings she was determined to ignore.

"But nothing. I won't let you throw your life away."

"Who says I'll be throwing it away?"

She turned her face away. "You know you don't love me like that."

"I could—"

"Look at me!" she exclaimed, pointing at her stomach. "I'm a beached whale, for Pete's sake."

"No, you're not." His eyes softened, and he offered a tender smile.

She could feel her chin quivering. A knot lodged in her throat.

"Cut it out. And stop looking at me that way. We're just friends, and that's all we're ever going to be."

"I don't know why we—"

"Because I don't want that kind of relationship with any-body! I just want to get through this pregnancy and get on with my life. Stop trying to change my mind."

Before she could stop him, he cupped her face, forcing her to meet his gaze. "Please, just think about it."

She jerked her chin away and heaved a loud sigh. She did not want to talk about this kind of stuff in the middle of the grocery store.

"I love you. Just not that way."

She pondered the irony of her statement. It wasn't that long ago that Dan kept telling her the same thing, and she refused to listen. How much her life had changed in such a short time. But there was no going back to the way things had been.

A former boyfriend from her sophomore year in high school entered the aisle where they'd huddled in the corner. She wished she could shrink and hide behind Jeff, but Mark had already seen her and headed in her direction. She'd been so in love with Mark, but then he'd dumped her for a new girl.

"Hey, Susie. I didn't know you got hitched. Congrats, girl!" He turned and offered his hand to Jeff. "Do I know you?"

Jeff received his hand and quickly let go. His neck reddened to his ears, and he directed a quick glance at Susie. "I'm Jeff . . . um, Susie's . . . ah . . . friend."

"Nice to meet you. I'm Mark." Her former boyfriend's gaze strayed to Susie's hand. "Then who'd you marry?"

Susie's throat squeezed. It wasn't the first time someone assumed she was married because she was due to give birth. "I'm not."

Mark's gaze strayed to her protruding belly, then returned to her face. "Oh."

"Jeff and I are good friends. We go to the same church."

Cocking his head to the side, Mark asked Jeff, "So where do you attend?"

"First Christian. You?"

Mark straightened. "My family goes to the Ward on Fourth Ave. I'm LDS."

An awkward silence ensued. Susie remembered going to church a few times with Mark when they'd dated, but she'd never felt comfortable around his family.

"Well, it was good seeing you again, Mark," Susie said in a rush. "Maybe I'll see you around."

"Maybe, but I doubt it. I moved to Washington. I'm just visiting my family for the week. Well, bye." Flicking his wrist, he turned the corner without looking back.

Susie exhaled. "Wow," she said without enthusiasm. "He still looks the same as he did when we were sophomores. That's pretty amazing."

Jeff laughed. "Well, of course he does. You're only twenty. It hasn't been that long since you graduated." His smile faded. "You like him?"

"We dated in high school." Susie gasped and bent over, clutching her stomach as a strong squeeze radiated through her abdomen.

Jeff stood behind her and put his arms around her to hold her up.

She felt a strange sensation. Without warning, her water broke, spilling the clear fluid all over the floor.

"Oh no!"

His eyes widened. "No way. Not here—"

Heat suffused her cheeks. Of all the places to have her water break, why the grocery store? She tucked the folds of her long skirt between her knees in an effort to contain some of the amniotic fluid.

"Jeff, can you get the manager? See if he has a towel or something."

"Sure." Jeff darted around the corner and returned moments later with a towel, trailed by the store manager. Jeff gave the concerned-looking man a quick wave, then took her arm and guided her toward the door. "Hang in there, babe. We'll go straight to the hospital. Wait right here, and I'll go get the car."

"Like I'm going to take off," she muttered.

She hardly got the words out before another pain reverberated through her. She wrapped her left arm around her abdomen and dug the fingers of her other hand into Jeff's arm. What felt like a long menstrual cramp—only more severe—stole her breath until her eyes filled with tears.

Why didn't I sign up for those Lamaze classes? Then I'd know what to do.

"Hurry!" she gasped.

Giving her a scared look, Jeff gave her hand a quick squeeze, then darted out the door and sprinted for his car.

Susie watched him run, and a wave of loneliness washed over her. He had been so good to her over the course of her pregnancy. She knew it had been out of guilt at first because she had been raped while drunk during a party at his place. But the more time they spent together, the more things improved between them until now they really enjoyed hanging out with each other.

But once her baby was placed with Passels, she didn't know where that would leave her and Jeff. She could only pray he would still want to be friends. That he wouldn't be angry with her for giving her baby up for adoption.

This life-changing decision was hard enough, but if she lost her best friend she didn't know how she'd make it through. She didn't want to admit it, but deep down inside she knew she needed him. And that terrified her.